John P. O'Connell
1613 North 201st Street
Shoreline, WA 98133

NEW YORK MOSAIC

NEW YORK MOSAIC

THREE NOVELS BY

ISABEL BOLTON

DO I WAKE OR SLEEP

THE CHRISTMAS TREE

MANY MANSIONS

STEERFORTH PRESS
SOUTH ROYALTON, VERMONT

Do I Wake or Sleep first published in 1946 by Charles Scribner's Sons;
The Christmas Tree first published in 1949 by Charles Scribner's Sons;
Many Mansions first published in 1952 by Charles Scribner's Sons.

Library of Congress Cataloging-in-Publication Data

Bolton, Isabel, 1883–1975
[Novels. Selections]
New York mosaic : three novels / by Isabel Bolton. — 1st ed.
p. cm.
Contents: Do I wake or sleep — The Christmas tree
— Many mansions.
ISBN 1-883642-28-0
1. City and town life — New York (State)
— New York — Fiction.
2. New York (N.Y.) — Social life and customs
— Fiction. I. Title.
PS3525.I553A6 1997   97-18480
813' .52 — dc21   CIP

Manufactured in the United States of America

FIRST EDITION

CONTENTS

INTRODUCTION

IT IS ONE OF THE ACCEPTED TRUTHS of the publishing world that many good books appear, are critically praised but attract few readers, fall between the cracks of their time, and are never heard of again. So, for me, it is a pleasure to see, resurrected and restored to print, these three novels by Mary Britton Miller who published them under the pseudonym of Isabel Bolton.

A few years ago I sent a copy of *The Christmas Tree*, one of the novels you now have in hand, to my editor, a man of very good taste. I hoped he would consider republishing the book, especially in the light of new public interest in gay fiction (*The Christmas Tree* first appeared in 1949). He returned the book with a note saying it was "a bit old-fashioned" for his tastes.

In 1978, I came upon the name of Isabel Bolton in Diana Trilling's collection of her reviews from the pages of *The Nation. Reviewing the Forties* contained the admission that she had been pointed toward Bolton by a hymn of praise to *Do I Wake or Sleep* by Edmund Wilson in *The New Yorker*. A few months earlier he had written:

> She [Bolton] has cut to roundness and smoothed to convexity
> a little crystal of literary form that concentrates the light like
> a burning glass . . . Her writing rarely shapes or paints; it either
> makes people talk or talks itself, but it does have its own per-
> sonal tone, a voice that combines, in a peculiar way, the lyric
> with the dry; and is exquisitely perfect in accent; every syllable
> falls as it should . . .

Trilling went on to extol the same novel, by the woman writing under a pseudonym, in what some must have regarded in that time as hyperbole:

> Whoever she is, she is the most important new novelist in the English language to appear in years . . . *Do I Wake or Sleep* is quite the best novel that has come my way in the four years I have been reviewing new fiction for this magazine. (1946)

◆   ◆   ◆

Do I Wake or Sleep was published by Scribner's, then a most distinguished house, when Mary Britton Miller was sixty-three years old. (Her previous work had consisted of five books of poetry and one novel, all for children.) Adopting a pen name was one way of signifying that she intended to remain anonymous, autobiographically disassociated from the novels of her late maturity. When asked by her editor for jacket copy about herself she wrote: "Here it is, the book over which I have thought deeply and worked hard. What more is there to say, except perhaps to add that I have lived some time in Europe, that I was brought up in America, and that New York has been my home for many years?"

The fortunate reader who comes upon *Do I Wake or Sleep* for the first time, fifty years after it appeared, will, at first, see traces of Henry James's Isabel Archer in Millicent, Bolton's point of consciousness, of Virginia Woolf's stream-of-consciousness technique in *Mrs. Dalloway*, and more than a little of the acute sensibility of Elizabeth Bowen in *The Death of the Heart*.

But ultimately it will become clear that Bolton's style is entirely her own. Her treatment of contemporary New York scenes, from the 1939 World's Fair to the cocktail party gatherings, drinks at the Algonquin and dinner at the memorable Chambord, the visit to a Newsreel Theater — most, alas, long, long gone — as well as her subtly critical treatment of the shallowness of the literary chatter of that time, all strike me, who lived through those days and in those places, as accurate and evocative. Tragic echoes of Hitler's rule in Europe hang over the frivolity of this odyssey in the day of a sensitive and charming middle-aged woman.

A short novel, *Do I Wake or Sleep* did not evoke universal admiration. Lesser critics like Anne Freemantle in *Commonweal* ("I slept," she reported) and Dorothy Sparks in *Book Week* found the story well written but unsuccessful and plotless, unprepared as they seem to have been for the subtle and unexpected manner of revealing by hint or mere suggestion the underlying truths of the story. What incidents there are — Millicent's past with British Christopher Henderson, the brilliant and "modern" young Bridget's tragic child in Hitler's hands, the fragile novelist Percy Jones's unhappy, lovelorn, drunken day — are encased in Bolton's fine evocation of the charm and mystery of the city she loved. It is a celebration of place that was to continue three years later with the publication of *The Christmas Tree*.

♦   ♦   ♦

As I have already suggested, *The Christmas Tree* is my personal favorite of the three books. Parts of the first two chapters had appeared in *The New Yorker*, I suspect, through the influence of its then book critic, Edmund Wilson. Bolton, with unaccustomed (for her time) insight and sympathy, describes three days and nights during the Christmas season of 1945. World War II had just ended. The story is colored by the sensibility of another middle-aged protagonist, Hildegarde Danforth, whose little grandson, Henry, her daughter-in-law, Anne, and Anne's new husband, an Air Force captain, are gathered in the high, terraced New York apartment to celebrate the holiday. The arrival of Mrs. Danforth's beloved, gay son, Larry, father of Henry, and his gay lover bring about the awful climax of the story. All the unspoken, suggested strains of these complex and ultimately tragic relationships are here again bolstered by the beauty of skyscrapers and the glamorous midtown streets of New York.

Edmund Wilson was as enthusiastic about *The Christmas Tree* as he had been about Bolton's first novel: "[It] seems to me even more remarkable . . . She is a poet of the noblest kind who uses the compression and the polish of her fiction to focus human insight and to concentrate moral passion." And Diana Trilling wrote in her review of *The Christmas Tree*: "With her second novel . . . Isabel Bolton establishes herself as the best woman writer of fiction in this country today."

xii ◆ NEW YORK MOSAIC

◆   ◆   ◆

Margaret Sylvester, in *Many Mansions*, is a very elderly woman living in New York City in 1950 (the book was published in 1952). The story of her life is told as she rereads, in manuscript, an autobiographical account she had written some time ago. Set in a Greenwich Village hotel, it allows for the inclusion of young Village types and a fine re-creation of the condition of old age. As in the other two books, Bolton's main character is her customary well-to-do, upper-class woman with cherished memories of her favored childhood, and a past that holds secrets buried too long ago and too deep to be part of her present. Margaret Sylvester's young womanhood, partly spent as a volunteer worker among the sweatshop working women of New York, reads as autobiographical revelation, and was the first time Bolton had shown an interest in another class in her fiction.

So much of *Many Mansions* rings true that I found myself searching in its pages for hints of the life of Mary Britton Miller, a question given ground by the author when she observes in the novel: "And here we were, hawking our souls about, writing novels, our own little autobiographies (all novels were, in one way or another, autobiographical) . . ." Was she describing herself, I wondered, when she wrote of her heroine's deepest love for her friend Mary whom she loses, in a way, to marriage: ". . . there had been a hollow in her heart . . . There had been the queerest void . . . had not this deep, this steadfast friendship for Mary been the one human relationship where love had never failed to nourish and replenish her?" Did she, like her heroine, bear an illegitimate child in a convent in Italy, and then lose him to adoption? I fear I will never know.

◆   ◆   ◆

Nineteen years later, when Bolton was eighty-four, she wrote her last novel, *The Whirligig of Time*, a touching account of the lives of aged Blanche Willoughby and her very old friend, David Hare, coming together at the end of their lives after both had lived lives marked by the deprivation of their love by his marriage to an heiress, Olivia Wildering. A vision of this unfortunate union of attractive, servile

David to demanding, heavy, selfish Olivia recalls the poignant glimpse of a similarly miserable marriage in *Many Mansions*.

Again, reputable critics praised the book, but the somewhat grim and old-fashioned subject matter and style did not interest a public now more absorbed by the fiction of John Updike and Bernard Malamud — both *Rabbit Redux* and *The Tenants* appeared that year.

◆   ◆   ◆

The three novels in this volume appeared when I was young and had lived all my life in the beloved city of Bolton's memory, but I was ignorant of her and her work. She was a writer who pursued her craft without any desire for personal appearance or publicity. She wrote one memoir, *Under Gemini* (1966), about her childhood with her twin sister who drowned when they were not yet in their teens. No other autobiographical volume was to follow.

Under Gemini was dedicated "to my incomparable friend Tobias Schneebaum." As luck would have it, I knew Toby from our stays at Yaddo artists' colony, so what little more I have learned about Mary Britton Miller was provided by him. He met her, he told me, at Yaddo in 1959. She was then in her seventies, a rather grand, elegant nineteenth-century lady, "a vision," he said, in her long white dress and large straw hat, walking about in the rose garden.

As she aged she had developed a serious eye affliction and could not read for any length of time without great pain. Toby offered to read to her and went on doing so until she died in 1979. In New York she lived alone, finally at 81 Barrow Street in Greenwich Village in a charming, ample four-bedroom apartment. She was secretive about her past, even to Toby, who describes her as imperious, sharp-tongued, demanding, witty, often a delightful conversationalist, and always difficult (she once fired a reader on the spot for stammering in embarrassment over the word "fuck"). He was told she had spent some time in Italy, but there was no way of knowing if the Italian events in *Many Mansions* are autobiographical. She never married; in earlier years she had two close women friends (to one, Virginia Stevens, she dedicated *The Whirligig of Time* "with love and gratitude"). But whether her unusual compassion for the gay son in *The*

Christmas Tree was evidence of her own sexual orientation we have no way of knowing.

Schneebaum remembers her holding a large drawing pad in her lap on which she wrote poems, not her own but those of T. S. Eliot, W. H. Auden and others. Near the end she enjoyed having contemporary literature read to her: Saul Bellow's *Augie March* and James Joyce's *Ulysses*. She died in the way she had assigned to the heroine of *Many Mansions*, of a stroke suffered in her apartment. She was 92; the last thirty years had been the most productive and successful of her long life. The fortunate reader of this gathering of three of her novels will have the pleasure of encountering, most probably for the first time, a unique (if somewhat "old-fashioned") writer of originality and great power.

Doris Grumbach
Sargentville, Maine
April 23, 1997

DO I WAKE OR SLEEP

O N E

───────

WITH HALF OF HER ATTENTION Millicent regarded Bridget and with the other half looked out upon the scene surrounding her.

There was, she thought, a magic, an enchantment — these myriad rainbow lights, now soft and low, now deeper, stronger — all the stops and chords and colors played like organ voluntaries, over the moon, the clouds, the grass. The fountains with their leaping jets and pyramids of spray, the fairylike palaces (states and empires of the world met here in conclave on the green), all seemed illuminated, just as though the heavens were opening to receive them, with an uncanny radiance — a gravity.

How graciously the lovely little Dutch building stood up in the strange light; that ostentatious marble structure with the meaningless cascades descending its façade was Italy; what a happy achievement the miniature Greek building — white — classic, and very pleasing next to it, sending out its unbearable appeal to your sympathies, Czechoslovakia; and directly across the way the great sprawling British Empire, and there at some remove from the other European states the marble palace of the Soviets, rising with so much authority, and lifting into the night those two youthful figures that ran, following the star that guided them, lightly upon the air.

What with the wine, the laughter, the moon, the wetted flowers, the smell of wet grass, the music of a stringed orchestra (was it Gluck's *Iphigénie?*) and Bridget St. Dennis in her lovely leaf-green dress talking to poor infatuated Percy — the three of them together here at the French Pavilion — life seemed as insubstantial, evanescent as a dream.

There she sat delighted as a child, eating her slice of melon. "Oh, how beautiful," she said, "it's the color of an apricot and frosted all over with little silver stars."

How skillfully she wove her charms about them, extending them in every direction, so that you had the sense that not only Percy, tied and bound and fatally enmeshed, but the occupants of all the tables were caught up and spun around with the invisible, gossamer threads.

Now she was laughing. Percy was leaning forward eagerly, looking at her with that expression of sheepish, abject devotion. He was making a pass at her hand; and to watch her was to move into a realm of private and interior speculation, for to think about her at all was, of course, to draw comparisons.

Bridget all flash and emanation, turning the facets of her heart around with such swiftness as to make it uncertain which emotion was striking out at you, seeing so many flashing all at once — paying out her lines with the unconscious ease, the effortless industry of a spider at work on his intricate task — never holding on to anything too long, hovering, flying off — distributing her fascinations with such largess and simplicity.

As for herself, always living at the center of her own emotions — keeping hold, clinging on (saying yes when she intended to say no, and no when it had been her firm intention to say yes), concerning herself too much with feelings, pitying people too much, dangerously engaged in compassion; and somehow always managing to arrest the flux, the flow.

Compassion threw you back on silence, on solitude — in a word upon yourself — hoarding in your heart so many unconfided griefs and guilts and attributes — longing to tell everything, to make mutual avowals and confessions, but thrown back instead on scrutiny, on pity, and in a curious manner isolated, quixotic — never expressing quite what you had intended to express, or receiving just what you had expected to receive.

But what was she saying to Percy — coming out so swiftly, so explicitly with all these startling announcements?

Her grandmother had died very suddenly in Florence. Little Beatrice had been sent to Vienna. She would have no income now. The allowance on which she lived had come to her from Ireland — a part of the old lady's income. The estate was entailed; the principal reverted to an uncle. He'd as good as cut her off. And without money what in the world was one to do?

And Percy's exclamation, "But why, my darling girl, did little Beatrice have to go to Vienna?"

Frau von Mandestadt lived in Vienna. Perhaps the priests had finagled it. And anyway, where else could they have sent the poor child?

Frau von Mandestadt was the mother of Bridget's first husband, Eric von Mandestadt. Though she'd been born a Rosenbaum, she'd married an Aryan (she'd used the ridiculous word as though it had been incorporated into all the European tongues). But what would that do to exempt her little Beatrice? Shrugging her shoulders, spreading out her hands. This was the world in which one found that one must live.

Her darling grandmother; darling granny! She was afraid she'd broken her grandmother's heart. She wished that she could give them some idea of her, not as she had been in those final tragic years, but as she used to be; why, at over seventy there wasn't a man in the whole world she couldn't, if she'd set her mind upon it, have captured, manipulated and wound right round her little finger — moving her beautiful hands as though to demonstrate these accomplishments.

She extended her nets to include a certain young man in the far corner of the pavilion; she sent word to an old gentleman staring at her outrageously that she thought him odious; she told the waiter that the melon was exquisite — "absolument exquise." She was, she said, a beauty in the great tradition — a genuine grande dame — a good deal of a child — completely captivating. She was, in fact, incorrigible. She flirted with men; she flirted with women; she flirted with the entire world. She could no more arrest her coquetries than a bird could stop its singing or a dove could stop ruffling its feathers.

But she wasn't completely frivolous either — very far from it. She had great capacity for love; and the poor darling had had many sorrows — her favorite son killed in the Irish revolution and that fatal marriage he'd contracted shortly before his death. She'd never known the truth about her mother; she was Spanish; she was reckless; she was beautiful. She had mysteriously disappeared. Just where and in what manner she had died had never been disclosed; it had all been very secret, scandalous — tragic, and she could only recount with accuracy that she'd been left, and at an early age, an orphan in her grandmother's charge. She'd been the apple of her eye and the poor darling had probably read from the beginning the tea leaves in the bottom of the cup, knowing her mother's blood was racing in her veins and all that Irish yeast fermenting, too.

However, she was a determined character. She had a fixed obsession, and had gone about in her own peculiar way to outwit those three implacable ladies paying out the weave. She used to hear her grandmother say, before she knew the meaning of the words, "Bridget is born for diplomacy" — a quaint idea, but one that seemed to obsess her. She was very old school and of course, expecting her to be endowed with all her own accomplishments, she felt it most important she should marry a diplomat — in diplomacy beauty, coquetry, and wit could be put to valuable uses in the world.

And with this in view she sent her to a convent when she was very young, such a beautiful place, near Avila, with a landscape from her window very grave, and certain trees and flowers flaming in it like the burning bush; and bells chiming at morning and in the evening; and those pious nuns at their devotions, walking with them in the sunshine, in the shadows under the plane trees, working at her studies with the nuns — a not unhappy time; and all that fascinating literature; what poetry resided in the lives of the saints — the earthly and the heavenly realms as close as light and shadow! There she'd stayed for nearly seven years.

And then suddenly her grandmother sending for her to come to Rome, where she'd established herself in a fine old palace with all her threads in hand; and if they could believe what she was about to tell them, which they probably could not, the poor darling had all but got her married to the diplomat of her selection. She'd given him a great deal of consideration; she'd followed his career — she'd gone to Rome in quest of him. There, my dears, he was — Eric von Mandestadt, first secretary at the Austrian legation, the son of her old friend Mathilda von Mandestadt, nee Rosenbaum. He was rich, he had a brilliant future — he was not too old. Had they any idea how her grandmother had gone about to set the trap for her?

No, she was certain they would never guess. She'd had a little, a very discreet little affair with him herself. It was cold; it was calculated; it was perfectly planned.

When she had him exactly where she wanted him, terribly afraid he'd compromised himself too far, that he'd never be able to escape from her embraces, that was the moment she'd been brought into the picture. Everything worked with miraculous success. She was young, she was undoubtedly innocent, she was marriageable, the grandchild of his mistress — just Eric's dish of tea.

"*Bon! oiseau magnifique*" (examining a beautifully browned and breaded guinea hen, and apparently not at all loath to let the waiter into the story, carefully selecting the bits of breast he recommended), going on to say everything had worked so fast and smoothly that she was married before she even had a chance to know she was betrothed, altogether a most bewildering experience for so young a child.

There was something about the way she told it, keeping herself as carefully removed from the range of your sympathies as she'd managed to remove the situation itself from any suggestion of sentiment or self-pity, marching along to the tune of her grandmother's plots and affections, as though it were a kind of natural music and accompaniment to her dilemma; and Percy not only so terribly shocked but bottled up and overcharged with indignation and pity and affection for her, longing to burst out and let her know just what he felt about it all; and Millicent aware of every nuance of his condition, struggling herself with two conflicting resolutions — the first to go along with Bridget and show no signs of either sympathy or surprise, and the other to join up with Percy in a perfect orgy of feeling sorry for the girl, while he managed to work off some of his emotion on the waiter.

No, he wouldn't have any guinea hen — dismissing him with an abrupt, an angry nod, and as soon as he thought him out of earshot, asking Bridget, and not without a certain severity, how old she'd been when she married Eric.

Just seventeen, and if they could imagine a man who possessed in about equal parts the qualities of fish and tiger, perhaps they could guess something of her feelings for him. He was cold; he was passionate. And she did not intend to dwell on those Roman years — they were the unhappiest of her life.

But there had been that February afternoon she first encountered René. How well she remembered it — it was her twenty-fourth birthday — little Beatrice was just three months old; and coming into that party at the French legation with the Italian officer so much in love with her — and there he was staring at her from across the room, much she expected as Romeo had stared at Juliet. She'd stared back; they couldn't take their eyes from each other.

It was love at first sight. She'd known nothing about love. She'd had her little affairs of course, and who in her place would not have had them? But this experience! It was so new, so surprising — a Vita Nuova — everything was transfigured; and Rome in the early spring; and going out into the *campagna*, and all the asphodels, and all those little larks springing up out of the ground, not like Shelley's skylark, just one at a time singing in the sky, but thousands of them, literally thousands — the sky filled with them. To find oneself perfectly happy when one had never in one's life been happy before!

What could you do but capitulate? You bowed to the god when he appeared. She burned her bridges without a qualm; she left her child. She broke her grandmother's heart; could she have done otherwise?

Fortunately, René had plans and resources.

Had either of them ever been to the Dutch East Indies, the islands in the Java Sea? And suddenly looking as though the sun were shining in her face. If you wished to find the perfect location for Eden, you'd place it right there on René's property — one was reminded of the sixth day of the created world when God made man and woman and set them in their garden to enjoy themselves. There was an innocence about it; something so completely candid, with the blue sea and the beaches so incredibly white, so divinely curved. The palm trees were tall and straight and they moved in the wind like music; and the waves, the beautiful Pacific waves with their perpetual murmur — sometimes they were large with the white foam streaming, sometimes they were small and crystal clear, hut always they were sculptural, turning, shaping themselves to fall. One saw within them colored fishes, seaweed, shells. And the shells one gathered on the beaches — far more fabulous than flowers! You bathed, you slept, you lived and loved outdoors; and you were accompanied by a mysterious sense of having, long ago, way back in the very dawn of life, experienced it all before — the slow warm days, the quick twilights, the sudden dark, the miraculous stars, the long slow night, the dawns.

But one woman, no matter how much he adored her, was not enough for René. He had to have variety. And as for those Balinesian women, they wore flowers in their hair, laughter was on their lips and they had in their eyes a kind of wonder, an eternal childhood; who was she, shrugging her shoulders ruefully, spreading out her hands — who was she to compete with those Balinesian girls?

There was her little maid — such a beautiful young creature! She used to help her dress and undress; she'd spend hours brushing her hair. René would sit and watch them, the brown girl and the white girl in all those lovely attitudes. How he raved. He made them lie down together in all kinds of postures, just as God had made them, in the sunlight, in the shadows — for the real sorrow of René's life was that God had not endowed him with the genius of Gauguin; and if he didn't have genius, he certainly had the artistic temperament; he was an artist to the marrow of his bones.

And she supposed she should have been prepared. When she looked back on that time she recognized how utterly naive she had been; but her astonishment had been complete — that day she came upon René and the little creature making love in broad daylight under a great palm tree on the beach. If he'd run at her with a sword and stabbed her in the breast she could not have been more wounded, more surprised; and then his not being able to understand her jealousy — taking it all so lightly, insisting that his making love to the little beauty had no effect upon his devotion to her; why he said she was, she would always be, the only woman he really loved — for to be never bored was to be always in love. This was a trump card he always played whenever she argued with him — and they must admit it was the ace of trumps; they never bored each other. But then when she discovered there was another lovely little creature — a child of fifteen, Nianna's aunt — it seemed more than she could bear, and she made one perfectly dreadful scene and said that she was not going to put up with it — that everything was over between them, and that she'd decided to return to Europe and leave him to his brown girls. To her great surprise he didn't protest, and before she knew it she was in the toils of her own hasty decision. He never lost his temper, he was very generous and philosophical about it; he bought her tickets, he promised to send her money, he even traveled with her as far as Batavia, where he put her on the boat. And to this day she'd never be able to understand how she'd resisted him when he bade her goodbye, there in her stateroom — putting his arms around her, kissing her with so much passion and that overpowering impulse to forgive him and return with him to paradise; and she had never been any good at resisting her impulses. But resist them she did. And off she'd sailed for Europe; and there he'd stood on the pier waving to her till she was unable to distinguish him from the rest of the crowd. How her heart had ached!

And Percy's breaking in, trying to get her back to little Beatrice, suggesting that it must have been some comfort to her at least — going back to see her child, for after all, that must have been an awful wrench. How long had she been in Java, and how old would little Beatrice be and surely she must have had tremendous eagerness?

No, frankly she had not been comforted, and as a matter of fact, she was not going to see her child — not then at least. She wasn't headed in that direction; she was going to Paris to stay with her friends, the Van Nords. Paris was as good as any place to try to recover from a broken heart — and one had somehow to start again.

But was little Beatrice in Vienna with the von Mandestadts? Was she in Rome with Eric — was she with her grandmother? And where was her grandmother? Had she remained in Rome?

No, she was living with little Beatrice just outside of Florence, in the villa where she died — a lovely place among the hills and vineyards. She had not yet advised her grandmother about her quarreling with René — coming back to Europe and all; she was waiting for the proper moment to break the news to her. And then what did they think occurred, and only a few months after her arrival in Paris?

René put in his appearance! He was charming and repentant — they could imagine how happy she was to see him. And the extraordinary thing about it was he turned up at exactly the moment her solicitor and the von Mandestadts' emissaries had finished all that tiresome business about her divorce. She was free, and René so impatient he couldn't wait a moment; they must get married at once. He used the most eloquent reasoning; they never bored each other; he even went so far as to promise perpetual fidelity. And as for her, she was always a reed in the high wind as far as René was concerned; she had little faith in his promises, little faith in the future; but those months of separation had taught her what life without him could be.

Percy all the while so impatient to learn about little Beatrice, trying to interrupt her. What about little Beatrice, wouldn't she tell him before she went any further what had happened to the child? Had the von Mandestadts insisted on getting custody?

Oh, dear no (and had Millicent seen a shadow as swift as the flight of a bird flit over her face?), nobody wanted little Beatrice; she had remained where she was — with her grandmother in Florence.

She hadn't been there yet?

No, she was waiting for just the right moment — she wanted to go with René, for they had, as soon as the necessary papers were in order, gone off one pleasant morning with the Van Nords for witnesses and got themselves properly married; not such a marriage as her grandmother could approve of, for it was without benefit of the Catholic church, of course, but still a perfectly respectable legal tie.

It was extraordinary the delight they, both of them, felt at finding themselves man and wife. They went to Greece for their wedding trip. She'd never been there before — they could just imagine how beautiful that was; and then after it was over, they decided to go straight to Florence and make a clean breast of everything. René was really so charming, so handsome, so cultivated — just her grandmother's dish of tea; they'd even planned that if the old lady showed any signs of trying to fascinate him he could go as far as he wanted to in responding to her charms. He seemed to be looking forward to the encounter.

But, ah, they weren't prepared for the change that had overtaken the poor old lady. Darling Granny (crossing herself in a quick, an almost furtive manner). That visit had been terribly poignant. Her fascinating, worldly, capricious old grandmother had, she could describe it in no other manner, moved out of one room of her soul, locked the door upon it and now resided in another. She had always, in a purely punctilious and routine kind of way, been a religious woman; she'd gone to mass; she'd confessed her sins. But the piety she practiced now was an entirely different matter. Even her appearance had changed. She wore over her head and framing her beautiful face a black lace mantilla; it was vastly becoming to her and lent her a kind of melancholy grandeur, for she could never escape being the *grande dame*. She moved about the villa like a sort of Mater Dolorosa and her only associates were priests and prelates. The whole place smelt of piety and prayer and penitence, and what was even more distressing, a sort of resigned and disciplined sorrow. She and René didn't seem to have any defense against it. They had gone expecting to implore her forgiveness — they found themselves forgiven. It was very strange, very depressing indeed, a most melancholy visit; and with the nightingales singing all night in the cypress grove behind the villa and the fragrance of iris and gelsomino always drifting through the air — all that magic of the Tuscan June wrapping them round in ancient, penitential grief. God! They weren't able to endure it! They only stayed a week.

Hurrying on quickly, as though determined not to allow any comment on her failure to even mention little Beatrice; and poor Percy rendered completely speechless by such flagrant neglect of the little creature, giving up the struggle to bring her back into the headlong narrative; just letting her go on, with the poor child left like a ghost among the shadows in the cypress grove, or out in the sunshine in the paths between the iris and the gelsomino, running in and out of the great rooms of that melancholy villa; uncanny —

On she went, trying not so much to justify her affections, her out-and-out infatuation for René, as attempting to explain her response to him, her delight in his companionship.

She wouldn't go into it all too deeply. He had his prevailing sin, weakness, call it a misfortune if you liked — perversity; he couldn't keep away from women. As for herself, perhaps it was callousness; she'd suffered the initial consternation; but really, she got so that it didn't trouble her too much — perhaps it was necessary to be married to René to learn to adapt oneself to his vagaries, to be able to forgive him. As a matter of fact, the whole thing had a less poetic aspect than in Bali, for those brown girls were so beautiful — they had their poetry, certainly. These affairs were different. She'd have to confess it, she even found some interest in them; he'd developed a penchant for the ugly, the perverse, the slightly corrupt — and always now discussing everything with her — there was a certain interest in analysis — dissection.

It was the companionship she shared with René that was so personal, so unique a thing. Why, in his society everything came to life. And what wonderful things they enjoyed together. There was the Russian ballet; they followed it all over Europe. And what music they heard! René's knowledge of music was really, for an amateur, immense — all the great quartets and symphonies, the operas, he knew intimately, carried in his head; he'd hum and whistle the most complicated arias, the most intricate themes and variations; it was such a joy to hear him every morning in his tub. But of course his greatest love was art; they'd travel anywhere to see a picture he wanted to become familiar with. What pictures did to make one understand the world in which one lived! They made a practice of studying faces — everywhere, in trains, in cafés, in the queerest places; for they were always searching out the shabby, the shady, you might say the out and out disreputable haunts. To find the "face arresting" — that was the quest that they were after; and if you found it and looked at it long enough, you almost always discovered its replica in some great masterpiece; and when you'd found the counterpart, your knowledge of that face, that masterpiece, that character resembling it increased your knowledge of the world, of human nature generally — of life itself. This relating of life, of experience, to art was one of the richest pleasures they enjoyed together. They invented all manner of interesting games around this practice; every city had its game — and there were country games — and the slightly shady and disreputable games. She couldn't enumerate them all. René's capacity for wresting initiation out of knocking about was extraordinary. And, of course, they must always remember that he had, and to an extraordinary degree, the artistic temperament — this insatiable curiosity of his — this need to taste, experience, clutch at everything; and all the fruits on all the trees almost, you might say, within his grasp; and knowing as he did the jig was nearly up.

And then there was (her face suddenly grave, meditative, as though lost in certain depths she could not presume to fathom) this disturbing desire he had to paint, a kind of straining beyond the reach of any natural gift or capacity — a sense of frustration — and, being as lucid as he was, knowing he was an amateur and not able to leave off trying, plunged sometimes in deepest gloom. When they were off on their expeditions he always took his painting gear. His water colors were charming — not strong enough in line or color, weak; but charming, charming. She really did her best to show an interest; but she couldn't lie to René. She was not convinced.

It was this passion to paint that finally did her in — that summer in the Balkans, in such a ravishing, a quite undiscovered place and where she least expected competition; indeed it was a situation she never dreamed she'd really have to face; but that summer in Petre she encountered a genuine, a fatal rival. She didn't know to this day what her nationality was, Rumanian? Bulgarian? Perhaps she was a Greek, a Serb. René never told her — she never asked. But she got her hooks into him very deep indeed. She was fat, she was ugly; she was very neatly twice his age; she was extraordinarily corrupt. But she was an unmistakable painter. Her talent was indisputable. She told him his work was remarkable; that she could make a painter of him — that his only excuse for living was that he had a gift — a genuine gift.

In the face of all this (shrugging her shoulders, lifting up her hands), come now — what chance had she? She knew that when René found a mistress whose society he enjoyed in broad daylight as well as after dark, there was genuine cause for alarm. He began to take her off on those ravishing little trips and journeys that they were always making together; and then — behold, one fine day, and without a word of warning, he carried her off to Bali.

Yes, with the help of her solicitor and emissaries from her grand-mother she divorced him. She supposed it had been her desire to hit back. The gesture was contrary to her nature. It was hard for her to be angry long with anyone and, as for René, there was little at any time she wouldn't have forgiven him. To tell the truth, she was utterly miserable as soon as all those knots had been untied and, of course, a European woman twice divorced was in none too enviable a spot.

What did she do with herself? She managed to pretty well fill René's own prescription — "Eat, drink, and be merry, for tomorrow we're all over the cliff." She had several bizarre little affairs; but really bizarre. The only thing she regretted about them was that René wasn't on hand, so that she could talk them over with him. They were, they would have seemed to him — amusing.

And then one lovely day in Paris, it was two days after Chamberlain had returned from Munich — she remembered the afternoon so well, the late afternoon sunlight streaming through the Van Nords' drawing room — and they were drinking tea and eating croissants when in he came, as gay and musical as a lark, and whether the Van Nords, who perfectly adored René, had been in the plot or not she never knew; at any rate, they could imagine how glad she was to see him.

After the happiest week in Paris, doing all the galleries, hearing all the music that was possible — never a word of anger or reproach did either one have for the other, everything amiable and charming — after the happiest of weeks, René appeared one morning flourishing two tickets for the *Normandie* — a bridal stateroom, no less. He had decided that she must sail with him and at once. Europe was about to crack. It was finished — kaput — and he wasn't going to have her remain behind when he had gone; he wanted her in America, only so could his heart be at ease. She needn't tell her grandmother anything about their escapade till she'd arrived in New York. Then she could look around her; she could open up a correspondence with the old lady. She must persuade her to cross the ocean with little Beatrice. It was the only safe place for them all; and her grandmother would live to thank him for his sagacity; he'd assist them to the limit of his powers, which she knew were none too great, as he'd about run through everything he possessed. And there was that Balkan woman, that Serbian, Rumanian — whatever she called herself — waiting for him in San Francisco.

So here she was.

And she got up abruptly in that way she had of erasing with a gesture, an inflection, the emotions contained in what she considered was a finished situation, offering her attention fresh and innocent of entangling climates to the next experience. She wanted, she said, to go again to see the pictures — there were so many she hadn't seen at all thoroughly; and there was that lovely little Van Der Weiden, the adorable Goya. One couldn't see them often enough.

She beckoned them to come; she started off at once, moving with her slightly indolent gait, a little ahead of them, humming the aria from *Iphigénie*, over the wetted paths, over the grass in the strange light of the moon, the artificial illuminations, the broken rainbows.

T W O

———

MILLICENT LAY IN BED and looked out.

To the right and to the left of her, tiers and tiers of windows — clusters and bevies of little lights flickered, fluttered, floated off like sections of bright beehives in the blue night air. That sense of unreality she had experienced at the French Pavilion increased; it very nearly overwhelmed her.

God, there were moments when she wanted to shout to heaven her utter unbelief in it — this life, this world reared up around her — being here — clutching the ropes, grabbing the rings; and tonight especially with Bridget's story so fresh in her mind, and all these hives, homes, these bevies of little lights positively flying in through the open windows.

And there was upon one this spring a mood of tenderness and terror. You carried it about with you wherever you went — what with the season so gentle and the lovely days following each other like a reassurance — summer so far ahead of time. And the Fair going on over there on the Flushing meadows. Hitler had occupied Austria. He had moved into the Sudetenland. Chamberlain had offered us peace in our time. Tomorrow she would go to the Lenny Weeds' cocktail patty. She would doubtless meet Paula Downs and old Mr. Andrews. She would drink more cocktails than were good for her. She would be strident and unacceptable, even to herself.

A clock struck twelve. She counted the strokes. Blown over from Long Island, from New Jersey, the fragrance of grass and young green leaves, lilacs, apple blossoms floated vaguely through the town, came in at the open windows. The moon rode high above the skyscrapers.

Mists rose from the sidewalks. In the East River the tides ran strong; gulls dipped and plunged. The tug boats wove their river symphonies. In the North River the *Normandie* pushed out into the stream. Crowds waved from her decks; handkerchiefs waved from the pier. In the cornices of the Metropolitan Museum the pigeons slept, their heads beneath their wings. They covied, across the street, in the cornices and window ledges on Fifth Avenue. They slept in the niches, the cornices of the Forty-second Street library. The skyscrapers — choirs and choruses of lighted windows, human hives and cells swarming round her in the night, cities of glass and iron — flickering, fluttering like bees, like fireflies, seemed to sing together, celebrating something strange and not to be quite credited.

Why, if you chose to think about it — the unbelievability of it — being herself, in whom sleigh bells still reverberated and to whom the slow plodding of a horse's hooves, wherever she might hear it, carried her back to a time as remote from now as the days of Elizabeth, or any other period of history. And considering all this — the transformations that had taken place in the landscape of her life since she was young — she might venture to think that she had extended her journey beyond the usual boundaries of memory and association; for there were moments amid the excitement — the frantic rush of today, when all that she was experiencing seemed to exist in an empty space filled with sound that had no vibrations in the memory; one seemed severed from one's roots; one groped, one tried to find one's way.

And how could anybody who had lived, as she had, that enclosed, parochial life of her childhood and early youth exist in the world today without perpetual amazement, not to say dislocation of one's soul — turning on the radio (as you chatted, carried on your small pursuits), twisting the dial — voices from all the continents and islands of the world. You went to the movies; to the newsreels — unimaginable scenes of horror passed before your eyes, cities bombed and women eviscerated, and children murdered at their innocent games. You saw the inhabitants of every continent. You traveled through jungles and arctic circles and saw the aborigines of hitherto unvisited lands. The world had cracked; it had cleft apart, it had opened up before your astonished eyes, all its teeming cells and hives and tenements seemed to be turning out their populations for you to gaze upon. And wasn't it the case that you felt some queer, indefinable, yet authentic sense of guilt, responsibility, as though you were yourself implicated in the whole awesome and terrible business?

You ran about in motor cars, you boarded ocean liners, crossed the continent in Chiefs and Super Chiefs — airplanes, you dashed here, there, and everywhere — attempting to grab, to see, to snatch everything, as though every sight, every experience were accessible to you if you only hurried fast enough, while all the time there was this yearning upon you to go back, to retreat into the darkness, the dusk, into the backward and abysm.

Awful and vertiginous the pace, the beat of it, with the great war, the great boom — the crash, the great depression, and the present moment so filled with terror and tenderness, and experiencing every day such a queer intensity. Wondering so often who you were and what you were and who it might be necessary for you to be the next moment, with all the different roles it seemed to you at various times you had to play and having to behave with this group thus, and with that group like quite a different person, and everyone engaged in trying to get out of everyone else a little more than anyone was quite prepared to give, and the heart so hungry for heaven knew just what, so unassuaged, so void.

For almost anything might happen to you in New York — almost anything might occur — one seemed to be asking for everything (or almost everything) and with everything within the reach (or nearly within the reach) of everybody; and the fabulous city like a great Christmas tree, so brilliantly lighted, with so many glittering gifts perpetually being handed out; and all the rush and competition — all the frenzy, wearing your mind to frazzles and your nerves to fiddle strings — grinding out the articles, the inferior little stories, which, if you must be honest about it, you found difficult without genuine humiliation to acknowledge were your own, grinding them out, sending them off for the rewards that grew in proportion to their triviality more and more immense — switching you off, as they appeared to have done in the most unexpected directions — trafficking with Hollywood, while all the lawyers, managers, publishers, contracts, agents spun around you the most bewildering web of engagements and adventures, speeding you up and, before you quite realized what was happening, to the amazing tempo at which you lived, so that the whole thing seemed somehow to have occurred more by accident than by design.

You wouldn't call it the natural climate of your soul. You went here, you went there; you laid yourself open to the most abominable habits of the heart — this snobbishness of names, achievement — the need for personal identification — it seemed to be in the air you breathed, it got into the very bones and muscles of behavior — the cold little nods, the wandering eye, the embarrassing enthusiasms suddenly poured over you, enough to wither the heart within you. And so frequently finding yourself adopting the same manners, snubbing this person, trying to have a word with that one. Longing as you were for some display of natural warmth and friendliness. Loyalty and kindness seemed, and almost without one's realizing it, to have dissolved in gossip, analysis — sophistication. And who was to blame and how this had occurred, it would be difficult to say.

And if the heart ached for something it did not receive, where did it take itself with all its obstreperous needs? Personal relationships seemed to have lost their shape and outline. One grasped at nothing tangible. There was hunger, there was immense curiosity, there was solitude. And one was very busy. There was an urgency. You must do this and that; you must go here and there. And, strange as it was and impossible to define (for were we not involved in this together?), there was a certain fidelity. Everyone must keep going; nobody must falter, for if you displayed courage, a certain perseverance, you might get through with it and on to something else perhaps. But what it was and when it might be realized, who was there to say? Who could predict concerning these possible, these vaguely guessed at eventualities?

Yet there were these sudden, these unaccountable moments — being overtaken by love — feeling it rush into your heart like an annunciation, coming to you here, there — everywhere — on top of busses, in crowded concert halls — sometimes on winter evenings with the skyscrapers floating, flickering above you — that rush of the great wings, that outpouring, that generous gift of all that you possessed of love, allegiance — merging with the crowds, examining the faces. This sense of brotherhood. You buried your loneliness in it. At times you were persuaded that it was larger than any personal stakes you had in happiness.

Millicent raised her hand to brush away the tears that to her surprise were streaming down her cheeks, and allowed herself the luxury of their warmth and tenderness. She closed her eyes and let the warm breeze fan her cheeks and throat.

Out there in New Jersey, over on Long Island, in Bronx Park, in Van Cortlandt Park, on into Connecticut spring was silently, softly passing into summertime — crossing the threshold, changing her icy greens and frost-white blossoms for the darker dyes of summer. And these sensuous, tender images trailing along with them the remembrance of Bridget St. Dennis, she saw her arrayed in that perfectly lovely leaf-green dress, the chic and innocent black hat, with the birdlike bow perched beside the spray of apple blossoms, setting off her white face and soft dark hair.

You always had with her a peculiar sense of emergence, surprise; her nerves tuned to the most subtle perceptions, she seemed to be perpetually moving from one climate, season of the heart, into the next. Those great dark eyes, flooded, as Percy declared, with their deep, their Mediterranean gravity, which wasn't of course half their story, since the Irish strain bestowed upon her by her father scintillated, at times positively snapped, within their irises — this compound of Irish and Spanish conspiring to set something grave, informed and watchful over against a recklessness, a gaiety and wit the girl possessed; and the two tendencies held in perfect equilibrium.

Add to these elements of day and night, very likely bestowed upon her at birth, those more accidental qualities incident on her being completely of her day and generation, and she somehow held you in suspense. You saw, behind her, glimpses of Europe tottering on the brink of destruction, more open and inviting, more ready to be enjoyed and investigated than at any other moment of its history. The whole of it, you might say, spread out before her like an enormous garden of enchantment — all the lovely cities, their opera houses, concert halls, casinos, restaurants, churches, cathedrals, museums, bars, bistros, thrown for her diversion into a kind of private pleasance, traveling about so swiftly and prompted by the most freakish whims to run from capital to capital, this determination to explore the esthetic and sensuous, the intellectual response having become, for her, not only the exciting, but the important and essential business of existence.

Suddenly startled — severed abruptly from her thoughts — Millicent reached her arm across the bed, grasped the telephone receiver; for the telephone was ringing sharply, insistently, tearing through her like a knife, cruelly exposing her nerves to its insolent demands.

Good God; what it exacted of you — interest, sweet temper, the required inflection, the ability at any moment to tune yourself to whoever had need of you.

"Yes, Percy," she said, "certainly, my dear." (And how did he have the nerve and at this hour? Was there no moment of the day or night he didn't feel that she was at his beck and call?) "What is it that you want to say?"

He couldn't rest, thinking of Bridget's plight — thinking of little Beatrice. He'd no sooner taken her home than he'd gone off to telephone her. He'd asked her to lunch tomorrow at the Algonquin. She said she'd come on one condition — that Millicent came too. And would she telephone the first thing in the morning to confirm this date?

"What — I'm not interested? Why of course I'm interested, Percy!" — divining by his voice the exact condition of his nerves and laying over her face an expression that combined both patience and exasperation, leaning back on the pillows, closing her eyes with the receiver clamped to her ear.

He could do nothing but worry. He was almost frantic with anxiety. What was the meaning of Bridget's silence on the score of little Beatrice? There was something strange about it — ominous. The von Mandestadts were going to kidnap that child. This was his theory. And Millicent must remember that little Beatrice was a fourth part Jewish. That she must keep in mind. Had she come to any conclusions?

No, she had not? She must promise to assist him tomorrow at luncheon in getting to the bottom of the mystery. They'd wrest it from her together. Her silence on the subject was peculiar. Surely there was something they could do for the poor girl in all her trouble.

"What — you say I don't want to come? Don't be childish, Percy. I'll be there sharp at one. Yes, I'll telephone to Bridget." She hung up the receiver, she'd have to admit it, very abruptly.

From where, she wondered, had he telephoned?

From his favorite bar, his club, his own apartment? He'd certainly been drinking heavily. She had undoubtedly offended him — hanging up like that, or practically hanging up on him. It had been his intention to talk to her for hours. She tormented herself with all sorts of doubts.

She rarely cut his confidences short. She liked to have him stand in need of her. And now, with his passionate attachment for Bridget about to end in disaster, turning to her for help and guidance as he undoubtedly would, how much of herself was she prepared to give to him; and could she if she tried to, patch him up? Could she make a whole man of Percy Jones?

She didn't know. She honestly didn't know.

He was profoundly involved. And this clinging so closely to his notions about Bridget's child was of course all a part of his absurd romanticism. Why, she was a little composition of his own heart, a sort of invisible agent at work on his behalf, banking as he did on Bridget's devotion to her, inventing all manner of situations — going to Europe to rescue her, and just in the nick of time.

She'd seen him through so many of these infatuations, his disastrous marriage and all the rest; and the exasperating consistency, breaking his heart on all of them, suffering so unnecessarily. What a gift he had for suffering, endowing him really with a touch of the ridiculous — always getting into the same traps, falling in love with the same beautiful creature, as remote from his grasp as a star in heaven, doting on her subtlety, variety — for he never fell in love with just a pretty face — there had to be brilliance, personality. But always wanting her fixed in terms of his own notions about her — "stop there, my darling, while I go on and complete the beautiful story" — always yearning to render some extravagant act of devotion, to lavish upon her in her emergencies all the treasures of his soul. And all of them so much younger and compassed about, as they always were, with romantic entanglements.

The present dilemma resembled the others, except, of course, that Bridget was incomparable, and in his being so much more passionately involved and having with equal intensity to pay for all of it, and moreover, behaving as he was in this somewhat novel manner, approaching his plight in this new, and to her own way of thinking, exceedingly unbecoming spirit. You had only to look at him — those pleats and folds, the little lines appearing around his mouth, those sullen cheeks, the general droop and sag of his expression — challenging fate to do him in, determined this time to get ahead of fate, to frustrate her usual tricks and pranks; and all this playfulness and jocularity — an overassertiveness, a kind of boldness and truculence utterly out of harmony with his character; and drinking even more than ever — you practically never saw him that he wasn't drinking, trying to wrap himself round in these naive dreams about protecting her, bringing her child back from Europe (simply fixed upon that little girl), and his undisguised sorrow and disappointment over her story; the symptoms were all there; you couldn't mistake them. A crisis was approaching.

After which, and all to be gone over again, the usual orgies of analysis — confession, turning on himself, rending himself. And finally, his misery somewhat spent, and trusting her, as he invariably did, not so much to lay the blame on him as to comfort him with a sense of her understanding, her general pity for the poor, irrational human heart — its tendency to reenact the dramas that destroy its happiness — and the bonds of their affection curiously strengthened, open as she would be to his persuasion, his need of her. And the question this time to be decided once and for all. Would she, should she, and indeed did Percy really want her to marry him? He was always on these occasions thoroughly convinced that he did.

But did he, did he actually want her to?

What Percy needed was a mother, someone always ready to understand, to advise, to help, pity, and encourage him. This role she'd played too long, too well. And was he beginning to show signs of a sickness for which there was no remedy? Could marrying Percy make him whole?

She didn't know; she honestly didn't know.

One way or another she'd managed to escape the personal entanglements. There was something — this tendency she had to make the lives of other people root themselves within her heart — become a part of her own growth and inward flowering, the vicarious experience enough and more than enough for her. Queer thing — this sense of being bent on some strict interior quest, yet never free from the profoundest grief at her own meagre share in life — the real, the warm, the flesh and blood and human business of living, crowning your own sex with all its earthy anguishing and palpable rewards.

And here then she was — swinging on the ropes — grabbing the rings.

The towers crowded round her — tiers and tiers of lighted windows, beginning now to dim, to disappear, to float her off among them in the soft spring night. She seemed to rise, to fall.

And were these wings attached to her ankles, or, like the wings of angels, to her arms, for surely she was flying, gently, windlessly levitated above the loveliest city in the world, which apparently lay below her like a garden arrayed in sun and space and greenery, clouds colliding, bursting, burgeoning, distributing their mother-of-pearl and moonstone luster, chestnut trees — green, white, and crimson plumes blown vaguely about with clouds and shadows, with lilac and wisteria; and all the monuments placed at proper intervals — the Tuileries on one side of the river and the Luxembourg on the other and (apparently just where it should be) the Place de la Concorde, throwing up its jets and pyramids of fountain spray.

And was that Bridget seated among the flowers, the fountains, the artificial illuminations dressed in the lovely vestments of the spring?

No, this was neither Paris nor the Flushing meadows. This was New York. She was here, in her own bed. Hitler had occupied Austria. He had moved into the Sudetenland. Chamberlain had offered us peace in our time. And should she go tomorrow to the Lenny Weeds' cocktail party? Should she wear her new spring hat? The tugboats wove their river symphonies. Motors blew their horns. A taxi roared through the street. An airplane went over.

T H R E E

WAS SHE DREAMING OR REMEMBERING, Millicent wondered, as feeling the comfortable mattress supporting her — conscious of the morning sunlight filling the room and of the city gilded, all blown over, with the blue and amethyst mists of spring, hearing the tugboats in the East River and the hum and drum of the city far below and, making a drugged and drowsy effort to orient herself, she fell, plunged, sank deeper into her dream, and losing consciousness of time and place and floating, though not entirely disembodied, in an element that allowed for curious extension of scene and bodily condition, she saw that face clearly recognizable as the face of Christopher Henderson leaning out of a gabled window which, with its chimney pots, its irregular roofs, seemed to duplicate itself many times, and thus to reproduce a series of streets, of sounds, of smells and all drenched in the aroma of pleasure, sharpening, intensifying her recognition that here, then, she was in London, with Christopher, wearing a sunbonnet and smoking a corncob pipe, calling her from his upper window; and though she was undoubtedly out of doors and responding to the London streets, the sounds of horses' hooves on the cobblestones and the smell of fog, of cannel coal, of pavements soaked in wet, she was nonetheless seated in a beautiful Georgian room, with many books ranged round and portraits on the walls and Christopher himself by the fire continuing to shout at her, while her voice growing louder and still louder, she retreated farther and farther from London and appeared to be standing in a wide field with birds rising and dropping down into the grass, raking up little mounds of new-mown hay and looking for daisies, cornflowers and poppies, stooping now and again to pick them and twine them into garlands and, at the same time, watching the processional of great white clouds that moved above her in the sky — marmoreal clouds in which she discovered the head of Michelangelo and the perfectly lovely outline of a little ram running on the wind, and white angels trumping on their horns and suddenly Jehovah, perfectly immense, riding the blue waters of the summer afternoon. There then she was, half in the heavenly meadow picking cornflowers, daisies and poppies out of her rake, and half in that fascinating ambient — London — with Christopher, now a part of the cloud processional, now hanging from the top story of that Georgian house, now in the big chair by the blazing fire and the smoke from his pipe disturbing the fragrance of the meadows, rising to the surface, sinking, falling, floating off again and finally emerging to find herself once more on her comfortable mattress and repeating, "was it the dream or was it the memory," looking about her.

This was her room, her view, her towers and tenements and peaks and pinnacles.

Attempting deliberately to move from the condition of her dreams into the mood and climate of those old memories out of which they so mysteriously were wrought, she lived again through that romantic, perplexing, difficult visit.

Staying with the Underwoods in Cornwall, hearing the gulls cry and the waves break, haunted by memories of the sea (Yseult's sea, Malory's, Tennyson's sea), seeing it there before her, marvelously streaked with green and blue and purple eddies, the white sails, the wings of gulls, the crests of the waves all flying up and off into the blue, and the great cliffs, blown round with spray, retreating down the shattering coast, her heart filled with that perpetual ache of adolescence, that expectation, restlessness; and never being quite able to believe that she was part of the social and human drama going on in that large, romantic house — carrying it off, of course, with a high hand, and acting to the best of her ability the fabulous role in which she found that she was cast, with the dressing for dinner every night and the young men coming down from London for the weekends and that extraordinary idea that had taken possession of Claire and Hall Underwood — that Christopher Henderson, who was there for a fortnight, was completely entranced with her.

She knew, alas, that this was not true. She knew that young men were never entranced with her and that, fascinating as she thought they were, and as much as she yearned to attract them, those mysterious little nets woven round most young women, filaments so vibrant that she could actually feel the air quivering whenever two people of the opposite sex had begun to spin them together, would never be spun around her — something was lacking, in as much as, long as she might for these moments of penetrating sweetness — this mystery to weave about her and someone of the opposite sex — she was incapable of paying out the first fine filaments. Something was amiss — and considering all this, how difficult it was to carry out the fiction that Christopher Henderson was head over heels in love with her, even though Claire and Hall Underwood assumed that this was the case, and diligently persisted in their matchmaking, persuading Christopher, whenever they had him alone, how clever, how very unusual she was, greatly exaggerating her income as well as her charms, and laying especial emphasis on her independence from family ties — presenting her in fact as a perfectly splendid match; and with the same scheme in view taking her aside, telling her all about him, his family connections, his interesting friends, his exclusive clubs — the great success of his first remarkable novel.

She'd read the novel, of course, and without great enthusiasm; but she had liked, had been considerably impressed by him, and the whole scheme, it could not be denied, was filled for her with unspeakable fascination — living in England, meeting all these remarkable friends. The idea that she was going to marry him was indeed seldom out of her mind. Every night before she went to sleep she fitted herself with his name for life — Mrs. Christopher Henderson — Millicent Henderson. It sounded very well indeed. She imagined herself launched in London and gathering about her a group of the most brilliant people. Naturally, she'd have a child, very likely a large family. There was nothing indeed that this marriage did not seem to hold within its gift, and its consummation began to seem to her as not only the most desirable and exhilarating, but the most inevitable thing in the world.

Nevertheless, the more certain she felt of it all, the more embarrassed she became in Christopher's society. He was a dapper young man, somewhat frivolous, perhaps, for he was light and airy in his movements and walked on the tips of his toes, and had a habit of turning a phrase in such a manner as to make it almost compulsory for her to laugh at everything he said; and this, forcing her to be extremely witty herself, straining beyond and outside the secret mood that nourished her excitement (the tryst with Malory and Tennyson, the sea, the waves, the cliffs) and longing so much to invest their relationship with some touch of all this melancholy beauty, rendered it exceedingly difficult to keep the whole thing going — just sitting around from day to day as she was, being so bright and gay and witty and waiting for him to propose to her.

And then one day, sure enough, he did — call it a proposal if you wanted to. There the two of them were, and on the last evening of his visit, alone in the long drawing room, and the sea stretching off beyond the terrace to the sky and the late afternoon sun illuminating the grass and the flowers in the borders with a peculiar grave, clear light, the windows open and the sound of the waves breaking far below at the foot of the cliffs, neither of them making any attempt to be amusing, and the silence, so unusual between them, growing extremely embarrassing, making up her own mind that she would on no account break it, and guessing that Christopher had made a similar resolve; and then, when it had drawn itself out to perfectly intolerable lengths, Christopher's suddenly rising from his chair, going to the fireplace, knocking the ashes from his pipe, crossing the room and standing beside her in the embrasure by the window, taking her hand and saying in an embarrassed, but a very determined voice, "Miss Munroe — Millicent. I want very much that you should be my wife."

What with waiting so long for it to come and feeling so relieved, so more than anxious to meet him with gratitude and enthusiasm, and being so ready, so perfectly delighted to accept his offer, how astonished she was, how utterly unable to believe it — that she was drawing her hand away, that she was folding it over the other hand, that she was saying, almost as though she couldn't help herself, as though some power not her own were forcing her, "how good of you, how really wonderful of you, Christopher — Mr. Henderson — asking me to marry you. But no, I can't. I don't even know why it is, but I can't, I simply can't." He'd looked astonished enough — insulted; however he hadn't persisted; he'd turned quickly and gone out of the room and, except for having to sit next to him that night at dinner, she'd never seen him from that day to this.

Freakish it certainly had been; but then freakish her behavior often was — unaccountable; and though she'd regretted, she supposed, a million times or more the extraordinary rejoinder to what had been after all the best chance that life had offered her for fulfillment, marriage, family ties, nevertheless, though so far away, dreamlike as that visit seemed, and made in an era so different from the present moment as to render it almost impossible to believe she had lived it at all; and though that young girl in her trailing skirts, her large romantic picture hats, that girl with the large romantic eyes, the adolescent, hungry and expectant heart, was a creature as different as possible from the woman who lay here tonight remembering her, they did certainly share in common the same wayward behavior of nerves — reflexes set invariably in motion at the touch of certain springs, the freakish denials, choices, abstinences that had so often shocked her with a sense of being trapped in snares of her own invention.

But what a strange dream — and having it just now, with her mind so occupied with Percy and Bridget. She didn't think she'd given Christopher Henderson a thought for years — seeing him there, dressed in his sunbonnet; smoking his pipe, hanging out of that gabled window, and then moving with him to the splendid room in the Georgian house, and lastly transported to those heavenly meadows. What a sweet, particular music and fragrance moved in her heart when she remembered this last part of the dream — those clouds and the angels trumping on their horns, with Jehovah in the midst; and the little rams that ran upon the wind, and everything so blue and halcyon. Very mysterious this underworld of memories — the night, the morning dreams playing on them in much the way the morning sunlight played on the innumerable, anonymous little drops of dew that hung on every leaf and blade — turning them round, extracting from this one, from that, what varieties of sparks and colors, what intricately crossed refractions — rays . . .

She might if she lay there and speculated longer make something out of it — the dream, the memory. But she must get up; she must bestir herself. The city was already washed in morning splendor — what with the mist, the warmth, the sunshine, and all the bright dust whirled up into the air, it was filled with as much speck and spark and gilt and gold and fire as an opal; and it seemed impossible that the weather could continue to be so lovely — one day following another, more exquisite than the last.

She was going to telephone Bridget, she remembered. They would lunch with Percy at the Algonquin. And perhaps Bridget would tell them about little Beatrice — very likely she would not. But in any event she could never rise to meet a new day without this sense of expectation, curiosity — excitement . . .

FOUR

IF SHE DECIDED TO WEAR THE OLD HAT, she'd come home after lunch; if she decided on the new one she'd make a day of it and go to the Lenny Weeds' cocktail party. The first was old and shabby and the second, though chic and modish, was unbecoming and ridiculous. But if she was trying to compete with Bridget St. Dennis, it didn't matter which she wore. For who in the world at any age could compete with Bridget?

Poor girl! Over the telephone she'd seemed calm enough. She would be at the Algonquin at one. How nice, she'd said, of Percy to ask them. How she could, in the midst of her great anxieties, remain so cool and apparently unruffled was a major mystery. It was because you were unable to fathom Bridget that she held you always spellbound. So explicit about all she said, and yet so essentially mysterious. She made apparently a genuine effort to convey the truth about herself. At any rate, she never seemed to be lying. Yet the lies to which one was accustomed were so much more transparent than this baffling candor of Bridget's.

She'd had, she said, no more news. She had not slept. In a few months she'd be stony broke — penniless; but if the worst came to the worst, she thought she could adjust to it. She would not allow herself to get scared. Think of the Russian princesses; there were the dressmaking establishments; the milliners. And moreover there was always Hollywood. Her friend Northrop Eames (Bridget somehow seemed to know people in every corner of the globe waiting to pull wires, open doors for her) had told her that if she ever thought seriously of getting into the movies he'd lend her the necessary money. If she were really serious, he'd stake everything he had on her. She had, she believed, some talent in this direction.

Millicent had never seen her do her little skits? She didn't wish to appear vain; but they really were good. They put, so Northrop Eames declared, Beatrice Lillie in the shade — very gay, naughty — satirical; but in spite of this, there was depth — seriousness. However, first she must get her child across the ocean — that was her great preoccupation.

No, she wouldn't wear the last year's hat — too dowdy, with that faded wreath of poppies, cornflowers and wheat halfway round the brim. She threw it on the bed and put on the chic, the modish — the ridiculous little confection which was not only ludicrous and unbecoming but which, she must remember, committed her to the Lenny Weeds' cocktail party, where she really did not want to go.

And translated suddenly to that wide meadow, raking up the grass and flowers while Christopher Henderson called to her from the house with the gabled windows — hearing the waves beat on the Cornish shore and her own voice refusing his offer of marriage, she selected her gloves, took up her purse, a pocket handkerchief, left her apartment, descended in the elevator, walked out into the street.

The morning was even lovelier than she'd imagined. There was a smell about New York this time of year; you'd know it anywhere — the streets just watered and a dash of pavements, a dash of sidewalks, a breeze in from the bay bearing a faint smell of the sea, and though you'd hardly believe it, that hint of apple blossoms and lilacs floating over from Long Island, from New Jersey.

And look, ah look! She stopped a moment to bless the little row of plane trees. The leaves were out full frill; they were actually casting shadows on the sidewalk; and regarding, not the leaves, but the shadows at her feet, their effect upon her was instantaneous — filmlike, impalpable she could feel them, not there on the sidewalk, but within her own heart, shade moving over shade, shadow lightly placed above shadow, and behind these the processional moments — songs of birds, leafy trees, flowering meadows, waving grass — music, fragrance, measure, as though the pageant of spring eternally stepping into summer dwelt within her, capable of infinite revival — going on and on.

> And the heart grieves, and the heart remembers
> And leaps into the green glade like a hind —
> Leaps into the green glade to recover

Forgotten dreams behind the dream remembered,
And shadows laid on shadows in the shade —

She improvised, and the words seemed to confirm her in that curious
sense she had of walking through her dreams — memories. "Shadows
laid on shadows in the shade," she said aloud.

But at this instant she was almost run over by a taxi, and her knees
trembling, and her legs hardly able to support her, she decided firmly
not to prolong this particular intensity of rhymes, meters — words; for
if she did, she'd never reach her destination without an accident. The
day she had before her admitted of nothing of this sort. She was going
to a newsreel; she was going to the Algonquin; yes, she'd made up her
mind, she'd make a day of it; she was going to the Lenny Weeds' cocktail party.

"Shadows laid on shadows in the shade" — muttering the words,
crossing Fifth Avenue, walking along under the elm trees by the park;
and oh, but what a day it was, lovely, ethereal. Seen through the tender
lace of leaf and mist and blossom; everything — the walks, the roads,
the lawns, the trees, with the motor cars flashing in and out, and that
great row of tall hotels and apartment houses on Central Park South,
with the awnings, the terraces, the irregular roofs and façades, had a
light, an airy gaiety, as though about to bow, to smile and blow away
into the blue — the pedestrians, the little groups of people floating off,
like bouquets of brightly colored flowers thrown about at random.

She'd stop and have a look at General Sherman. How jaded he looked
on his jaded horse; but for all his weariness, he resembled a winged victory, with the winds of his long march blowing back his hair, and the
heavy folds of his great cape and the golden angel rushing on before
him, her golden palm upheld. Set about in his semicircle of sycamore
trees he accommodated himself with enormous dignity to all the skyscrapers that crowded round. She glanced from the golden general to
Pierre's, to the Squibbs Building, and some happy accident of light, of
shade, of depth and mass piling them up before her eyes in a most brave
and challenging composition, she marveled; she exulted in them.

Did one ever get used to New York, she wondered, as she continued
down the avenue — the energy, the daring — the surprise! It laid its
spell upon one certainly. Sometimes you admired, you loved it so; and

at other times you couldn't hate or fear it enough; you were unable to put your trust in it. Always it seemed unreal, ephemeral.

And as for this! For she was now standing in front of Rockefeller Center — brought up short by it, her eyes following the amazing central shaft, traveling up and heavenward with it. Why, it was one of the most astounding buildings in the world; it shot up so spontaneously, propelled like a rocket, like a fountain straight into the sky — upward it lifted heart and eye — and furthermore, it set the feet in motion, it positively drew them like a magnet down this narrow alleyway between the French and the English buildings, where the red tulips flamed so bright in their boxes and Manship's dolphins measured out so accurately their broad ribbons of silver water; it took you for a run-around and never left you for an instant free of its command to follow with your heart, your eye, that startling thrust into the blue, stopping to admire the flowers, looking into shop windows, strolling about with the crowd, diminished as you were to midget proportions, running lightly, lightly, on your tiny midget's feet.

Yes! Mr. Rockefeller's City struck the authentic note. Right here at the very center of the town — a metropolis within a metropolis— above the ground, below the ground. It teemed with life, with superfluity; those subterranean, neon-lighted shops, arcades, art galleries, plazas, rialtos, restaurants, from which one could emerge into the light of day to find oneself still within the new Jerusalem, with further shops at one's disposal — theaters, plazas, art galleries, pleasaunces, ramps, skating rinks, flights of stairs, fountains playing, dolphins spouting, flowers blooming, gardens on the asphalt, gardens in the air, and tiers and tiers of offices, choirs of windows, lifted up on every side.

Imagine, if New York should some day be composed of cities on the general order of this! Some existing buildings would remain, of course: the beautiful New York Hospital, the Medical Center, St. Bartholomew's and all that aerial magnificence that rose around it — others one might choose. But the central scheme, the gorgeous plan, should be these ghost-gray cities in the air. One could visualize it. They should be placed at proper intervals — uptown, downtown — to the east and to the west — cities that for each community provided offices, banks, and shops and theaters, churches, cathedrals, art galleries — lofty dwelling places, homes with windows looking out on unimaginable views — the North River, the Fast River, the great bay, the bridges and the boats; for in between the cities there would be gardens — space and prospect, trees and green lawns and lights and shadows, sculpture, vistas, song of birds and the laughter of children; there would be music, men and women strolling arm in arm — not rushing as they did today, walking about in a leisurely manner, enjoying the parks, the gardens — marveling at the cities. It was possible; anything was possible in this extraordinary town, which was always being demolished, rebuilt, and certainly there was much one would most gladly see torn down forever. But these cities, these ghost-gray cities would be here to stay.

But maybe Percy was right, she thought, examining a pair of neat little rabbits, half-a-dozen faence angels, a couple of Kewpie dolls in pink and blue china, America had little to offer the world but the heart of a ten-year-old child — a little old ten-year-old baby; for it required more than youth and wealth and energy — always crossing frontiers, getting out beyond skyline and landfall — beyond all the horizons — out there in the blue, seeing everything huge, gigantic. It required something more than this — vision was necessary — love. And suddenly, the beautiful verse out of *Revelation* coming into her mind, "And he that talked with me had a golden reed to measure the city and the gates thereof and the wall thereof," she repeated it, she condensed it into a line of her own — "Place in my hand a golden reed" — thinking of William Blake, drifting off with the crowd — pulled irresistibly down to the railing overlooking the skating rink.

Below her a few enthusiasts on roller skates (boards now replaced the artificial ice) were practicing their skill — executing their forward leaps, their backward swings, circling round and round; in front of her the massive gray buildings with their various levels and terraces were all disposed in proper relation to the great central shaft which, still exerting its peculiar influence, drew up her eyes, her heart. She loitered with the other onlookers. The sun was deliciously hot; masses of tulips bloomed in fine array right round the balustrade. Over on Forty-ninth Street a combustion engine was breaking up the rhythms of her body, interrupting the rhythms of her thoughts; all the little midgets on their tiny feet seemed to slip, to slide down the steps — over the pavements, across the street.

Suddenly she became aware of an intense feeling of oneness with the crowd surrounding her, and then, as though the larger inclusions were implicit in this feeling, of union with everybody in the world. This sense of oneness, identity, was, she knew, a not uncommon experience with many people today. It was probably what St. Paul referred to when he said we were all members of the same body; only today how much more terrifying, how much more certain the evidence that we were members, not only of the same body but of the same soul.

That was our modern dilemma, receiving the many into the one, having the world thrust with such violence into one's breast — going to the newsreels, listening to the voices from the four quarters of the earth — participating wholesale in the physical and spiritual tragedy of our age — implicated in the pride, the folly and the crime; stepping aboard airplanes and ocean liners, stepping out each day, you might almost say to gird the world. It was altogether too much of a good thing — too much experience, too awesome an idea to entertain; but there it was, at times overtaking us, overwhelming us altogether — a sense of oneness — implication.

Just how this sense had come about, one would be at a loss to explain; but it was with us, we weren't likely to escape it. The Russian novelists were perhaps responsible in part — Dostoevsky had contributed to the dilemma, and certainly living in the era of Freud, and all these soul-dissolving novels we read, melting down the very sinews of our pride, while we assisted at the process, going down into all the infernal circles, visiting all the depths and levels, the dreadful pits and terraces; and then emerging suddenly to see, like Ariel let loose from our own hearts — a bright bird, a flowering branch, a cloud, a breaking wave — soaring up and off with Ariel into the wonder and the ecstasy, always subjected to such heights and depths, being jerked right up and down the scales so violently.

For wasn't it the case that this moment, this living moment, here — now, was fraught with a heavier burden of awareness than the soul (for she supposed that she was thinking of the soul) had ever been called upon to sustain? Hadn't the attack upon one's sensibilities become more violent, and wasn't the range and variety of the sensibilities attacked at one and the same moment tremendously increased; and if the soul was to survive at all this attack upon its capacity for readjustment, wouldn't it be necessary to develop a new muscle, or at least for it to learn to develop muscles not hitherto put into play?

A muscle of the soul! What a novel, what an exhilarating idea. And why not, she questioned, turning down Seventh Avenue at Forty-eighth Street and hurrying to her conclusions excitedly; why not? The life process was certainly a series of adjustments, and if a mollusk, a monkey? But she was getting out of her depth and was probably thinking the sheerest nonsense.

And here she was at the little glass booth outside the Griffin Theatre. She handed the peroxide doll in her little cage behind the glass window a ten-dollar bill. The doll took the bill, regarded her shrewdly, and gave her back exactly seventy-five cents. Without the slightest realization of the ruse just practiced upon her, Millicent put the change into her pocketbook and marched through the vestibule, handed her ticket to the official at the door and walked through the long lobby into the orchestra.

In the celluloid twilight she searched for a seat, and spying one just vacated, she made a dash down the aisle to the accompaniment of marching feet and soldiers goose-stepping through the streets of Vienna; and catching sight of a Satanic face under the visor of a military cap, a smile, a sneer, a bit of a mustache, and filled with mingled feelings of consternation, curiosity and terror, and muttering, "Excuse me, I beg your pardon!" she pushed past a variety of knees and finally sat down and composed herself, as the planet moved on its axis round the sun, for an hour of the most extraordinary entertainment, traveling at vertiginous speed through landscapes of the ear and eye and the imagination calculated to crack the stoutest heart.

She saw the skies above Chungking, and planes dropping their bombs upon the city, and the inhabitants of the city with their rickshaws, their babies, their goods and chattels, fleeing from the terror in the skies. She saw a biblical, a desert landscape, the barren hills, the primitive dwellings and little men and women, dressed apparently in their nightgowns, fleeing from the terror that flies by night and by day; and sitting there in her comfortable chair she beheld cities in Spain reduced to ash and rubble and amid the rubble, the desolation, little children murdered at their innocent games. She looked upon women crazed with grief, weeping over their dead; villages in ruins, cities smoldering. Then, behold — suddenly, a beautiful half-opened rose (for it seemed that one participated in the heavenly and the infernal symbol at very nearly one and the same instant) made, with an authentic gesture of divinity, deep obeisance — then silently, precisely, unfolded its matchless and immaculate petals, laying one over upon another until all the delicate threadlike stamens were exposed and each, tipped with its divine essential grain of pollen, quivering, shivering there before her eyes.

And, being in a state of the highest excitement, words came to her lips —

> *Only the star*
> *The rose abide*
> *Within the soul*

And it seemed to her that the emotion that filled her heart had charged those three brief lines with sufficient feeling to bring to her lips and without further effort on her part a little poem complete and flawless; but it was impossible to go on with it. The visual images jostled and pushed at each other rudely — ("The dove has flown out of the ark — Into the world's great dark"). She turned distractedly to regard her neighbors, who sat stolid, unmoved, with rather bored, emotionless faces. In front of her a thick-set man, his head dropped on his chest, snored audibly. She thought of Rome, of the days of Caligula, the days of Nero-Heliogabulus. Surely those ancient Romans were not more inhuman, callous than we? It was their habit to sit and watch their Christian brothers thrown to devouring lions. Yes, to be sure. But weren't the most monstrous crimes, the most unspeakable agonies, conveyed to us from all the awful arenas of the habitable globe? Her lips began again to move:

> *"Beautiful flowerlike children*
> *Bombed at their innocent games;*
> *But my colosseums are*
> *on a scale to beggar these;*
> *In a chair I sit at ease*
> *And see my Christian brothers thrown*
> *To Lion the devourer."*

And now, for she seemed to be regarding further miracles of nature — whales, if one could believe one's eyes, suspended in the waters beneath the seas; and one picture dissolving quickly into the next —

> *Aqueous copulations — sports,*
> *Never spied upon before,*
> *Carried on beneath the seas,*
> *On the ocean's emerald floor;*
> *Seals on desolate rocks I saw,*
> *Snake attacking jaguar —*

It was utterly distracting and that little poem still moving in her heart — waiting to be uttered. She closed her eyes; her fingers beat lightly on the air. Now she felt sure she had it whole; now she'd lost it completely. But she needed a pencil. It was necessary to get out into the lobby, where she could write down the little lines.

And so, the program having come full circle and Hitler standing erect in his open car and holding up his hand in a salute that exposed his palm like the atlas of the world, she pushed her way to the aisle and to the accompaniment of marching legions out into the lobby, where she seated herself on the long upholstered bench against the wall.

What if she didn't have a pencil? She searched for one nervously. Yes, thank the Lord, here it was. And here was the back of an envelope. Quickly, and in an almost indecipherable hand, she wrote the little lines:

> *The dove has flown*
> *From the ark,*
> *Into the night,*
> *The soul's great dark;*
>
> *The heart too small,*
> *The soul too wide —*
> *(The rose, the bird,*
> *The star abide*
> *Within the soul —)*

But she didn't have a poem at all — merely broken fragments; and what was that line about the olive leaf, and something about the intolerable scroll —

> *Oh, messenger —*
> *Oh, dove,*
> *Where can you fly,*
> *Or go, to hide —*

Was it grief or shame or pride or the intolerable scroll? She put the envelope back in her purse, for there was no time to meddle with it now. It was very late. She grabbed her purse and hurried out into the heat of the blazing sidewalk.

The clock on top of the Paramount Building disclosed the awful fact that it was half-past one. She hailed a taxi and, shouting the address, jumped into it, repeating as she sat down, "Aqueous copulations — sports . . . But my colosseums are . . . Seals on desolate rocks I saw — Snake attacking jaguar . . . Beautiful flowerlike children . . . killed at their innocent games" — and the lines beating out the rhythm of the motor and the jagged rhythms of her thoughts, she was brought up abruptly in front of the Algonquin.

Heavens, were they here already? On the sidewalk she searched nervously for her purse. Good God, where was that ten-dollar bill? As far as she could discover, she was the possessor of only seventy-five cents. She said something of this to the driver; an hour since she'd had a ten-dollar bill, now she only had seventy-five cents. She handed it to him vaguely, and as it covered a very substantial tip he pocketed it, telling her that she was, Lady, a little crazy in the head — "nuts," he said, tapping his forehead.

This she conceded him. She was, without a doubt — crazy in the head. And so, adjusting her hat and trying to gather her scattered wits, she went into the hotel to lunch with Bridget and Percy.

F I V E

SHE COULD SEE HIM AS SHE CAME IN, alone at one of the small tables in the lounge, his hands folded in front of him and his head bent over four empty cocktail glasses, and a waiter arriving with a tray removing the glasses and placing a fresh martini on the table.

She'd wait; she'd have a moment to pull herself together; she'd have a look at him. Poor fellow, he'd evidently given up their arrival and was allowing the cocktails to take care of his disappointment. Day-dreaming, mixing fact with fancy; nourishing his forlorn hope, and sipping (was it his fifth martini?) he appeared to be engaged in dressing up the unsatisfactory evidence with romantic notions of his own.

But here, just as he was finishing his cocktail, was Bridget, fresh and smiling — lovelier than ever. Who could possibly have guessed that she'd spent a sleepless night? She didn't look as though she had an anxiety in the world. And she was arrayed in the delightful leaf-green dress that made you think of shadows and pale-green leaves; with that small black hat, so chic and yet so innocent, perched on her lovely head, she seemed like Botticelli's *Primavera* to be strewing buds and blossoms in her path — there was a fragrance — there were circulations.

"Oh," she said, kissing her on both cheeks, "Millicent! Late too? How nice!" But she mustn't let Percy's wrath descend on her; she intended, she said, to take the blame.

Very well, she could, said Millicent. And just on the point of complimenting her on her beauty and the success of the green dress, she looked up to find herself involved in the most confusing and unexpected situation, for two very gay, very splendidly arrayed young men who, it would appear, had suddenly joined them, were now taking part, most naturally and in a perfectly casual manner, in their salutations. She had never met either of them, but the elder of the two, who was at the moment shaking her hand with the utmost cordiality, she knew by sight and reputation (as who did not, since he was possessed of one of the largest fortunes in the entire world?). "My dear Miss Munroe," he was saying. "How nice."

He had, he told her, just been calling on his old aunt, Hortense Westbridge, who had said the most charming, but *the* most charming things about her; and, of course, she remembered seeing the old girl at the Wingates' the other evening? And what a remarkable character she was — *remarkable*.

It was all very easy and gay, and Bridget, who by this time seemed to be sharing in the flavor of Aunt Hortense's personality, and was already in the very smile and gesture of receiving an introduction, casting her enchantments over both young men, as well as offering them congratulations on the success of their enterprise, was certainly to be held responsible for what followed. For, though Millicent knew neither the Westbridges nor the Wingates from a hole in the ground, and was perfectly well aware that young Price was practicing an impertinence, not to say an unpardonable trick upon her — that he had very likely just bet his friend that he could pull it off with the greatest of ease — though she knew all this and was fully determined to snub him roundly, to put him at once in his place, to say that she knew neither him nor his aunt, nor the Wingates, there was Bridget, to all intents and purposes intimately acquainted with everybody concerned, and there she was herself, and to her utmost dismay and astonishment begging to be allowed to present the young man; and the introductions successfully achieved, the four of them were talking together in the easiest and pleasantest manner possible.

She was angry — disgusted with herself. She could have died of cha-grin. Why was she always so irrational, saying no when she wanted to say yes, and yes when it had been her firm intention to say no — her behavior never chiming with her intentions? She was hopeless. And, of course, Percy would have every right to be furious with her, for there was no knowing how far these cocksure young men were likely to go —

probably barging in uninvited on their luncheon party, appropriating Bridget for the rest of the afternoon.

He'd been watching the little scene suspiciously and was now, Millicent observed out of the tail of her eye, getting to his feet — (just how drunk, she wondered, were they likely to find him?) — with considerable difficulty, pulling from his pocket various bills — a handful of change, leaving these among the cocktail glasses and cigarette stubs on the table. Once successfully on his feet, however, he seemed to know quite well what he was up to, and lost no time in executing his plans.

"Hollo, Beautiful!" he said, striding up and taking both Bridget's hands in his and ignoring the two young men with a thoroughness of which she had herself been utterly incapable. "We're getting out of here; I'm lunching you elsewhere; come along."

But, pleaded Bridget — please; she'd come to see the celebrities; she adored the Algonquin — she didn't wish to be torn away like this.

"Well, I'm the only celebrity you'll see today, Beautiful," he said and made for the door without further explanation. "Come on, Millicent," he commanded curtly, for he was, you could see, ready to take it all out on her. "Come, Millicent, it's getting late."

Bridget seemed in no hurry to obey his orders; she pulled a rueful countenance and remained a few moments talking with the young men; she was going after lunch, Millicent heard her say, to the dressmakers and then on to the Lenny Weeds' cocktail party. Would they by any chance be going there too? It would be nice to catch a glimpse of them.

Young Price didn't know the Lenny Weeds; but that would be okay by him. He could crash that party with the greatest of ease. He'd be there.

"How nice," she said; she smiled; she waved her hand.

Whether Percy had heard all this Millicent was unable to determine, but she thought it very unlikely, bent as he seemed to be on carrying out his own schemes. And when they both joined him on the sidewalk he had already procured a taxi. "Get in," he ordered peremptorily, and ducked in after them, giving the driver directions where and at what speed to proceed.

Off they dashed at a pace that indicated his intention to get a start on the two young men, for craning her neck to look out of the back of the car, Millicent was just in time to see them hail a cab and disappear into its depths before it leaped after them like a greyhound off the leash.

The escapade was childish; it had that mad, that utterly unreal quality that often attended one in New York; but life being what it at the moment was, a series of utterly bizarre and unrelated adventures, it did not seem to disconcert any of them, or to interrupt the light, the playful conversation in which they were engaged. No mention was made of the breakneck speed at which they whirled through the streets, nor of the two young men in pursuit, the business being to elude, to escape them and, if possible, not to be held up by the red signals, to take advantage of the green. They turned suddenly south, they swerved to the west, they turned north, they wheeled around east and, like one of those sequences at the movies, escaping death at every turn — the spring hats, the gay spring dresses, the taxis, the shop windows, the bright awnings, the window dressings, the brownstone fronts, the pavements and the pedestrians flashing into view, disappearing, dissolving into the long vistas of the streets; the skyscrapers, the dusty shafts of sunlight and strips of pale-blue sky revolving round them in kaleidoscopic patterns, the wonder of it all being that they weren't caught up by a pair of traffic policemen on motorcycles and arrested on the spot.

Bridget lighted a cigarette; she wanted to know where they were lunching; she pleaded to go to the Rainbow Room — to the Tavern On The Green.

"No," said Percy.

Then might they go to the Fair? She wanted to see the Future Amara — The Bitter Future — "Futurama — Future Amara — I adore yer," she chanted, tossing off her grim little pun as gaily as though she were throwing a handful of confetti into the air.

"No," Percy declared. The place was chosen; he was going to treat her to the best filet of sole she'd ever put into her mouth.

To which she replied that he must be taking her across the Atlantic, as there was no sole in America; you could get cod; you could get halibut or codfish cakes — but never sole.

Oh, yes, my little B, he insisted; they were brought over on the *Normandie* in a tank filled with salt water, and kept here in New York just so that she could put them into her lovely little mouth at the restaurant he'd chosen.

"The darling *Normandie!*" What favors she said that ship was always according her; first a bridal suite and now a tank full of sole.

The driver turned around. "Okay, boss," he said, "we've given them the slip." The taxi slowed down to a more normal pace.

Percy gave directions; he turned. "Now, Beautiful, we're set," he said and leaning forward put his hand on Bridget's knee. "Hungry?" he asked her, and there spread over his countenance the look of a beggar holding out a cup for alms. He abandoned himself to the needs of his heart. "Give me, give me — just a crumb of assurance that you need me; give me an inkling, only an inkling, that you can trust me to help you. Tell me about little Beatrice," that was in substance what he was trying mutely to convey and there was so much unappeased adoration and sentiment and supplication in his bearing and expression that Millicent found it impossible to look in his direction.

But Bridget, obviously an expert in managing the behavior of mendicants and doubtless as well aware as Millicent of all he was trying to say, took his hand and without changing the mood of lightness and frivolity in which their adventure had been launched laid it down again upon his knee, and glancing out of the window at the Chrysler Building (for they were now coasting down the Third Avenue car tracks), asked how anyone could possibly conceive of it — placing on the top of a skyscraper a lady dressed in hoopskirts balancing an icicle on her nose; whereupon she suggested a game of her own invention — "Of What Do They Remind You?"

Of what, Percy asked, did the Empire State put *her* in mind?

She reproached him; he mustn't be so obvious. Everybody knew that gentleman. But, really, had they ever looked at that building from Eighth Avenue through Forty-fourth or Forty-third Street? Seen thus, it was superb — a tall crusader riding a tall horse, with visor up, the Black Knight — Richard Coeur de Lion.

She was incomparable — incomparable, he said; but she was taking an unfair advantage of them; she'd played the game with herself; she had all the answers.

Well, yes, she admitted, she had; but could they guess her name for the wonderful, the incredible central shaft at Rockefeller Center?

No, not possibly.

Well; she hoped they'd both agree; it was this — "Give Me My Arrows of Desire." Pure William Blake.

"Little B, you're incomparable; you beat the Dutch," and he leaned over and kissed her, just as they were piling out; for they'd turned, they'd reached their destination — between Forty-ninth and Fiftieth Streets.

Oh, and she looked around her at the low tenement houses, the sidewalk shops, the elevated tracks above her head — "Restaurant Chambord. How charming." It reminded her of Paris.

Where one always, added Percy, had an opportunity to enjoy the Third Avenue trains as they roared through the Latin Quarter.

"Exactly, dear Percy."

Lending himself to the mood of extravagant gaiety which so betrayed the tender and anxious distress in his heart (thinking of little Beatrice, thinking of Vienna), he spread out his arms with that air of boisterous enjoyment so peculiarly unbecoming to him and positively shooed them into the restaurant. "Come along, girls," he shouted, "come along."

Everything seemed to delight Bridget. You couldn't mistake it, she declared — the goblets, the wineglasses shining like mirrors, the napery bleached as clean as snow; and that smell; she sniffed the air, testing, sampling it; yes that smell was authentic. She might as well be in Paris.

The compliment and the smile that accompanied it was at once appropriated by the head waiter who, bowing and dancing around them, and fully aware of the electrifying effect that her entrance had on everyone in the room, nimbly played his part in the drama of getting them seated and provided with wine lists and menus. You could actually hear the sensation she caused. A hush ensued; conversation stopped; knives and forks were laid down, coffee cups suspended in air; everybody frankly stared, and an old gentleman with a red face and the eyes of a codfish screwed his head right around and allowed himself several minutes to take in every detail of her face, her hat, her gown, her figure, and he might as well have been shouting as he stared at her — By George, I never saw anything like you — you're perfection.

Discussing the wine list, the menu, and not unaware of the sensation she was causing, vibrant and alive to every little quiver in the nets she spun and industriously setting up her various lines of communication, she laid her hand lightly on Percy's arm — and begged him not to spoil a beautiful repast with another martini; and having, with that peculiar gift she had in these matters, established a partnership with the head waiter that made him a champion of every preference she entertained, she begged on behalf of everyone for apéritifs instead of cocktails.

But Percy rebelled; though the European contingent was lined up against him — and she could have all the apéritifs she wanted to order — he must beg to be allowed his favorite beverage; and Milly too, he knew her tastes. A dry martini for each of them. That sipping and savoring, tasting and testing one's enjoyment — never exhausting anything, hadn't yet been cultivated in America, where everything must be taken swiftly, grabbed, and gulped down. He was for the quickie — the immediate draft of enlightenment; for little B would have to admit it, she needed some catching up to, always tasting, as she was, and testing. How could he possibly catch up with her on just a single glass of sherry, a Pernod, or Porto? No, not he. Not Millicent. She must have some mercy on them.

The trouble with the quickie was, she said, the knockout came too soon; she'd admit the advantage of that first fine sprint; but for keeping in the race, perhaps . . .

Right she was; right she always was; but let him have his quickie.

Then would they think it too naive of her to ask for a bottle of Vouvray to accompany the sole and asparagus? She knew nothing about years and dates and vintages — this she'd leave to the head waiter; but the mere mention of Vouvray reminded her of that month she'd spent with René at that divine little island in the Mediterranean; had any of them (she included the waiter) ever been there — Isle de Port Cros? They'd shared a bottle every night — sitting at the table by the open window — looking out on that little harbor, perfect in every detail, the curved white beach, the scattered houses, that splendid Chateau Fort against the sky, the moon, the first bright stars, and slowly, noiselessly, the yachts, the fishing boats stealing into port . . .

The waiter bowed, "Oui, Madame," he knew Port Cros, an earthly paradise; and he knew exactly what she wanted — not too sweet and not too dry; he pointed with his pencil. A year unparalleled.

And would they think it very childish of her — for she didn't want hors d'oeuvres or turtle soup, or chilled consommé — if she suggested Persian melon; exactly like that they'd had at the Fair last night? She gave the waiter an exact description of its beauties.

He promised everything — the little silver stars, the exquisite texture, the color — the taste.

And then, if everyone agreed, after the fabulous sole (she listened attentively while the waiter told about the passage in the *Normandie*. How wonderful! Preserved in brine; she'd never heard of such a thing), could she suggest romaine with a French dressing, a delicious ripe Camembert, then coffee — liqueurs?

"*Bon. Parfait.*" He would mix the salad himself. And off he went with his lists and his menus.

S I X

———

AFTER ALL, IF SHE WAS DETERMINED not to refer to her child, what could Millicent do about it, with Percy giving her all these dark frowns and woeful signals, nudging her foot under the table? This gaiety was out of place. He wanted her to know he wouldn't let her off. She could, if she made the effort, *do* something — change the conversation — make some attempt to help him out. Little Beatrice was in Vienna. And she knew as well as he did that Bridget faced the direst emergencies. They were here to learn about them. They were her friends; they wanted to help her. It was no use going on like this.

But what *could* one do about it with Bridget controlling the ropes, keeping the conversation so deftly in the air, allowing him all manner of little privileges in the way of badinage and flirtation — using his devotion as a kind of springboard from which to launch her smaller engagements — paying out, lengthening, distributing her lines? You couldn't wring her neck and force her to stop her charming practices and look squarely in the face of little Beatrice, who was (she couldn't disguise the fact that she knew it as well as they did) haunting the festive luncheon like a ghost.

It was not only that she was a natural-born flirt, that there reposed within her springs, retorts, antennae which apparently put into action, and without volition on her part, little waves, vibrations, delicate recordings on the air, these gossamer engagements rested on a broad basis of experience, a knowledge of human behavior in general; and this knowledge, insight — imagination, lent a flight and fling, a kind of winged quality, to the enjoyment of life in her society. She forced you to go along with her, to share with her all the give-away expressions, the telltale gestures, the whispered asides she set so skilfully in motion, receiving, decoding, sending out her airy messages.

Would they look at the couple in the corner — the man watching her under cover of downcast eyes, and the woman in the big hat? He had crossed with her in the steamer coming from Batavia — an international crook, a card-sharper; he had a false mustache; his hair was dyed. They did these things so cleverly. But she'd swear it, the identical man. He had recognized her too. Couldn't they feel a disturbance in the air — people fearing, suspecting each other? The couple were eyeing her most insolently — challenging her. He was telling the lady in the hat about Batavia — that crossing on the same ship—making up fantastic lies.

And Percy lifting her hand, kissing it awkwardly. She drew a long bow, he said — such a long, long bow — adorable little B.

Look at the way they were whispering. Come, he must admit it — there was this suspicion — antagonism, in the air. Look at the woman in the hat.

Undoubtedly a Nazi spy — a Hitchcock villainess.

Not at all unlikely; life was beginning to imitate the movies. But if they wanted something that resembled a little story by Anton Chekhov instead of a Hollywood thriller, would they please regard the old man with the eyes of a cod?

What, Percy asked — the ogler?

Yes, the ogler — the Eater. Would they look at the manner in which he addressed himself to his food? When they ate like that, there was but one conclusion to draw.

"What was that?" asked Percy.

That their score with the ladies was zero; their score with life was zero — in short; there was nothing now for them but food.

But why did the old cod ogle? Why did he wax his mustache?

That she said was the little story by Chekhov. Everybody had to live with some kind of a picture of oneself. And who could bear the image of a hog? This old gentleman lived all alone in a dreary hotel room. While there he spent the larger part of his time in front of his mirror waxing his mustache, practicing this lady-killing business. But what he really was preparing for, and with an impatience Percy could scarcely imagine, was his rendezvous with the roast duck, the lobster thermidor, the crêpes Suzettes. Just look at him.

The old fellow was eating with a gluttony that defied description, stuffing his mouth with lobster, mopping up his face — shouting to the waiter to bring him the menu.

"There," she said triumphantly, "he wants more lobster. How ashamed he is, seeing us watch him ask for it." And she turned quickly away.

And when he had a chance to do so, would Percy look around at the woman making most outrageous love to her? Oh, no — not that old girl in the tailored coat and hat with the self-conscious, awkward, masculine behavior; she was just another story by Chekhov, very pathetic and inhibited — the pretty young one in the ruffled gown, with the big liquid eyes. Also, there was an elderly gentleman making most unseemly proposals to the young fellow directly behind her; he pretended he was flirting with her, but not at all; he was merely using her as a blind to carry on the more important communications.

Did she wear her eyes, Percy asked her, in her shoulder blades?

Yes; she'd have to admit it; she saw everything; she had Argus eyes. And then (was it because she knew that Percy's attention was wandering and that unless she wished immediately to be confronted with the ghost of little Beatrice she'd have to shift her tactics at once, or merely that she'd hit on a subject she wanted to discuss?) she suddenly grew thoughtful and, abandoning the mood to which she'd so vigilantly kept them pitched, said, speaking slowly and as though doubtful of being able to convey her meaning, that it was an extraordinary thing. They might themselves have had the same experience, but it came down to this.

She had been in her brief existence two distinctly different beings, and one of these was the creature she was before and the other the creature she had become after reading the works of Marcel Proust. No, but really; she wasn't joking. From this experience she'd emerged with all manner of extensions, reinforcements, renewals of her entire nervous system — indeed she might say that she'd been endowed with a perfectly new apparatus for apprehending the vibrations of other people's souls. She was saying all this most awkwardly, she knew, but she often wondered if we sufficiently realized the effect that Proust had had upon our awareness of one another, for whether we liked it or not, we were forced to take about with us wherever we went this extraordinary apparatus, recording accurately a thousand little matters of which we had not formerly been aware, and whether she was glad or sorry to be in possession of so delicate and precise an instrument, she had never been able to determine. And would Percy and Millicent give her their opinion — that is, if they didn't think she was talking rot? Were they glad or sorry to be thus equipped?

Then quickly, allowing neither of them an opportunity to think out an answer to so sudden and complicated a question — leaving it in the air, she flashed on them another facet of the discussion under way. For she supposed, she said, that Proust was the novel to end all novels. What was the use of carrying analysis any farther; or indeed could it be carried any farther? And weren't we now able, since we had within ourselves the means of learning the hitherto undivulged secrets, not only of our own thoughts but of our neighbors, to read our little novels as we ran — to extract them from the passing moment? Was it plot we wanted? We could go to the movies for that excitement — we could read a mystery story; but for the insatiable curiosity about the human psyche that lay at the bottom of one's novel-reading needs, hadn't Proust preempted the field — equipping us, as he had, with means to make our own discoveries? What was left for future novelists? What in the world was there left for them?

Oh, come, Percy interrupted, could Bridget expect him to subscribe to that idea? The novel to end all novels! Where was he to come in — and what was to happen to the other American novelists who were flourishing at the moment like the green bay tree?

She laughed gaily; it was, she said, her outrageous habit of exaggeration that generally helped her along with her discussions. He'd put his finger on just the point she'd wanted to make. For a long time she'd been anxious to discuss with him the difference between American and European novels. What she'd intended to imply was merely this, that the European novel had, and didn't he agree? — about run its course — completed the cycle. What more was there — (she shrugged her shoulders and threw out her hands with that gesture so characteristic of her) — it could possibly say, that is, when it came down to talking about the human heart?

But with the American novel — she looked up at him, as though she expected him to confirm her statement — it was an entirely different matter.

She meant to imply, he suggested, now thoroughly interested and for the moment entirely forgetting little Beatrice, that all we had to do was to make again the same old discoveries, like that squirrel in Yeats' poem running round and round his cage?

Well — she'd appeared to say that, she'd admit; but here was her point. American novelists weren't, or so it seemed to her, quite ready to accept Human Nature on the same terms on which Europeans accepted it. Europeans were old and wise and without illusions. They'd been documenting the human heart for centuries — they'd crystallized its gestures. Why, European literature was like a great cathedral, its beast and angel symbols — the earthly, the heavenly elements — all displayed; you had only to read the great masterpieces — all the attributes, the hierarchies of the poor old heart placed in their final niches, until at last one had only to say — Behold the human family — the human heart, its innocence and corruption, its vices, its virtues, its needs, desires, passions; and, furthermore, behold — its subterranean depths — the thoughts that lie here unacknowledged; the duplicities, the villainies, the hidden, the sensuous imagery — and above all and always to be considered, its need to be forgiven. . . . Why, one was reminded of a priest telling his beads, counting the familiar attributes, worn smooth, familiar to the touch — telling them over, mumbling the litanies.

"Yes, yes," he said, "go on, little B," and he regarded her with his eagerly questioning, searching eyes, hoping, Millicent felt sure, that she was about to say something about his own work — taking it all very personally.

Would he say, she continued — did he really believe that American novelists were ready to accept, to celebrate the same creature, the same human heart? It seemed to her that they were always trying to reshape, to remold the creature according to some pattern they desperately yearned to have it conform to — or perhaps she was stating it the wrong way round, they were too occupied in railing against the conditions that had shaped it to keep their eyes on its familiar antics. Would he agree with her that American novels seldom went deep into the realities of character — weren't they dealing more with circumstances, places — epochs, environments? They came boiling up out of the decades — out of the twenties, out of the thirties — out of Pittsburgh,

Chicago, the Deep South — New York, New England — and with an intensity, a grief, a lamentation and love that was very moving, very sincere indeed. American novels were, she thought, so full of a kind of feverish protest — how could she put it? A morbid, an almost neurotic determination to lay the raw nerve bare — something even a little sadistic perhaps, as though these novelists had suffered so acutely themselves that they weren't going to let you off a jot or tittle of the agony; there was always this protest — the surface realism so sharp, so unadulterated. But for the inner, the spiritual realism, did Percy find it in anything like the same degree in which it was to be discovered in Europe? It was almost as though the American artist stopped short of handling it — as though he actually balked at handling it, believing very likely that if he continued to rail away on superficial, on environmental levels long and loud enough he might, perhaps, sometime have a new, a more perfected creature in his hands.

And that she declared was all right by her. "Okay," she said.

She went, said Percy, so fast it was difficult to keep up with her; but if she was implying that at bottom American novelists were moralists, he'd be inclined to agree with her.

Why of course, certainly, that was exactly the point, and she hurried on, delighted to have him help her along so explicitly — look at the biggest of them — Melville, Hawthorne, Henry James — always coming at you with the moral issues, never getting so directly, so frighteningly at the poor creature himself — actually treading, like Dostoevsky, for instance, the awful labyrinths, detecting with that cold, that meticulous scrutiny his social dishonesty, his terrible darkness, loneliness and fear — taking a strange, a cathartic solace in getting it all down. Who could really call Henry James in comparison a good psychologist? He contrived his situations with a matchless brilliance and probity; for what he was really doing was voicing his own innocent, indignant and upright response to the vulgar, the brutal, the material aspects of society that so profoundly disturbed him. (He was a very great gentleman indeed.) But if you tried to compare him with Dostoevsky, he was a child, a holy innocent. And hadn't Dostoevsky, in that uncanny way the artist of genius always had of getting there first, prepared the way, like a John the Baptist, for modern psychology, for Freud and the exploration of the subconscious? He was the traveler in the desert of the soul. Wasn't he the first to lay before us the map, the terrible landscape of the soul, and in so convincing, so truly terrifying a manner — all its realms and kingdoms opened to the view — that kingdom of Heaven, that kingdom of Hell that man creates within himself? And the extraordinary test of his truth being simply this — that you never had to leave the well-recognized boundaries of your own heart to know just where he was, and just where you were, too. This was the fearful thing that Dostoevsky had done for us. And would it be necessary to do it again? Hadn't he perhaps preempted the field — done it up brown, once and for all?

Good God! Percy covered his face a moment with his hands. She went so fast — give him a chance to think it over.

She laughed again. She always did. She couldn't keep up with herself. But wouldn't he admit that in this matter of dealing with the interior life the Americans were, for one reason or another, miles behind the Europeans?

"How about Faulkner?" he asked.

"Faulkner — my dear Percy — *Faulkner!*" She'd heard him called, she said, "the Dostoevsky of the Deep South." He wrote about the Deep South certainly. And what a style he had; with what positive necromancy he managed to give off atmosphere — describe a house, a landscape — declare a mood; which, of course, and without a doubt was his method of grieving over the South, its sadness, decay — disintegration. But when it came to Faulkner's characters; come now, she asked, could anybody be convinced by them? Bogies hung about, with all the Freudian perversions — afflicted with every imaginable sexual habit and desire. Bad dreams of men and women. But did anyone ever suffer with and for them? Was one ever able to locate them here — she laid her hand an instant over her heart — right here within the human breast? Certainly not — the unrealest characters, the most unconvincing in literature.

For with Americans everything was, she went on, so intense — immediate, so personal. Time seemed to be torn up by the roots, so that this could be inspected and that. Here. Now. Pittsburgh. New York. Chicago. The Deep South. And every American tragedy so stark and unadulterated — so unique an American event. Character was never developed, or the joy, the sorrow that stemmed from human relationships, as a universal theme, flowing through time, through history, but kept right here — right here in the passionately implicated heart of the novelist. It was his grief, his personal grief, of which one got so strong a flavor — very moving. . . . She'd thought about this a great deal and didn't it probably come from the fact that American novelists were, *au fond*, as they had both decided, moralists? Did it induce a tendency toward neuroticism — and was this tendency perhaps increasing somewhat? Was it not obviously the case?

What did she mean by neuroticism? She'd used the word several times.

Was there a running counter to American destiny, she asked, to the national psyche perhaps?

He would have to ask her again to be more explicit.

She knew she was getting very complicated. But just let her give him the impressions of one poor exile, running almost like Lot's wife out of the burning cities — seeing America, she meant, and at such a moment, for the first time. For here it was — young, vigorous, exhilarating, with the clear bright air and everyone in such a hurry; and that sense one received of something new in process under the sun — all these skyscrapers, these cities of glass and iron and bright illuminations, the highways looping them together, and the great bridges. Think of it all — think of Boulder Dam, of the TVA. Think of the bridge across the Presideo — all the bridges, all the dams and highways. Think of the Fair in Flushing. (No, she wasn't joking), think of the Futurama.

Here it was. And in startling contrast, here was this despair, these unhappy writers — this unhappy literature; this necessity for the quickies. Was there no one left to go along with Whitman, to do some shouting, to exult about it all, not anyone to hand at least one little nosegay to the architects — the engineers — no one, of course, except that little ten-year-old of Percy's? Must he be the only person to display his glee? As for herself, she'd often felt inclined to shout, to sing, hearing so many little poems by William Blake — "Give me my arrows of desire." You had only to take one look at that beautiful central edifice at Rockefeller Center. Wasn't that a kind of symbol — apparently in America they couldn't help these cosmic gestures — shooting off like that into the blue.

Had she ever read the poetry of Hart Crane? What — she hadn't? Well, she must. A most remarkable young poet, who would have known what she was driving at — a lineal descendant of Walt Whitman; he'd left behind him a great — a magnificent, an uncompleted, very likely an unachievable poem — "The Bridge." Like Whitman, he'd lived in Brooklyn. He'd plied his way across the river — back and forth between the cities. He'd made an attempt, a truly amazing attempt to span the mystic distances — to throw a bridge between the present and the future — between (who knows? he was pretty obscure) the intervening spaces. She'd have understood his symbols. But the poor fellow had committed suicide — jumped off an ocean liner one dark night into the waters of the Caribbean Sea. She must read this poem. She must read this young man's biography.

Poor fellow, she said very gravely; and she paused a moment, apparently trying to reassemble her ideas — to pursue her argument from another angle. She wished she could explain a little more clearly what she'd implied by this neurotic tendency. And might she go back again to Proust? He was a neurotic certainly — nobody could deny this; think of that cork-lined room in which he'd lived; think of his last years. He was married, like so many other Europeans, to the death wish. But on the whole wasn't it a happy, certainly an appropriate marriage? Think of Proust's objectivity. Think how completely impersonal he was. He wrote about a dying civilization, about himself, and he was dying too. But there wasn't this personal note of anguish — despair. He'd been interested in it all, you might say positively enchanted with it, up to the last minute. But why, she wondered, should America, since she hadn't passed through Europe's tribulations, stopped at any of these Stations of the Cross, be sending off so many people on their journeys to the grave, and since she wasn't old in every seam and sinew of her soul, why must they turn their backs with such abruptness on their youth? Wasn't it terribly imprudent — wasn't it as a matter of fact very dangerous?

And there was this she'd noticed too. How should she express it — a kind of false sophistication — something overweighted with sophistication; think of the *New Yorker*. Was there anything like that anywhere on earth, brilliant, brittle, sensitive to the point of private language — terrifying? It scared the daylights out of her. It was sick, it was neurasthenic; it was old before it had given itself a chance to enjoy its youth.

Poor little B with all her sophisticates — all her disconsolates.

All those desolated dogs — the devastated men — the devastating women; the battles of the sexes and the souls; they'd almost finished her. And, she might add, they weren't at all what she had crossed the ocean expecting to encounter.

What! Had she been prepared to find only the little ten-year-old?

He shouldn't be so frivolous. That little ten-year-old could never have conceived these miracles. And if, by some peculiar distribution of talents, America had something in her bone and marrow that made her capable of designing plans for New Jerusalem, you couldn't put the blame on him.

She was incomparable, he said, she beat the Dutch; and he leaned across the table and took her hand in his and there appeared on his face the exact expression he'd turned on her in the taxi — hungry, beseeching, like a beggar holding out his cup, "Give me," he seemed again to be crying out, "some assurance that you need me — that I can be of help to you."

He'd finished, Millicent saw, with all this evasion, hedging; fascinating as she was, successful as she'd been in holding his attention, he was through with it — the spell she'd cast around them; he'd make the situation his — he'd not depart until he'd learned from her the plight of that poor child. Here was the luncheon hour all consumed, and here they were, practically ready to leave, and not a mention of this situation in Vienna; well, come what might, he was prepared to keep her here until he'd faced her up with little Beatrice.

Drawing her hand away and looking with great attention at a couple just preparing to depart, she asked if either of them had by any chance observed those two. Ah, they hadn't? Well, about them a long, long story might be told. She'd learned it all directly from the husband. Look at the devoted manner in which he helped the lady on with her wrap; see — he was picking up her glove; he was lighting her cigarette. What a slave! he was her ape, her monkey. He had not, all during lunch, expressed an opinion contrary to hers. He aped her every preference — and he'd poured her three-fourths of that beautiful bottle of Burgundy; he'd given her his melon when she'd finished hers. He never spoke, except to celebrate her preferences. But he was sick of it. He couldn't endure another day of marital devotion. And this he'd been engaged in telling her from the moment she'd entered this room — oh, dear — such a stream, such a flood — he'd simply poured his misery over her. All sorts of the most private and delicate confessions — terribly embarrassing — she'd never seen such hunger in the eyes of any man.

And then, this couple passing out, she was forced to stop commenting on them, for the poor starved gentleman, maybe because he was in fear of his wife's detection, maybe too abashed at what he'd already told her, never raised his eyes in confirmation of her story.

Poor man, she said, she felt so sorry for him. She turned round to scan the restaurant, and seeing that the guests, except for a few people sitting at the bar, had all cleared out, that they were the only ones remaining, the tables all presenting that abandoned, littered look, with the waiters busy replenishing silver, glass, napery, sweeping up the crumbs, whisking off the tablecloths, and every gesture a kind of shooing them off, a hustling them away, and little Beatrice there beside her plucking at her sleeve and Percy determined to have her face the ghostly presence, and all the ropes she'd used so skillfully to keep the conversation in the air collapsing, indeed the whole apparatus of her animation suddenly breaking down, she lighted a cigarette; she poured herself another cup of coffee, she emptied her glass of cognac.

How tenderly he forced her into it, leaning over, taking her hand again and in a voice trembling with feeling, but unmistakably determined, calling her his child, his dear, dear Bridget, as though he knew she'd let him be her friend and elderly protector — saying it all so eagerly. He'd been waiting to hear about her child, her little Beatrice, ever since she'd told her story to them at the Fair. She remembered, didn't she, she'd broken off and left the child in Vienna with the von Mandestadts? It was, he knew, an anxious, a dangerous business — a terrible moment for a mother: he didn't want to intrude; but she must tell him about it; she must tell him all the facts. He might be able to advise — to help her. For if there was anything on God's earth that he could do . . .

Yes, she said, of course; and there appeared on her face that look of fright (or was it hesitation?), like the shadow of a bird, gone before you'd seen it. "Of course," she repeated; but there was little he could do to help; she really had regretted even mentioning it.

And could Millicent believe her eyes? She watched her in amazement, for she seemed to be employing, by way of explanation, a kind of
pantomime — cool, precise, explicit — lifting her hands to outline,
somewhat grotesquely, a face, a head, stiffening her neck, her forefinger. And was it gallantry, she wondered, or just this habit of lightness
she assumed, as though to say, if it's a matter of one's private life, and
in the face of all that one has learned about existence, why view one
calamity with greater seriousness than another? For there wasn't a
doubt of it, her hands were attempting to give the impression of shape,
of size — a certain distortion, and she undoubtedly was saying, in her
cool, unhurried voice, "My little Beatrice has a very large head; she
points; she mutters; she makes strange sounds." She was actually attempting to bring the little creature before them bodily, to give them,
as much as she might be able to do so, the full experience of little
Beatrice, sitting there together over their coffee and cognac. She made
a few uncouth sounds; she rolled her head to the right and to the left;
she pointed a finger. "I'm afraid I must tell you, my dears," she said, "my
little girl is something of a monster; it's too distressing, but my little
Beatrice is, I fear, an idiot."

"Oh, my darling!" Millicent could have bitten off her tongue, for she
knew that the last thing that Bridget wanted now was an excess of sympathy. She'd struck the note — it was up to them to tune their speech
to hers.

As for Percy; well, she didn't have the courage to look in his direction. Apparently he was also attempting to express himself — and she
saw him fumble for Bridget's hand — try to cover it with his.

She drew it away quietly and folded both her hands on the edge of
the table. She had been told, she said in a level, matter-of-fact voice,
she had been told — and she had every reason to believe that it might
be true, for the news had come through a friend recently returned from
Vienna, and here she made an effort to empty her face of all expression;
she had heard, she repeated, continuing without changing the emotionless quality of her voice, that the Nazis had begun to make a practice of exhibiting the child, tricking her up in some grotesque costume
— cap and bells or something of the sort, slinging a sign around her
neck — *Kleine Jüdin*. This, she said, they must remember, might be all
trumped up; but then she wouldn't put it past the Nazis.

Millicent thought that she was about to faint. The room tipped, it wheeled around and the waiters, the tables, a young couple sitting at the bar, Bridget and Percy, seemed to be going round and round in a circle, like swans and horses and children in a carousel. To keel over under the circumstances was unthinkable. She could not; she would not allow herself to faint. And she fixed her eyes with great resolution on Bridget's hat and kept saying to herself — that is Bridget's hat — I am looking at the bow on Bridget's hat. Presently the dizzy waltz slowed down. The room stopped going round. The people in it took a perpendicular position. Thank God, she had saved herself. She looked at Percy, she looked at Bridget. There they were erect.

She heard Percy saying that something must be done about it and at once. Would Bridget consider letting him go with her to the German consulate? They could all go together *now*, and didn't Millicent think this was an excellent idea? And wouldn't she go with them, for something, of course, must be done, and at *once!* She could see the poor fellow wanted them all to stick together. They were Bridget's friends, and he wished Bridget to understand they didn't intend to desert her.

She pulled herself together. Yes indeed, she said, Percy's idea was splendid. Her afternoon was free — she'd go with them at once.

Bridget smiled at them a little ruefully, but with apparent appreciation of their good intentions. She said that she had been there several times already and that you might as well try to move Gibraltar from its foundations as to jar the imperturbability of those Nazi brutes — that the only thing that would be of the slightest avail would be a large, an immediate sum of money, but that the three of them together could not, with all their resources, raise what would be required. They were darlings — they were perfect darlings — but . . .

Percy would not be daunted. He said he'd hit on a new idea. Bridget knew about his novel; it was just about to appear. His publishers had great hopes for it, and so, as a matter of fact, had he. Indeed, he felt quite sure that on the strength of their expectations they'd give him a handsome advance on royalties if he asked for it, and if Bridget would come with him, if she could bring herself to tell them about little Beatrice and her terrible plight — they were decent fellows, they had hearts, he felt quite certain they could this very afternoon have a substantial check in hand.

She was touched, amused, and she turned to him as though he were a very generous little boy who had just offered her his dearest possession. It was a charming, a most generous, an adorable idea, she said — but really if he'd written *Gone With the Wind* it wouldn't be of much avail. There were no publishers in the world they could ask for such a sum as would at present be necessary.

She glanced at her watch — good heavens; she was late, it was half-past three. She had an appointment at a quarter to, at the dressmaker's. She must be off. She searched for her gloves, for her bag. She summoned a waiter. Would he be able to find the gloves, the bag? She had an unfortunate habit of consigning everything she possessed to the floor — oh, there of course they were, under the table. She thanked him with her brightest smile. She took a little mirror out of her bag; she inspected her hat, her face. Certainly she looked a fright. She straightened the hat and she declared that she must begin to make herself up a bit. One should never allow nature to get ahead of one.

Certainly, thought Millicent, she must know something of what Percy was undergoing. You had only to look at him. How could she let the poor fellow down like this — telling him her story, confiding in him and then dismissing him? All these quick perceptions, these amazing nerves the girl possessed, were they completely severed from the life, the climate of her heart? What a birdlike heart she had — never still — always in flight — always in motion. And could such an instrument be named a heart at all? You couldn't fathom her.

Would Millicent, she asked, if she could spare the time, go with her to the dressmaker's? She had such discretion about clothes. She'd like her opinion on this dress, this absurd little hat she'd got herself in for — as a matter of fact, there were two absurd little hats.

Percy, meanwhile, in a dazed, mechanical manner was paying the bill, tipping the waiter . . . Millicent could only think of one of those pugilists — knocked completely out — staggering up from the blow — making the motions with the gloves. Under no circumstances, she thought, should she desert him — leave him to his own devices. What would he do with himself? Turn in at all the bars along Third Avenue — go to his publishers with some quixotic suggestion?

Yes, she said, she'd go with Bridget, if she could be of any assistance; but when it came to passing judgment on her hats and dresses, she felt quite unequal to that task — think of the responsibility . . .

And then in a few moments, and to her utter amazement and distress, there she was climbing into the taxi behind her — deserting Percy — leaving him high and dry on the sidewalk, with that dumb, that stricken look on his face. Life carried you along in the most relentless manner — and this feeling one so frequently had that it was all a dream.

She had an impulse to say, "Come along, Percy, with us — Bridget needs your judgment on her hats — not mine." But instead of this she said, and in a voice sufficiently loud for him to hear her, that she believed Bridget was going to the Lenny Weeds' cocktail party, and if this were the case they could both go on together.

Oh — was Millicent going there too? How nice — how very nice; Bridget leaned out of the window, gave Percy her hand, nodded to the driver — "Goodbye, Percy," she called back. "Thanks for the luncheon" — the filet of sole was more than he'd promised.

And away they drove, Millicent's heart aching intolerably, knowing something of the bruise that Percy carried off with him — feeling for him such excruciating sympathy; and moreover, suddenly tortured, thinking of that tip she'd given him about the Lenny Weeds. What a fool she'd been! As though this temporary relief she'd thrown after him, giving him Bridget's program for the rest of the afternoon, weren't likely to bring about the most disastrous consequences. In what condition would he arrive, for heaven's sake? And seeing Bridget with those two young men. She seemed to have a genius for doing the wrong thing — a perfect genius for it — and as for helping Percy in his plight — listening to Bridget prattle on about her little hats and that dress she wanted her to cast her eye upon.

S E V E N

THE LINE, THE CUT, THE MOVEMENT were perfection, declared the head fitter, clasping her hands and lifting up her eyes and calling on the various members of the establishment gathered round to bear her out; this costume, the striking red hat, the purse, the smart little shoes, the perfectly fitting dark-blue dress, with the touches of red applied with such subtlety and finesse as to be almost invisible, was not only perfection — it was, moreover, the complete, but *the* complete expression of Madame St. Dennis' personality.

Staring at Bridget's reflection, catching her smile in the mirror and oppressed with an almost unbearable sense of the tragedies that enveloped her, Millicent seemed suddenly to see her emerging from the South Pacific waves as naked and innocent as the dawn, for there was — in spite of all the evidence to the contrary, in spite of the incredible domains of her experience and sophistication, something of peculiar innocence and simplicity about her — something quite independent of time or custom or behavior — free even of tragedy — you couldn't define it; but you gave it your instinctive allegiance — and perhaps, she concluded, one needn't suffer so much about her.

Yes, she said, smiling back at the reflection in the mirror — the head fitter was right — the costume was a masterpiece — the cut, the line, the movement. And what did Bridget think?

She wasn't so sure — she hadn't made up her mind; but of one thing she was certain, Millicent herself preferred the little green number she'd just taken off.

The head fitter repeated that this was, however, the complete expression of Madame St. Dennis's personality. The green and white, she admitted, was exquisite, it had a certain poetry that became Madame admirably. But after all, this was a matter of a cocktail party, and they must remember that the costume in which she was now arrayed was not only a masterpiece — a great work of art, it *was* a cocktail party in itself — the very spirit and essence of a cocktail party. Had it not been named by those who knew the secret of these matters the Dry Martini? There was no question about it, Madame St. Dennis must wear it off with her. She positively must appear in it at the Lenny Weeds' party.

Bridget moved away from the mirror. The question was decided, she said. What could be more fitting than to go arrayed in a costume commemorating Percy's favorite beverage, the dry martini? It was sublime. She asked for the bag that accompanied her former outfit. She transferred to the scarlet pocketbook a few necessary articles. And was there a handkerchief to match the gown? Oh, yes, here it was. How enchanting! She unfolded the little square of cambric smartly bordered with blue and with a blue-and-red cock emblazoned in each corner. "How charming! *pour le cocktail!*" and she flourished it gaily, folded it solemnly and, declaring that she had never set out so perfectly arrayed for any occasion, bade them all an appreciative "Au revoir."

And the entire establishment accompanying her to the door, she waved them goodbye, running down the sidewalk under the awning and jumping, with Millicent behind her, into a taxi waiting at the curb.

Would the driver wheel along as fast as he could without breaking their necks? She searched in her bag. She gave him the address.

"Okay, Baby," he said, keeping his eyes on the little mirror that framed her face — "Okay," but he'd like to be whirling her all the way to Frisco.

She leaned back. She took a long breath of the warm air. What a lovely evening. This was the first spring she'd ever spent in New York and she must admit that for a city without trees, without open spaces and only a few rags of sky above your face, there was something of extraordinary charm about it. You had your summer in the air — way up there among the tall buildings. What lovely lights and shadows. She laid her hand in Millicent's and there she kept it lightly poised, and whether this was by way of saying to her that her heart was breaking but that in this utterly intolerable world there was nothing for it but to be gay, frivolous, and gallant, or whether she merely wanted to share

with her the momentary pleasure and excitement of going to a cocktail party in the greatest city in the world, Millicent was unable to determine; but she appeared to be experiencing a series of the most
delicate, the most precise sensations, as though stars pricked through,
as though little flowers were putting out their petals in her heart.

Would there be many at the party? Bridget asked.

She drew her hand away; probably, she said, there would be an awful
jam. Had she ever been to one of these affairs?

Yes, she had. They were priceless. They always featured someone or
other. There was an exhibition piece for every party.

Was Bridget the feature today? Millicent suggested.

Oh, no. She alighted, paid the driver. The Lenny Weeds were fea-
turing an old lady — an old great aunt or somebody. It said so on the
invitations.

Millicent hadn't read the invitations, or if she had, she'd forgotten.
She followed her into the apartment house, through the hall and into
the elevator. She was tired; she was mortally fatigued.

E I G H T

THE COCKTAIL PARTY WAS IN FULL SWING, rushing up like a wave —
the smell of alcohol and cigarette smoke, the clap and clatter of
tongues, those shrill little shrieks that seemed to fly about detached
from the general babel, the deeper undertow — voices, laughter,
crowds. Walking down the shallow steps into the big living room
with Bridget beside her, Millicent was filled with an ominous sense
that something fearful was going to occur (Percy's turning up drunk,
as she felt certain he would — finding the two young men, and
Bridget laying herself out to charm them). Why, she wondered, had
she come! And couldn't she, even at this late moment, manage to escape? The Lenny Weeds were bearing down on Bridget like a pair of
hounds.

'Ah, here she was; and more beautiful than ever!'

'And what a gown; it knocked the eye out!'

'The Dry Martini! Wonderful!'

'They were waiting for her!'

What an effort poor Bridget made to drag her into the dining room
along with them; but unsuccessful — unsuccessful. This was her
chance to get away. After all, there was no reason in the world for her
to stay. Let Bridget and Percy and the two young men work it out together. Trust Bridget to handle the situation.

But here, alas, was old Mr. Andrews, with that rather ministerial look
he wore on these occasions — always wanting to help somebody out,
to come to someone's rescue — ("What, my dear lady, can I do for
you?") and like a prestidigitator drawing rabbits from his sleeve, waving a whole tray full of cocktails in her direction.

There they were — most tempting, shining, icy-cold; the beautiful old-fashioned with the slice of orange, the slice of lemon, the bright cherry, the cubes of ice; the mahogany-colored manhattan; the tempting martini. Of these latter she needed more than one. And before she realized what she was up to, she'd taken a glass, she'd gulped down its contents, she'd made a sign to the waiter, she'd put the glass back on the tray, she'd snatched up a second. Mr. Andrews must excuse her; she was very dull, she was very tired; everyone had had a head start. And one needed one's courage at these parties, didn't one?

Yes, he said; would she like another?

What he really wanted to know, Millicent realized, was who she *was* and what she *did*; for old Mr. Andrews worshipped artists, writers, creative people generally — and one must give one's credentials. He expected everyone to *do* something, to *be* somebody. And never feeling quite at ease with her own titles to distinction, she decided not to reveal them.

She could, however, appease him with names of illustrious people of her acquaintance and current gossip about them; and this would not only reward him for supplying her with the cocktails, but chain him to her side a little longer — for who liked being abandoned at these affairs? And though, if there was one thing she deplored more than another it was this particular variety of snobbishness — showing off, giving oneself a bit of prestige to which one hadn't the slightest title, violating your inner grain and instinct (for she was really most reticent — most unpretentious). And feeling completely disgusted with herself (these parties had the strangest effect upon you — the strangest), she asked old Mr. Andrews if he had heard that her dear friend Percy Jones was bringing out a new novel — a very remarkable book?

Oh, *did* she know Percival Jones? He was delighted to hear about the novel. Percival Jones was, in his estimation, one of the outstanding literary figures of the day; and he began moving his hands about, in that way he had, like a seal flapping his fins, attempting as he was to outline the proportions of Percy's talent. In his belief, he was one of the great ones — one of the giants. What was the novel to be called? *The Last Romanticist.* How interesting! He got out his notebook and wrote it down. Out this week. He'd order an advance copy.

Well embarked on the horrid business of riding her way to importance on the back of Percy's fame, she said, yes — and, as a matter of fact, Percy was likely to be here this afternoon. She'd just been lunching with him and she believed she'd heard him say that he was coming.

Oh, she didn't mean to say so — she'd just been lunching with Percival Jones?

Yes, she said, she and Bridget St. Dennis had had lunch with him at Chambords.

"*No,*" exclaimed old Mr. Andrews. "*No!* not really, you know *her,* Miss Er-Miss Arr? You mean to tell me that *she* is here this afternoon? La Belle Dennie — you just came from lunching with them? I'll find her in the most striking of costumes — The Dry Martini; how awfully funny — the dressmakers like their little jokes." He trumped up an enormous laugh.

And then there followed exactly what she might have known, if she'd had any discretion at all, was going to happen. Old Mr. Andrews again got out his notebook, his pencil. He wanted to give a party — a party in honor of Percival Jones — in honor of his book — in honor, moreover, of La Belle Dennie and of course in honor of her (my dear Miss Err — my dear Miss Arr), for he had, as everyone knew, the most naive, the most childlike delight in giving parties for celebrities. And how angry Percy was likely to be with her for helping to trump this one up she didn't even wish to imagine; he hated Mr. Andrews's parties — he never, if he could help himself, got roped into them (and arriving here drunk, as he undoubtedly would) and why, my God, had she managed all the afternoon, when she wanted so desperately to be of help to the poor fellow, to do exactly those things most likely to irritate him?

This was just the season of the year for such a party, continued Mr. Andrews; the flowers on his terrace would be in bloom. And, of course, she knew his penthouse? He'd seen her many times at his parties. Why, yes, he remembered last spring having a long talk with her. She'd admired the terrace, the fountain, the view, and in especial his little pear tree; he remembered it all perfectly; and then — triumphantly — he'd hit on it at last — "Of course, Miss Err — Miss Arr — You *paint!*"

She'd not bother to enlighten him, she'd let it go. And so — for she'd got herself in for it, she couldn't extricate herself now, she applied her mind to the perfectly preposterous business of helping him make up his party — the birthday party he called it, of Percy's book — making out the list for him, just tossing him, as though they were her private stars and galaxies, names — any amount of famous names, tossing them around in this familiar manner, juggling as she was with the shining constellations. And certainly of all the snobbish, the cheeky, the un- becoming performances this was the worst — Percy's friends — not hers at all — not even his friends; why, she was going in for mere ac- quaintances — just so that she could pluck one and then another star and toss them to Andrews and watch him write them down. And could anyone be responsible for the way one behaved at these affairs — something about it — a snobbishness — an inferiority — a superiority — something, ending up the horrid business with this last imbecility — tossing him — of all people in the world young Prentiss Price (she'd never spoken to him until this afternoon). Yes, she said, he was a friend of Bridget St. Dennis's — a great admirer.

Mr. Andrews closed his notebook. There was no doubt about the pleasure she'd given him. He was as delighted as a child, and he made no attempt to disguise his excitement. Now he must go in search of Percy and La Belle Dennie; they must be consulted about the day — the hour; they would all confer, they'd talk it over. If she would excuse him (my dear Miss Err — my dear Miss Arr) he'd take a look through the rooms, he'd find them all, he'd bring them back — he wouldn't be gone long — only a minute or two; and off he went, pushing his way with a great deal of purpose and importance through the crush.

What a fool she was, what a fool she'd always be! This was her prize display of folly. For doing exactly the reverse of what she wished and intended to do she certainly took the cake. But with all these little streams that had begun to flow through her mind from heaven knows what tributaries of exhilaration, what did she care about anything? Why worry — why worry about a single thing? How the cocktails tapped the sources of intuition — enlightenment; and it was more than likely that Percy would not turn up at all — even possible that the two young men had decided not to follow up their escapade; and if she wanted to, she could escape before Mr. Andrews returned; it would be the easiest thing in the world. In any case — why worry — why worry about a single thing? Just one more cocktail and she'd be able to carry off whatever situation developed. How they relaxed the tensions; how they eased the strain.

And had she very discreetly beckoned the waiter, or had he, without any summons from her, just obligingly stopped there in front of her — offering her the choice of those shining, icy glasses — the old-fashioned, the Manhattan — the martini? And did it matter if this appeared to be the same waiter from whom, and in that shameless manner, she'd snatched those first two drinks? For here he was and she seemed to be going through the pantomime again ("Thank you, waiter, very much indeed"), gulping down the first, taking up the second, trying to be excessively ladylike (she could, if occasion demanded it, command the grand manner). She dismissed him. He must not think she was one of those aging ladies headed so surely for dipsomania one saw everywhere today.

This, her fourth, should be, she resolved, her last — and she would sip it very slowly, very slowly indeed; for certainly the rarest, the most multiple perceptions dawned upon one — all the minute subtle behavior and gymnastic of the heart set so actively in motion by these beneficent beverages, duplicating, extending your speculative faculties, your thoughts flowing one into the other and each flashing such penetrating light on the one that followed it, and being so observant and watching everybody with so much attention — chimes ringing, lights flashing, vistas extending, widening, opening up, and associations linking this with that — accumulating what a wealth of remarkable ideas, bringing you what an excess of initiation — insight.

There was Paula Downs trying to attract the attention of Slade the correspondent, who definitely didn't want to be snared; there was Loeb the painter (how nice he was, how unaffected), and there, wandering glass in hand, was Brodansky — the great Brodansky. The Lenny Weeds *had* pulled it off this afternoon; so many celebrities you couldn't count them — they circulated freely, poets, artists, journalists, musicians, novelists. There was the beautiful Rosa Locke, whom one so seldom had a chance to see. With what adroitness Brodansky was separating himself from Mrs. Ross Taite — slipping into the dining room for another drink. And were, she wondered, the highballs as potent as these martinis?

Well, here together we were. Here we all were — the celebrities and the lesser lights; and if she wasn't greatly mistaken, everyone consumed with an acute uneasiness — a hunger of the heart wanting something, from oneself, from one's neighbor, from the moment, that certainly was not being yielded up — turning like the inhabitants of a famine-stricken city for the necessary bread and meat, to the beneficent beverages to fill the void, to staunch the ache (eyeing the tray, beckoning the waiter, grabbing the glasses) and the yeast of these queer, these unsated hungers at work on all the flushed, the slightly disintegrating faces.

Would you call it entirely pleasurable? Look at the groups, the couples — everyone up and on their feet, chatting, gulping, sipping, the cocktail glass in one hand, the cigarette in the other, shifting from foot to foot, puffing the smoke into the face of the vis-à-vis, allowing the eyes to wander, the attention to travel, the heart to yearn; and in these rushing, grabbing, competitive days, fame almost, if not quite, within everybody's reach; and when one considered the touch-and-go and trigger business of emerging suddenly into the magic beam and blast — the whole elaborate apparatus of publicity — the profiles, the blurbs, the babble — radio, screen, and press assisting to produce, and on so large a scale — to mass-produce you to such an extent that wherever you went you appeared, not only to those who beheld you, but to yourself as well, to be seen as through a thousand reflector mirrors, your voice heard as echoed from countless whispering walls and galleries. Was it to be wondered at that in the presence of all these celebrities, exposed to so many at once — there was a certain disturbance in the heart — a malaise and awkwardness in the approach of one person to another?

Feeling suddenly free of all trammels, filled with initiation and enlightenment, and each face she looked at seeming to reveal to her something of extraordinary importance — some state, condition of the heart, and her mind summoning, in their various hierarchies and orders, her own feelings, impulses — desires, marshalling them to the sudden, the surging, the triumphant belief that there were within her (*in vino veritas, in vino veritas*) certain recurrent and dominant needs, aspirations worthy of the utmost consideration, isolating these and determined to traffic no more with the distracting, the disturbing; the gregarious and trivial, but to stick to her secret goals and purposes, and under no circumstances to grudge herself the cost of these firm resolves.

Scanning the faces — feeling aloof, independent — beginning to hum some little tunes of her own invention — "Tra la la — Fortune frowns on Paula Downs," — (still trying to capture the attention of Slade) — "not at all, Mary Paul — not at all — not at all" (turned down by Loeb a second time). "And Mrs. Ross Taite must stand and wait — must jolly well wait — at the pearly gate; Tra la, la-la-la la," noticing the remarkably fine features and the expression on the face of Swensen, the Danish cartoonist (so unassuming, talking so quietly to the lady in black), and suddenly shifting her attention to the strange gentleman Marcia Weed had just brought in (for there was something that drew her gaze in his direction. Where had she seen him before?) And aware that Freddie Macauliff, whom she so intensely disliked, was sidling up to her, a hand pressed against his cheek in a manner to suggest a certain urgency and excitement, nodding cordially (for who liked to be abandoned on these occasions — who could endure it for long?).

He offered her no greetings, but announced, as though he expected her undivided attention, that he had a wonderful idea; he must tell her all about it; she would, he knew, be interested.

Doing her best not to show the effect he had upon her, for he was an unmitigated bore and why he always sought her out she was at a loss to understand, trying to appear as interested as possible, she asked him to tell her about it — his wonderful idea.

Well, here it was; he'd give it to her for what it was worth. Wouldn't it be fascinating, but perfectly fascinating — to write a comedy in the style of Wycherly with the setting (and here he took his hand away from his cheek and waved it around inclusively), just this — the Lenny Weeds' cocktail party? It could all be so beautifully stylized — instead of fans, cocktail glasses, cigarettes (replacing his hand, regarding the scene). He had a splendid, a naughty little plot, which he could not, of course, think of revealing, but he intended to develop it through the wittiest dialogues — little conversation pieces, formal bouquets which should conceal, intimate, suggest, like the fans and furbelows, and all charmingly accompanied by movements of the cocktail glass, the cigarette, the delightful, the libidinous wit of the Restoration — which, after all, and didn't she agree with him, very much resembled the hint and innuendo of today? He proposed to give his characters symbolic names — Lydia Libido — Ida Id — Prysilla Psyche.

It was certainly a most amusing idea, she said; but frankly, if he wouldn't mind her being honest with him, she didn't think that our manners today at all resembled Restoration comedy, where everyone hewed to a formal pattern, where sex itself was harnessed to rules as formal as figures in a dance. Here we all did our little *pas seul* — a riot of conflicting steps, conflicting egos. Had he ever seen the ego so rampant — attempting to take this shape, or that or the other, to be somebody other than one was, to get something other than one had, to see oneself in all the shapes, the attitudes, the gestures of fame, celebrity — success? For, after all, anything might happen to one in New York, where the gifts were fabulous, the rewards astonishing; and exposed to so much glamour — exposed, to be specific, to the Lenny Weeds' parties. Might she suggest Eric and Erica Ego as even more symbolic of the occasion?

But what, he asked, did she mean; he was afraid he hadn't understood — would she please explain?

Yes indeed, certainly, if she wasn't very much mistaken, and she looked around the room — nobody was exchanging anything with anyone. And weren't we all engaged in the most melancholy of trysts — communing exclusively with ourselves? If she were to invent the proper conversation pieces, they would all be monologues — everybody talking to himself, nobody listening to anyone else. For herself, she found a cocktail party the most solitary ordeal.

He said again that he was afraid he hadn't understood — hadn't got her. Would she explain more carefully?

"Why yes — please, Freddie — look around you," she begged, "regard the various faces."

That was, he assured her, his usual habit; and restraining with great difficulty an impulse to turn and leave her, he asked if that wasn't the great Brodansky coming into the room — did she see Brodansky?

Yes, she did indeed; everyone was aware of Brodansky. Everyone was aware of Rosa Locke — of Loeb. And this was exactly what she was driving at. Would he look at them all? Would Freddie just look at the various groups and couples? Who was really conversing with anyone? They chatted, they laughed, they laid on and off the necessary smiles, they made the appropriate gestures. But couldn't he see that everyone had the roving eye — the traveling attention? Nobody was really listening to anyone. Look at the unappeased, the hungry expressions mantling these faces. The moment should, everyone felt, be yielding something more satisfactory than was actually the case — something really immense. Look at them! They puffed their cigarettes, they laughed, they talked — but they were absentminded, the eyes wandered, the hearts yearned — exactly, she wanted very much to say, as yours is doing now, my dear Freddie; but instead, she asked him if he could tell her who the pretty girl was talking to old Professor Jenks in the far corner of the room.

Yes, he said, she was Frances Templeton — a very warm friend of his — a young writer of exceptional talent.

The Professor, she continued, with a perfectly sadistic desire to give it to him straight, was holding forth at length — and his little Miss Templeton was aware of so many illustrious people with whom she longed to be talking that she'd dropped every pretense of listening. Now come, wouldn't Freddie admit that his little friend was frankly bored, and didn't he think it was likely that she was saying to herself in a perfect frenzy of frustration and desire: "There is Whittridge Knight, the novelist, here at my side is Slade, the correspondent, and over there is Mary Paul chatting with Geoffrey Bains; and if I could have the attention of one of these people I might perhaps grasp my moment — my chance to further my own career; for I too have gifts, doors are about to open to me, I am about to pass over thresholds — into magic rooms. But how can I escape my old professor, how can I get away from this intolerable bore?"

"How can she?" asked Freddie, making no attempt to disguise his irritation.

"Mary Paul," she went on, giving in completely to her desire to irritate him further, "looks hopefully in the direction of Slade; 'we are people of parts' she says to herself, 'we should not be stuck with such nonentities.' But he continues to avoid her eye. Paula Downs allows her eyes to roam. Look — she's bowing to the great Brodansky. And how skillful he is — always managing to escape his admirers and give his undivided attention to the cocktails and canapés. And there, coming into the room and in the most bizarre of costumes, is the famous Mrs. Green. In she strides; she gives us all the once over, she rejects us — but no, her eyes have fallen on Brodansky. She decides she'll stay. Come now, Freddie — what resemblance does this bear to Restoration drama?"

"None at all" (conceding it childishly), "that is," he added, "if you wanted to interpret it in this particular manner," but he never cared to go in for all these asides — too obvious, too obvious. And suddenly alert, interested, nodding an invitation to Paula Downs, who, clad in a bright-blue bolero and a variety of smiles, dashed out of her corner, cigarette and cocktail glass lifted in a gesture of salute, and executing the most fantastic little pirouette, a foot kicked out to the left, a foot to the right, advanced to greet him.

"Freddie," she gasped, falling on his neck, "Freddie Macauliff."

"Darling," he rejoined, righting her position, straightening her hat, "how *are* you?"

She gave Millicent a belated nod. How did she find herself? And what she had come, she said, all the way across the room to inquire was, could either of them tell her *who* Marcia Weed had got in tow? He had an Oxford accent and he was just *too* amusing — who *was* he?

Hearing explosions of laughter, Millicent turned to regard the gentleman in question, who held the little group around him entirely enthralled. He seemed to be telling a story with all the tricks of the professional wit, keeping his face completely shut, allowing not a smile to escape it, and giving the impression of reciting something already learned by heart. Amid the merriment he was creating he stood poised with his hand held to the back of his head. But the fascinating, the truly arresting thing about him was that he did not appear to be present at his own recitation, for the living, sentient self — the pretty, the darling creature having been brusquely pushed back, shoved away from any contact or traffic with the smartly dressed, the very dapper middle-aged gentleman scoring off his carefully calculated points — had slipped right away from him and was running off in front of everyone's eyes, fluttering, waving her handkerchief, holding onto her veils, reaching for her ribbons, catching at her hair in a coy, an entirely successful attempt not to let any of her feminine charms escape her; while the recitation nearly over, his hand still held to the back of his head, shoulders slightly lifted, eyes still rolled well up under the lids, failing to acknowledge the enthusiasm of his audience (everyone was going off into gales of laughter), he leaned forward, finicky, ladylike, and placed his glass on a table at his elbow.

Suddenly down came the eyes from under the lids and, his face still expressionless, they roamed the room, they rested vaguely on Millicent and fixed her for a moment with a bland, a blue and innocent stare.

She looked him squarely in the face — oh, certainly not, it couldn't possibly be — certainly *not*.

And now there was a new distraction — exclamations of delight and astonishment were breaking out all over the room. For a very, very ancient lady — one could see with what pride and delight at the mere feat and effrontery of her performance — was approaching on Lenny's arm, dressed in a full black skirt, black bodice fitting tight as a glove, little buttons straight down the front, snow-white cap on snow-white hair, white ruche at her throat and wrists, and a large black onyx brooch, with big pearls in a cross down its center, striking the religious as well as the decorative note. She came in at quite a clip, her beaked nose and her sharp-beaked upper lip lending her a formidable resemblance to a parrot. Leaning lightly on Lenny's arm, her skirts flying out in all directions and her high cracked voice hitting a different key with every word, she gave the impression of perching there on his wrist like a falcon, while he proudly held her up for everyone to admire.

A florid lady in a salmon-colored dress, accompanied by Myron Heartly, the Egyptologist, pushed against Millicent for a better view, the young man declared that to have such an old girl for a great aunt was indeed a social distinction. He'd never seen anything like her, unless perhaps under a weeping willow in an old, old cemetery. "Priceless, priceless — a Victorian relic if there ever was one," said the lady in salmon, while Millicent, attempting to get a look at the exhibition piece, found herself whirled up into the little drama with a suddenness that allowed for no preparation whatever.

"Too good to be true," reiterated the florid lady.

"Unbelievable!" said the Egyptologist.

"What an air!" exclaimed Freddie Macauliff. "What an aristocrat!"

"How long has Lenny kept her up his sleeve? The best show they've put on yet," said Paula Downs.

"My dear," cried Lenny in his most imperative voice. And bringing Millicent, as he lifted his hand, into the very forefront of the performance, "Aunt Harriette insists on it. She insists."

"Milly Munroe," shrieked the old parrot, flying off her perch and directly into Millicent's face and pecking her first on the right cheek, then on the left — "Milly Munroe!"

"Miss Harriette Howe, of all astonishing things!" she exclaimed as she returned the old lady's kisses. "Miss Harriette — my dear Miss Harriette — *how* extraordinary."

The apparition tapped Lenny on the sleeve. She shook an angular finger. She wasn't at all surprised, she said, to find this little girl, the child of her oldest friend, here among his celebrities. And what did she *do?*

"Nothing, Miss Harriette — nothing at all."

She needn't tell her that. The finger shook emphatically — a remarkable child — with her love for little things — for very, very little things. How she'd loved the little things. She shrieked it out at Lenny — at the entire room, and her voice rose to a high, a perfectly delighted shriek — "the very little things."

"What kind of little things?" inquired Freddie Macauliff.

Oh, she said, archly, coquettishly — attempting to invest Millicent with the aura of her childish eccentricities — grasshoppers, crickets, ladybugs, butterflies, caterpillars, ants. Did Millicent recollect how she'd always snooped about — lying there at the edge of the meadows, listening — eavesdropping? "We were always shooing her off," she declared — going through the pantomime, "shoo-shoo."

Yes indeed, Miss Harriette, said Millicent, she remembered; she remembered very well.

She mustn't say Miss Harriette, Lenny corrected. This was Madame Greenfeld — the distinguished Madame Greenfeld, introducing her with a great flourish to her audience.

On they went with it, Miss Harriette declaring that if the dear child still wished to call her Miss Harriette, by all means let her continue to do so, and Lenny insisting, with that emphasis on the frivolous and decorative that made him such an excellent impresario, that she deserved all the honors of her estate, bowing to her gallantly, the old lady carrying out the role in which he had cast her, returning the bow with an antique curtsey, while Millicent begged to be excused, for she never would be able to think of her by any but the old familiar name — and Paula Downs arriving on the scene and Swensen, the Danish cartoonist, drifting up with Loeb and Mrs. Green, and all clamoring for a word with the old lady, every one of them under the impression that she was deaf, shrieking in the loudest possible manner.

Paula Downs shrieked at Miss Harriette that she was marvelous, and she shouted at Lenny that she was a perfect model for a "Profile" in the *New Yorker,* and didn't he think that it could be arranged — wouldn't Madame Greenfeld like a "Profile" of herself?

She'd prefer a full face, she cackled back. She never liked her profile — too much like a parrot.

At which everyone screamed with delight, and Paula tried to explain to her about the "Profile."

Doubtless — doubtless, said the old lady — it was hard for her to receive more than one idea at a time, and she hadn't recovered yet from her astonishment at finding the world so small — for here in her nephew's apartment, only think of it, little Milly Munroe, the daughter of her old friend — an extraordinary coincidence. And they had no idea what an exceptional child she had been — always so interested in little things — in very, very little things.

And then, suddenly, in the way that situations had at these parties, of dissolving, one into the next — opening and closing so swiftly the shutters of emotion, presenting such vistas and landscapes of the heart — leading you down such varied conversational byways, there she was conversing with Swensen, the Danish cartoonist, who it seemed took a great interest in the flora of foreign lands and had, he told her, once bought at a florist's a tight pink bunch of very small flowers, the smell of which, he declared, had translated him to realms of indescribable delight. Could she tell him about them? Where did they grow? And had she ever picked them herself?

"Arbutus!" she said, and she felt as though she and this amiable Dane had been carried away from everyone in the room to enjoy a private kingdom where for a moment or two they might share together a sheer, a flawless experience. Yes indeed, she had picked them many times. They grew, she said, in woody places and often when the snow still lay in patches on the ground — and suddenly overcome with a desire to describe the exact locale — that uncanny excitement — that sense of waiting on the revelation — down on one's knees in the April woods, tugging at the stems, loosening the roots of ferns — scattering the mold, the pine needles, with all the wet surrounding plants still in their lifeless winter raiment — smelling the earth, the melting snow, beholding them there so pink, so perfect, reticent, precise, their fragrance on them like a sacrament; not knowing of course what, or if any, of all this, she had said, and feeling it all with such intense emotion.

Nothing, said Mr. Swensen, like the small flowers of the northern springs. He could, he assured her, find no better words than hers — reticent, perfect, precise — and he talked to her about his native flowers, choosing a few specimens — giving them their Danish names and describing them with an accuracy and economy that was, she reflected, both poetry and botany — and was she familiar, he asked her, with those lovely flowers of celestial tints that grew on rather limp and silken stems.

Hepaticas — oh yes, certainly, and she felt exactly as though she were taking them out of his hands, with hues upon their petals of the morning and the evening clouds — dawn-pink, amethyst, dusk-blue — hearing Miss Harriette Howe still cackling, protesting in her cracked, her parrotlike shrieks that she'd prefer a full face to a profile — and Lenny shouting at Paula that she'd love it — Aunt Harriette would love it — sitting for her "Profile"; they'd make her famous overnight.

There was, she said, Star of Bethlehem — or Quaker Lady — Innocence — he could take his choice of names: they were petalled precisely, like arbutus — but of an evanescence, a fragility — color of the air, the mist, the April shower, and with a nearly invisible, thread-like yellow stem. The Innumerables, the Hosts — the Multitudes she called them — for they grew in such crowds — such quantities and one could almost watch them grow (remembering it with such vividness, that afternoon in May when she had stood among them in a shroud of rain and rainbow — seeing them springing up all fresh and stainless at her feet).

And rushing headlong into summer, did he, she wondered, know pirella, pipsissewa — and the strangest of them all — the Indian Pipe — uncanny — like an apparition — wrought of frost, of snow — the thick snow stem, the thin sepals of ice at every joint, the heavy, sculptured snow bell — that stamen ring of dull gold — like the touch of gold upon the everlasting (Immortelles). It was, she said, the little ghost, the *revenant* that came to haunt the August woods.

He wrote down, very meticulously — Indian Pipe — ghost — *revenant*. Yes, he said, he thought he knew it. It was he believed a mushroom growth. It turned black soon after it was picked. Uncanny,

uncanny indeed. And a clock striking half-past five, he put his note-book in his pocket. He was afraid that he must go. Their talk had kept him beyond the time he should have stayed. But how often did one have a chance for such congenial conversation? He bowed; he thanked her with great courtesy, with gratitude. Then he left her and went to his hostess, bade her goodbye, bowed himself out.

She watched him depart — the nicest gentleman she'd ever met, she thought, and it seemed to her that her heart, the room, the entire world was starred and gemmed with little candied flowers.

But all at once she felt them blighted by a sudden frost, for there coming in from the dining room and followed by young Price and his anonymous companion was Bridget, and directly behind them old Mr. Andrews, gaily waving one hand to announce the arrival of his troupe and with the other firmly gripping Percy by the arm, trying to regulate his gait, urging him forward. And catching the unmistakable expression of fury spread across Percy's face, she recognized instantly that his anger was directed against herself. All the irritations she had caused him since they'd met for lunch had gathered to form in his mind a violent, confused, and drunken conviction that she had deliberately set about to trap him into his agonizing, his ignominious plight. (For hadn't she been responsible, not only for getting these young men here, but for getting him here, and finally for this incredible bit of impertinence — roping him into Mr. Andrews' ridiculous plan to give a party for his book?) Watching him with dread, with consternation, and also aware that Marcia Weed was calling Bridget, she saw Bridget stop, she saw Andrews stop a moment, relaxing his grip on Percy's arm. She heard Bridget's sharp exclamation of surprise.

"But Christopher — Christopher Henderson!"

Her eyes were riveted on their greeting. (Then it was undoubtedly Christopher Henderson.) She saw him lift his shoulders, take her hand, raise it to his lips; and Bridget, with that inimitable gift she had for extracting from every incident all it held of human comedy (tossing off her little skit with a lightness, a skill and delicacy that ran no risk of letting him see that he was being frivolously, almost affectionately caricatured), allowing him to kiss her first on one cheek, then on the other, repeating his exact words — "Fancy finding you here," raising her hand to the back of her head, as though to arrange a stray lock, subtly, slyly, for the private entertainment of the two young men, who stood aside and watched her, completely captivated.

"My dear young woman," gasped Christopher, simulating a swoon, "my dear young woman, *how* extraordinary."

Millicent staggered back. Was it a sensation of scalding heat, or of stinging cold, on her right cheek, on her left? The calamity that was upon her and the grim, incredible incidents that comprised it had neither sequence nor validity, but appeared to be happening, like those fatal flashes of lightning, simultaneous with the clap and crash of thunder, all in an instant. There was Percy hauling off, preparing to lunge at her a second time — "Millicent, you fool, you blooming fool!" And Bridget like an arrow darting up to him — "How *could* you, Percy? Millicent's your friend" — striking him full across the face. And young Price with one violent, well-directed blow knocking him down, knocking him over, neat as though he'd been a ninepin. "Cad, you goddamned cad!" And everything crashing, falling, splintering — cocktail glasses, books, a chair, a shining table made of glass, a great bowl of dark-red peonies. And Percy on the floor, covered with the blood-red petals of the peonies, and the blood streaming from his face and forehead, as good as murdered, as good as murdered, she decided, seeing the sharp edge of the broken table and discovering that she was down on her knees assisting Bridget in turning him over, staring at him and hearing the screams of Miss Harriette Howe and the loud aside of Paula Downs — "The best show they'd put on yet" — and young Heartly's rejoinder — "They got the breaks — think of all the people — think of all the names!" While Bridget, dabbing Percy's forehead with that absurd little square of cambric embroidered with red-and-blue cocks, assured her that he was going to be all right — the injury was not serious, the trouble was that he'd had too much to drink, filled with the forlornest sense of woe, believing she was to blame for everything, taking a handkerchief from somebody or other, attempting helplessly to bandage Percy's head — praying from the depth of her soul that he might immediately regain consciousness and imploring him to forgive her for all her blunders — all her ineptitudes; for certainly she alone was to blame for this calamity.

N I N E

IT WAS LIKE A NIGHTMARE, with the breeze coming through the windows, stirring the curtains, bringing in that smell of summer, that drone of the city streets below them, and Bridget sitting there at the window, her striking costume drenched in blood, and poor Percy unconscious on the bed, the blood seeping through the bandages, running down his cheek, staining the pillows, and the noise of the party in the next room continuing unabated.

Did she feel, Millicent asked, that they were dreaming it, and that presently they'd wake to discover none of it was true?

We'd not, she answered, wake from the nightmare till we woke from it together. It wasn't a matter of this macabre incident or that. The performance was continuous — all in it together, running to the brink of the precipice. And one was as responsible as another. There was something personal, insatiable — wanting everything, receiving nothing. Perhaps when the anguish in the heart was deep enough.

When did she think young Price would be back? It seemed to her he'd been gone an eternity.

She glanced at her watch. He'd only, as a matter of fact, been gone a quarter of an hour. Surely there must be a doctor in the building. He'd bring one back in just a moment.

But, Millicent questioned — would he? It wasn't so easy to get one in an emergency — and it was just their bad luck to have every doctor they knew out of town. "Wouldn't it have been better to have sent him off in an ambulance? All the doctors in the vicinity were probably sitting down to their dinner. Try to pry one of them away from the table."

Bridget got up and crossed the room. She slipped her hand into Millicent's. She mustn't, she said, allow herself to get so worked up. There was one chance in a million that this was a mortal wound. It was, of course, a nasty business. And that poor unfortunate boy, so afraid he'd murdered him, very nearly beside himself with fear. But she believed he'd be all right. Just get a competent doctor to sew up his wounds and give him something to bring him to.

The blood was seeping through all these bandages. She didn't like it. Why should the wound continue to bleed so profusely?

Oh — it was a good sign, Bridget assured her — much worse if it wasn't bleeding. The artery had certainly not been cut, for in that event there'd be fountains of blood, which obviously was not the case.

Millicent tried to find his pulse. It seemed to her very weak and intermittent; but then she didn't know much about these matters. Certainly his face should not have gone this strange, gray color and the skin so puffed and coarse.

Death, declared Bridget, was always a reverent sculptor. In the hands of death a face took on such gravity — beauty. There was always nobility. But at the mercy of this drunken sculptor the human countenance became positively gross, indecent. A merciless artist. How hungry, vulnerable — unappeased poor Percy looked.

One wished, said Millicent, to cover up his face.

The trouble with him was, Bridget continued, he tried to live in contradiction to the movements of his heart — that was Percy's undoing, his perpetual tragedy. He was a great romantic, the core of him all sentiment. He couldn't bear it that she had so little feeling for her child, that she knew so little of maternal love. Few knew less of it than she. And yet, when that news had come out of Vienna, she'd felt something so fierce, so passionate. She wouldn't be able to explain it, knowing as she suddenly did that there was nothing — nothing on this earth that she would stop at — no stone she'd leave unturned to get her little cretin to America. Was it rage, was it indignation? She wouldn't know. But understanding Percy's feeling for the little creature — not wanting to hurt him; and knowing he was in no position actually to come to her aid, deciding not to shock him with the brutal facts — coming to lunch as she had, with her mind made up to evade all further mention of her difficulties; and when he'd faced her with it — for there'd been no alternative — he'd forced her into it — being so drastic, so brief and unadorned, so realistic — that had been too much for him. It was her method, getting through with it — avoiding sentiment.

And she'd never as long as she might live forget that offer he had made about his royalties. Millicent didn't know how far he'd gone with that idea — rushing off to the publishers, while they were at the dressmaker's — making the most extravagant suggestions. He'd asked them to give him, then and there, an advance on every novel he was likely to write up to the day of his death. He'd offered them in short a most enticing gamble on his life. They were, he'd said, considering it; he'd promised them best-sellers to the end of his days — that was all he was good for anyway. He'd almost done it once by accident — and if he really put his mind to it, there was a fortune in the gamble. Drunk as a lord, of course, and young Price there and listening to all of it. Good God, the expression on his face when he saw that boy. Then old Andrews coming up about the party for his book — getting all that business mixed — telling the poor man that Millicent knew Price and what's-his-name — that they were great friends; thinking of nothing but how he'd rescue little Beatrice.

Then that Algonquin episode, all so quick, like a kind of God-sent intervention — being presented with her deliverer when she least expected it. And of course without Millicent, who had effected the introduction, she might never have been in a position to have the young man's millions at her disposal; for, indeed she'd have to confess it, as soon as she heard his name announced she'd entertained no doubts, either about her methods of procedure or her ability to harness all that money to her enterprise. But how quickly she'd had to act — giving him that tip about the cocktail party, and only a second to pull it off in, with Percy doing his best to snatch her from salvation. Then everything working out so well, even in the matter of Percy's spilling the beans in that painful drunken speech about his publishers and her poor child — young Price being there and hearing just enough to make it quite natural for her to tell him the entire truth whenever he should ask for it. And their dining out tonight and all.

It filled her heart with grief to think that, where she had come off in the whole affair with what she could only call her usual luck, here was poor Percy the tragic victim of her strategy. Millicent had only to look at him to know how badly she must feel.

No! protested Millicent. Bridget must not blame herself. It was entirely *her* fault. She should never have given Percy the information about their coming here. She'd felt so sorry for him. That was always her undoing — feeling sorry for people.

Suddenly the door burst open and, ushered in by Lenny and Marcia Weed and followed by young Price, a stocky little gentleman, carrying his official bag and somehow managing to separate himself completely from the anxiety of his companions, crossed the room without so much as opening his mouth, and, showing in his face the violence of his spleen, went directly to the bed.

Here, thank God, was the doctor!

He moved Percy's head abruptly — petulantly, towards the light and announced, as though he were handing out an indictment: "Intoxicated — drunk."

Of course, burst in young Price — wild-eyed — distraught — apparently at the very end of his endurance. They all knew that. Couldn't he say something to reassure them? The man's condition wasn't critical, was it?

He unwound the bandages, drenching as he did so the pillow and Percy's cheek with blood; the wound was, he said, abominably bandaged and his voice, even his hands, shook with petulance and irritation. Would someone bring him a basin of water at once?

He couldn't, insisted Marcia Weed, couldn't possibly imagine the anxiety they all felt. The patient hadn't been seriously injured? The wound *couldn't* be mortal? Nothing so shocking as that. Poor Mr. Jones was, as he had pointed out, a little intoxicated — a wonderful man, a writer, a very famous novelist — Mr. Percival Jones, whom he must know by reputation.

It might very well be, said the little man, remitting none of his petulance, that Mr. Jones had received a mortal blow. The wound was in the vicinity of the right temple; it was at just such parties that these violent scenes occurred. They led, God knew, to the breaking of all His commandments, including the Sixth (he took the bowl from Lenny). Now he would have to ask them all, with the exception of his host and hostess, who could be of some assistance to him, to clear out of the room. He must examine his patient; he must sew up this ugly gash.

Good God! cried young Price, couldn't the doctor recognize his state of mind? He'd merely knocked this poor man down for insulting a lady. He hadn't intended anything more than just to bring him to his senses. For he had taken, as everybody recognized, too much to drink. The poor fellow was drunk; he'd only wanted to bring him to his senses. Any gentleman would have done an exactly similar thing. Couldn't the doctor treat him with a little consideration? Didn't he realize the state of his nerves?

He must repeat what he had told them before. He could make no announcements till he had further examined his patient. He did not make a practice of attending such cases. He had no relish for them. These parties were uncivilized. We lived in a cocktail age. Society was nourished on alcohol. A Babylonian moment. He wished to repeat his request. Would everyone but the assistants he had designated clear out of the room?

There was one chance in a million, declared Bridget, standing there in her blood-stained garments and fixing him with a level stare, that the wound was mortal — the chance was more likely to be one in ten million. He had made a diagnosis with which they all agreed. Mr. Jones had had too much to drink. But, and she was willing to stake all she possessed on this, as soon as he regained his consciousness he'd be as sound as ever.

She turned. She laid her hand on young Price's shoulder. "Come, dear boy," she said. "Come, Millicent."

T E N

———

MILLICENT FOLLOWED BRIDGET and young Price back to the cocktail party. Her sense of walking through a nightmare increased — the belief that she was approaching its supreme moment of terror.

There in a corner was Christopher Henderson talking to Andrews, with white gulls flying up from the waves, and the cliffs of Cornwall retreating behind him, and the high cracked voice of Miss Harriette Howe, heard above the din and chatter, presenting her with a succession of little pictures — a house on a hill, a meadow full of buttercups and daisies, an old maid with a formidable pompadour — the extraordinary capacity of the subconscious to extract realms of beauty and terror from the phantom voices, faces — those peculiar landscapes, vistas of the heart, into which they dissolve, bestowing upon everything that occurred the antic and terrifying semblance of a dream.

The room was charged with excitement — melodrama. Questions flew at her from all directions. They seemed to hit, to stun her, like so many missiles directed at her heart. Rumors were afloat. Speculations swirled and eddied. Someone declared that Percy had died. Someone else said, no — he was dying. An ambulance was waiting. The police were about to enter the apartment. Questions continued to fly.

"What was the doctor's verdict?"

"Would it be murder?"

"Manslaughter?"

"Would the police be called?"

"Wasn't it shocking?"

"Terrible?"

"How *could* it have happened?"

"And to the Lenny Weeds — "

"Of *all* people?"

"They'd have to be questioned?"

"Held as witnesses?"

"Imagine it — "

"Going to court."

Bewildered and unable to say a single word, she turned for help to Bridget, who, she saw to her astonishment (how did she dare to say these things?), was dealing with the situation in the most easy and casual manner imaginable.

There — her hand still on young Price's shoulder — she stood, reassuring everybody on every score. "Murder?" she repeated, "manslaughter! Dear me, no — nothing so melodramatic as all that! Who said the wound was fatal? Quite the contrary was the case. The doctor would have to take a few stitches. Mr. Jones had, of course, and very obviously, had too much to drink. But when this matter was attended to, when he regained his consciousness, there would be little occasion for anyone to worry. Indeed, the person most to be worried about was this poor boy."

She took her hand from the young man's shoulder. He must, she insisted, be in need of something —

"Whiskey — brandy — rye?"

The effect of her words was instantaneous. Expressions changed; you couldn't exactly say disappointment was discernible, but that look of readjustment, of unwillingness to forego the high pitch and tension of melodrama — a deflation, a kind of blank and unbelief of first response. And then, suddenly, nerves adjusted to the drop in tension, a spontaneous display of all those pent-up and silenced egos — a need on everyone's part to be conspicuously helpful — everybody wanting to do something — anything for somebody, for anybody.

And how impressively Mrs. Ross Taite was saying, "Give it to him neat," trotting off with that self-important walk of hers — wanting to see he got it neat and followed by half-a-dozen other people, bent apparently on the same merciful errand.

A new group closed round, avid to be of assistance, to extract, if possible, a crumb of information from the source . . .

"Did she want a cigarette?"

"Would she have another drink?"

"How about an aspirin?"

"She must sit down!"

"She preferred to stand?"

"Would she tell them something — "

"Anything about it?"

"Extraordinary!"

"Out of a clear sky?"

"He was her friend!"

"How splendidly she'd acted — "

"Such coolness — courage!"

A gentleman she did not know said Miss Munroe was wonderful — a most remarkable woman; and Paula Downs, flourishing her cigarette, sipping her cocktail, agreed emphatically — "A remarkable — a wonderful creature."

"One of the great ones," said Mr. Andrews, coming up with Christopher Henderson, whom she saw arrayed in a sunbonnet, leaning from the upper windows of a Georgian house, smoking a corncob pipe, simultaneously borne off with him to the sunny meadows, the little ram running on the wind, Jehovah and the angels trumping on their trumps clearly discerned in the clouds as she raked the new-mown grass and pulled from her rake poppies, cornflowers, daisies.

And could he, inquired Andrews, introduce an author internationally known? He must have heard of her inimitable little stories; he'd surely seen them on the screen — a writer of script, beloved of Hollywood — a writer of witty articles and famous tales — a very great lady — Miss Millicent Munroe.

She put out her hand. Could it be possible that once, and she looked into those vague, peculiarly focused blue eyes, she'd gathered into a sheaf, to be laid on the altar of marriage — happy, safe, with children and a Georgian house and exhilarating friends — all the treasures of her romantic heart: poetry, sorrow, love for wind and wave and cloud? And if she'd regretted turning down that proposal once, certainly she'd regretted it a million times.

"To a visitor from England, equally distinguished — Mr. Christopher Henderson — the Mr. Henderson," continued Andrews, rounding off his introduction with a flourish.

Living contented ever after, as one believed one would in those naive and far-off days when one was twenty-two and knowing nothing of this and that and all the other things of which one was aware today — turning him down in that extraordinary manner — rebuffing him for good and all.

"How jew dew," he said, raising his shoulders, lifting her hand, and — for he evidently had no intention of admitting by so much as the flicker of an eyelash that he'd ever laid eyes on her — regarding her with that peculiarly focused, that vague blue stare — "how jew dew," offering, as he explained, a salutation to Hollywood, bowing, kissing her hand — "Miss Millicent Munroe," saying the name twice over and not without a certain irony.

Had he, she asked — and the question escaped her mouth before she could suppress it — continued his career as novelist?

What! interrupted Andrews, he was a novelist besides all his other accomplishments? She didn't mean to tell him that he *wrote?*

Christopher protested; he drew himself back, fending off the assertion with both his hands — his one wild oat, he said — his very wild, wild oat; and how remarkable that a charming lady from Hollywood should have been informed of his greatest indiscretion.

She remembered it very well — *The Key in the Rusty Lock;* she'd enjoyed it extravagantly on her first visit to England; she'd really, as a matter of fact, never been able to forget it.

"One never knew," he said, achieving again that distant, decorative bow.

And Andrews engaging her attention, she tried to listen to his apologies — he hadn't, he said, lowering his voice very confidentially, realized Percy's condition. He should never have brought him up to her; he should have taken him directly home. He had learned from the beautiful Madame Bridget — and thank God for this — thank God for it, that the accident was not in the least grave (how had Bridget *dared* to make these declarations?) — that as soon as the doctor had taken a few stitches — administered a few drugs, there'd be no occasion for anyone to be alarmed. They could all congratulate themselves. But on the other hand, he owed her the profoundest apologies . . .

"No! Mr. Andrews," she declared impetuously; she alone was to be held responsible for what had occurred. She should never — never in the world, after luncheon, when they were leaving the restaurant, have given Percy that information. She should indeed have realized in what condition he would appear.

Her audience had heard it all, of course; she found herself beset again —

"The information — "

"What information?"

"She'd been lunching with Percy Jones?"

She'd confess it. She'd been terribly foolish; she should never have told him about it — that they were coming on to the party. He'd not known of it. He'd not even been invited. They'd been lunching to-gether — the three of them. (Would nothing stop her — could nobody shut her mouth?)

"They'd been lunching together — "

"Which three?"

"What three?"

"Mr. Jones was *not* invited?"

"He didn't *know* the Lenny Weeds?"

"Would she continue?"

"They were lunching together?"

"Certainly," said Mr. Andrews, "Miss Munroe and Percival Jones and La Belle Dennie had all been lunching together at Chambord's."

"What — at Chambord's — "

"No! Not at Chambord's?"

"*How* interesting!"

"Was he tight, at Chambord's?"

"No," she said, "he was perfectly all right; he wasn't tight at all." They'd separated after lunch. She'd gone with Bridget to the dress-maker's and it had been just then, just as they were separating, that she'd told Percy they were coming on together. She should never have told him about it. Never in the world; about the cocktail party and their coming here together. This had been her fatal blunder. If she hadn't given Percy the address, this dreadful, unspeakable catastrophe would never have occurred. It was entirely her fault. Poor Percy — poor darling Percy could hold no one else responsible.

"Poor Mr. Jones."

"He was to be pitied."

"Poor Percival Jones."

"And so clever — "

"Such a brilliant writer!"

"One of the great ones," said Andrews. "One of the great ones. And his new novel about to appear. Had they heard about it? Coming out in a day or two — *The Great Romantic* — something of the sort."

On the nightmare went, tossing up the phantom scenes and voices, the apparitions, forcing her into the weirdest blunders and confessions. And if she screamed could she not put an end to dreaming? Would she not wake up?

She looked about her. Scenes shifted; figures changed. There, sprawled on a sofa, was Brodansky, a handkerchief over his face, an empty cocktail glass held delicately in his long beautiful hand; there was the lovely Rosa Locke, wandering about, talking to herself, grimacing horribly; and here, approaching on the arm of Freddie Macauliff, her skirts flying out in all directions, shrieking at the top of her cackle and dissolving into her element of memory, was Miss Harriette Howe — becoming, as she flew off her perch and kissed her, first on one cheek and then on the other, a meadow full of flowers — a little girl — a summer afternoon.

"Milly, my dear child," she shrieked. "What an outrage!"

She did her best to calm her, to assure her that it was all an accident — that Mr. Jones's injuries would not prove serious. She must not alarm herself. The doctor was taking a few stitches; he would adminis-ter a few necessary drugs.

As if she cared a fig for Mr. Jones! It was this little girl she was anx-ious about. Why, and again she addressed the entire room — if they'd only known her when she was young — so sensitive, so full of feeling — wrapped up in nature — always so fond of little things.

The hive swarmed, the world dissolved — one was everybody. One was nobody. And here we all were together — the Nobodys — the Somebodys — the Everyones. There was Geoffrey Bains; there was Brodansky; there was Rosa Locke. And here now, suggesting that she'd perhaps like a shot of brandy — neat, or maybe a nip of rye, was Freddie Macauliff. "No, thank you, Freddie — not a fan, not a furbelow." Accepting a fresh martini from the hands of Paula Downs (for one grabbed at the glass, one gulped down the cocktail — to staunch the ache, to appease the hunger. And we were all implicated. We shared a common ignominy — as Bridget had said, there'd be no waking from the nightmare till we woke from it together), hearing Miss Harriette chatter away about her childhood — her love of little things — butterflies coasting, birds singing, daisies floating and everything progressing to the accompaniment of this increasing fear — this mounting terror, her sense that there was nothing for it but to scream — to scream at the very top of her voice, inquiring of Christopher what it was that had brought him to America.

He had come in connection with the Fair in Flushing — an important exhibition — fabrics — it seemed, for he was an expert in fabrics — textiles. He knew all there was to know about them. (She seemed to see him in the very act of wrapping himself round with yards and yards of delicate fabrics.) The modern textiles, he said, would be ravishing — really exquisite beyond imagination, and wrought of such surprising ingredients — wheat — glass — milk; making up her mind to scream — deciding that now — *now* the moment had come, hearing Miss Harriette's voice pitched to an excruciating note of interrogation, asking her sharply if she hadn't, when she was a young woman and shortly after the demise of her parents and while visiting the Underwoods in England, refused a most desirable offer of marriage — a man of excellent family and Position — Henderson — if she wasn't mistaken; yes, she was sure of it — the young man's name was Henderson — yelling back at her (why did you invariably yell at her? She wasn't deaf) that the name was Matthewson — not Henderson — hastening to assure her that Mr. Matthewson had never asked her to marry him — nothing of the kind — the young man had been a novelist — a charming fellow, but never in love with her — all cooked up in the minds of Claire and Hal Underwood.

And then suddenly, waves breaking, gulls circling, crying, a door opening — closing, seeing a maid in a plum-colored uniform cross the room.

She was making straight for her; she was here. She was at her side.

She was touching her on the shoulder.

"Was this Miss Munroe?"

Yes, she said it was.

Would she come into the big bedroom? Mrs. Weed wished to speak to her. She wished to speak to Mr. Prentice Price — to Madame St. Dennis.

E L E V E N

THERE WAS MARCIA WEED IN THE DOORWAY, just beyond the passage leading out from the living room. Millicent saw her as though she stood at the end of several retreating passages and were retreating with them, while the various groups of people drew back and Bridget emerged with young Price from the crowd surrounding them. They joined her as she crossed the room.

Bridget had her hand on the young man's shoulder. "Brace up, dear boy," she said to him, for his face was the color of ashes and a wild, almost hysterical, expression of fear was spreading over it.

And although Marcia Weed seemed to be retreating with the passages, there by the open door she still remained. She beckoned them in a stealthy and furtive manner — like a conspirator, thought Millicent — exactly like a conspirator.

All three went into the bedroom. Marcia closed the door behind them.

Millicent looked quickly around her. The nightmare sight of Percy she'd braced herself to see had vanished from her dream. The bed was empty. The pillows and the blankets were drenched in blood, the mattress still held the impress of his body. But Percy had disappeared. The doctor had disappeared. Lenny Weed had disappeared.

She saw Marcia Weed sink into a chair.

"But where," shrieked young Price, "where," he shrieked hysterically, "is Percival Jones?"

"Where," demanded Bridget, "is the doctor; where is Mr. Weed?"

Marcia heaved a tremendous sigh. She threw out her arms in a gesture of explanation. "My dears," she gasped, "my dears — "

Bridget tried to steady young Price.

"For God's sake," he shouted, "for God's sake, Mrs. Weed — "

"That infernal little man — that infernal little man," she wailed.

"For Christ's sake, Mrs. Weed — "

"But what had happened!?"

"Where was he?"

"Where had he taken Percy?"

"Tell the truth — "

"Where was Percy?"

He need not have scared them all so terribly, she wailed, breaking down altogether — bursting into tears. He'd done it simply to be infernal. It was the most terrific hour she'd ever spent — to the end of her days she'd never forget it — for up to the last moment that little man had made them expect the very worst.

All the strings in the weird orchestra of nerves seemed suddenly to snap. The macabre scherzo ceased. The tension broke. Millicent saw young Price stagger to the end of the room, lean heavily against the wall; she saw Bridget cross herself. She sank down on the edge of the bed, praying gratefully, "Thank God for it, thank God for it," unable to say a word and listening to Marcia's broken recitation and the eager questions of Bridget and the young man.

"But where had the doctor taken him?"

"Where had he gone?"

"He hadn't taken him anywhere; he'd gone home."

"Who had gone home?"

"Percy?"

"The doctor?"

"They'd both gone home."

"My God, Mrs. Weed." The boy left his position by the wall and stood beside her, shouting at the top of his lungs — "'My God!" Did she mean to tell him that Percival Jones, practically a goner, had got up from that bed and walked out of the room on his own two feet?

That was exactly what he'd done; Lenny had helped him a bit, of course. He'd got him a taxi. He'd taken him home; but he'd stood up — he'd walked out of here and on his own two feet.

"Well, he'd be damned; he'd be goddamned."

"But how had the doctor consented?"

"What had the doctor *said?*"

"How did he explain himself?"

"It made no sense."

Conversation wasn't the doctor's strong point. When he'd finished his job he'd turned round; he'd gone into the bathroom to wash his hands; he'd come back; he'd packed his bag; then he'd walked to the desk and made out his bill. He had taken his hat. "If Mr. Jones wanted further assistance he could call another doctor." He'd suggest a psychiatrist, or better still, "a minister of God"; as for the work that he had done for Mr. Jones, he could vouch for it; the forehead would heal; if he needed further dressings he must go to someone else. "Good evening." That was all he'd said. She hadn't looked at the bill; it was probably preposterous.

"But we've not heard half of it."

"What had he done to Percy?"

"How had he brought him out of it?"

"Could she tell them what had happened?"

Impossible, she said, to give them any idea of it. She was so angry with the impossible little man — so shaken and washed up by the whole experience. Why, they had no idea what she and Lenny had suffered at his hands. He'd taken a devilish delight in torturing them — never a word to ease their anxiety. You'd have to have seen it to have believed it. And every move he'd made so deliberate — washing his hands, laying out his instruments, getting on his rubber gloves, working away in that awful angry silence. Give him this, give him that — displaying, she'd have to admit it — remarkable skill, stanching the blood, taking those careful, expert stitches — administering his evil-smelling drugs, actually making something human out of Percy Jones, who looked already dead, stewing all the while in his own spleen — giving them such a taste of moral indignation as nobody would wish to swallow; why, she and Lenny had been made to feel exactly as though they had murdered the poor fellow themselves. And then suddenly and to their utter astonishment, Percy's opening his unbandaged eye — coming out of it, giving them that one-eyed stare.

"But what then?"

"What had happened next?"

"What had he said?"

He'd said very little. He'd rolled his one eye right round the room. He'd wanted to know where in hell he was. "You're drunk, Mr. Jones," the nasty little man had said to him; just that. Then, exactly as she'd told them, he'd gone into the bathroom, washed his hands, packed his bag, made out his bill, taken up his bag, left the room. It was the damnedest thing she'd ever seen.

But, pleaded Bridget, couldn't she tell them anything more about Percy? Did she believe that he remembered what had happened? Did he seem distressed? What did she think was in his mind?

That, Marcia said, she wouldn't know.

Of course, reflected Millicent, Marcia Weed could not be expected to know. But she herself could feel every shade and nuance of poor Percy's misery — just what he must have felt waking up in this strange bed, rolling round that single eye — putting together the fragments of his recollections, piece by awful piece — how he'd struck her in his blind rage, twice across her face, and then that blow from Bridget, and young Price rushing at him, knocking him down, knocking him out — all these brutal, these unbearably brutal events, flooding in on the grief that was oppressing him — his passion for Bridget, his consternation at the fate of little Beatrice, his sense of frustration and his sullen anger against fate. Oh, she felt it. There she sat, enduring every nuance of it all.

Meanwhile, the lugubrious atmosphere of the room had changed. Bridget and young Price were talking in a gay and even frivolous manner — exchanging compliments. They seemed to be light of heart. The color had returned to the young man s face; he'd regained his assurance. Tragedy had brushed him with its wings; it had flown away.

It appeared that everyone had acted splendidly — indeed just as they should have acted; there was a kind of exuberance — talking it all over. Young Price sang her praises to the sky; he called to Millicent to confirm his story. Hadn't she been wonderful? Hadn't she been superb? Never turned a hair of her beautiful head, never batted an eyelash, just sailed through it like a fine ship in a high wind.

She resolved to go to Percy at once, for to leave him alone in his apartment was unthinkable — alone with his memories and his misery. How much liquor, she wondered, was there in the place? And would he drink himself into another stupor? Or would he decide to put an end to his misery? It was quite possible — anything was possible. Yes, she said, Bridget was superb. She hadn't for a moment imagined that she had been scared.

She tried to rise; but it seemed to her that she was paralyzed. If she could only reach him, and in time, of one thing she was certain. There would be no further question in her mind. She saw everything as clear as daylight. She would marry Percy. If she had to force the issue she would marry him at once. She was prepared to devote the remainder of her days to saving him. Nothing else mattered. There was nobody besides herself to give him any assistance. He had need of her. And if she had to stay with him all night to persuade him that this was the case, she was ready to do so. This was all that mattered to her now. It was her passionate desire to give up her life to saving Percy Jones.

Was it, she questioned Bridget, all a bluff — carrying it off in that carefree manner? How had she really felt?

She'd confess it; she'd been petrified — scared out of her wits in fact. But something had taken hold of her — sheer audacity. And seeing all those people so exhilarated had determined her to rob them of their little murder — to snatch it away from everybody. And it was extraordinary how, once launched upon her assertions, she'd begun to believe in them herself — flying in the face of disaster like that; but when the little maid had come to summon them she'd realized just how sure she was that Percy was a goner.

"Never turned a hair of her beautiful head — never batted an eyelash," young Price reiterated. "She'd simply cleared the air of melodrama — sailed through it like a fine ship in a high wind. And the way she'd stood up to the doctor — when he'd sent them packing — like a queen.

Anyone could see through that little man, she said. Nevertheless, there'd been something about Percy's appearance — stretched out on that bed and the wound so near the temple and all; and bleeding so profusely. It had looked dire enough.

"Dire as death — dire as murder — dire as life imprisonment," said young Price, making a long arm and reaching for the slip of paper on the desk and announcing gaily that he proposed to be the first to look at this little document, disengaging his arm from the hold that Marcia had upon it — Marcia snatching, clutching for it too.

Saying to herself that not a moment could be lost, she must put an end to this chatter and frivolity, she'd go at once to Percy, for to wait another moment was simply to court disaster, Millicent watched the little scuffle impatiently.

"As the perpetrator of the crime," the young man said, deftly pocketing the bill.

She got up. Awkwardly, abruptly, she put out her hand. She'd have to say goodnight. It was very late.

But suddenly she dropped her hand; she fell back, for there was Lenny bursting in upon them, jovial — vociferous, filled with the prevailing exhilaration.

He'd delivered Percival Jones to the elevator boy. He was okay — perfectly okay. The elevator boy had taken him up; he'd given him a tip; he'd put him in his charge — cost him five bucks. Not a damned thing to worry about. They could take it from him, Percy Jones was perfectly all right.

"But was Lenny sure of this?"

"Had he actually walked out of the taxi?"

"Had he *walked* to the elevator?"

"What had he said?"

"Had he offered any apologies?"

"How perfectly awful he must have felt!"

"Really, Lenny," insisted Marcia, "what had Percival Jones *said?*"

They'd talked of quite indifferent matters. As a matter of fact, he didn't believe, if you asked his opinion, that Jones remembered a goddamned thing about any of it. He'd gone suddenly stony. His mind was a blank on all of it. Good thing, too. Imagine the poor man's humiliation.

And now for another round of drinks, he suggested, "Eh, what? Wouldn't they all come into the other room and have another round of drinks?"

He put out his arms as though to gather Bridget up and carry her off with him. What did she think of making a night of it? The evening was still young.

"Yes," pleaded Marcia, "why *don't* we make a night of it?"

The idea that this was the party to cap all parties and that there was plenty of excitement still to be squeezed out of it had so taken possession of Lenny that he'd practically mustered them all into processional array. "Come," he commanded, urging Bridget, taking her forcibly by the arm.

But to Millicent's unspeakable relief Bridget drew herself away. Oh, no, she pleaded, they must both of them excuse her. She was dining with this "poor boy," and again she laid her hand on Price's shoulder. And look at her, she exclaimed, look at Millicent Munroe. Look at their garments. She owed it to this poor young man to change her clothes before he took her out to dine. And indeed it was growing very late for all of them, for she knew that Millicent must want to take a look at Percy Jones, just to make sure they hadn't murdered him.

Freeing her from any further effort to get away, and speaking as though she were well informed about her eagerness to be gone, Bridget turned to Millicent. She insisted she should come along with them: they'd drop her at Percy's apartment, which was directly on their way.

Free, free at last to go to Percy! she kept muttering all the way out of the apartment — all the way down to the street.

T W E L V E

SITTING BESIDE HER, CHATTING WITH YOUNG PRICE and giving, as they both of them appeared to be, the surface of their minds to the conversation that engaged them, flitting from this to that and partaking in the young man's infatuation and delight in simply being there, in her lovely ambient, Millicent became suddenly aware of the singular communion that had established itself between herself and Bridget, for each seemed to know, by some peculiar grace the moment offered them, exactly what the other thought and felt and questioned. Relying on a series of the most delicately communicated vibrations to convey every shade of their queries and replies, each was most gently, most subtly, able to say to the other that thus — far more than had they been relying on the devious medium of speech — could they this evening, by some curious miracle of nerves attuned, prepared for the event by who might say what previous music and vibration, share for a few brief moments in the secret fluctuations of each other's thoughts.

The taxi turned into Fifth Avenue, sped along beside the park. Bridget lifted her face to the sky — the view, and the breath of young green leaves, the fragrance and freshness blowing suddenly about them, she exclaimed, "Ah, look! New York!" With all the little lights and all the little windows and the towers twinkling — really it often had, she said, a way of surpassing itself. For being something other than it was, something out of dream and fancy — for creating its illusion — Venice was not to be compared.

And she turned suddenly on young Price. Of what did it remind him; of what, just at the moment, did it make him think?

Completely bewitched, content to sit beside her, listening, staring; and bewildered, horribly embarrassed at being asked to take these threads of fantasy she offered him and weave an independent pattern, he said quite simply that he wouldn't know; he'd have to admit it — he really wouldn't know.

She laid her hand on Millicent's and an ache of tenderness, regret, stirred and fluttered in both their hearts, recognizing as they did that in a few moments they would be bidding each other an ultimate good-bye. There would be no more meetings, no more lunches and dinners and telephone calls, for by an agreement they had arrived at in silence it was best — considering everything and estimating Percy's plight, the sorrow Bridget brought him, and young Price about to play that part in the rescue of her child which he had yearned so much to play himself — to terminate their friendship altogether; what with wanting poor Percy to recover from his anguish and Millicent pledged to help him through his crisis, this was, then, they felt, the time to turn the leaf upon the little chapter of their friendship — to say goodbye, to go their separate ways.

It reminded her, she said, elaborating the conceit and choosing her words, the very inflections of her voice, with deliberate intent to further ensnare the young man (for time, she seemed to hint, was short and every moment must be used to good effect) — it reminded her of a bubble launched from the windows of a city in some unimaginable dream; for look — it was all reflections, all little pictures, one floating lightly upon another; look at the celestial colors, the lights, the windows, the palaces upon the air, the little cloud — that first bright star — everything about it unsubstantial, ready to evaporate — to blow away. Certainly she felt herself that she was floating off in it, and if one searched the little pictures one would surely find the taxi and the three of them, tinted gold and opal and amethyst and amber — topaz, chrysoprase, she finished, smiling at the young man, with what was in reality only the fringe of her attention, preoccupied as she was in telling Millicent that she must not worry on her account.

Saying in substance, beware of pity — it slays the heart, it grows into a kind of watching with yourself; and as for her, for Millicent to worry over her was quite ridiculous, since she never worried about herself; she lived in the living moment — she lived in flight, she never stopped on any bough or branch to look back with sorrow on the regions she had traversed; she had her rules; she stuck to them: never hesitate, make decisions on the wing, have no regrets. And would she marry this poor youth? Well — that she was not yet prepared to say — everything waited on tonight, and to what conclusions her designs upon him were to lead must be determined by a variety of delicate and not quite to be foreseen contingencies — she must work through the maze as she prepared the threads; but it was probable — it seemed to her more than probable that so it would work out; and if the boy were with her — if the young man and his bank account were actually at her disposal, there in Vienna, with all the gruesome obstacles to overcome — it would seem to her she had the best chance of success; and to get him there as quickly as might be, would, she imagined, be to marry him; for of course all that really mattered was little Beatrice and time was of the essence. . . . The lightning filled the cloud; and whether they could cross the ocean before the storm burst upon them was indeed a question.

Then turning to young Price as though to illustrate the perfect flow of their secret dialogue, and their communion still in full tide, she asked him if he'd thought where they should dine. Where did he think, dear boy, that they should dine? Perhaps Millicent might offer a suggestion.

Ah, but the young man cried, he'd decided that. He needed no suggestions, he'd chosen just the place.

Would it be quiet? Could they eat in peace? No dancing, no saxophones — no floor show? And just the proper menu, for even with her costume changed and all these stains of their late murder washed away, it wasn't going to be easy for her to trump up an appetite. She needed something delicate to eat — a discreet and quiet, an intimate, environment.

He assured her passionately that he'd taken all these matters into consideration; he'd made the proper choice.

Dear boy, she said, how very thoughtful he had been. She would, just for tonight, put herself in his charge. And she took her hand from Millicent's and laid it again on the young man's arm. It was good sometimes to feel protected.

Thinking how unprotected she was, how daringly she was improvising this precarious rescue, trying to imagine her married to the youth (actually married to him — why it was incongruous, simply incongruous), Millicent turned to look at the beautiful, pale profile, cast, even while she chattered gaily away, in the mood and mold of extraordinary gravity, and that uncanny sense of, carrying on with her an intimate and secret dialogue increased.

Would he allow her to have ten guesses, she asked him, and if she guessed it the first time — ten dollars, if the second, nine dollars — and so on, down to the last guess?

A thousand dollars for the first — nine hundred for the second, and so on. To the last guess, she'd never hit on it.

Restaurant Chambord, on Third Avenue between Forty-ninth and Fiftieth Streets, she said.

He very nearly jumped out of his seat. How had she known it? How in the devil had she known it? He didn't think she'd ever heard of the place.

Her choice — her place.

She could, she reassured Millicent, take the young man in her stride, and if marriage should prove to be a necessary part of the scheme, that was the last thing to worry about. What, after all and at the present moment, did one thing matter more than the next? Was one husband much to be preferred to another? And Millicent must not forget her astonishing luck in encountering the young man and all his millions, and though she was completely prepared to cast her die on the rescue of her child, neither of them could forget it — all the lovely cities waited underneath the cloud; and the cloud was filled with lightning and a million arrows ready to let fly. For who could deny it, civilization hung in the balance and none of the thresholds over which one stepped were to be relied upon. One passed from one to another, and hoped to be on the right side of the crashing timbers; and if she appeared to be, like Lot's wife, fleeing from the burning cities, her little cretin in her arms, it was not her intention to look back. She'd go right on with it. Hitler had occupied the Sudetenland; he had occupied Austria; in Spain, they'd pulled off their fearful dress rehearsal — all the arsenals, in the air, on land and on sea, were preparing; and if she managed to escape the burning cities, to cross the various thresholds and return to America, it was just a matter of waiting. For, even here, were the girders — the iron cities — the windows and the towers and the palaces insured against disaster?

We were all in it together — all implicated; and the little nightmare they'd just passed through, of which they so gaily had taken leave, was merely another symptom of the general disintegration.

Now they were waiting at Sixty-first Street, with the green lights flashing their signals all the way down Fifth Avenue, and the Sherry Netherlands, Pierre's, the Plaza delicately pricked out with lights — the great block of apartments and hotels to the south of them as beautifully unreal as though some celestial goldsmith had devised them to decorate and frame the picture with that inconceivable display of bright aerial workmanship; and the tender twilight fading into tender dusk — and the park dispensing, casting over them, a poignant sense of spring, of breaking buds and fluttering blossoms and vagrant, vanishing emotions that trembled on the brink of tears.

She asked the name of the Sherry Netherlands.

Young Price gave it to her.

Oh, yes, of course, she said — she sometimes forgot — she gave them names of her own invention.

What was her name for it?

The Trinket.

The Trinket? Why the Trinket?

Because of that ridiculous little decoration on the top, so trivial — irrelevant — like something one might wear upon a chain. But she wouldn't cavil at it tonight; she wouldn't cavil at anything. It was all enchantment — beauty — with the first star like a flower in the sky — the entire scene so evanescent — so unreal.

The lights changed — the taxi, like a greyhound slipping the leash, was off; past General Sherman, past the Plaza, down into the canyon of Fifth Avenue they sped.

The ache of parting in her heart increased, charged as it was with such intense emotion — with so much apprehension, tenderness; and again she felt the light touch of Bridget's hand on hers and knew immediately that her intuitions were at work — that they were searching her through and through, that she was moving about lightly, expertly, among her sorrows, her chagrins, her habitual absurdities, going backward, going forward — that in sum the girl had, and about the most secret matters, informed herself, and that she was offering her, a little gently — humorously, and as though to laugh it half away —

sympathy, understanding, asking her discreetly why she had to take it all with quite such seriousness. But since she did, since that was what she so constantly persisted in doing, might it not perhaps be possible that this was something imposed upon her by her psyche — some specific demand her psyche continued to impose? And if this were actually the case, wouldn't it be folly to attempt escape? For there was, after all, a kind of abdication in failing to be faithful to these mandates.

Take now, she seemed to be intimating, the two of them — for she was undoubtedly approaching this delicate matter of Millicent's inability to spin the webs, distill the elixirs (winding meanwhile inexorably around the young man at her side the chains and fetters of her fatal charms) — if here their differences were, to put it mildly, startling, might there not be also a certain fate they shared in common — that neither of them could, so to put it, help themselves? As for herself, if she'd continued practicing her talents, if indeed she'd made an art of them, perfecting them through this very swiftness, this taking life on the wing, examining it with what she chose to call her Argus eyes, but letting go of her discoveries, clinging to nothing — passing with all the quickness of a bird from one thing to another, and, if still persisting, she'd been no more able to help herself than her poor dear grandmother had been before her, might it not be that both of them were, if she could put it thus, the victims of these mandates from within?

And going on to press the subject a little further, asking if, as a matter of fact, she had scrupulously kept faith with them. Hadn't she struggled, protested, tried, and yet without conviction, to go counter to them? And hence, and of course saying no when she wanted to say yes and yes when she'd intended to say no — and so often finding herself in equivocal relationship to this and that and the other situation? The psyche was of course inordinately cunning and, when cheated of its required loyalties, capable of the most astonishing rebellions — outbursts.

Certainly Millicent's position was infinitely more difficult than her own, since it had to be with Millicent a matter of abstinence — sublimations, choices; and in her own case, by some happy distribution of the gifts, she'd found it unnecessary to worry much about the choices — it had been unnecessary indeed for her to do very much more than just to exist in her own beautiful being, flitting from fiery branch to fiery bough — singing her song, keeping her eyes alert. And poor Millicent, perpetually hungry — searching for perfection, and turning after every disappointment with fiercer hunger, intenser vision toward that perfectibility — beauty, which she somehow, and without much warrant in experience, continued to believe was accessible.

Touching so lightly and yet with what amazing insight upon all these intricate, private, and subtle concerns, and yet at the same time, and before they parted, wishing to tell her — from one who had been responsible for what strange and terrifying blightings and with-erings, what sudden fiery burgeonings on the bough — that she had read her like an open book. And then an instant of sheer miracle occurring, as though she'd gathered up her little divinations, twined them in a wreath — given them back to her — for there was literally nothing of which she was not aware (and even in this matter of Christopher Henderson it was probable she knew it all — "No, not Henderson, Miss Harriette — the name was Matthewson), suggesting almost casually, yet with that uncanny authority she had, that there were certain souls who found their flowering in flame and others (pirella, arbutus, pipsissewa, hepatica) consigned to blossom only in the shade.

And did she really think that she was likely to marry Percy Jones? Without a doubt she was going to him prepared to give him everything she had, to sacrifice even her solitude, her loneliness — integrity; for her pity for him was more than she could well continue to endure — and if she could help him, if she could by any chance help him to pull himself together. But did she honestly think she could more than patch him up? Did she believe she could make a sound, a whole man out of Percival Jones?

How jealously he nursed his wounds. He didn't want to be cured of them. It was out of his sickness, out of his wounds, that he pressed all the essential elements one discovered in his books. Look at the girls — think of the dream girls, the never-never ladies of Percy's novels. Did she think she was going to cure him of his insatiable habit of taking these girls, these fictions — fabrications of his mind — of taking them around with him to all the bars, the bistros — weeping over them in restaurants and cocktail lounges — drinking himself into states of the highest sensibility?

For the peculiar fascination of Percy's writing was that it was equivalent to half a dozen dry martinis — achieved with his nerves, his sensibilities rather than his deeper centers — this little vignette and that — and the whole of the disintegrating universe of bars, cocktail lounges, pubs, bistros, dives, which in the depth of his soul he feared and desperately deplored, and which nevertheless had become an absolute necessity to him and to his art, was the familiar, exquisitely sensed backdrop and decoration for the dream girls, the never-never ladies.

This was Percy's sickness, she must remember, as well as the cloth out of which he'd chosen to cut his books — underneath was certainly that generous, simple, extremely romantic and tender heart over which she knew that Millicent was yearning — the heart she wanted to cure and put together. But did she honestly believe that she could do it? And of course these were merely suggestions — fugitive thoughts, formulated quickly — moving about in her mind — thinking of them both — of her and of poor Percy — wondering, speculating. And what did Millicent think — what would be her answer?

Waiting now at Madison Square, with all that masonry of life insurance to the left — the Mutual, the New York Life, the Metropolitan tower, glittering and wavering a little, behind the tender leafage of the trees, and ahead the Flatiron Building pushing up into the traffic at the junction of the two avenues, like a ship among the busses and motor cars.

Of what did it remind him? she asked.

Of a flatiron, he said humbly.

Oh, no! not that — it was a Nike — a beautiful Nike.

A what? inquired the young man.

The Winged Victory.

Exactly that! How wonderful to think of it.

The Victory of Samothrace, she amended, and returned to the question of the menu, for they were engaged in a lively discussion of what they'd order for their dinner.

What should they have for dessert?

Would she like zabaglione — that was very light and delicate.

But it was Italian. Couldn't he think of something French?

Crêpes Suzettes, perhaps?

Oh, no — not that. Certainly not crêpes Suzettes.

Ah, he'd got it; he'd thought of just the thing. He'd keep it a surprise. How much if she could guess?

A hundred dollars. She could have ten guesses and for any one of 'em a hundred.

Was it rice pudding? Was it strawberries in wine?

They were crossing Fourteenth Street. They'd turned into Thirteenth — they'd reached their destination.

Twelve West Thirteen, she said — south side of the street. She looked around — so this was Percy's place. What an odd spot — among so many warehouses.

There were lots of funny places in New York, said young Price.

But so nice when you arrived. Had she never been here? Millicent leaned to say goodbye.

No, never, not so much as once. She kissed her first on one cheek, then on the other, quickly, like a bird. "Goodbye, Millicent," she said, "be good to yourself — pity nobody too much."

Millicent kissed her and, turning hurriedly lest she should see her eyes were filled with tears, got out, bade her a casual goodbye.

The taxi drove away. Bridget waved; she blew her a kiss on her fingers. She turned to the young man.

Millicent watched her carrying him off, placing, she wondered, what stakes on her desperate gamble with their destinies.

"Goodbye," she said, "my dear — my dear"; standing on the sidewalk she repeated the words until the taxi turned into Sixth Avenue and was lost to view.

T H I R T E E N

HAD MR. JONES COME IN? she asked the colored boy who took her up in the elevator.

"Yes, ma'am, shore — he done come in."

"Had Mr. Jones gone out?"

"No — ma'am — no; he done stay in."

"He hadn't rung the bell; he hadn't asked for anything?"

"No, ma'am, no."

Whatever thoughts he might have entertained about Percy's condition and her own ghastly appearance he was determined to keep strictly to himself. These colored people, how imperturbable they were.

"Had he seemed all right?"

"Yes, ma'am; he had a bandage on the head."

Very nonchalantly he let her off at the seventh floor; but failed, she noticed, to take down the elevator — standing there in his steel cage and staring at her through the grillwork as she took her key ring from her pocket book, selected the proper key.

She put it in the lock, turned it and went into the apartment.

Her knees and her hands shook violently. Slowly, as silently as possible, she closed the door behind her.

Of what was she afraid?

The place smelled of formaldehyde — that awful stench that had filled the bedroom at the Lenny Weeds. There she'd hardly noticed it. Here it almost knocked her over. It was, she knew, something they gave to alcoholics. But what did it generally do to them? Did it wake them up — excite them, or did it send them off to sleep? In what condition would she find Percy? Why, she wondered, had she come?

She waited a moment, trying to steady her nerves. She took a few deep breaths. Of what was she afraid?

Finally, on tiptoe she went into the living room, where she thought it not unlikely she'd find him, mixing himself more martinis, or half seas over again, an empty bottle at his side. The lights were off and the room had a spectral appearance, with all the shades up and the Empire State building dead in front of her like an enormous lighthouse of the sky, those lurid red and blue and purple illuminations outlining the tower. She stood staring at it. Finally she turned, she looked about. There was no evidence that Percy had been here. There was a kind of silent, neon-lighted ghostliness — the big bookcases, the familiar furniture — the usual disorder. In that sideboard between the windows Percy kept his liquor. It was closed; she saw no glasses, no cocktail shaker — no bottles.

So far, so good. But why was she afraid to go into the next room, and her heart beating so fast, her knees still trembling? Certainly she'd passed through a great deal in the last few hours.

She called. "Percy, are you there? It's I — Millicent. May I come in?"

There was no answer. The Empire State still held sway. It was rather monstrous at times — lit with those lurid colors — menacing. Was it, she wondered, the tallest building in the world? And would they ever build them taller?

Why did she remain here staring at it? Couldn't she find the courage to go into Percy's bedroom?

She called again.

No answer.

Marshaling all the fortitude that she possessed (and she had little. Imagine Bridget hesitating like this), she turned her back on the Empire State and went into the corridor. Here she stopped, her courage failing her again.

Imagine it — finding his room empty. It was possible. Possible indeed. But no. She'd not allow these morbid fears to run away with her.

"Percy," she called, "it's I — it's Millicent."

And receiving from him no answer, she went in. The lights were also off and there was less illumination from outside. For several minutes she did not dare either to turn on the light or glance in the direction of the bed. She scarcely dared to stir, but becoming finally aware that

Percy was breathing heavily, tossing up little grunts and snores on every breath, she put out her hand, switched on the electricity.

There he lay, much as she had seen him stretched out on the bed at the Lenny Weeds, only that the wound was bleeding no longer and the bandage that covered half his face had a clean, professional appearance, and he'd lost that ghastly death-like look that had so terrified them all before.

Should she wake him? Should she let him sleep it off?

She spoke to him, but very softly, as though she didn't really expect he'd answer her. "Percy, it's Millicent. I just wanted to know how you are. Are you all right, Percy?"

Should she shake him? Should she wake him? Should she perhaps leave him and go, without so much as even allowing him to know she'd been here? She reassured herself. He was safe — apparently sleeping it off quite comfortably.

But then — imagine it, his waking up quite by himself, remembering those terrific moments — slapping her in the presence of all those people; and Bridget paying him off; and young Price knocking him down. Would he remember? Or would the whole hideous, violent drama, as Lenny Weed had assured them it would, remain forever buried in unconsciousness? She hoped so. She fervently hoped so.

And a great sense of pity, tenderness, overcoming her (pity no one too much; that had been in substance Bridget's final mandate), she decided that she'd wait. For she could not, no — she simply was unable to think of it, leaving him here alone — to wake up and face remembering.

She'd sit in this chair by the window. And perhaps that light she'd left shining directly in his eyes would wake him. The outlook here was pleasant — overlooking the low houses, the backyards on Twelfth Street, and those ailanthus trees. How many times she'd sat right here; and what a deep affection one acquired for ailanthus trees — so tropical, fernlike; and at this season, with that somewhat sickly fragrance. There was a nostalgia — those sticky budding boughs. After tonight, whenever she smelled them there'd be Bridget, little Beatrice — Europe. How life accumulated associations around sounds, fragrances!

The spell of that curious communion was still upon her, Bridget's penetrating her thoughts with such swiftness that it had been impossible to disentangle the subtle threads (which were hers, which were Bridget's?), sitting there beside her in the taxi — asking her, would she marry Percy, summing the whole extraordinary situation up in perfect silence, and with such clarity — such emphasis, asking her, would she marry him; for it appeared that Bridget had known better than she had known, herself, that at the bottom of her mind the question, in spite of her certainty at the Lenny Weeds', was unresolved.

Would she, wouldn't she?

At the moment, he seemed peculiarly in need of rescue. Poor, unfortunate Percy. Was his sickness, as Bridget had intimated, incurable? Did he love it as passionately as she had suggested? Was he bent on clinging to it, and under all circumstances (short of the impossible one — his rescuing little Beatrice) determined to drink himself to death? And her eyes falling on that photograph that stood on the bureau in its leather case, tilted up against the mirror amid the litter of books and papers — cigarettes, neckties, pipes, heaven only knew what else besides, she reached for it; she took it up and scrutinized it carefully.

What a fine face, and how honestly Percy's square-cheeked, smiling mother, clad in her ample print dress and apron, apparently just emerging from her kitchen and shooing some hens out of her garden, a silo and the corner of a large barn in the background of the photograph, and the flowers, the kitchen door, the back porch and upper windows of the unadorned frame house in the foreground, declared herself for exactly what at that time she must have been, a vigorous, hardworking, happy young woman. And certainly the arresting thing about her (the picture was an enlarged snapshot taken many years ago) was her startling resemblance to Percy; for though there wasn't a trace in that countenance of the queer, harassed, smoldering life of which you were always conscious when you looked at him, the structure of the bones, the broad brow, the square cheeks, the deep-set eyes were still the same; and something more — that look of inherent generosity, goodness, which still with Percy, and though overscored, underlaid with the nervousness, unhappiness, turmoil that seemed perpetually in opposition and conflict, managed somehow, and very poignantly, to persist in shining through.

Poor Percy! How far he had traveled from that particular belt and section of his native land, the simple, kindly people, the silos, the barns, the unadorned frame houses, the grain elevators beside the railroad tracks — those horizons, fields, miles on miles of cultivated acres — corn blowing up the skies in the warm smother of the summer days, drinking up the rain from the clouds, sucking up the sunlight, throwing out from the rustle of green blades and ripening ears what darts and arrows of intense strong life.

Drinking his martinis at all the bars, sipping his aperitifs at all the bistros, seeing it tough, earthy, feeling it soft, sentimental, testing the sensations with so keen a relish, tramping the hill towns, strolling about the European ports — watching the silhouettes, sketching the gestures, listening, savoring, tasting, hearing the chimes, the voices on the air, dialects, languages, street cries, sampling the smells, chestnuts roasting in the braziers, smoke blowing on the wind, the subtle permeations of garlic and grape lees — tasting the vinegars, the herbs, the lettuces, sipping the wines, watching the sunlight in the wineglass and the shadows of the vine leaves on the tablecloth, on the crumbling walls — thinking to extract from his passion for all these things some authentic breath and emanation from the ancient world, the ancient, classic customs, and all caught up and tangled in a mesh of confused sentiments and emotions — repudiating something he was not ready to repudiate, denying some source and substance of himself — fabricating the romances, clinging tenaciously to the dreams. For hadn't the whole intricate weave and complex of his emotions been wrought of his anger, protest, indignation with America, selling her soul to the gadgets, the mechanized, the mass-produced existence — life in the towns he hated so intensely, the ugly houses, the breakfast nooks and tiled bathrooms, with tinted toilet paper — pink, blue, and violet to match the towels, the Kewpie dolls with swans-down petticoats, and Whistler's Mother and the Mona Lisa and September Morn all reproduced and ranged together in the scheme of decorative values, the women's magazines, the advice, the advertising, the traveling salesman offering upon a shoestring speculation opportunities to possess an automobile, an electric icebox, a washing machine, a vacuum cleaner — the Encyclopedia Britannica, President Eliot's ten-foot shelf of books?

How we all tore ourselves up by the roots, how we repudiated and threw away our heritage of customs, precepts, memories — and how life had become an almost simultaneous process — denial and assumption, grabbing, clutching, taking on, throwing off — reading all the books, seeing all the pictures, straining for all the music — moving along with all the cults, the preferences, the prejudices — passing through the tumultuous decades, allowing each to vibrate in the heart, to move the intellect in this direction and in that, and our hungers increased by denials, espousals, our idealism heightened by our increasing skepticism, and one thing canceling out another, till the very core, the center of our hearts (the still place at the center of the whirlpool) was tortured by a sense of guilt. Guilt for all the betrayals, the denials, which, even realizing, as we did, that these required certain choices, the employment of certain honesties (standing, as we knew ourselves to be, upon the brink of one tremendous threshold that who might have the fortitude to cross?), continued to increase within our hearts.

For, as Bridget had said this afternoon, it was all of it a nightmare and one from which no one would awake unless we woke from it together.

But why had Percy stopped those smothered grunts and snorings? He seemed to be breathing easily — like a child. And would this mean that he was about to wake up, or rather that he was sinking into a deeper sleep? She didn't know. There might even be, she thought, a possibility that he was awake, lying there conscious of her presence in the room, but unwilling to face it out with her — too chagrined, humiliated — miserable.

"Percy," she said, "are you awake? It's Millicent."

There was no response, and as far as she was able to perceive not a flicker on his face to indicate that he was trying to deceive her — lying there pretending sleep. She returned to the scrutiny of the photograph.

With what a triumphant gesture, as of someone doing exactly what she enjoyed the most, Mrs. Jones was shooing the hens away from the dahlias, the asters, the golden-glow, stepping out for a moment to enjoy the sunshine, the smell of the autumn weather — the sense of her own domain, the bright light on her apron, on her face and hands; for surely all that vitality, that bounty of joy and generosity and kindness must have been nourished at some deep source of love and tenderness, of pride in beautiful responding love, dependencies, staking as she had so much on getting him prepared for life — sending him East to school, to college and all the rest of it.

And little of his life today that she could share — less that she might wish to investigate too carefully. There were of course the dutiful, the essentially truthless, meaningless letters that he wrote with such regularity and his occasional visits, and each of them realizing in the silence of their own counsels that something on which they both depended, as one depends on a necessary limb, but which when it is amputated one must, in one way or another manage to get on without, had vanished altogether from their companionship. You hardly dared to think how maimed, impaired they must have found their old dependency — being together, or how they passed those self-conscious, distressing days of his brief visits to Missouri. For how was it possible that she could understand, have any conception of the hungers that had snared his heart, hung up, treading the perilous ropes that stretched between his life on the one hand and his writing on the other, snared in such subtle trammels his sensibilities and his simplicity, his repudiations and his allegiances, and all so perilously woven through and through with filaments of substitution, daydream, fiction — trying to escape the tangled meshes which the world in which he lived had so industriously spun around his generous, large, and essentially simple nature? And if he had formed, at her gentle dictates, habits of dependency, having to rely on someone's interest, love — belief in him, to find sufficient self-reliance to get through with it at all, how doubly painful to discover in her society, and with her loving hands stretched out to him with the large, the so familiar gesture of giving all she had to give, to face the bitter fact that there was nothing — absolutely nothing she could offer him.

She had, she realized, examining that strong, expectant, happy face, become a substitute — a kind of ineffectual understudy, knowing so much about his life and living within the frame of his literary and emotional references, and having offered him so long her over-ready sympathies, always waiting around for him to turn to her — trying to patch him up, to make him whole again. She put the picture back, tilting it carefully against the mirror. How confidently it seemed to dominate the disorder, as though Percy's placing it there amid the books, the papers, pipes, keys — odds and ends from all the pockets, heaven only knew what further evidence of his neglected state, had in itself a special eloquence.

For wasn't the great discrepancy between the love and faith — the hunger in the heart of Mrs. Jones, and the insatiable, the restless hungers in our hearts today occasioned just by this — we had, and without sufficient courage to acknowledge it, lost faith in our reliance on anyone to see us through with it? Begging meanwhile in all directions, asking, beseeching. No one capable of sacrifice — capitulation; separate, unique — unwilling to give up a jot or tittle of uniqueness, individuality; each for himself, for herself — treading the satanic mills, crying out to all the pilgrims on the bitter road, "Look, this is I — myself; behold, listen to me; give me some token, something — anything, everything. Reassure me," standing up revealed, quite stark and naked, in the aureole of self — stretching out empty hands, lifting up ineffectual voices, afraid that death might overtake us before the gifts were all distributed.

But we'd not awake from the nightmare till we woke from it together — the personal legend dissolved, impersonal — anonymous. She repeated the words; they seemed to comfort her enormously, as though in saying it over — "impersonal, anonymous," she got some sense of it — anonymity — love in general circulation, being nourished from innumerable living springs — sitting here alone with Percy and somehow queerly convinced that he had waked up and was regarding her with his unbandaged eye, hesitating, dreading to turn and look at him.

For what was there that she could say to him with any conviction? And with this sense so strong upon her, that there was nothing she could give him — absolutely nothing, since the minor sacrifices, the personal immolations had lost their power to be of any helpfulness — being in it as we were together — having to go through with it alone until such time as we should waken from the nightmare — smelling the fragrance of those ailanthus trees — thinking of Bridget, of young Price, of little Beatrice, wondering at what moment the lightning would leap from the cloud, the thunder roll along the great horizons — turning at last to look at Percy and seeing to her enormous relief that she had been mistaken — that his single eye was not upon her, but apparently closed in sleep.

She got up and walked over to the bed.

Was he pretending?

The light fell full upon him, and that half of his face uncovered by the bandage showed no tremor of recognition; the heavy breathing, the little grunts and snores had recommenced. She could not be sure, of course; she'd never actually be certain of it, but somehow she believed that he was acutely conscious of her presence beside him, and that he did not wish to have her stay.

Life was strange — ah, stranger far than fiction, and what a travesty the moment was on those romantic situations so frequently devised to end his books — the beautiful young heroine, the dream, the never-never girl appearing, and at just the most sordid, the most crucial moment, to sacrifice herself for the almost foundered, the all but desperately finished young man, so thinly disguised as Percival himself.

She leaned over and kissed him lightly, for a sign to make him think, in case her guess about his having waked were right, that she believed completely he was sound asleep, for whether the conjecture was correct or not, she knew that neither he nor she would ever speak of it — her having come to him tonight.

She reached for the switch; she turned off the light, and very softly, as though attempting not to wake him, left the room. Cautiously she closed the door, she tiptoed through the corridor; she let herself out of the apartment.

F O U R T E E N

AT THE CORNER OF THIRTEENTH STREET and Fifth Avenue Millicent hailed a taxi and was just about to get into it when she remembered she didn't have a penny in her pocketbook. That miserable peroxide blonde at the Griffin Theatre had deprived her of her last cent. She dismissed the driver. No, she said, she'd decided she would walk. He drove away muttering crossly and she stood there on the corner, bewildered, almost ready to burst into tears.

What could she do about it? Should she go back and borrow ten cents from the elevator boy at Percy's apartment? Should she beg her bus fare from somebody on the street? With her dress so blood-stained and the generally suspicious appearance she presented, she'd hesitate to draw any one's attention to her plight. Perhaps if she went to Washington Square and sat down on a bench she could muster sufficient courage to ask somebody or other — and, besides, it would be very pleasant to sit awhile in her favorite square among all the Italians up from Sullivan and Bleecker and Thompson Streets, enjoying the warm air — the summer night.

But in spite of deciding to go, even making up her mind just what she'd say in the matter of begging for her fare, she seemed to be keeping right on — she had already crossed Fourteenth Street — and there was apparently nothing for it but to continue walking in this semi-trance-like condition, succumbing to the mood that was upon her. For it was not so much that she was thinking of Bridget and of little Beatrice and their danger (the lovely European cities waiting underneath the cloud), as that she was suddenly, overwhelmingly assailed by it — this sense of her love for Europe, walking in the loll and stride of summer up the avenue — the European climate blowing round her like an element.

That ache and softness, that sudden draft of sweetness poured into the heart; for there was something more than just the aesthetic, the intellectual response, there was a powerful physical sensation, as though you'd been dealt a sweet and aching wound in the vicinity of the heart — the age, the beauty, the organization. The first sight of the old cities, the towns, the villages — churches and their spires and campanile, the monasteries, convents, palaces, the gardens, the chimes and clouds that floated through the air, knocking softly at the heart — the streets, the cries, the ancient tongues; and those sweet, suave glimpses of the countryside — valley, river, mountain range, lovely little terraced hills that lifted up, crowned with their fortresses and towns, vineyards, orchards, farmsteads, every inch of the earth wherever one beheld it stripped and striped and squared with cultivation; the peasants going to church, going to market, working in the fields, the great white oxen in the furrows and little donkeys in the roadsteads with panniers harnessed to their sides; and then behold, the architectural trees, the cypresses, the sycamores, the poplars planted as they were to lengthen out a vista, to follow the line of a river, a hill, a long straight avenue, lending to the landscape a final elegance, a strict design; and every scene enclosed, kept within a well-proportioned frame, complete within itself like a well-loved and cherished work of art.

How could Europeans possibly understand this response to all these accretions of the centuries, to all this gracious, slowly matured loveliness? How it refreshed and soothed the hearts, the souls of people nourished on vast, exposed, uncultivated spaces, on waste, on haste, on some urgent necessity to exploit a great continent, to get everything accomplished with vertiginous speed — cities built and wilderness cleared — rushing headlong toward something new — gigantic, without limit or design, felt in the nerves and the intuitions rather than in the heart, the memory. Impossible to describe to Europeans our exact feelings towards the older, lovelier lands — always crossing our own frontiers, wanting to arrive at some unchartered destination, beyond horizons, beyond sea-rim and landfall, right out there among the stars and skyscrapers building something on our own.

Think of the Italian cities where you never for an instant escaped the memories — the evocations. How instantaneously one acted on the other. How the ancient palaces, piazzas, baptistries, churches, duomos, the very streets themselves, reverberated to the great names, the epochs. How even the *contadini* in their wine carts as they clattered over the cobblestones seemed to compass you round with memories of orchards, vineyards, olive groves — never in these cities long without remembering the ancient, classic harvests — bread and oil and wine. And think of the ampler, opener cities — Paris, Vienna, Budapest — the assault, the play upon the sensibilities, planned as they were with such subtle logic, monuments, squares, parks, avenues all laid out like architectural gardens to set in proper vista and perspective the tragic and inexorable march of history; and all together, monuments, trees in blossom, rivers, bridges, clouds, vehicles, restaurants, sidewalks, children, leaves, and shadows, somehow involved in it — in memory, the long accretions of the centuries.

But here you walked in a vacuum. There were no echoes, no reverberations. She stopped abruptly, allowing her eyes to travel up the windows of the Empire State, story by story, to the tower at the top. It was the tallest structure ever built. It dwarfed you to midget proportions. It was as tall as a mountain. It was one of the wonders of the world. Nevertheless she didn't (and how many people she wondered did) even know the name of its architect. It rose above you, innocent of fame or fable. To the east, to the west — all the way up Fifth Avenue, in the side streets, up Madison Avenue, up Park, up Lexington they arose, the great ephemeral edifices — immense, astonishing, sprouted like mushrooms overnight.

What a strange, what a fantastic city! And yet, and yet; there was something here that one experienced nowhere else on earth. Something one loved intensely. What was it? Crossing the streets — standing on the street corners with the crowds? What was it that induced this special climate of the nerves?

Ah, there was a young man with a straw hat. How pleasant it was to see the straw hats reappear! And all these summer dresses, the bare arms, the open throats, the light upon these faces. There was something — a peculiar sense of intimacy, friendliness, being here with all these people, and in this strange place. They brushed you by, like moths, like flowers, they brushed against your cheek, they touched your heart with tenderness and you felt yourself a part of the great flight and flutter — searching their faces, speculating about their dooms and destinies.

Certainly Bridget had been right when she declared that Americans could not afford to get away from this youthful, strong, and dominant music that ran along the nerves, the arteries; and Whitman singing his exuberant stanzas crossing Brooklyn Bridge had, whether we chose to recognize it or not, left us a wealth of treasure buried in the heart — little themes, variations, a sort of unconscious folk music. It broke from one spontaneously — crossing the streets, waiting on the corners. Nowhere else on earth was there anything quite resembling it — this questioning, challenging the faces. Who are you? Where are you going? From where do you hail? What is your doom — your destiny? And nobody being placed in any permanent niche, none of the orders, the hierarchies arranged, and everybody so frankly curious — expectant — and, for a moment, out and abroad and on their tiny midgets' feet, in this strange place, among these walls, these canyons, just perhaps as good as anybody else. And everybody going somewhere at such a head-long pace.

But where, she wondered, thinking fearfully of Bridget, with her little cretin in her arms, crossing from one frontier to the next, where were we going? Could anyone discern our destination?

And seeing suddenly, as though in a magnified and inconceivable vision of the Apocalypse, all the choirs of windows, all the tiers of little lights, the towers and terraces and tenements — the bevies, the hives, the sections and intersections and cross sections of human habitations collapsing, toppling, falling, one upon another, and all together in their downfall proclaiming the final judgment and annihilation; and crying out against the awful answer, invoking from the very depth of her heart that young and innocent and as yet unchallenged faith and love and generosity, which somehow, and in spite of all evidences to the contrary, she guessed, still lay deep-rooted in the American psyche to deliver us from death — remembering the Fair on the Flushing Meadows, the Futurama (sponsored by General Motors and displaying with such naive assurance the chart and prospect of these United States — valleys and industries and towns and cities all at peace, the bridges

spanning the great rivers, the great dams performing miracles of elec-
trification, planes accomplishing their destinations in the skies above,
and motor cars, like locusts, traversing the national highways), she
walked, with knees shaking from fatigue and emotion and a heart
beating very irregularly, past Rockefeller Centre, where the great
central shaft shot like an arrow upwards towards the stars, past the
Cathedral, where the pigeons, their heads beneath their wings, slept in
their niches beside the saints and the apostles, right on up the avenue,
until, and much to her surprise, she found that she had arrived at
Fifty-ninth Street.

Would she continue homeward or should she cross the street and sit
on one of those inviting benches, there at the entrance of the park? It
was a late, a peculiar hour to be out alone on a park bench certainly,
and her dress all stained with blood, and disheveled as she was; but she
was beyond bothering about her appearance; what she needed was to
sit down — to rest.

Taking advantage of the traffic lights, she managed to get across the
plaza and presently she was seated on a bench beside a derelict old
Irishwoman, looking vaguely up into the boughs of a young maple tree.

What a perfectly lovely sight it was, with these delicate golden
leaves, bells, buds, blossoms trembling on the air, and behind them the
electric, incandescent sky; she'd never seen anything more exquisite.
And was she thinking of Percy or of Bridget; or was she thinking of
Christopher Henderson, or of Miss Harriette Howe, or of Mr. Swensen
the Danish cartoonist, or was she thinking of herself freshly issued from
the mint of this extraordinary day?

She did not know. Her thoughts had become merged with the flux,
the flow — with wind and leaf and bud and blossom; and she seemed
to see the great pageant and procession of the spring — the fruit tree
boughs, the shadbush, the dogwood trees, the oak and elm and beech
and birch and maple trees, color of blood, color of the doe, fawn-
colored, rose-colored, coral-colored, color of honey, color of the rain,
carried off and away, floating over the hills, over the valleys, across the
plains.

And if she looked long enough into the blue sky behind the golden
bough she could, she perceived, watch the little stars emerging one by
one; on and on they shone, one behind another; on and on and on.

THE CHRISTMAS TREE

PART I

O N E

THE CHRISTMAS SEASON, thought Mrs. Danforth, pacing up and down her living room, did queer things to you, compassing you round with all your memories — remembering other Christmases, you might indeed say other existences; for she was one to keep an eye on her own mortality, and the sum total of her experiences gave her frequently the oddest sense of having led many different lives and passed through many periods of history. Not only had she seen astonishing changes take place in the exterior, the material world, but what startling revolutions seemed to have occurred within men's souls — the gestures and gestations of the spirit, the morals and manners of today! Lord, if you allowed this accumulation of memories and impressions to play over you — if you returned to thinking of the days when you were young.

One waited, she remembered, her memories of Christmas beginning to dissolve into a sense of a far-distant past, and watching the fine small snowflakes whirled round the corner of her high balconies and terraces from one December to the next, and all the days between flavored with just a bit of Christmas expectation. There had been those fabulous, practically legendary New York winters, the horse cars and the horse-drawn busses on the Avenue and frequently sleighs dashing through the Park in a bright scatter of snow and simultaneous sleigh bells — and the sound of wagon wheels and carriage wheels creaking in the cold, the plonk, plonk of the horses' hoofs — all the streets so very orderly and given over, to use that worn-out phrase, to "people of one's own class," the snow so very clean, piled neatly up on either side along the curb, lying along the area railings, and along the brownstone balustrades, with few buildings higher than the familiar church steeples on the Avenue, and coming as one did at Forty-second Street upon the reservoir surrounded by the high stone wall so sparsely grown with ivy, and all the sparrows twittering.

At this point in her perambulations, Mrs. Danforth stopped a moment to take a look at her little grandson who was stretched out on the window seat completely absorbed in some game or other that apparently involved a piece of wood, a wire, and a bit of string, and deciding as she regarded him that she would give him this year a Christmas tree, she visualized it — there in the center of the room, lighted by real candles and resembling, if possible, the kind of tree she used to have when she was young.

Poor little Henry, she thought, resuming her walk, a rather mean time in many ways modern children seemed to have of it. No stability around them — hardly a bed to call their own — what with their cramped manner of living, dwelling in apartment houses and all. Now, when *they'd* gone to visit Mrs. Constable, when the aunts and uncles came to visit them, what a difference there had been!

She looked around her living room. What a pleasant place it was — her own. She'd quite let herself go in creating it — the walls so carefully painted for that effect which had been far from easy to achieve, as though the vague blue of a summer afternoon, like the lights and shadows in an oyster shell, were blowing through and taking cool possession, everything harmonious, remote, with the pictures floating in just their proper element of light. She derived great comfort from it. Frequently she felt there was little else she could call her own. It always seemed a refuge; for she had somehow managed, with a certain flair she had in this direction (spacing, composing, framing), to invite the skyscrapers in — to make them more than just dramatic outside properties, but hers, a part of her interior scheme. At night, in the daytime, at any hour that she wished to look around, what with her books and flowers and pictures and the East River all looped in — the gulls, the passing boats, the strong flow of the tides — it had its peculiar magic.

Infinite pains had been taken with it; but she'd certainly not had Henry in mind when she called in the decorators. It had been, she guessed, the expression of herself that she was after — her personality. One tried today, in one way or another, to express oneself.

Was there anything, she wondered, about those old homes as she remembered them — those stolid brownstone houses, those newer, more pretentious mansions with the plate-glass doors, the grillwork and the European flourishes, to suggest a need for individual expressionism? They seemed to bristle somehow with the importance of family ownership. In all those parlors, bedrooms, dining rooms, what an accumulation of miscellaneous property, and everything held in such high estimation as being handed down or about to be handed on and inherited or given away — the very pose and attitude that they presented as they stood facing each other across the cobblestones intimating somehow the dynastic, the permanent. Here we are, they seemed to say, to document a golden era, to announce to the whole world the wealth, the solidity, the huge importance of the families who dwell within.

When she thought of those town houses and country houses, those drawing rooms and tea parties, the afternoon calls, the lawns and the tennis courts and billiard rooms, those endless games of croquet — the ladies moving about in their leisurely manner, their long rustling dresses, their graces and their laces and their perfumes, the frivolous assurance of their laughter, and the gentlemen with their mustaches or their elegant little beards, those wondrous monogrammed handkerchiefs, so pleasantly scented with cologne, their gestures, the inflection of their laughter, the very cadence of their speech implying a certain arrogance and assurance, as though they knew themselves to be the chosen and elect of the Lord! For those were the days when people really believed in their wealth and special privilege — the days of the big new houses and the ample ways of life, of the many servants and the negligible wages, the days of elegance, of arrogance, of ignorance and what a rashly planned security.

How well she remembered her own sense of privilege and protection. Fires were lighted, lamps were filled, gas burned in frosted globes, shades were pulled up and down; outside were the day, the night, the city streets in winter and, in summer, lawns and gardens, terraces. And over these domains had reigned that personal beneficent God, introduced to her by her parents, so secure in their good fortune as well as in her own as to make it appear that His principal care was to keep her perpetually provided with all the blessings that surrounded her.

Resting in this sense that He was guarding her, feeling quite sure that He conspired night and day to keep her cloistered in the safest, kindest, most comfortable world, lying in bed and hearing at five o'clock in the morning the furnace man shaking down the furnace, hearing the logs dropped into the baskets by the firesides, thinking of her security and of the safety of those other guardians, her parents, asking God to bless them and all that they possessed, to give to them, and thus of course to her, more and more and more abundance; for also it would seem to lie within God's province to bring her, like that other benefactor to whom one prayed at Christmastime, a pony, a doll — anything that one might covet most; and though often confused in His identity, seeing, as she so frequently did, His apparition in the flower, the star, the lightning in the cloud, and disposed to watch and wonder and to ask for more astounding answers than those which she received; nevertheless, inclined to rely on the parental word that all was ordered and assured.

Yes, God's eye was on her, He knew all she did. He made the heavens and the earth and the waters underneath the earth; He made her. He declared that she should do this, but by no means that, and that if she was a good little girl and obeyed His edicts she should have her rewards on earth as well as in Heaven; and His edicts coinciding so perfectly with her parents' sense of what it was proper to do or say, or think, and loving them as she did and with such a pathetic dependence upon them, and her father assuming a somewhat Godlike role himself, dispensing his dollars and his discipline, dangling his seals, radiating importance, rushing off to his office, to directors' meetings, reading the *Wall Street Journal* and certain portions of the daily papers with such concentration and attention — there she was, in the world that they had created for her, her mother dispensing her more delightful comforts and assurances, the swish of her silk petticoats when she came into the room, that sense she seemed to give one of a world of ease and grace and pleasant, almost endless leisure to loll, to watch, to give your thoughts full range of fantasy.

If she compared her childhood with Henry's, Lord, what a contrast it presented! — this little universe of hers protected from harm or sin or wrong, closed round as it had been with such beneficent assurances, and only, to use that ugly phrase again, "people of one's own class" allowed the privilege of entering it, buttressed round as it had been with fortunate and charming relatives (her Uncle Lionel living in the same city block in winter and her darling Aunt Adelaide, her Uncle Philip, only a meadow or two away in summertime). When she compared her fidelity toward everything and everyone surrounding her, her utter trust in life, with Henry's complete lack of faith in any kind of security — for as far as she could see there was no safety for him anywhere, taking as he had completely for granted this change and that goodbye, the next reunion, adapting himself as best he could to whatever freakish novelty life might present to him, and hardly ever knowing what sort of bed he was likely to sleep in from one month to the next, and possessing, if she recollected correctly, neither aunts nor uncles to buttress up his faith in a toppling world — when she came to think of it all, which little soul had been the best prepared to meet the events in wait for it?

However unable she felt to answer the question, Henry should, she decided, have his Christmas tree. What might occur in the interval between then and now, or where the child was likely to be, whether sheltered by her, or by his mother and the Captain, or even, perhaps, claimed at the last moment by his father, it would not be her business to determine. But at least she could arrange this little celebration. She'd invite in a few people; she'd make it gay and festive. Henry should have his tree.

Not that children felt today the way that she had felt about Christmas in her childhood, for along with all the other changes, this change in the Christmas spirit she definitely believed had taken place. Though there was all manner of evidence of the season — New York producing it, as it produced everything else, on its own colossal, mass-production scale, all outdoors and public and promiscuous, with a tree in almost every park and square, all the churches turning them out properly lighted and arrayed, the great central civic spectacle there in Rockefeller Center, the tallest Christmas tree erected on this earth, standing up in all the majesty of its broad green boughs, with those beautiful balloons floating like celestial bodies of blue and gold and silver all around it, while from below, in the skating rink, with crowds and crowds of people listening, one heard, right through the night, those deep strong voices singing the familiar hymns.

Christmas had been, as she remembered it, a private and interior, a family, almost a dynastic affair, with the larger houses, the larger families, the aunts and the cousins, the uncles and the grandparents all gathered together so enormously well provided for and at ease in their secluded world, the Christmas happiness spreading from heart to heart and a sense prevailing that the Lord blessed every gift and every grandchild.

Heavens, the joy was truly terrifying, sitting there with eyes upturned, as though those candles, those brightly colored baubles, those green boughs and tiny scintillations, one behind another, and Christmas bell and ball and star, reflecting, flashing back the happiness, were saying, "This is, my little one, the tree — the mystic tree of joy on earth. Behold it hung with candy cane and cornucopia, with dolls and skates and ponies, with little dogs and donkeys and darling pets to be your very own, hung, in fact, with all you ever asked your parents to bestow upon you. But do not snatch, my little one; for there upon the radiant tip of your miraculous tree, behold — the Christmas angel, the trumpets, and the wings outspread; see, all the candles lighted for the festival."

She used to sit wide-eyed and gaze. She did not grab or even touch a single bauble; and what images went through her mind she would not now be able to recall — perhaps Santa Claus with all his packs and presents, his reindeer shaking Christmas bells — a sense of waiting on miraculous occurrences, being there and not being there, and thinking very likely of more mysterious things, of forests far away and snowflakes falling, and maybe squirrels, rabbits, snowbirds, antelopes.

And she would not now have recognized one festival occasion as differing from the others, all merging in her mind to brew this Christmas ravishment, had it not been that, searching through her memories, she remembered the little lifted and exalted sense she'd had of something beautiful past comprehension going on that night between Aunt Adelaide and the delightful, the almost too fascinating young man with his auburn beard and periwinkle-blue eyes, so soon to become her Uncle Philip, making this Christmas Eve stand out for her as more important, somehow, than any other she had known.

Dressed in her sheer white frock with its blue sash and in her white silk stockings and her patent-leather pumps, there'd been something about the way she'd felt — six sleek shining curls hanging over her shoulders, down her back — that had given her, starched and soaped and scented as she was, and standing there among the cousins and the uncles and the aunts (each and every one of whom confirmed her in it, with their smiles and acquiescent nods), a sense of waiting, angelically prepared, on ceremonials of a nature far surpassing earthly joy.

They were turning off the gas in the hall, in the dining room; someone behind her, and on tiptoe, was putting out first one lamp and then another. The light on the stairs had been extinguished. There was the encircling dark, the all-pervasive hush. And everyone (and all together) drawing in their breath. The double doors between the two large rooms were rolling back; and then, as though escaping from everyone at once, the great, the general "Oooh" — the "Aah, how *beautiful!*"

And was she taking the hand of her Aunt Adelaide, arrayed in cloudy grey and silver while Aunt Adelaide's companion, in all his elegance of shining shirtfront and surprising auburn beard, held her other hand and urged her to look at it, just to look at it — or was she standing there apart, alone, the rapturous "aah" still warm upon her lips, struck dumb and speechless by the wonder?

There stood the tree — the great, the green, the fabulous hemlock — with all its layered boughs reaching out into the room, filling it with greenness, tapering upward, till its tip almost, but not quite, touched the ceiling, and distributing a Christmas incense which the warmth of the room, the heat of burning candles drew out to such a fine intensity of Christmas sentiment. There it stood before her, garlanded, looped round with ropes of snow-white popcorn, with rainbow-colored chains of paper bracelets, with silver tinsel and with gold, hung with blue and red and gold and with silver balls and bells and silver stars so cunningly faceted as to receive and flash back, from bell and ball, from star and candle flame, from the upper and the nether ornaments and trinkets so many tiny sparks and scintillations, so many beams and filaments of light, as to create in all the boughs and branches a mesh and maze of brightness, the candles with the blue candle-centers all together flickering, traveling upward to a point of highest ecstasy.

There it stood, fixing her in a trance, rendering her incapable of detaching this little picture from that, or one moment from the next —

kneeling or sitting down, smiling, getting up, walking round, around, the blessed instants blending, melting one into another, becoming, and even as she gazed, memory, message, meaning.

For here, under the white sheet spread out to save the carpet from candle grease and hemlock needles, were all the Christmas gifts, of every shape and size, wrapped with white or silver paper, tied with white or red or silver ribbons, embellished with holly and mistletoe and inscribed with loving dedications — "Hilly from Mamma and Papa"; "Hilly, Merry Christmas from Uncle Theodore"; "John from Aunt Sally"; "Hilly from Mamma and Papa"; "Adelaide from her father" — and all and everybody searching to find their own particular presents — package heaped on package, and each one for somebody, with love from someone else, and all presumably from Santa Claus.

And oh, the smile and grace and glance and gesture of it — this charming episode and that, the voices, the salutations, while the walls of the two big rooms faded away into dim corners and that sense, with the snowflakes pit-patting on the windowpanes, of the snow accumulating outdoors, of the mystical preparation for tomorrow fringing her thoughts with such a strangeness, such a flame of joy. And not being at all certain whether she was unwrapping her own Christmas presents or assisting at the unwrapping of someone else's — being so lost in the idea that everybody was kissing, or receiving, or giving or thanking, hearing so many exclamations; Aunt Bessie crying out to Uncle Lucien, "How *could* you have known?" and her mother embracing her father and taking a small slip of paper out of a tiny envelope, declaring that it was *far* too much; he should *never* have thought of such a thing; and old Mrs. Constable trying to tell her something about a piebald pony, just arrived and waiting in the stable, and not at all sure that she hadn't seen it, saddled with silver and bridled with gold, drawing a little jewelled pony carriage round and round the room; but on the other hand not at all certain that she had. For was she not carrying a miraculous doll that opened and closed its lids and said distinctly, "Mamma-Papa" whenever you pulled a string hidden beneath its long lace petticoats; and hadn't Aunt Adelaide's companion just plucked from the Christmas tree a little darling candy cane and a cornucopia filled with Christmas candy and presented her with both; and was she not at the moment sucking a barley Santa Claus, walking round and round and thinking happily how the world for many days to come would be a perfect paradise of spun sugar and chocolate bonbons and wondrously striped and twisted ribbon candy?

And, moreover, wasn't she all the time and at every moment wondering whether her beautiful, her beloved Aunt Adelaide was "in love." The words (she had heard them for the first time in her life on the lips of her Uncle Archie — "head over heels in love with the fellow") running in and out of her mind together with all manner of hints and intimations as to what they really meant. And if a part of this hallowed Christmas was having her Aunt Adelaide in love with this delightful creature with his auburn beard and strange blue eyes, she was determined to lay herself open to every breath and beam and smile of their condition. And this need they both displayed of being in her society, and so tremendously happy as they were, was almost, she felt, as though they'd wished to use a little girl in a white dress and a blue sash, with bright hair and eyes, as a kind of medium — a way of saying to each other that perhaps some day they too might be possessed of just such a little treasure of their own.

And now they'd gone off and left her with her doll, her speculations and her barley sugar. And was this just another of these Christmas fantasies, hung up like magic-lantern pictures in her mind (her doll in its lace petticoats, the pony prancing round the room)? There, without a doubt, was her white-haired Great-aunt Sarah, in a velvet dress and with a paper cap upon her head, waltzing about the room with her handsome papa; and that was her grandfather, holding in front of him and with an expression of absolute astonishment a pair of pink pajamas. And had she, or had she not, caught that glimpse of them in the deep bay of the windows and behind the marble statue of Susanna — the gentleman bending over Aunt Adelaide, taking her in his arms, kissing her so fervently on the lips? All was shift and change and one bright tableau imposed upon another. But surely the little hoarded sense she had of the way these two had been behaving all the evening was part of the strange, the quite unearthly happiness now spreading in her heart.

For in the next room they had gathered round the piano — Mamma and Papa, Grandpa, the cousins, the aunts and uncles, old Mrs. Constable — while the familiar words, all bright and touched with an angelic gravity, came floating in to her:

"O little town of Bethlehem!
How still we see thee lie — "

carried back through all the years and being there in person in those
dark and silent streets, while overhead the stars silently, so silently,
passed by; and receiving one by one those Bethlehem pictures — Mary
and Joseph kneeling there in the stable, and Jesus in the manger with
the crown of light around His little head. And then — the chords
breaking, the tune changing —

"Silent night, holy night,
All is calm, all is bright — "

received again into the Here, the Now, and appreciating with such
rapture that, outside these brightly lighted windows, and all in com-
memoration of that miracle accomplished centuries ago, the clouds
had cleared, the night was blue and frosty underneath the Christmas
sky —

"It came upon the midnight clear,
That glorious song of old — "

discovering a cow, a wise man, a shepherd, and there, somewhat higher
up, the Infant Jesus; and finally lifting her eyes, beholding on the top
of the fabulous tree and raising silver trumpets to his lips the herald
angel with his wings outspread —

"Hark! the herald angels sing
Glory to the new-born King — "

And could there be imagined, wondered Mrs. Danforth, stopping
again in front of her little grandson, a joy so pure, so bright, so inaccessible?

T W O

———

"WHAT ARE YOU DOING?" she asked, regarding the little boy on the window seat.

The apparatus that engaged his attention might, for all that she could tell, have been an airplane, a battleship, a tank, an atom bomb. He was completely absorbed in it, and as he twitched his wire, which she saw he'd fastened to his bit of string and attached to his bit of wood, now resting on a book, she thought to detect upon his face emotions not altogether innocent of cruelty; there was a rapture of initiation — an absorption.

"What *are* you doing?" she inquired a second time.

"Charging this electric chair," he said.

"Oh."

"I'm electrocuting Dr. B."

"Who is Dr. B.?"

He mentioned a name almost unparalleled in the history of crime.

"Where is he being electrocuted?"

"Sing Sing," he said.

"Where is Sing Sing?"

"Sing Sing," he repeated, in a voice that indicated surprise at her ignorance.

"But where *is* Sing Sing?"

"*Sing Sing,*" he said, making it plain that if she asked again he'd enlighten her no further.

She continued to regard him — wondering, speculating about it all. What a lovely child he was, with his sand-colored hair, his intensely blue eyes, the fine structure of his head and brow; but springing you surprises, bringing you up short with the rudest shocks and jars and causing you not infrequently to wonder at the queer, the crowded content of his mind.

He never, as his father used to, asked unanswerable questions —such as, for instance, "Who made God?" "Who made me?" "What does God look like?" He surrendered himself too completely to his enjoyment of the world, just as he found it, to have time for abstract questions and was by way of offering information and enlightenment rather than wishing to be informed himself. "Look, Grandma" (or "Daisy Mae," as he more often called her), "this is a B-29; here's a Grumman Hellcat. This is the best tank ever made — the kind they sent to General Patton. See all the guns? See this turret? Bang-bang! Do you know how quick they fire? Bang-bang-bang!" etc. He was informed about such a startling variety of things, what with something being always plugged in, or turned on, or cranked up for his amusement and instruction and being taken, as he was so often, to the movies.

Never would she forget the first time he'd gone. She could see him now watching those celluloid embraces and tossing off that odd question — "Grandma, why didn't *you* get married?" sitting there too spellbound to press the matter further and oblivious of the laughter he had caused, straining forward while the screen continued to offer him the most vertiginous entertainment, lights flashing on and off, voices issuing from the dark, pistols pointing, men and women falling dead upon the floor, blood flowing, lovers kissing, and all so breathless and enthralling that his gaze had remained fixed, his silence absolute. And even when these spellbinding scenes of murder, mystery, and passion had been exchanged for the fiction and fantasy of a Disney cartoon, he had endured the transition without protest or expostulation, quite at home in this mad world where nothing could surprise but everything exhilarate. With what proprietorship he had taken to his heart those millions of elongated dogs, of kaleidoscoped cats, of Mickey-mice and Donald Ducks, erupting, as though from exhaustless cornucopias of delight, from frying pans, from bedclothes and clocks and kitchen stoves, to caper about in a series of bewildering escapades which whirled them over precipices, over the sun, over the moon, down into the sea, up above the clouds, with Donald drawing them along with him to almost certain doom and, at intervals, blowing up not only himself, but the entire Disney universe. On and on it had gone, at a pace so fast, so furious, so utterly magic-crazy-mad as to convince him that this magic carpet of ten thousand weird events would continue to transport him forever and ever through scenes of unimaginable novelty. And when the program was at last reeled off and his mother was urging him to get up and put on his coat, so firm had been his belief in the fabulous carpet and so great his incredulity at her unwillingness to stay, that he'd done his pitiful best to persuade her to remain. "You wait; you see — it's going on. It hasn't stopped," he insisted, and it had been with tears and protests and the deepest disappointment in her lack of faith that he'd been finally bundled into his clothes and literally dragged out of the theater.

Perhaps that had been, she thought, the beginning of his assumption that life was preparing for him an endless sequence of enthralling joys, for, having learned this trick of walking back and forth, with no disturbance to his sanity, between the two dear worlds of his delight — the world, on the one hand, of Gargantuan sidesplitting mirth and multiplication of merriment, and, on the other hand, the hair-raising, the bloodcurdling, the nightmare world of horrendous crimes and plots and punishments — his demands had grown exorbitant. And here now, at six years old, and having learned, in some miraculous manner, and in spite of the conspiracy against his efforts in this direction, how to read, he'd placed "the funnies" at his own disposal and, perfectly acquainted with their language and landscape, had suddenly acquired a style and humor bordering, she believed, upon the exquisite; while, as for the other world of his delight, that underworld of fearful pleasure, he had, of course, the radio —Dracula-like hands stretched out to him, weird orchestral sounds, intimations of fell deeds about to be committed, green dragons glowering, sinister hornets circling, and invoking every night the benison of these devilish mechanisms, taking himself off to bed to be visited, she wondered, by what dreams, what apparitions?

Watching him, still intent on electrocuting Dr. B, his stubby, pliant fingers twitching at the wire, and that expression she'd noticed before, if not of actual cruelty, certainly of intense and inward absorption on his face, she recollected how he'd come early this morning to her room, resembling in his long nightgown a bright angel, the fair hair like a nimbus round his face, the blue eyes innocent of guile, and carrying in his hands an assortment of small cardboard airplanes. Did she want to see his airplanes? he'd asked. He had a big array of them and knew each one by name — the number of its engines, the speed at which it could fly, its function in battle.

"Look, Daisy Mae — here's the B-29. This is the P-27. Oh, goodness, *no*, not a bomber. Can't you tell the difference? A Grumman Hellcat — that's a fighter." Prattling on most knowingly, and then, all of a sudden and without warning, staging a battle in the air, very swift and dramatic — a flying, a buzzing, a bombing, a booming, a zooming, with sounds of flight accompanied by all manner of bombardments, collisions, explosions, hissing of rockets, tat-tatting of flack. "Look, there's a kamikaze; look, look, they've got it. Look, Daisy Mae, there's another. Bang-bang." Rockets, hisses, explosions. "They've got it, Grandma! They've got it."

The battle accomplished, the victory with the AAF relapsing into silence, preparation. And, finally, his voice tremulous with glee, holding aloft a single plane, the B-29 on its way to Hiroshima with the atom bomb. "Look, Daisy Mae, you look now, you wait — they have to drop it very accurately. You wait."

"Now, Grandma. Now they've dropped it. You listen; you wait."

She'd listened; she'd waited.

Then he'd produced it, all by himself, the fearful cosmic blast, his voice shaking with excitement, with a positively devilish glee. "Listen," he'd commanded, "it's exploding, it's killing all the people, Grandma, all the people."

He seemed to dramatize his games with such intensity; he was still occupied, she saw, with Dr. B.

"Get up, Henry," she said, hoping to divert his attention, for she had a surprise in view for him.

He continued to jerk his wire.

"I'm going to give you a surprise," she urged. "How would you like to go this evening to a restaurant, just as a little Christmas treat?"

"Oh, boy!" he cried and got up with alacrity. "To a restaurant, Grandma?"

"I think so, dear."

"Oh, boy! Oh boy! We'll go to Schrafft's!"

"Perhaps so, dear; it's rather far."

"But we can take the crosstown bus. That's very near."

Well then, get on your things."

"Can I have ice cream?"

"I think so, dear."

"Hot dog!"

"No, dear," she corrected, "ice cream."

"Hot dog," he cried, running into the bedroom ahead of her.

How clever he is, she thought, watching him in the mirror while she put on her hat — pulling on his galoshes, buttoning up his reefer.

"Help me on with my coat, dear," she commanded.

But he was off. "Door bell," he cried, dashing into the hall, cap in hand, to answer it.

She adjusted a veil, dabbed on some rouge, powdered her nose, struggled into her coat.

Telegram, telegram," she heard him shouting in the hall.

And in he ran with it, excited, expectant. "Telegram, Daisy Mae."

She took it from him, opened it, her face paling under the rouge as she read it, carefully, several times over."

Your father is coming, Henry," she announced; "he's arriving tomorrow."

"Oh, boy," he said; but suddenly his face looked troubled. "Isn't Captain Fletcher coming, too?" he asked.

"I don't know, dear"; and then, for she wanted to learn just how much he knew about it all, "where are they now — your mother and the Captain?"

"Reno," he said.

"Oh, and where is Reno, Henry?"

"Reno," he said, "Reno."

"Come, dear," she urged, "it's getting late. You shall have as much icecream as you can eat."

"Oh, boy," he shouted and ran ahead of her to hold the front door open till she came.

THREE

MRS. DANFORTH SWITCHED ON THE LIGHT — jumped out of bed. It was, she saw, glancing at her watch, approaching midnight. The wind was blowing a gale and the storm increasing. She put on a wrapper, shut the window down and went into the next room to see if the bedclothes had slipped off Henry and to close the windows there — having spent the larger part of her life in Europe, she was not one to believe too much in the cold air at night. The Europeans were, she thought, right about this as they were about so many other matters.

After tugging at the windows she managed to get them down and, turning, went to the davenport to have a look at Henry. She found him fast asleep, with the blankets pulled up around his neck, and on a chair beside him his beloved Grumman Hellcat, his B-29. She brushed his cheek lightly with the back of her hand and regarded him tenderly. He looked very much as his father had at the same age — that sand-colored hair, the faint flush and the fair skin, the fine structure of the head and brow.

But Henry was a little alien number; she would not presume to guess about him. The world surrounding him was too strange, too wrenched out of any path or track with which one's feet had hitherto become familiar.

She stooped to kiss him. Poor child, he was not *her* problem. Difficulties likely to entangle his emotions were at the moment being wound around him. She must try, if possible, to keep from interfering. No, she told herself severely, she would *not* interfere; however, she worried. She worried inordinately. And since receiving Larry's telegram, there'd been this sense of dread — apprehension settling down on her like ten thousand bricks.

Why was he coming at this crucial moment? If he'd been coming at all he should have made his visit during Anne's six weeks in Reno. To return just as she was arriving with Captain Fletcher was perverse — it was sheer perversity on Larry's part. And who knew better than she how he was capable of acting? Who better understood this emotional instability against which he struggled and from which he suffered so horribly himself — habits of behavior repeated so frequently as to make them appear, like muscular reflexes, quite beyond his own control, and which resembled exactly, as they had long ago when she'd first become aware of their development in him, the actions of a spoiled, an overindulged and idolized little boy?

Suddenly she burst out, in that way she had, which she so thoroughly deplored, of talking aloud — asking Larry, just as though he were there beside her, how he could, so sensitive himself, behave so cruelly to other people. "I know you, darling," she cried, "and Anne knows, Anne knows. Still she doesn't somehow blame you. Your behavior hurts you so much more than the victims of your cruelty; there's something you possess — an intelligence, a depth and fullness; and all of us in one way or another trying to shield, to forgive, to go on loving you."

She sat down, closing her eyes, the better to concentrate upon her thoughts. She wasn't one to flinch from the accusing finger. And mothers were eternally compromised, always searching their own hearts to discover the origin of their children's faults, getting back, at every signal of distress or tragedy, to the fearful question: Weren't these repeated plights and crises inherent in my failure, in my fault? That was the great maternal grief, having to bear the burden, assume the guilt.

And if she had had to endure having everything explained to her in these bald Freudian terms, being called to look at herself as the primal cause of all the misery, still she had, with reservations naturally, for she was sick to death of all the clichés, accepted the verdict that Larry was the victim of a mother-complex or fixation (one could take one's choice). And though she had her special knowledge and could have made out for herself her own excuses, she had listened; she had not contradicted Anne. She'd remained her friend, thank God, throughout. In her own queer, tortured kind of way she'd been her ally — taking her side in the matter of the divorce and even cutting across Larry's headstrong ideas on several matters of adjustment.

They led, these modern girls, such hazardous lives. There was nothing they seemed afraid of experiencing. And Anne's professing to know — well, all there was to know about poor Larry, talking about it with such disarming frankness, coming out so boldly with all the facts; for, it seemed, there were today no secrets one must bury in the heart. He was, she'd said, the type she always fell for — the invert, the schizophrene, the artist. Men like that were never normal sexually.

She'd been admirably courageous, poor girl; she'd gone through with it till it had got too much for her. There seemed to be no stumping these intrepid young people of today. Life was merely a matter of going from one situation to another, gathering tolerance and enlightenment as they went, and if they found it necessary to turn to a psychiatrist for assistance, that was a necessary part of the process, looking round them, getting themselves divorced and married again with an apparent growth of wisdom and maturity, and, as far as she could see, no residue of bitterness or rancor in the heart.

As cool, as expert as she appeared to be, and getting everything so admirably arranged for everyone's deliverance, even to lining up a second husband in the person of her handsome young wing-commander who, she understood, was, whether married or unmarried, at the present moment traveling back with her from Reno, was not Anne, Mrs. Danforth speculated, still desperately, very nearly incurably in love with Larry?

How many times she'd heard her declare in that confident, emphatic way she talked about it, "My dear Hilly, it's over. I'm incapable of thinking about him with the slightest emotion. I'm outside of it altogether — outside the nice little web I've spun myself. That's what my analysis has done for me. It's broken the pattern once and for all." And by breaking the pattern she had, of course, meant that she had not only recovered from her infatuation for poor unfortunate Larry but cured herself of her fatal tendency to fall for, and think to help, protect and eventually reform, a charming, perverse and incurable neurotic. Hilly had only to look at Captain Fletcher. Did he resemble a young man who needed protection? No, not Captain Fletcher! He was the sort who simply had to offer protection to others. Responsibility was an essential part of his strong and simple make-up. It cost him no strain; it presented no problems. It was the center of the young man's character. She'd done with the subtle, the divided, the complex. George was a perfectly adjusted human being. And, furthermore, he was just the sort of father Henry needed. Hilly had no idea how much George had already done for the boy. Henry adored the ground the Captain walked on.

She got up abruptly, lighted a cigarette and began to walk about the room. If she had shared with Larry in the past a communion that had been almost telepathic in its intimacy — exchanging, as they had, most of their thoughts in silence by means of intuitions, signals, nerves — it made her relationship to him at present and under the stress of all that they'd undergone the more hazardous. Larry had a manner of withdrawing, saying in substance, "just so far you go, but not a half inch further"; however, in one's solitude one carried on the reconciliations, one repaired the differences.

And it could *not* be possible that he intended shutting her permanently out of his life? For over a year she had not laid eyes on him. The peace in Europe had come; VJ Day had passed. There had been some correspondence — whatever letters he had written had been strictly confined to his domestic problems; they had been cool and businesslike and left her with the painful impression that she was to be severely punished for the part she'd played in the matter of his divorce, assisting Anne in the battle they had had for Henry, going even to the lengths of putting down on paper certain evidence — acting, as it had seemed to her, in the only honorable way she could have acted in so delicate and difficult a situation. Larry was not, and this he knew quite as well as she, the proper guardian, even in a case of divided tenure, for a little boy. One must consider Henry; one must keep one's head. You could not sacrifice your grandson for the love you bore your child.

"We must," she cried aloud, "consider Henry. You know this, Larry, just as well as I. Then why, my darling, just at this moment — tell me why?"

Had he learned, she wondered, of the Captain's trip to Reno? Anne must have written, surely. And was Anne married at the moment to the Captain, or would they perhaps wait till they got back to town?

As for Larry, she wouldn't have known his whereabouts had he not sent that telegram, which had undoubtedly come from Washington. He was, she'd heard, though she wasn't at all sure that this was true, still in uniform. He'd apparently done good work in the ordnance department; he knew a great deal about modern weapons; he'd executed

some fine drawings, written some good reports; he was a first lieutenant. He had kept his apartment in Alexandria; he was, she presumed, continuing his relationship with that young man, Jerry Styles.

No, that was not the name. What was the young man's name —
Stearns, Stephens? No; Styles — it *was* Styles, Gerald Styles.

"Oh, my darling," she again cried out, "forgive me the mistakes I've
made! I was so young. I did not have the enlightenment about these
matters that we have today. What I wanted for you, my dear, was all
that I had lacked — love, understanding, tenderness, the chance to
grow a soul. You can't imagine, Larry, the way they pushed us round
and tried to create us in their image, offering us a God who echoed all
their prayers and prejudices, calling it love, their determination to give
us wealth, position, a sense of our dynastic obligations, marrying us off,
dedicating their lives to accumulating the dollars. Believe me, darling,
I thought that I was going to give you something better than I'd had
myself."

And if, she reflected, falling silent and sitting down again, she'd chosen Europe for her child, wanting to give him values different from
those that had been imposed on her, could she have been blamed for
failing to understand how difficult it was for an American girl, brought
up as she had been, to find the values she was searching for? When she
recollected it all, how inaccessible they had always been. She'd found
environments — resorts, hotels, American colonies; and what with all
the other expatriates, what with the relatives, and never having been
taught that working hard for anything you wanted desperately was one
way of procuring values — everything so easy and delightful — just
giving the poor boy Europe, allowing him to feel and vibrate to it
through her own delight in its charms, giving him languages, the
leisure and the languor, making of him in fact a congenital alien, an
American, but not an American, a native of Europe, but never, never
a European, a young man with the most nervous and acute, the most
overdeveloped aesthetic tastes, nurtured as he had been on so much
art and scenery, seeing and feeling everything, as she had somehow
succeeded in making him through her own ravished sensibilities —
keeping him always with her, feeding him so deliberately on her quick
ecstasies and enthusiasms, her passionate response to all the treasure
and antiquity and loveliness. If there had grown up between them a

closeness, an identity of response, a need to rest, each in the other's presence and acquiescence, it had been so gradual, so gracious; and with the relatives so frequently at hand to assist in the spoiling and what with Larry's having been so beautiful a child and for a long time so amenable and gentle, was she to be blamed too much for it — not seeing what was happening? In those earlier years we had been without these new enlightenments.

And, she wondered, at about what moment had she developed this state of enlightenment which, for lack of a better way to think about it, she'd call a modern intelligence — this new surprising equipment of nerves and sensibilities? Just when had she thrown off her earlier innocence? She seemed to have plucked initiation from the air. She'd read so many books; she'd engaged herself so much in probing and analysis, treading the nervous tracks and pathways, watching the emotional designs and patterns of behavior laid down, threaded into the warp of human character; seeing, as she had begun to, even in herself and her own child the busy shuttle working on the tragic loom of their relationship. It had been, roughly speaking, in those years that followed the First World War and accompanied by the premonition that one had of watching some great apocalyptic melodrama gradually unfold; reading as one had about this time those magnificent and terrifying novels of Marcel Proust, devouring them one by one, living at the moment then with Larry in that little flat they had beside the Panthéon while he was still at the lycée — a kind of half-caste you might have called him, talking French with such ease and fluency, but retaining in his bearing and physical appearance something unmistakably American, wearing with such peculiar awkwardness the regulation costumes of the French schoolboy which were, like the youths for whom they'd been designed, so weirdly grown-up and at the same time so extraordinarily infantile — the short trousers, the bare knees, the little berets, the carefully tailored coats.

And there had been Pierre — short, swarthy, with the dark down on his upper lip and the voice already emitting the deeper registers; and something from the first a little mysterious about his relationship to Larry, his parents, as they were, connected with the fashionable world and living in a hotel of some pretension in the Faubourg. Certainly she had never laid eyes upon them, no exchange of calls had been in order, and Pierre's manner to her — an overelaborate politeness almost as excessive as an apology — suggesting that her graciousness, her hospitality, even if a little out of the way and so uniquely American, was utterly adorable, since it was most unlikely that either she or Larry would ever find their way to his domestic interior, these matters of introductions and invitations being laid down in France with such solemnity, and with who might know what fine drawings of social distinctions and discriminations, and contrasting so sharply with her own desire to invite and immediately welcome Larry's friend to their little flat in the Rue d'Ulm and her pleasure in discovering a youth of such keen intelligence, such genuine European culture and education. But coming there, she somehow suspected, without his parents' cognizance, becoming gradually aware that the boy combined, together with his delightful attentions toward her, his flattery and effusiveness, a good deal of erotic enjoyment (inviting those kisses, which she didn't quite know why she had begun to bestow upon him — much as she might have bestowed them upon Larry), and realizing slowly that (very subtle it had been and most difficult to define) all manner of intimate, induced and sensuous undercurrents had begun to flow through this strange triangular relationship, as though being in her ambient, courting her caresses and attentions, Pierre derived an exquisite, an ever more and more romantic attachment to her boy.

Then that awful evening in the pleasant spring twilight, listening while Pierre played the "Moonlight Sonata" with such an extraordinary blending of depth and brilliancy; for a boy of his age, she'd thought, observing how the tempest and the passion of the music swept across his countenance — remarkable, remarkable; and the music's stopping with such abruptness that it had startled her; Pierre's rising and going to the window where Larry sat entranced and speechless; seeing them staring at each other; and divining instantly the truth about the boys' relationship.

The consternation she had felt, she'd carry with her to her dying day. She would question, every time that memory revived the scene. If she'd acted differently, if she had made an issue of it, might she perhaps have altered the sequence of events in Larry's life? But in these great emotional crises one had so little time to make decisions; they somehow made themselves, out of — God knew what other scenes and memories.

She'd watched the boys exchange their glances. Larry had made a movement as though to embrace Pierre, had then embraced him, quickly, passionately, and she'd thought, "My God! he's not sixteen and Pierre scarcely a year his senior," knowing without the shadow of a doubt that Larry was aware she'd divined their secret and that, somehow, Pierre also realized she had guessed it. So there they were together, with the windows open and those weirdly affecting Parisian street sounds drifting up to them, their hearts shaking with the secret she had apprehended.

"Bravo, Pierre," she had said, "you play so beautifully." She'd crossed the room, turned on the lights, gone to the piano. "Come, Pierre," she'd urged, turning over the music on the piano and discovering a favorite Chopin waltz, "play something now for *me*."

And he had come and kissed her lightly, in that endearing, almost feminine way he had, and then he'd played the lovely nostalgic waltz with a light evocative touch, just as it should have been played, his head swaying slightly and his body moving in unison.

Strange, probably — she would not know; she'd felt no censure of the boys, she'd had no inclination to reproach them. She'd only felt an immense love, an overwhelming pity for them. And oh, she questioned passionately, how much could she herself be held responsible for Larry's inclinations? How much had she been implicated?

She got up and, throwing her cigarette into the fireplace, went to the window and looked out, noticing that the storm had increased and, still with something of the Christmas magic haunting her, she struggled against the onslaught of another painful memory and the invariable question that accompanied it —had Larry, or had he not, remembered it? It was most unlikely, she always reassured herself — he was less than three years old; and yet somehow she always suspected that he had — there was something quite uncanny about a child's exposure to certain situations, that queer way they had of plumbing the nervous and erotic depths when confronted suddenly with passion; and, at any rate, she'd never, as long as she might live, forget that he'd been there — a little silent, wide-eyed witness; he had heard the cry that had escaped her, "My dear, if we succumb, we're lost," and he'd seen her bury her face in her hands and heard that other voice, dominating, passionate, "Try to escape it, Hilly, if you can. Impossible, my dear"; he'd watched while the tall, the too-familiar figure took her roughly in his arms and forced her to receive those brutal, burning kisses; seen her wrench herself away.

There, shaken, trembling all over, she'd stood in the path by the mimosa bushes, seeing Larry; perfectly motionless and silent, watching them. All three of them completely speechless, till Larry turned and ran away.

She would never ask him. He would never tell. And if he had remembered — well, if he had?

It was snowing heavily. Even at this height she could see the silent fall and slant of the snow against the lamps. How beautiful it was — the sidewalks thatched with white and the roofs of the cars in the streets below, the terraces and water tanks and radio antennae, the tall buildings standing up like phantoms in the storm. All over the city, the boughs of every meager tree and all the trees and shrubs in all the parks, the fountains and the pavements and the palings were arrayed in white for Christmas. Out on the rivers the snow fell on the cabooses of the tugboats, on the long flat barges, on the pilot boats, on the decks of ships.

She listened. The streets were muffled in silence, but in the river below she could hear the foghorns and the abrupt, interrupted hootings of the smaller boats. In the North River there'd be louder groanings, moanings, the wails of sirens, and out in the bay the boats would signal their positions. The snow was dangerous, like the fog. She thought of all the ships — the perils they encountered, the long sea voyages, their arrivals and departures.

Thank God, they were no longer carrying tanks and planes and jeeps and guns and troops and airplanes. Thank God that the great convoys were no longer assembling, stealthily augmenting their numbers out in the larger waters of the bay, while that formidable array of war matériel, darkly massed and swathed in brown tarpaulin, slowly whitened on the decks.

How many nights she'd lain in anguish, thinking of the enormous theaters of the war, of the blood shed daily, hourly, on the world and of the young men fighting those outlandish battles — in deserts, in the center of great cities, in the green jungles, in the mountain snows, upon beaches and on tropic islands, and in the skies above these combats, on the seas and in the waters underneath the seas — and, though

Larry for reasons never mentioned, but known to both of them, had not been called upon to join these battles, actually envying, oh, in a queer excruciating way, those other mothers who had been called upon to sacrifice their sons. For when it came to participating in anguish of such huge, such universal dimensions, one felt a kind of shame for having private and particular griefs.

Well, it was over. And she did not have to stop and ask herself: How many young men *now*, this instant, killed in battle in the air, the ocean, on the land? How many cities bombed and burning? It was over, God deliver us. And here we were. We prayed; we waited. Where was our security?

Thinking of Henry in the next room, with his beloved B-29 beside him, Mrs. Danforth burst into sobs, standing there with her face buried in her hands. For, though she'd not seen Larry for so long, of one thing she was positive; she could rely on one thing. Their hearts ached with the same anguish. About this world in which they lived they shared the same sentiments. Larry felt, he loved, he suffered.

"You are, my darling, on the angels' side!" She allowed the cry to escape her, although she was, at the moment admonishing herself severely — "Don't be a fool, control yourself" — crossing the floor, turning out the light, returning to her bedroom.

Here she wiped her eyes and managed to subdue her emotion; but she stood beside the bed irresolute. Should she; shouldn't she? Would it be wise, or would it be exactly the wrong thing to do?

Finally, she sat down at the table by her bed and, taking the receiver from the telephone, dialed the central office.

"Yes, operator; I want to send a telegram.

"Is this Western Union?

"I wish to send a telegram to Alexandria, Virginia.

"Yes, that's it — to Mr. Lawrence Danforth." She gave the number and the street. "Yes, Alexandria. Certainly it is in Virginia. 'Better not come now, dear. Love.' Signed 'Mother.'" She gave her own telephone number. She asked them to repeat the message.

"Yes. Be good enough to leave out the 'love.' 'Better not come just now.' Leave out the 'dear,' too; insert the 'just.' Yes; sign it 'Mother.'"

She put the receiver back on the hook.

F O U R

MAKING UP HER MIND THAT SHE WOULD NOT WORRY, trying every device of which she could think to get off to sleep, remembering lovely summer sights and sounds — birds singing, clouds sailing, winds blowing over the grasses, Mrs. Danforth suddenly found herself lying in a meadow at the edge of a lawn, near her mother and old Mrs. Constable, while the two sat under the oak trees, talking together in lowered voices; and a fresh breeze moving in the trees shifted the boughs so that here the leaves became light, transparent like mica, and there dark in their own green shadows, and all lay side by side, changing hues and textures, opening and closing upon each other, exposing the blue sky, shutting it out again; and the birds among the boughs singing, just as though the trees themselves gave out their tunes and breezes, showering them down on her while she lay filled with incredulity and horror, hearing what they said and longing above everything else on earth to run to her mother for consolation, imploring her to tell her that not a word she'd heard was true.

"Hush, Hatty. I don't want Hilly to hear all this."

"She can't hear at such a distance; and even if she could she wouldn't understand."

"She should *not* be lolling about in the long grass."

"Hilly" — the beloved voice was harsh and disapproving — "get up out of the grass; run away and play."

The heat waved over her hands and face and the air rippled all around her in little rings and circulations of summer tunes. She put out a finger to deflect an emerald beetle climbing a blade of grass and watched it spread its pretty double wings and fly away; there was a long

procession of ants running toward an anthill; spiders spun webs; a but-
terfly opened and closed its wings; the clover, the daisies, the devil's
paintbrush, the sorrel and timothy nodded above her and gave her a
peculiar sense of being, herself, a meadow full of grass and flowers and
little flying, crawling, humming creatures. Lying there and listening to
what they said, she realized quite well that if what she heard was true,
the world as she had hitherto known it would simply cease to exist;
precedents would vanish; and God would fail to keep His promises. Life
itself would have a nightmare quality. For such a thing as this could not
possibly happen in her family, where everyone was so perfectly charming, so happy and good and fortunate; and that her Uncle Philip, of all
living people, could have committed this mortal sin, the unspeakable
nature of which and the secrecy that clothed it, together with the urgent necessity of listening, had suddenly revealed to her in all its awful
solemnity what was really involved in breaking the Seventh
Commandment. Oh, no. Oh, no — it was not true; and, furthermore,
they could not require her to believe that because a baby who should
never have been born at all, having been born dead, and because of the
baby's mother (who was not, it appeared, Aunt Adelaide) having also
died, and because Uncle Philip had in his medical capacity administered certain drugs that he, her favorite uncle, was — oh, God, she
could not say it — was an out-and-out murderer. "Oh, no; no, no, no."
   "In the charms of Philip Davenport I never put my trust."
   "But you must admit his fascination."
   "I repeat: I never trusted him."
She was blindly, crazily compelled to investigate the matter for herself. If she saw them, if she spoke to them, somehow she would know.
She rose to her feet, hearing her mother call her to get up from the long
grass and, at the same time, filled with an intolerable longing to run to
the shelter of her arms and beg her to say that not a word of what she'd
overheard was true, she started to run, across the lawn, down the slope,
into the road, and up the hill, terrified at the thought of what she'd put
on foot.
   Would her uncle kiss her? Would he not? She'd say, "Good afternoon, Aunt Adelaide. How do you do, Uncle Philip." If he kissed her,
she would know somehow that everything was all right — that he
wasn't a murderer. But if he failed to do so — well, then he was. As fast

as she could go she went, the birds dipping and skimming, rising up out of the grass, scattering their notes like flowers, carrying them up onto the air to twine them into wreaths above her; and on one side of the road the ox-eyed daisies far outnumbered the white ones, and on the other side the white ones went floating off in drifts like stars.

When she reached the locust avenue that led to the house, the fragrance of locusts seemed to drench the very air in all the crimes of Uncle Philip. She knelt down to pick up the tiny shell-like blossoms, slowly, one by one, a thousand pulses beating in her heart. She began to pray: "Don't let it be true; don't let it be true."

Then she saw them both approaching and she ran quickly to meet them.

"Hilly, dear little Hilly," said Aunt Adelaide and folded her in her embrace.

She turned to her uncle.

And hearing his light, his positively frivolous voice ("Hullo, Hilly. How does the world treat you?"), saying, as she had decided to, "How do you do, Uncle Philip," keeping her voice as steady as possible and taking the hand he offered her, she knew without a doubt that everything was true.

There they stood, the three of them together, the sunlight shining on his beautiful red beard.

Good gracious, with what vividness she'd lived through it again. But then — why not? thought Mrs. Danforth. So much else was trammeled up in it. It had surely been the most crucial experience in her childhood. Its effect upon her character had been drastic — drastic. And what, she wondered, would the psychoanalysts have made of it — what wouldn't they have got her telling them? Keeping it all so strictly to herself and strengthening her in that habit she had of hanging around, observing, listening, mixing fear with fascination. How stubbornly, perversely, determined she'd been to ferret it all out.

She had never been able to understand why her parents had not suspected her of knowing something about it — that the sudden disappearance of an aunt so dear and an uncle so unusual had gone completely unremarked should have given them an inkling — and that they could have believed the explanations they offered her ("Your Aunt Adelaide and your Uncle Philip have gone off on a long journey.

Of course, they'll be coming back; but not at present, dear") completely satisfactory seemed singularly lacking in imagination and insight, sending her off, as they used to, on those little improvised errands
("Hilly darling, won't you go upstairs and fetch me a pocket-
handkerchief," etc., etc.), just as though they expected her long train-
ing in docility and good manners had rendered her entirely impervious
not only to curiosity but to feeling.

Her very silence should have warned them that she was initiated. But
no. She was a little girl who must take as gospel truth everything they
saw fit to tell her; and there an end of it, as far as they were concerned.
It had not apparently occurred to them that it was singular for a sensitive and inquisitive child to take without question or wonder the fact
that the house on the hill had simply ceased to have any connection
with their day-to-day existence, the shutters so suddenly tight closed
and the front door nailed up and barred across, the leaves unswept in
the avenue, the whole adjacent property going so swiftly to rack and
ruin, with a crazy sign up in the meadow and an equally crazy one on
the lawn — "This Property For Rent or Sale." Aunt Adelaide had gone
to the South of France to stay awhile with Uncle Philip — a lovely
place that Hilly must herself visit some day —moving among them, as
she had, as innocent as a May morning and pretending so vigilantly
that she hadn't heard a word, didn't know a thing while, with her uncanny ability to sit quietly in their midst and pull right out of the air
they breathed this little dreadful fact and that, she'd finally, bit by bit,
pieced together the whole appalling story.

How the mother of the baby had been somebody with whom she was
well acquainted — pretty Miss Millet, who had always come in the
spring and autumn to sew for Aunt Adelaide and Mamma — and how
that poor baby, born dead (an anomaly that had tortured her, whenever
she'd put her mind upon it), lay buried beside Miss Millet in the green
and shady cemetery not so many miles away from their own house at
the Meadows; how they had managed somehow to "hush it all up" and
get Aunt Adelaide and Uncle Philip off to the South of France (where,
presumably, she would go some day to see them).

For years she had been haunted by the strangest dreams and her
mind harassed by thoughts she scarcely dared pursue; and she'd been
afflicted by the queerest compulsions, being forced again and again

against her inclinations and her better judgment to run up the hill, through the locust avenue, to peek through the closed shutters of the house, saturating herself in the sorrow and shame and challenge of the still unfinished story and even, on one occasion, setting forth alone and without permission for the cemetery and there hunting for and finding the obscure and tragic little grave — sitting on the grass and weeping copiously and leaving behind a small bouquet of violets and snowdrops, in atonement for her Uncle Philip's crimes.

If she had had a little understanding from her parents this would have been of great assistance to her emotionally, but though they were always telling her that she was "all they had" and assuring her that they lived only for her, she had, she suspected, realized all along that their parental love was meted out on the oddest possible terms and that the only conspicuous evidence of their affection for her lay in this habitual declaration that she was all they had on earth; though she received, of course, those kisses bestowed upon her in the ordered routine of greetings at night and morning — "good morning, Hilly"; "good night, my dear."

Her need for her mother's love and tenderness bordered certainly on the neurotic and, in a very peculiar way, her mother's beauty entered into it, for it had the effect of inclining her toward love as toward some miraculous moment of grace and healing; and out of what wells of need and loneliness she must have drawn that fruitless little prayer — "God, let her come; make her come up tonight." How perfectly beautiful she had seemed to her, and how distant; and her father, as so often she had heard it rumored, so "madly in love with her." She used to say the words over to herself, distilling from them a fascinating secret life of her own. For her father she always entertained a feeling of the profoundest awe, combined with a very definite embarrassment when too long in his society (for there was something about a male being, in those days, very difficult to define); and had she not on one occasion, watching him from behind a glass door, seen him grab at her mother's arm and print on it, from the wrist right up to the elbow, a succession of quick and furtive kisses? Mamma had snatched her arm away — "Pull yourself together, Leonard; not *that*; not *now*.

She was always lolling in her vicinity, watching her gestures, listening to her conversation; and there floated from her, seeped and crept out of her laces, her tea gowns and undergarments, certain fragrances — French soaps, sachets, delicious essences from Paris — and these combining with the inflections of her voice, her laughter, to give her a sense of being in some fabulous garden filled with the rarest, the most exotic flowers, not one of which she was allowed to pick.

She had, she imagined, spent the larger part of her childhood simply hanging around her — always on the fringes and outskirts, never really partaking in her enjoyments or sharing intimately with her in anything. She was content merely to be near her, to listen and observe. She was generally allowed to watch her preparing to go out into society, or she could, on those Tuesday afternoons at "the Reefs," when she was at home to the callers who used to drive out in throngs to the tennis parties on the lawn or the tea parties on the breezy veranda, actually play her little part in the entertaining of society, arrayed in one of those exquisite white dresses and conscious of herself only as a tiny fragment of decoration in the graceful and delightful scene, passing glasses of lemonade and plates of cake, moving about among the various groups, shy, reticent, drawing back a little from the kisses and flattery, but with a kind of eagerness, an intensity of desire to please Mamma, waiting for her commands, hearing her voice emerge from that pleasant airy sound of general chatter, prettily cadenced and with the small trail of laughter that ran through it and seemed somehow to accent not only the triviality of her conversation but the light and frivolous quality of her soul — "Hilly darling, there's a gentleman here who wishes to make your acquaintance," or "Pass Mrs. Constable the cakes; Mrs. Archbald would like another sandwich." Fetching, carrying, bowing, smiling, enduring the kisses and the sallies, and acutely aware that it was only as her mother's daughter, only by that extraordinary grace and dispensation, that she was suffered to be present at all, while the breeze distributed the laughter and the voices, shifted the lights and shadows on the lawn, blew over the grass in the surrounding fields, and the heavenly encirclement of blue sky and bluer sea arching over, beyond and around her gave her that curious sense of being compassed round by some large beneficent element into which, and at any moment, she and the ladies and the gentlemen and the queer little ache of beauty in her heart might dissolve and blow away with the mist, the breeze and the laughter.

In this feeling she had for her mother there was undoubtedly something more than just a little morbid, waiting as she always seemed to be on some completion or fulfillment of her adoration, and it was when she came in, like someone admitted to the most exotic rites and ceremonies, to watch her dress for going out that she felt her need and yearning expand and grow in her heart as the elaborate preparations progressed.

There she'd sit before her mirror, while the maid behind her combed, brushed, gathered up into strands her beautiful bright hair, deftly erecting, as she fastened it with jewelled or amber combs and hairpins, an aureole of golden pompadour, and on the dressing table in front of her such a bewildering array of cut-glass bottles, silver mirrors, silver hairbrushes, buffers and boxes, little silver-topped jars and silver-bottomed pincushions, powder puffs and orange sticks and implements of steel and ivory, strewn about in a kind of opulent disorder and ready for her hand as she sat polishing her nails, turning her head to right or to left at the bidding of her maid, opening or screwing up one or another of the little jars, applying a touch of rouge here, a dash of powder there, powdering her neck and her arms, smelling the stoppers of various bottles, taking up her hand mirror at intervals to see herself from every angle, directing her maid — this curl should be moved a trifle to the left and here, on the temple, the hair should be lifted considerably; now, that was exactly right.

Then suddenly she'd rise; there she'd stand — tall like a white rose or a lily — in those unparalleled petticoats, flounced with lace, run through with pure-white ribbons, the lacy, monogrammed corset cover very low in the neck, revealing to the limit of propriety her full round breasts, the blue veins like shadows beneath the soft white skin, and, before there had been half enough time to take her in from her shining hair to her satin slippers, Martha would have brought from the big double bed, where it had been so conspicuously laid out, the wondrous glistening ball gown and with the deftest imaginable movements and without disturbing a single hair of her head have sheathed her in its shining folds.

Arrayed in all her glory, slipping on her rings, pulling on her long suede gloves, while Martha buttoned her up, pulled her in, invited her to hold or to let out her breath, she'd turn.

"Will I do, darling? Do I look all right?"

She'd hold out her arms; but that longed-for embrace, wrought of all the perfumes of Arabia and all the devotion in her little daughter's heart, usually failed to come off.

"Oh, darling, you've crushed my dress; you must learn to be more careful."

One would have thought, reflected Mrs. Danforth, trying to figure it all out, that flying so many flags and banners and captivating invitations, positively drenched in seductions as she was, that she was out to capture all the gentlemen in creation; and yet, when you stopped to consider it, and looking back upon them both, Mamma and Papa (the words were conjoined in her mind) displayed a moral propriety and deportment which, contrasted as it was with the low-necked dresses, the jewels and laces and perfumes and petticoats, seemed not only ridiculous but almost unbelievable; there'd been a kind of partnership about it, managing — as they had — to preserve a chaste, an inviolate, a perfectly inhuman attitude toward sex.

"Leonard, not *that*, not *now*."

She remembered Papa's face on that memorable occasion and how, after a moment of what must have been a severe test of his ability to "pull himself together," he had complied so obediently with her commands.

Was Mamma essentially cold? she wondered.

When she came to speculate about it — the paradox, the puzzle about those days, that behavior — she really could not do justice to its queerness. That Papa was "madly in love with his wife" she had recognized without the shadow of a doubt (in that uncanny way that children get these things) as far back as she could remember; but that he should, high-tempered and authoritative and accustomed to power as he was, have yielded with so much docility to the abstinences and denials she must have imposed upon him was certainly a tribute to her power over him. Rules there must have been, rigidly imposed and vigilantly practiced, between them. Range through her memories as she might, she could never remember having heard them quarrel, nor did she ever remember seeing her mother deliberately attempt to captivate another male creature. It might possibly have been that she was not captivating; here she must confess that she was in the dark.

But that all that exquisite array of lace and lingerie, those privacies and seductions of her toilet, should on the emotional and sensual plane have served no other purpose than to heighten and at the same time suppress the sensibilities of a little girl had about it surely a queerness, a quaintness. That ample double bed, on which those beruffled, beribboned drawers, those corset covers and petticoats and dresses were so seductively laid out, had, she felt quite certain, been but rarely placed at the disposal of those connubial pleasures for which it had so obviously been designed. Papa had had his private apartments — a bedroom and a dressing room — and on the rare occasions that he did, while the mystic rites of preparing Mamma for "going out" were in progress, knock at her door, there was such a hustling and scuttling and bustling about on the part of Martha (hanging up the petticoats, hiding the drawers, secreting the corset covers, and all in the name of modesty, covering Mamma in a wrapper or peignoir, and Mamma calling out, "You must wait just a minute, Leonard," or "I'll meet you downstairs, my dear") that one could readily infer that an informal access to her during these moments of preparation was considered entirely out of the way. It was in the finished product that he had to reap his rewards, waiting patiently for her at the bottom of the stairs or lingering discreetly at her bedroom door.

Poor Papa!

Mrs. Danforth closed her eyes, the better to invoke the picture of that little, nervous, decorative gentleman almost ludicrously brushed and pressed and polished and with that suggestion of tension and anxiety in his eyes and round his mouth which, even in his happier moments, he'd not been able to disguise. He certainly had his worries and, at times of financial crisis (he was then referred to, not as "Papa," but as "your father"), she used to watch him, studying the financial columns of the paper, or anxiously pacing the floor, fearing all manner of imminent disasters — that, for instance, they'd have to "give up the horses," or that they'd not be able to "take the house at the Reefs" or indeed, if the worst came to the worst, that they might have to sell "the Meadows" and go, all together, to the poorhouse. Acutely aware that the absent-minded, the almost disembodied quality of his good-night and good-morning kisses boded bad days for everyone, fearing his outbursts of temper, and watching the servants tremble in his presence (the roasts during these periods were always either too rare or overdone, the plates were too hot or too cold and reprimands flew about in all directions), she'd make up her mind to put up with it as best she could, awaiting a time when things might perhaps begin to improve.

And, sure enough, when she least expected it, they always did improve. She'd discover that the horses were to remain in the stables, and not only did they not have to go to the poorhouse, but they still retained "the Meadows" and would go for July and August to "the Reefs"; indeed, she'd perceive that a new era of conspicuous elegance was about to be ushered in, with new horses for Mamma, a new victoria, new liveries, and Papa "quite himself again."

In his happier moments, he treated her to a rather embarrassing affection. He liked to hold her on his knee, long after she was too old for such fondling, and he told her stories designed for an infantile intelligence; he made up little names for her and enjoyed telling her not to put beans up her nose and inquiring jovially, when she came in, whose chicken coop she had been robbing, and though such affectionate banter was distressing enough, it was on the whole welcome and reassuring as it so clearly indicated that things were to go on as usual and that they would not, after all, be so very poor; they could retain the beloved "Meadows."

Her poor parents, she could not think of them today without emotion!

F I V E

———————

WAS SHE INDOORS, OR OUTDOORS, was she walking through the winter-lit streets with her governess, or driving with Mamma in the afternoon sunlight, through the park, or shopping with her at Altman's or Arnold's or Lewis and Conger's, or was she perhaps drinking tea with her mother's guests in the big overfurnished drawing-room?

She did not know — the pageant and panorama passed before her and she seemed actually to be living again in that vanished era, re-visiting those streets and houses, seeing again, as they used to look, the Fifties and the Forties, Fifth Avenue and Madison Avenue, the serried ranks of brownstone fronts, uniform, respectable, built, apparently, to stay, with here and there a house introducing a foreign façade, or one like their own in Fifty-third Street, with the marbled, the plate-glass appearance, the impressive vestibule, the large front door, heavy and important, the iron grill protecting the glass. And, of course, those perfectly splendid mansions of the Vanderbilts — ducal, manorial — defying change and time.

Indestructible and baronial they looked as one passed them by of a winter evening, lighted for some festive occasion and the doors open-ing and the carriages rolling up and envious crowds staring on the side-walks. Indeed, all the houses in the neighborhood seemed, at a certain hour — with the appearance of the lamp lighter, with the appearance of maids in the windows, pulling down shades, lighting gas jets or switching on the electricity, and with the vistas behind the windows of chandeliers aglow, fires flickering, servants appearing — to give one a sense of an established order, of elegance, of black-habited, white-aproned, white-capped maids going about their evening offices, opening beds, bringing in tea trays, saying "yes, ma'am; no, ma'am" (knowing, as they used to say in those days, "how to keep their place"), and of butlers in dress suits, in discreet liveries, letting in their masters, letting in their mistresses, of carriages stopping and ladies descending, of footmen waiting at attention or hastily running ahead to ring door bells, carrying parcels, assisting their mistresses up steps, and of passers-by glimpsing the warm, lighted interiors, feeling in their hearts an ache which resembled, very likely, the yearning of the child beneath the Christmas tree, looking at all the baubles, the brightly colored balls, at that herald angel perched on top?

But there it was; there it was. And there was Fifth Avenue and the great, the truly astonishing procession of varnished victorias, broughams, landaus; and the two men on the box in their dark-blue, or buff, or plum-colored liveries, their backs so erect, the coachmen holding their reins so correctly, flourishing their whips, and the footmen so small, so rigid, their arms frozen to their breasts; and there, too, were the hired cabs, the hansoms with the somewhat raffish coachmen driving in their tiny crow's nest high aloft behind their passengers, who somehow looked, inside those quaintly rocking vehicles, so public and exposed. And always that uninterrupted rumble — that majestic pace and beat of the horses' hoofs hitting the asphalt; the beautifully matched horses, the roans, the bays, the chestnuts, all with their tails so stylishly docked, all with their shining, their silver mounted harnesses, and which pair the handsomest it would be difficult to say among so many of perfect gait and gloss, arching their necks, stepping out so splendidly and frequently flecked with foam, the coachman so proud on the box, reining them in at the curb! And those ladies in their victorias of such peerless elegance — the sable capes, the sealskin coats, the white suede gloves, the remarkable hats, with the ostrich feathers, the plumes of other splendid birds, the little fur, the velvet toques — going shopping, leaving cards or turning in at the Park for the afternoon circle, up the east side, down the west and out again at the Plaza. What a pageant! What a panorama, with midget footmen jumping nimbly to the sidewalks, nimbly ascending, standing expressionless by doors of carriages, lap robes over their arms.

Was it gay, was it glamorous, that incomparable decade?

One could, reflected Mrs. Danforth, certainly compare it with the Christmas tree, hung as it was with all those glittering balls and bells and baubles. Here on its branches were those thousands of parlor maids, chambermaids, waitresses, the black habits, the snow-white caps, the snow-white aprons; here were the regiments of coachmen in their handsome liveries, the little footmen holding the lap robes, carrying the packages; here were the butlers opening the doors, the vistas — lighted rooms with tea trays coming in; and here, behold, were other neighborhoods —that one so seldom mentioned but called by such a truly vulgar name, west of Broadway in the Thirties and the Forties, and the houses of statelier presence in better vicinities (known only to the gentlemen). Here were Lillian Russell and Diamond Jim Brady and the dance halls in the Bowery, here were the ladies one recognized but never bowed to; here was a great deal that was not spoken of, but, when one came to think about it, pretty well understood and very much on display, what with all the feathers and the flounces and the petticoats and corset laces, the chorus girls and Daly's and Delmonico's and the Peacock Alley at the Waldorf; here were the belles and the beauties and the Gibson Girls and the Bradley Martin Ball. Here, too, was Mamma; here was Papa; here were his business associates, his cronies, their seals and their gold watches, their cravat pins and excellent cigars, their polished boots and their cut-away coats and Prince Alberts, their top hats, their opera hats and capes, the fabulous costumes in which they drove their four-in-hands up and down the Avenue, their boxes at the opera, their yachts and yachting caps, their country estates and blooded cattle. Behold them, opening their dividends, cutting their coupons, sitting at their mahogany tables, combining this enterprise with that, consolidating their little empires of rails, of oil, of coal and iron and steel; and there, oh, look, close to the Christmas angel — the Statue of Liberty welcoming the foreigner to our gates, and the liners bringing in their steerage, day after day, boatloads of immigrants. Here was Andrew Carnegie donating his libraries and Mr. Rockefeller distributing his dimes and a chance for every man, if he proved himself industrious and learned to save, of becoming a millionaire in his own right; here were the little towns in Pennsylvania filling up with Germans and Moravians, and the larger towns with Scotchmen and Irishmen and Italians, and the towns in Massachusetts and Connecticut filling up with Dagoes and Polacks; and little towns in Calabria, in Sicily, emptied, literally emptied, of their folk, so that the rails could be laid, the road beds kept clean, the steel forged, the iron blasted, the oil be made to gush up from the bowels of the earth and the coal be mined in the ancient petrified forests under the hills.

The pick axes swung and the shovels were loaded, and at the blast furnaces and in the foundries men sweated and toiled; and the miners, with the picturesque little lights they wore in their caps, the little picks they carried in their hands, worked for long unregulated hours at their dark and dangerous tasks; and in the great cities men and women and little children worked for long hours at the meagerest wages in the factories and the sweat shops; and the thickly populated tenements spread out and became slums and dead-end areas, and the Central European Jews —Hungarians, Bohemians — the Russian Jews, increased in great numbers, the Italians increased, and the Germans and their dwellings were dark and squalid and there was scant room in their beds for their babies to be born or for their children to turn over in their sleep at night.

Meanwhile, these resplendent ladies and fastidious gentlemen sat through their endless dinners, eating the oysters, the game, the fish, the roast, the frivolous little sherbets and vol-au-vents, the timballes and fanciful desserts, the beautiful fruits and bonbons and, as noiselessly the priceless plates were changed, the appropriate wines poured into the proper wineglasses, they conversed with one another, agreeing, as she remembered it, on every subject, being as they were at one in all their creeds and criticisms and aversions; and if Mr. Gompers was, by any unusual twist in the conversation, mentioned or the horrid subject of labor unions touched upon, the same aversion was expressed by everybody, the same hatred — firmly the ladies echoed the opinions of their fathers, their husbands and fathers-in-law, angrily they shook their pretty heads, and it was agreed by all that there were dangerous elements abroad and that here in America, in this free country where free enterprise was above all to be extolled, the building up of our great nation into these tight little, right little family dynasties was the God-given task confronting them, that there was no need, no need at all for organized labor, that this was a free country where every man had his chance and that we must remember Mr. Rockefeller and Mr. Carnegie and, above all, that we must be suspicious of this European element —

these Hungarians and Italians and Jews. They were creeping into this country, they were undermining our liberties, patriotism, American idealism. God was invoked, and their own God-given prerogatives to regulate their own affairs.

How zealously they believed in themselves, in their wealth, their power and their paternalistic interest in the lower classes. Had Mr. James J. Hill not consolidated his empire of rails in the Midwest and was Mr. Collis Huntington not performing similar marvels on the Pacific Coast and farther to the north and east? And were there not the Goulds and the Vanderbilts? Were there not enormous fortunes to be made in steel and oil and iron? And was not this a great country, the resource and daring and enterprise of which they had only just begun to conjure with? Had not Mr. Horace Greeley said, "Go West, young man," and did not Papa sit with various presidents and directors at various mahogany tables and, although something of a dreamer and perhaps a little too prone to startle them with his ideas, perhaps too inclined to plunge and speculate, had he not at any rate and by dint of the most careful calculations set up this substantial block of gilt-edged stock against this, that, or the other blocks of a more speculative nature, the whole structure so nicely balanced, looking always into the future with a shrewd eye, thinking of his dear little daughter and of his perfectly beautiful wife sitting at the moment opposite him and agreeing with every word he said?

At ease they sat in Zion, secure in their belief that God was on their side. How piously they knelt in church! How bravely they rose from their knees! With what a righteous gesture they slipped their contributions into the box — always, she remembered, folded and placed in little envelopes to indicate that, with them, it wasn't a mere matter of loose and jingling coin, but of bills, carefully hidden from view and modestly presented (how much had they given, she used to wonder — five dollars or ten, or maybe a hundred?). She never had been able to ascertain the amount. But, at any rate, the zest with which they joined in singing the ensuing hymn might have led her to believe that it was quite as much as a million anyway —

> "Onward, Christian soldiers,
>   Marching as to war,

With the cross of Jesus
Going on before."

Their heads thrown back, their voices lifted, as though they, in the company of Mr. Collis Huntington and Mr. James J. Hill and his wife and children and family and all the Goulds and all the Vanderbilts, were marching together bearing the banners of Christ along all the defiles and declivities of the world.

And, meanwhile, on the great green boughs of the fabulous tree the Christmas candles burned blue and in an ecstasy of aspiration flickered upward toward that herald angel at the top. And outside in the night, as the skies cleared and one by one the stars went out — there, praying by the manger, Joseph and Mary with the wise men and the shepherds and their sheep beside them; and, thought Mrs. Danforth, closing her eyes and trying to remember the words exactly, Lincoln praying, with his beautiful grave smile, and Whitman dreaming his dreams, spanning the country from city to city with bridges of love. Then slowly, for she wanted to be sure she had them correctly, she repeated the lines:

"We use you, and do not cast you aside, we plant you
fervently within us;
We fathom you not, we love you, there is perfection
in you also."

Suddenly she jumped, startled out of her reverie, for there was a great banging at the door.

"Come in," she said, drowsily, "come in, dear," and she watched Henry switch on the light and cross the floor in his bare feet.

"Hullo, Daisy Mae," he said, jumping onto the bed. "Would you like to see my airplanes? I'll tell you some more about them — you're very ignorant; you need a lot of teaching."

There began the zooming and the booming. "Look, Grandma, can you tell me which one this is? Do you know its name?"

No, she said, she was afraid she did not.

"It's the big one; the big bomber, the B-29. You know, the one that took the bomb to Hiroshima."

S I X

———

"IT WILL BE A GREAT BIG TREE that reaches the ceiling, and we'll go this afternoon to buy it," she concluded.

But Henry was not at all interested in his Christmas tree. What he seemed determined to do was to go to La Guardia Field to watch the airplanes.

"But they won't be coming today, darling," she tried to explain. "There's been a storm; they'll all be grounded."

He ran to the window. "Oh, but, Grandma, the storm's over. Look — there's the sun. There'll be lots of planes. Plenty," he said with emphasis. What he was thinking about, obviously, was his mother and the Captain.

"Have you any special reason for wanting to go today?" she inquired.

"Well, yes," he said; "they'd be coming."

"Who?" she asked, pretending innocence.

"Mum and Captain Fletcher."

She thought, she said, that it was most unlikely they'd come by plane. There had been a blizzard in the West. One had to cross the Rockies. They'd arrive by train.

He remained unconvinced. "Oh, no, they won't," he said. For Captain Fletcher to take a train was as improbable as for a fish to travel overland or a bird to swim beneath the sea.

She followed him to the window. "I've not heard a word from your mother. Strange she didn't telegraph," she said.

"She'll be coming."

"How do you know, dear?"

"She promised she'd be here for Christmas."

"Did she, dear?"

"We're going to the movies," he explained. "Mum and the Captain promised me."

Standing beside him, looking through the windows, she was suddenly aware of a kind of eerie delight. The sun was out and the wind blowing. Whirled from the neighboring ledges, cornices, and balconies, innumerable rainbow-tinted specks of snow were spinning, gyrating in the air and forming, as they spun about, a delicate and spectral screen through which she looked out on the usual view. There, underneath the smoldering winter sky and looking as though fabricated of the most insubstantial materials and likely at any instant to be blown away with the winds and snows and clouds, stood the skyscrapers — some of them, like mountains with their summits hidden, only partially visible; and so fantastic, so fairylike and fabulous the scene appeared to her, standing here beside Henry, looking westward toward the streets that had been so familiar to her half a century ago (there, in Forty-ninth Street, Mrs. Constable had had her house; in Fifty-third Street her parents had built their substantial pretentious dwelling — and Uncle Lionel lived a little to the east), she felt a strangeness in her heart and a feeling mounting in her like a supplication, that there was no reality about it, that she'd dreamed it all — these skyscrapers and La Guardia Field and the Grumman Hellcats, and the B-29's, Hiroshima, Nagasaki, Captain Fletcher and her little grandson with his infernal playthings. They could not be true. There was no reality in them. Men could not have conceived all these things, and within one person's memory. No, she thought, there's nothing real about it. It isn't real, it can't be true — and whether she was addressing life or God or mankind she didn't know, turning to Henry and begging him to go into the bedroom and to get ready to go out.

"Put on your snow-suit," she said. "Delia Stone will be here in a few minutes and I think it will be nice for you to go to Central Park; there'll be so much snow; and you can buy yourself a shovel on the way."

No, he said, he didn't want to shovel snow; he wanted to go to La Guardia Field to watch the planes come in.

How curious, she thought, catching a somewhat arrogant look on the little boy's face. She'd never noticed *that* before. The child resembled Mrs. Constable. She had often seen a similar expression on the old lady's face.

"Go, darling, please," she urged. "Put on your snowsuit. Remember the cap with the ear tabs and the snow boots; it's very cold."

Much to her surprise, he turned and obeyed her, looking very crestfallen and sorrowful. Poor child, she thought, he was obviously worried about his mother and the Captain.

And then (it couldn't be possible he'd resemble Mrs. Constable — most unlikely, most improbable) she saw the old lady as though she were standing before her and experienced all the discomfort she used to feel in her presence; she heard the cracked, authoritative voice that had registered with such emphasis every shade of prejudice and opinion ("When I was a gairl — "), and she seemed to be looking straight into that cold, handsome countenance, bony, fine-drawn, as though the high cheekbones, the aristocratic thin-bridged nose, the well-cut lips, her lofty forehead and even the expression of her mouth and eyes had been exquisitely carved and executed in ivory — the skin, pulled over the ivory armature, well preserved and the hair piled high on her head, perfectly white above her black eyebrows, lending her large penetrating eyes a peculiar sharpness and brilliancy.

"When I was a gairl — " She used to wonder every time the old lady came out with it if it wasn't all a hoax, for obviously what she had been in her "gairlhood" was in every respect the exemplary young creature on whom Hilly was expected to model herself, and how never speaking unless one was spoken to, remembering on all occasions that a "gairl" was to be seen and not heard, becoming, in fact, docile and obedient to the point of self-extinction was likely to make out of anyone a belle, a creature capable of smashing the heart of every male in her vicinity, it was difficult to figure out.

However, her parents would have it that Mrs. Constable had been the most fascinating, the most capricious and beautiful young woman in seven counties. They used to say all kinds of remarkable things about her; she was a "great lady," a perfect woman of the world — being, as they'd go on to explain, "of it but not in it"; this small final phrase, she remembered, they had always emphasized, as though it let both themselves and Mrs. Constable off from any suggestion that they put too much store on their association with the merely mundane and fashionable.

They were under her spell and she both used them and dominated them. Papa advised her in all her financial affairs. She used to drive over from her estate, the Sycamores, some fifteen miles away, a long distance in those days, and she'd bring her maid and her bags and her little dogs. She and Papa would hold long conferences together. One could guess pretty well how the stock market had been behaving and what Papa thought of the future of his country by the timbre of their voices and the cadence of their laughter and badinage when they emerged from those long sessions; and the prevalent idea that she was going to "do something very handsome by Hilly" became, as a result of their conferences, as plain as day and as right as rain.

They had their schemes; and she'd always vaguely recognized it, being a tool in Mrs. Constable's hands. A hundred times she'd heard the story how she'd been widowed twice and how, her only child, a daughter by her first marriage, having died in childbirth, she had taken William — "poor William" — into her own home to bring him up in a station befitting his position in society.

Poor William Danforth. She found it impossible to separate her memories of him from her sense of Mrs. Constable, her house, her property and that peculiar climate into which one immediately stepped whenever one went on a visit to the Sycamores. Ten or twelve years older than herself, heavy, rather handsome in his inexpressive way, there he'd always be, allowing himself to be seen but not heard, coming regularly to his meals and sitting in stolid acquiescent silence.

With what vividness she recalled those interminable mid-day dinners — the large dining room, the great ugly sideboard, the huge table, the heavy carved chairs, the long French windows opening on the lawn, where the shadows deepened and the beauty softly led the eyes off and away to the view, between the tall guardian trees, of the river below them and a bend in the river and the hills beyond, while the singing of the birds and the wind in the leaves and the scent and sense of summer gave her always that feeling of having escaped in spirit with the shadows and the songs and the movement of the trees, beyond the lawn, beyond the river, beyond the hills, and of being at the same time imprisoned in the boring, intolerable moments, listening with an ecstasy of protest to the repetitious conversation, wondering would she ever again be free.

There he'd sat; and there had been her parents and Mrs. Constable and the other guests. She used to wonder how. William could stand it — always being under the ordinance and direction of the formidable old lady and, what with having stared at him so much and having accumulated so many pictures of him at those endless feasts, she could actually see him in the flesh, seated dumb and rather gluttonous through the splendid and ordered progression of the courses, rising when the meal was over to push back Mrs. Constable's chair, assisting her to her feet, saying "yes, marm; no, marm" whenever she spoke to him (she required this salutation from him, much as a monarch might require it from a subject). "Yes, marm; no, marm" — she could hear his polite and expressionless voice; and when, as was inevitable, someone would inquire, taking up one of the priceless plates, a goblet, or a wineglass, was it Sèvres, was it Meissen, or Venetian, or Bohemian, she could see him, turning the plate, holding up the glass as though he enjoyed this little office of inspection and dumb assent. He only spoke on the rare occasions when Mrs. Constable addressed him ("yes, marm; no, marm"). And there he'd sit, partaking abundantly of the rich delicious food and with a singular lack of animation on his handsome ruddy countenance. Hard to imagine a young man having, day after day, to endure it without protest — the examination of the glass and china, all that enthusiastic comment on the floral decorations, the compliments for Mrs. Constable, her jewels, her costumes, the preservation of her youth, compliments for the place, the garden, the gardener and the vegetables; and, like a major theme in the little symphony of polite, well-regulated voices, those compliments for the invisible Marinello — Marinello's pot-au-feu, his vol-au-vents, Marinello's sauces, his roasts, his potatoes and squash and peas, his lima beans.

William ate; he listened. Mrs. Constable apparently expected nothing more of him. She liked to have him there, opposite her, the head of the family, and she always referred to him as "my William" — my William thinks this, or my William prefers that or the other — which was perhaps legitimate, as who could tell what William really did think or prefer? When the meal was over, he would accompany her into the drawing room. Then he would disappear. He had a room consecrated to his own pursuits, "William's den." And here, quite alone, he spent the greater part of his time. There were pipes and guns, fishing rods, pictures of dogs and birds — everything, in fact, to substantiate the legend that had grown up around him and which, somehow, seemed to explain him and lend a certain color and prestige to his dumbness and solitude — "William loves the country"; it appeared that he was already, or was presently going to be, "the perfect type of country gentleman." He used to go out with his dog and his gun, and his capacity for solitude and silence was certainly formidable.

At this point in her ruminations Mrs. Danforth jumped as though she had been shot by a pistol, for there was the door bell; and here was Henry arrayed in his snowsuit.

"Door-bell, Grandma," he cried and disappeared.

Another telegram, she thought, and her heart began to beat violently while she waited for Henry to return (remarkable how many things he could do — only six years old and signing for telegrams); and the message was surely from Larry — oh, she wished she hadn't been so impulsive; it was a mistake to have interfered, a great mistake.

"It's another telegram, Daisy Mae."

"Did you sign, dear?" she asked, taking the envelope from the breathless little boy.

"Sure thing. It's from Mum and the Captain. You wait; you see. They'll be flying home."

She read the telegram, conscious of a curious relief in her heart, for it was not from Larry after all. "Yes," she said, "Henry, you were right. And I was right, too. They took a plane; but they're arriving nonetheless by train," and she read the message aloud: "Grounded Santa Fe. Now traveling home on Chief. Hope to be back for Christmas. Lots of love."

"Then they're married?"

"I should think so, dear."

"Oh, boy," he cried, "they're married!" but his expression seemed to indicate a little disappointment at the Captain's failure to arrive by plane. The air was his natural element. "How long will it take for them to get here?" he inquired.

She looked at the telegram, which had apparently been sent from the train. "Tomorrow morning, I should think, they'd be here," she said, trying to figure it out and wondering what they were doing in Santa Fe. "That is, if the storm didn't delay them," she added.

"When's Christmas?" he inquired.

"Henry Danforth! You don't *know?* Christmas is day after tomorrow. Tomorrow night is Christmas Eve. They ought to get here for our tree."

He agreed — they should be here for Christmas. They had promised to take him to the movies.

"But *what,*" she said, "has happened to Delia Stone?" And she regarded Henry and told him that he ought not to stay all bundled up in this steam-heated apartment. "You can go down if you wish to, dear, and wait outside with the doorman. And when Delia comes, bring her up for just a moment. I want her to do some errands."

"Okay," he said and was gone.

No, she reflected, Larry wouldn't telegraph; he'd just come along. He was just perverse enough; her telling him not to come had been a great mistake. A great mistake. But she must not worry or interfere. She must let events follow their own course.

And how utterly impossible it was, she thought, continuing her ruminations, for her ever to think of Larry as in any way connected with his father. Larry the son of Mrs. Constable's William; and this curious little Henry the old lady's great-great-grandson. Life was stranger than fiction; and why in the world she'd ever allowed them to get her married to William she would never be quite able to explain with any satisfaction.

There had been that great affair of her coming out and her utter inability to become a belle in society, and then that arid year of traveling about Europe with her parents, the resorts and the dressmakers and the cures and the plans and counterplans and returning home bored and disconsolate, on the verge of a nervous breakdown, and Mrs. Constable always at hand to consult and advise — telling Mamma and Papa so emphatically that she was not made for society, that like herself she was to be "of the world but not in it," and persuading them not to open the cottage at "the Reefs" but to have a long and restful season at "the Meadows"; and then, somehow or other, what with the advent of the automobile making visiting back and forth between the two places so much easier, and with William driving over so frequently either with Mrs. Constable or without her, she found herself definitely headed in the direction of matrimony.

He used to come over frequently and she'd preserved an indelible picture of him, sitting up very high in one of those funny old cars that you climbed into from behind, his cap and goggles pushed back from his forehead and a very foolish expression on his familiar countenance, self-conscious and at the same time determined, that made it as plain as a pikestaff that no matter how distasteful and out of his general stride this role of a suitor might be, it was his firm intention to go through with it dutifully, doggedly, to the end. He always came armed with a gay bouquet of many-colored flowers, freshly picked and giving off the scent of heliotrope, lemon verbena and rose geranium. This he presented, with a stiff, a rather courtly bow and, if unaccompanied by Mrs. Constable, with the compliments of "The Duchess" as he invariably called her (not jokingly but in all seriousness, believing as he did in the largest possible estimate of her grandeur).

He would generally stay for dinner or supper, and after the repast she would have to listen, sometimes chaperoned by her parents but often left alone with him, while he went on in his deliberate, his very earthy and bucolic fashion, to tell her about his plans for the future; for, assisted by Mrs. Constable and greatly encouraged in his enterprise by Papa, he had bought a place adjacent to "the Sycamores," which he intended to farm, thus making for himself an all-the-year-round home and becoming that perfect model of a country gentleman for which God and Mrs. Constable had so obviously designed him. On and on he would go — all about pigs and cattle and manure and the rotation of crops, and patiently she sat, patiently she listened.

What a sigh of infinite relief she always gave when he departed, and with what bored acquiescence she would listen to the references and innuendos. For somehow, somehow or other, it had got into everybody's mind that he was her beau (her swain, as they said in those days) and that he was paying her marked attentions. The visits became more and more frequent; but at just what point she became engaged to William she would have been unable to say, or whether, indeed, as they used to express it, he ever "proposed for her hand." He used to say, "That is a very pretty dress, Hilly" or "You're looking well this evening"; and there was so much talk in the air about what Mrs. Constable was going to do for him and how pleasant the old house on his property was going to be when thoroughly renovated and she took so many "spins" in his car and spent so many nights with Mrs. Constable, so many fragrant little bouquets were presented, so many affectionate little jokes were exchanged between Mamma and Papa and the friendship between the two families so firmly cemented that — well — there it was (to this day she could give no clearer account of how it had come about), she was not only privately, she was officially engaged to William Danforth. That everybody, William himself included, regarded it as a most suitable match there was not the shadow of a doubt.

So at long last Mamma and Papa were in a position to make for her benefit their final gesture of lavish extravagance — the gesture for which, very likely, all the others had been but mere tryouts and dress rehearsals — to "give her," as they very unctuously put it, her wedding.

Lord, what a wedding it had been! She didn't, in looking back upon it now, remember that she'd had any hand in the preparations, the whole stupendous affair, even to the choosing of the bridesmaids and ushers, having been planned and executed by her parents and Mrs. Constable. What she did remember, however, was that sense of tension — something electric and nervous in the air and Papa holding onto himself, for it was apparently one of those periodic moments of business anxiety, but whether it was the sudden drop in Anaconda or Amalgamated or the mines in Alaska she couldn't recall; something certainly was amiss.

However, on the ceremonial day both parents had been in the best of spirits — perfectly delighted with everything: the bride and the groom, the quality of the champagne, the beauty of the floral decorations and the lovely appearance of the bridesmaids. And why not? Had they not pulled off, for the sake of their dear little daughter (who was, as she had been so often assured, "all they had on earth"), their crowning gift and sacrifice?

She'd had, to be sure, the oddest sense of being an outsider at the spectacle, and she recalled going through with it, all in the clear June sunlight, with a smell on the air of trodden grass and fête champêtre, standing there under the elm trees on the lawn above the river, while the wind moved in the boughs and the scent of pollens blew in from the meadows, thinking not so much of the solemn nature of the vows which she and William were taking as of the lovely scene before her — blue sky, green lawns and leaves, the red-and-white-striped marquee, the gaiety and frivolity of the ladies' hats, their dresses, the gentlemen in their white flannel trousers, the bridesmaids and the flowers so fresh and frilled and perfect, the whole vivid and colorful picture as bright and precise as a Persian miniature.

Then, abruptly, the orchestra beginning to play the Mendelssohn march and the static quality of the picture breaking up and that sudden, disconcerting realization that she and William Danforth were man and wife — bound to each other for the rest of their lives — wondering how on earth it had come about and why she had ever lent herself to the appalling project. Nevertheless, knowing that she was in it up to her neck, shaking hands with all the guests as they came up in an endless line to congratulate her, hearing the compliments, receiving the kisses, while at very regular intervals Mrs. Constable shrieked out at the very top of her cackle, "She's a lucky gairl — William's a lucky young man," and saying "yes indeed, yes indeed" — regarding William going through with it stolidly, politely, and thinking of life as it stretched ahead of her, endless and monotonous, feeling a kind of panic dread overtake her at the thought of that wedding trip in the new automobile, all so nicely planned for them, right up into Canada and back again, dreading those first nights of being William's bride — haunted, she remembered still, by the thought of Uncle Philip and Aunt Adelaide who, in spite of all the tragedies that had befallen them, had once been so dead in love with each other; wishing, as she stood there receiving the compliments and the kisses, that she could turn tail and run away from this new life that had been so skillfully prepared for her.

But then it hadn't, Mrs. Danforth thoughtfully acknowledged, been so appallingly awful, after all. Few marriages could have been less romantic. She'd not been in love with William and certainly he'd not even pretended to be in love with her. And yet, the direct, the simple manner in which he'd taken what he so courteously referred to as "the pleasures of the marriage bed" was, whenever she thought of him, the thing about him that she'd liked the best — so honest and primitive. And she had allowed him those privileges, without passion to be sure, but with a certain luxury of relaxed nerves, a sense of faithfully fulfilling her contract with nature, that being woman had not been without sentiment and sanctity; indeed, there had been many moments with William fast asleep and snoring beside her when she had lain there praying he might awake and turn to her with words of tenderness and that she might, returning his embraces, learn from him a little some-thing of the mystery and poetry of love.

However, William had felt no need for either tenderness or romance. He seemed content with what he had — the pleasures of the marriage bed, a certain order and decorum, a well-kept house — these things, he felt, as a gentleman and Mrs. Constable's grandson, were his natural due. And the boredom that she had imagined as stretching out eter-nally ahead of her had not as a matter of fact to be endured, for when, after returning from their wedding trip, the real business of settling down began, there had been apparently plenty for them to talk about — the house and the farm and the planning of the garden, the disposal of the wedding presents; and how really delightful it had been to have, for the first time in her life, a home that she could in a measure think of as her own, to have her own garden, and her own drawing room, a front door through which she could enter her own hall — she remem-bered wondering, finding it all so much easier than she'd imagined, if there hadn't been involved in accepting it so easily some shameful ca-pitulation, the surrendering of every valuable expectation and desire.

Yet she hadn't questioned too much. She'd let the days go by. She'd suffered William to be himself, to go about the farm just as he had at Mrs. Constable's. Each day the same routine, the same old tweeds, old slouch hats, the same dull enjoyment of his leisurely outdoor life, and every night insisting on the accustomed decorum, sitting there oppo-site her, at the candle-lit table, a rather elegant, a very exacting gen-tleman, wanting everything ordered, formal — just as it had been at Mrs. Constable's — insisting on ritual, fuming if the plates were not sufficiently hot, or complaining about the roasts, having this platter sent away or that dish removed from his sight.

The days passed, not too unhappily (one flowed into another); the months passed. Then, in August, when the phlox was blazing in the gardens and the joe-pye weed and fireweed were blooming along the roadsides, she'd discovered her astounding secret. She'd kept it to herself; she'd guarded it with the utmost jealousy. She couldn't bring herself to tell William or her parents. Simply she'd not been able to tell a soul. Above all, to confide in Mrs. Constable had seemed impossible, for she realized she'd been preparing herself, for the first time in her life, if not for rebellion, at least to take her own stand and to be resolute in allowing nobody on earth to own the soul and body of her child. Looking back on those early experiences of pregnancy, how extraordinarily rich they had been — like a startling and appeasing exploration of her own soul, her own depths and the capacity within her to love. August went into September and September into the mildest October days.

And, finally, that soft and lovely autumn morning — William's joining her in the garden before breakfast (she was picking roses, she remembered), with those hideous emotions disfiguring his face — astonishment, anger, accusation — handing her without a single word the morning paper, and how she'd stood there staring at that picture of her father with the headlines sprawled across the page: Speculation, Bankruptcy, Suicide; and listening presently to William's voice, hard, indignant, accusatory, telling her with no adornment and no mitigation of the facts the stark and ugly truth about it — that Papa had, in fact, been using Mrs. Constable's securities for enterprises of his own; that he'd bought on margin; that he'd tried desperately to cover; he'd thrown good money after bad, Mrs. Constable's money. There had not been a suggestion of sympathy in his voice for either her mother or herself. There was the one calamitous fact to confront — Mrs. Constable's money was gone. He was going in his car, he said, to see "the Duchess." There might perhaps be something saved. He'd return as soon as possible and take her to "the Meadows." Her mother would want to see her.

And off he'd gone and she'd never laid eyes on him again.

There she'd sat in the garden waiting; she'd never known how long (minutes were hours and hours minutes, in such moments of shock), but presently — she couldn't say today whether it had been morning or afternoon — Taylor, Mrs. Constable's coachman, and his wife had arrived, bringing news of yet another disaster, for Mr. William, as they told her — Mrs. Constable's William — had been hideously, instantly killed at the dangerous railroad crossing by the river, rushing recklessly across the tracks to get to Mrs. Constable. She'd remained in the garden; and she'd had, she remembered, the illusion that she was holding a living child in her arms, trying to protect him.

From what? she asked herself, getting up to answer the bell (for Henry was punching it vigorously). And, actually feeling that Larry was pressed against her breast, she opened the door.

And here was Henry, followed by Delia Stone, bursting in with a new request.

Couldn't he, couldn't Delia — couldn't they both *please* go to Times Square? There was, it seemed, a captured German plane in the Square. It had lots of bullet holes in it; it had lots of swastikas painted on its nose. It was a honey. It was the real McCoy. Oh, please, Grandma, he pleaded. He didn't see why he had to go and shovel snow in the Park with a little sissy shovel. Please, Grandma, he begged. He hated it — going to the Park. That was sissy stuff.

PART 2

S E V E N

LARRY WOKE UP. He felt as though he'd been wrestling with an adversary too strong for him — trying to push off this heavy weight (was it the blankets or merely the misery in his heart?). Phew! he was exhausted. He took some long, deep breaths. Had he been dreaming or attempting to verify a memory? Could it, he wondered, actually have been a fact that on some dim occasion when he was scarcely two years old he had witnessed a struggle both violent and violating between them, there in the shadow of the mimosa bush and with the Mediterranean brimming the terrace wall, that big flood of breeze and sea and lovely morning flowing round them? And why, for God's sake, did he have to regard as at all authentic this vaguest of all his recollections? The only guarantee of its reality was simply this, that he could never smell so much as a whiff of mimosa without being at once assailed by a sense of sudden and startling initiation — sharing, as he seemed to be, with his mother and his Great-uncle Philip an emotional climate very disturbing and intense.

He wanted to share exclusively with Hilly that old garden on the Riviera. It was his lost paradise. He was always, in one way or another, attempting to return to it. There, as a matter of fact, he seemed to be at this moment, treading those walks and pathways, terraced back and out again, held so high aloft above the winding Corniche Drive, the hills billowing off and away into the hinterland and, before his eyes, vineyards, villas, fruit trees all in bloom, roses clambering over terrace walls, oleanders swimming off into the blue, the fresh sea breeze so excessively delightful, rifted with warmth and those exotic southern fragrances — mimosa, freesia, jasmine — while he and Hilly rounded that sharp corner and were so startlingly confronted by that view of the Mediterranean dropped sheer and far below them, brimming the terrace wall, carried up into wide gulfs of sky and air and stretching out before their eyes to the horizon's edge, the whitecaps flying off the waves and the sea gulls sailing into the mists and the ships and sailboats tossing on its breast, those recessional harbors all along the coast, with their quays and ships, their crescent beaches, the softly fading houses, bright in the sunshine, so gay, so parti-colored, so deliciously European.

He remembered how she had once, pointing to the Iles d'Hyères (there was Port Cros, there was Porquerolles, there was Levant), stretched out her hand and, opening it, declared that she always had the feeling in this particular spot that she was carrying the whole Côte-d'Azure in the hollow of her hand, and how he had at once visualized the pretty fancy, seeing the neat indentations of the coast, the harbors and the houses, the orchards and vineyards, the mountains, the wide blue Mediterranean itself, with the gulfs and ships and the islands, offered him in the hollow of her beloved hand.

And, actually, what an accurate symbol of her intentions toward him that had been — holding in her hand, and for his unique appreciation, Europe: all the landscapes, cities, towns, cathedrals, galleries; so anxious to absorb it with him, so bent on getting it woven into the very texture of their hearts, the process accompanied in the weirdest possible manner with a kind of heartache and homesickness, a sense of exclusion from the values she was seeking. For, in spite of their love, their almost idolatrous attachment (and brought the nearer to each other for the exclusion), they had always felt that they were strangers in an alien land.

There had been those journeys they'd taken together, he remembered, from his earliest childhood, going from Paris to the Riviera and then from home to Paris again — the stations and the voices, the arrivals and departures, with the ear trained to the conversations and inflections of his fellow travelers, and knowing, though French was his native tongue, and speaking it as fluently as any little French boy, that he and his mother were invariably taken for Americans. He had felt a sense of separateness in these designations (what should they be doing here, with such remarkably perfect accents, not French people, but Americans?). And what, he used to wonder, would be the mystery about it? For, indeed, there had always seemed to be something of peculiar mystery and sentiment bringing him over, as she actually had, to be born in Europe, "giving him" languages, "giving him" as much, poor dear, as she possibly could of the old countries, so young herself and so naive and generous and ardent, never as explicit as she might have been about the meaning of her gifts and intentions.

He turned on the light, glanced at his watch. It was one o'clock. He had slept only an hour or two and was not likely to go to sleep again, what with all these decisions he had to make, thrashing out his problems and trying to come to grips with himself. Now, why had Anne sneaked off in Reno and sent him that immediate message? What was the meaning of it? He fumbled among the books and papers on his table and found her telegram, read it aloud: "'Married Captain Fletcher AAF this morning. Very happy. Love. Anne.'" What the devil? He shrugged his shoulders. Was she inviting him to come and take a look at her young hero? What was she up to? Evidently she wanted to see him. Had half a mind not to go to New York, after all. Wished he hadn't telegraphed Hilly. However, the time had come for him to break with Gerald. He had made up his mind to this. He must sever his connections with Jerry. Didn't like to think about it. It was going to be devilishly difficult — hurting the poor fellow the way he had to; but then, it hurt them both a damned sight more for him to hang around here behaving so outrageously.

He got up, went to the window and looked out. Snow piled up on either side the street, white on the rooftops, white and frosty on the air, and over Alexandria, over Washington the stars very brilliant in the clear night sky. "To hell with it — to hell with all of it," he said.

For it was this obsession with his mother that was doing him in; it was at the bottom of all his despair — he was continually harassed by it, unable to forgive her, tortured by petty, irrelevant, ignoble grudges and resentments, accusing, blaming her, sometimes actually despising her; never assuaged without her presence at his side.

Oh, yes, he knew all about it; he'd gone over the ground scrupulously — not an inch of those old memories he hadn't traversed. Though Anne had spent hours with that idiot analyst, though she had all the words and could repeat all the rigmarole, the facts were in his possession. Hilly, too, possessed the facts; he could swear to it.

God, how much there was, if he went into it, for which he could hold her to account! She'd made such grave mistakes. And why, why the devil she'd ever believed that bringing him to Europe would accomplish such miracles of culture and character he'd never been able to make out — subjecting him, as she had, to the influence of those damned-fool relatives, Aunt Adelaide, Uncle Philip, her poor mother trailing around after them bewailing her diminished fortune, her fading beauty, pathetically attempting to keep up the ancient grandeur, dying pitifully in that big dilapidated villa at Cannes. What kind of an education, considering her background and her associates, had she been prepared to offer him? What had he derived from those weird Anglo-American colonies in Paris, Florence, Rome, Geneva, from all that indolent enjoyment of sea and scenery on the Riviera? To be sure, she'd been very young when she'd fled America and she'd hated from her soul the American scene as she had known it in her youth. For her to have thought that she could find a better substitute in the Europe she had offered him was, to put it mildly, naive. How tenaciously, poor darling, she'd clung to beauty, art, the aesthetic and cultural values. But why, why the devil hadn't she had the sagacity to perceive that such a banquet as she had prepared, served up with her own adorable charms, her quick untutored response to beauty in all its forms, could only have assisted her in completing the ruin?

He closed the window, pulled down the shade and went back to bed. Couldn't sleep; couldn't make his plans; was apparently obsessed with the memories. Aunt Adelaide, Uncle Philip moved in and out of his thoughts, brushed him with a sense of the past. He seemed to see them, to hear them speak.

Aunt Adelaide, large and florid, with a face and figure that declared her unabashed indulgence in every variety of good food and wine, her fading hair dyed a somewhat lifeless auburn, her brilliant complexion none too skillfully made up, still affecting the airs and attributes of an enchantress, speaking English with a slight French accent and French with a decidedly American accent, and with a fluency that failed to disguise her constant grammatical inaccuracies, never at a loss in any situation, always flattering and conversational and with something sensuous and insinuating about her every move and note and accent — the small caressing music of her laughter, her smiles, the amiable mur-

murs that constantly escaped her lips seeming somehow to imply that her only purpose in life was to captivate, to love and seduce the entire world — affectionate, expansive and sentimental. How happy she had been to embrace and take to her bosom not only her dear Hilly, who had so unexpectedly, so perfectly delightfully come into her life, but the even more to be cherished and desired little boy who was the light of her heart and the very apple of her eye!

And Uncle Philip, with his startling red beard and those extraordinary wide blue eyes, the slender grace and distinction he affected set off so elegantly by his tailor and the more careful restraint of his appetites, as well as by the free and easy manner in which Adelaide displayed all that she possessed of the round, the ripe, and the voluptuous, was a considerably more arresting character. How she doted on him — loved to make herself out the dumb, the uninformed, uneducated member of the partnership! "Philip knows everything; but everything," he could hear the lazy voice drawling it out. "Philip knows Europe like a book; so nice to have a Baedeker always in one's pocket." They made a great feature of his linguistic talents. He had, as a matter of fact, mastered none of the languages he spoke so fluently, but he found it easy not only to move from one tongue, but from one gesture and inflection, to another. Assisted by his various canes and hats and costumes and with a certain gift he had for imitation, taking on the small national foibles and mannerisms — the Italian play of hands and shoulders, the Frenchman's shrug and nonchalance — what a vivid, fluttering little figure he had cut. Wanted to make you the gift of his soul as well as the treasures of his intellect. Not an authority on any subject, or endowed with the slightest originality of mind, how glibly he talked and with what a sighing, gasping effusiveness he loved and hated! With his good memory for all the pictures he'd seen and every little town and church he'd visited and his manner of putting his soul so immodestly on display, together with Aunt Adelaide's excellent showmanship, the two of them had managed to establish quite a legend about him, his cultivation and scholarship.

Lord how they "adored" Europe — expanded in its ambient — and how happily, without a responsibility in the world, they sank into its easy graceful way of life. How fecklessly they fed their souls on this and that and the other thing — travel, art, scenery, indolence — and how they indulged themselves in diatribes against America, its haste, its waste, its "vulgarity." It was, they declared, ruined by money, business, materialism.

With their villa at Mentone so near at hand, their tips and their trips, their effusions and attentions, they'd certainly made life exceedingly pictorial and kaleidoscopic, filled it with change and movement, brightness, beauty. Why, the memory of his childhood was like a delightful pageant in which he had somehow always managed to play the most conspicuous role. Whirled along in carriages or motorcars, enveloped in clouds of dust, veils floating, parasols fluttering, Hilly on one side of him, Aunt Adelaide on the other, and Uncle Philip generally opposite, how like a small prince he'd felt, the ocean flashing out and disappearing again, clouds and mountains so serene and friendly, little landscapes smiling brightly in his heart; and finding himself so frequently in beautiful gardens or on sunny terraces under striped umbrellas, with vines and breeze and shadows circulating freely, gazing happily out on views, on lakes, on oceans, valleys, mountains (maybe the Mediterranean, the Aegean, the Adriatic, perhaps the Lago di Garda, or Mont Blanc and the lake of Geneva), while miraculously, and as though summoned for his particular benefit, there had appeared at his elbow cups of chocolate, trays of the most delectable confectionery in pretty fluted boxes, and everybody attending on the choice he made of these enticing delicacies, knowing many eyes were fixed upon him and that he was, without a doubt, the most charming of creatures, dressed in his sailor suit, his broad-brimmed hat, and with that way he had of making everybody laugh every time he opened his little mouth.

Yet with all this bounty and beneficence, had he, not always been conscious of a small lurking desire, subtly communicated to him by Hilly, to escape Aunt Adelaide and Uncle Philip altogether, to be off somewhere quite alone with her, entirely happy and appeased?

Just when he'd first become aware of Hilly's downright aversion to them he would not be able to determine. They had certainly been instrumental, at the panic time of the First World War, when all the securities and sanctities of life had been in danger of collapsing altogether, in having him sent to that phony boarding school in Vevey, coming almost at once to settle in Geneva, where Hilly had taken up her residence. During those years, what with his indispositions and ill-nesses, and being so often taken out of school on one pretext or an-other, he was frequently exposed to their doting, easygoing, pleasure-loving society.

Difficult for him today to think without anger of Hilly, so naturally fastidious and intelligent, having subjected him to what he would al-ways regard as the thoroughly perverting and corrupting influences of the relatives; and that she hadn't freed herself earlier from all the snares and invitations, the bewildering suggestions and "advantages" they were always offering, he'd never be able to understand.

She'd done so finally — drastically. How she'd managed it, he hadn't known. It must have been a difficult severance, though he couldn't for the life of him recall any definite quarrel or overt farewells. But that winter, when she so obdurately remained in Paris and took their small flat in the Rue d'Ulm, had seen the last of them. They'd simply ceased to figure in their lives. No talk about them, no shadow of regret at their departure — just a sense of freedom, emancipation, happiness.

That home in the Rue d'Ulm! No place in which he'd ever lived re-called such poignant memories — the view of the Panthéon from the window, the shadows of the leaves upon the pavements, the smells and sounds in the rooms, that sense of Paris, simply flooding in upon them. With what ecstasy Hilly had gone about furnishing, making the place attractive, as though the joy she'd felt in being there with him in a home which she was creating unassisted by the relatives could endow all her charming arrangements with a special grace and beauty of their own.

Then there had been his friendship for Pierre, so passionate and so intense and their gradual surrender to the erotic inclinations — the whole overwhelming experience bound up so strangely, so touchingly, with his love for Hilly; finding her, through Pierre's extravagant appre-ciation of her qualities, more beautiful, more beloved than ever, each of them in the most curious and tender manner in love with her and, in that climate she seemed so naturally to distill for them, all affection, harmony and grace, exploring and extending their natural gifts and tal-ents. The three of them so bent on the enjoyment of art and literature and music, it was a springlike interlude for all; for Hilly, he felt sure, the happiest period of her entire life, feeling, as she used to tell them so often, that she had acquired a second son, and so fascinated by Pierre's sensitive mind, the maturity of his nature, so eager to have his intelligence and the wealth of his references inform and influence her dear Larry's literary and aesthetic tastes and predilections, to give him, in fact, the benefits of that European education for which, poor darling, she'd been searching so fruitlessly and so long. How Pierre used to rave about her! He could hear him now. She was unique, so sensitive and direct, so filled with warmth and wonder and curiosity — an artist to her finger tips!

Then there had been that evening when Pierre had played the Beethoven sonata with such fervor and intensity, and that moment when, overcome by emotion and surely by some profound subconscious need to confess their relationship, he'd left the piano, crossed the room and come to him and embraced him with such gravity and passion; and the moment each had known that Hilly had divined their secret, the three of them waiting there, confounded by it, silent, trembling, while the soft spring air, the din and clatter of the streets below came drifting in through all the open windows.

God, to think about Pierre and, above all, to think about Hilly in her relationship to this experience was horribly disturbing. He wasn't at all sure that this crisis hadn't been a turning point in the whole difficult complex of his affection for his mother. Hilly had certainly failed him here. Hadn't wanted *her* feelings thrown at him, this sense he'd somehow received that *she* was suffering. No, hadn't wanted that. He had needed her counsel, her friendship. All this pretended ignorance of knowledge which they shared, knew that they shared in common; well, he found it difficult to forgive her for it — all so damned Victorian, so discreet. Something more courageous had been called for. He supposed she'd managed the superficial situation with skill as well as gentleness. She'd not attempted rudely and immediately to separate him from Pierre; she had relied on their sense of *her* distress, on their delicacy of feeling, their affection for her, to act as moral censor, and the deftness with which she'd kept this strange triangular affection going, on the intellectual and spiritual levels, had been both touching and effectual. But the error had been her continued silence — allowing him to see *her* suffer, her assuming ignorance of the fact that he was suffering also, that he needed more than all things else her assistance in alleviating the sense of guilt and conflict he carried in his heart.

Why had she shied off from the necessary frankness? Had it been pride, prudery or reticence that had kept her silent? Didn't her unwillingness to acknowledge personal acquaintance with a subject she discussed so frequently in a quite impersonal manner, and relating not only to characters in fiction but to the one being on earth for whom she really cared, indicate a kind of moral and spiritual cowardice — a fear of meeting these complex issues, having them out with him? Poor Hilly — he wouldn't know. Strange reticence had been set up between them, the freedom of friendship replaced not by the loss of love but by a loss of ease in its expression, a heightening of emotional tensions — love, you might say, in a curious way driven underground, and nerves, sensibilities, perceptions carrying on the traffic.

Oh, Lord, he thought, overtaken by a sense of enormous compassion, the traps and snares that those who love us most prepare for us.

E I G H T

"CAN YOU BELIEVE IT, ANNE," said the Captain, "our being here together, on this train, on our way to New York to see that kid?"

She smiled. "Yes," she said, "I believe it — here we are," and she
looked out of the window and thought how impossible it was to believe
either in her divorce or her marriage. A kind of nightmare, it seemed
to her — those six weeks in Reno — getting through with all that sordid business, the evidence she'd had to give, and fixing so much guilt
on poor Larry, appearing so victimized, and with the Captain turning
up at just the proper moment, so whole and hale and what you
couldn't but call "adjusted," so filled with zeal and passionate readiness
to take care of her, to make it all up to her; for somehow she had managed — though, God knew, it had not been her intention — to get it
firmly fixed in George's mind that Larry was an unspeakable bounder.
On she'd gone with it — married him only a few hours after the final
papers were signed and then stealing off, the very first chance she had
to do so, to send that unfortunate telegram to Larry (she'd regretted it
ever since): "Married Captain Fletcher AAF this morning. Very happy.
Love. Anne." When she'd asked herself whether a need to hurt him
further because of injuries sustained at his hands had prompted her to
send it, or maybe just the need she'd felt to communicate with him,
some sneaking hope that such a telegram might stimulate that tendency in him toward mischief and bring him on to New York to play a
little with her feelings, she had not been able to answer her own question. It was all most intricate. And as for believing in this honeymoon
— the two giddy days in San Francisco, and then that fearful plane
trip, running into the blizzard, with the passengers (all but George, of

course) scared out of their wits, landing safely at Albuquerque, that spectral drive to Santa Fe, the night spent there, and now crossing the desert and, as George had just reminded her, on their way together to see Henry — how could she be expected to believe in it?

She stole a glance at him. He was gazing out of the window, looking exceedingly drowsy. "Isn't it beautiful?" she said. "Isn't it strange and beautiful?"

"Swell," he said, "swell."

She regarded the big New Mexican landscape — mesas, lomas, mountains swathed in snow and rising out of the desert with an architectural splendor that simply took one's breath away; the distant mountains standing up against the great horizons, vibrating with such unearthly colors, such celestial lights. Oh, how Larry would have appreciated it! What it would have said to him. Seeing it now in all the splendor of the sunlight and the shadows and the snow. He would certainly have found something better to say than just that it was "swell."

Poor Hilly, she sometimes said that Larry should have been a poet. What an absurd, actually what an ironic remark, since it was very likely her own fault that he'd achieved, for all his gifts and talents, absolutely nothing. It took discipline, application of one's faculties, to write poetry, or, at least, the kind of verse that Larry would have honored by that name, and you couldn't say that Larry's early years had been conducive to any kind of discipline — goodness, when she thought of Larry's childhood!

But what was the use of going into it all again? They'd gone over it so many times. The blame had been laid at Hilly's door. Poor dear, she'd been generous enough about it, more than willing to admit her errors. And hadn't each of them suffered sufficiently, in all conscience, at Larry's hands? Why keep prodding the memories?

She'd be very grateful, however, if she could drive Larry out of her mind for more than half an hour at a time. She was, at the present moment, engaged in contrasting him with George, who, she saw with a good deal of satisfaction, had fallen off to sleep. You could hardly imagine two people who looked less alike —George so dark, with all that black hair neatly brushed and shining on his bullet-shaped head, everything about him well-knit and compact, the bones under the tight brown skin scarcely visible, and the face, without noticeable planes and angles, molded to firmness, rotundity, the features regular and well enough proportioned — a strong honest face, nothing at all arresting about it, except, perhaps, for that suggestion of character (tenacity, you might even say) that stuck out all over him. But to compare his face with Larry's was ridiculous. *There* was a beautiful, an interesting, you'd have to admit it, an arresting countenance — the blond skin, with that sprinkling of freckles around the nose, that seemed somehow to heighten the effect of blondness, that shock of sand-colored hair which, in an odd way, lent a kind of ruggedness to the irregular, the very delicate molding of his features. How well the flesh lay on his bones! There was something (who could deny it) very noble about Larry's appearance.

As for the expressions that played about his features — here you were up against the baffling enigma of Larry's personality. Those blue eyes, changing their shade and depth with the shift and change of his moods, sometimes cold and hard as stone; frequently, with the irises distended, of an exceptional depth and fluidity, and all that area of his face be-tween the cheekbones and the chin so extremely sensitive and subject, like the eyes, to sudden glooms and brightnesses. He seemed to have the capacity, if you could use such an expression, to close his face or open it at the dictates of his own caprice. It could be warm, generous, out-going, filled with an almost feminine ardor; and then, suddenly, it would shut up on you, shut down on you and become hard, sometimes cruel and ironic, as though to indicate that he'd had enough of communion, he wished to be alone. Had you bored, irritated, exasperated him? Just exactly what had transpired in these moments of exclusion from his society she was seldom able to guess. He was the most solitary person she had ever known and, though he was exceptional (oh, she'd stick to this — Larry was an exceptional human being), she sometimes sus-pected that he'd given very little to anyone and that, as a matter of fact, he'd taken from others even less. It was in his enormous concern for the general human plight that his affections were the most implicated; his love for humanity in the large impersonal sense was profound, had something deeply religious about it. It was, she imagined, his restless modern intelligence that did him in — his thoughts and perceptions so overscored that they rendered him the victim of his own sensitiveness. He was at the mercy of certain tricks and habits of bad behavior —

nervous reflexes which apparently he could not control — his sensibilities overactive, short-circuiting each other, no place he didn't get to
with his nerves. She frequently felt as though he were carrying on an intricate system of espionage, the way he got about in other people's
hearts — too many sympathies, insights, divinations — getting everything at once, and no defense against the reflexes.

How horribly he suffered from his own behavior, she knew only too
well; oh, it was this that made her always ready to forgive him — his
capacity to suffer that wrought upon her most and that had developed
in her a positively maternal affection for him; if she had to be honest
about it, her feeling for him very much resembled Hilly's. Hang it all,
she might lay the entire blame on Hilly, but hadn't she perhaps been
caught in Hilly's traps? For here was the oddest thing about it, as far as
Larry was concerned — everybody's getting caught in the same traps.
There were these young men he was always getting entangled with and
who seemed so capable of adoring him, no matter how badly he might
treat them directly his infatuation was over — always hanging round,
clinging on, long after they'd ceased to interest him. That was the
strangest thing — the hold he seemed to have on people and his somewhat queer and certainly exasperating inconsistency in expecting loyalty from those he'd injured most.

Surely, in this last affair with Gerald Styles, he'd tried her to the
utmost — so passionate about it all and so determined to set up that
little establishment in Washington. It was somehow the last straw,
knowing very well that if she kept on with him there'd be new affairs
and suddenly feeling she'd reached the last of her endurance and Hilly
herself taking her side in the matter; yes, a divorce was clearly indicated. But, really now, to have decided in such a hurry to marry
George!

There were moments when she was inclined to blame it all on her
analysis. That it had not had the liberating effect upon her heart she'd
professed to Doctor Brimmer and Daisy Mae, she'd known for a long
time. She had not, it was necessary to admit it, played fair with the
method, the analysis itself. Lying there on that comfortable, weirdly relaxing sofa while Doctor Brimmer listened and took down all those
notes, hadn't she somehow assisted him, consciously assisted him, in
piecing this bit of evidence with that, building up a final picture of her

case on which they both agreed? All those garbled fragments of dreams (how *could* anyone do anything but garble one's dreams?), all those not quite disingenuous confessions — selecting, maybe, rather than pouring out, the incidents revealed. One wanted to be honest; but then one wanted to be pitied a little too — to have one's sorrow understood and, at the same time, to appear very brave and strong and sensible — to get, if possible, one's ticket of release from pain, bewilderment.

And, oh, for God's sake, what an undertaking — revealing to another human being all the secrets of your all-too-human character! After all that spilling over and elaboration, after the whole damned business was, so one pretended, out in the open, shamelessly exposed, to boil it down into these Freudian terms —your behavior, Hilly's behavior, Larry's behavior. It was too easy, too simple, all this terminology. My Lord, when she remembered the way she'd agreed, her self-confidence, all the cocksure things she'd said to Hilly! And if she'd consulted her own heart as scrupulously as all these phrases she'd got down so pat, she might not have acted in quite such haste.

Why *had* she been in such a hell of a hurry to clean up the debris in her heart, to rush off from one marital experience to another? And how could Doctor Brimmer have allowed her to do this? If he'd been any good, any good at all as an analyst, he would have known, as she somehow felt that Hilly knew, how much she still loved poor old Larry. Heavens, after all she'd told him, after all those hours on that wretched sofa, allowing her to decide that it was high time somebody cared for her, loved her truly and unselfishly! As though he shouldn't have seen at a glance that George Fletcher was not the kind of man in a hundred lifetimes she would ever fall for. Granted: he was fine, he was a hero, he was modest and unselfish. Nonetheless, he was — even Doctor Brimmer would admit this — an extrovert, completely extroverted; he was naive, he was simple. Compared to Larry, he was — ah, well, she must not continue with these comparisons.

How soundly he was sleeping and how fatigued he looked. When she thought about his valor, his exploits in the air, really sometimes this modest unpretentious boy, so frightfully in love with her, wanting nothing more than to be her abject slave, struck her with positive awe. He didn't seem so much to be one man as a million incredibly heroic youths. He'd become a thousand millimeters, miles and miles of celluloid history, the whole fabulous drama of the airborne forces. Why, he stood for all the pilots, bombardiers, gunners, navigators, paratroopers that had passed before her eyes, fitting their helmets onto their heads, grinning, tossing off their jests and smiles, tightening their belts and straps, turning back their thumbs for luck, making the V-sign for victory, clambering into their battlewagons; he represented all those huge vehicles of air, hitting the runways, lifting up, flying off into the evening skies, crossing the Channel as the dusk descended, flying over the dunes and downs of Brittany, and then, their mission accomplished, streaking back at dawn. He was all the dead boys, all the wounded lads she'd seen assisted from their planes, and those still hale of life and limb who'd clambered out of them, all the fabulous battles fought in air, tracer bullets tracking their fiery pathway on the night, flares, explosions, rockets, young faces peering into the sky, gunners steady at their guns, navigators scribbling notes, pilots calm at the controls, boys with blood and anguish on their faces crawling from one perilous position to another, aiding their companions; goodness, all the planes, the little fighter planes, the reconnaissance planes, ascending, descending, clouds under them, clouds above them, executing spiral ascents, parabolas, tumbling, tossing in the clouds, righting themselves, soaring on steadfast wings, diving like birds of prey, bursting into flames, falling to earth, boys leaping into the dark, into the clouds of morning, into the innocent blue air. He was all the planes they'd shot from decks of ships, to fare forth alone over the great wastes of the Atlantic, the Pacific. He was the airborne invasions moving like dream processionals before her eyes, the bombers in their majestic formations, gliders towing freight ships laden with boys equipped with all the weird accoutrements of modern war; he was the parachutes drifting like beautiful flowers through the air, dropping the boys upon the beaches, on the deserts, on the islands and the mainlands and the mountains.

My God, had life actually evolved men capable of such incredible, such superhuman valor? Was it possible that she'd looked with her own eyes on these intrepid exploits? How could anyone be persuaded that such youths had lived on this earth? They were mythical, legendary creatures out of Jules Verne or H. G. Wells, or Milton or the Book of Revelation. Not real, she thought, not real. And she glanced at the Captain, who was still asleep with his chin reposing on his uniform, and began repeating to herself that concise and moving tribute to their youth and heroism, which, at the time of our greatest fear, had made them seem almost like saviors of the entire human family: "Never have so many owed so much to so few." Why she remembered how she used to feel a tremendous desire, whenever she passed some young airman on the street, to stop him, shake his hand, and speak her praise and thanks aloud. What romance, what glamour had then attached to them! Now here they were, many of them out of uniform, distributed round the country; you might see them any day selling you groceries at the A & P, jerking soda at the drugstores — young men in filling stations, boys sitting round the bars, having a snack at Nedicks, nothing distinguished about them. Here they were.

And to make life immeasurably strange, here she was — married to one of them herself, Captain Fletcher, wing commander. And when she looked at him and saw graven into his sleeping face the story of his ardor, his passion for her, dear me! When she thought of all he'd put into his big romantic love — their nights together, all he'd put into loving her — it did seem pretty intricate. How could she let him down? The world was in such debt to these young men.

Suddenly George woke up, staggered drowsily to his feet, moved a footrest, adjusted a pillow, looked at her with that doting, loverlike expression that so embarrassed her. "Are you all right, darling?" he said.

"Yes, George, of course," and she attempted to brush away the tears that were rolling down her cheeks, for she was, for Heaven's sake, weeping, and couldn't stop it. She was crying like a baby.

"Why, what's the matter, Anne dearest?" He took out his handkerchief and dried her tears.

"Nothing, George, nothing. I was thinking about Henry. We're sure to be late. We'll never get to New York for Christmas Eve. I want to be with Henry on Christmas Eve."

He reassured her. He took out his watch. "Even if we get to Chicago a little late tomorrow morning, we have a long wait there. We'll be sure to catch the four o'clock — and the next morning, early, there we'll be. A whole day ahead of time."

"But with all this snow," she blubbered, "storms everywhere. It will be snowing in Chicago. It will be snowing in New York — trains late all along the line."

He got up with alacrity, pulled a traveling case from under the seat, opened it and took out some little boxes which contained a variety of toy airplanes. He hadn't, he explained, intended to show them to her until Christmas. They were for that kid of theirs. He took up one after another, examined each one closely, and began putting them through their various turns and flights. They were beautiful toys, he declared, designed with real knowledge of the original models.

It was decent of him, she thought, his allowing her time to get hold of herself without further fuss. She watched him handling the little playthings with his strong, expert hands and thought what a fascination he held for Henry. She did wish, however, that he'd stop talking about the child as their "kid." It was undoubtedly her fault for letting him assume so much proprietorship. Henry certainly doted upon him. Nonetheless, the child had a father of his own, and George should not forget it. He simply waved Larry aside as though he didn't exist, and this also, she supposed, was her fault; for George, to her everlasting regret, had it all fixed up in his mind that Larry was a rotter and she, herself, the victim of great wrongs.

"Beautiful little gadgets, aren't they?" He presented her with a small silver bomber that flashed in the strong bright light.

"Yes, beautiful," she said, letting it drop in her lap and changing the subject with a suddenness that caught him off his guard. "Where did you spend last Christmas, George?" she asked.

"I was in France." His voice was laconic. They were, he reminded her, fighting the Battle of the Bulge.

"Oh, yes, of course; what an awful time! And the Christmas before last? Where were you then, George?"

"In the hospital," he said. "That was after my big smash-up." He shut his mouth rather stubbornly — didn't want to go into it.

He was always putting her off about his war experiences. Was this a private hell into which he was determined to descend as infrequently as possible? Or was it, rather, that those years belonged to a department of his life — bloody, valorous, brutal, masculine — which he did not intend to share with her? Probably there were, for George, two worlds — a man's world and a woman's world — and from the former he was determined to exclude her. There were the sacred and the profane departments. He wished to keep her pure, unspotted by reality. He was all up in the air about her. Lord, when she thought of the last few nights and how she'd done her best to respond to his passion, to the romantic key in which he'd pitched his lovemaking — good Lord! When she thought of the sentiments, the convictions, the misconceptions that lurked in this simple passionate boy, she couldn't help feeling a little frightened. This need he felt to protect her! To protect her from what, for Heaven's sake — from life, experience? The way he'd got her little Henry framed up in the picture — two people for him to protect. How could it ever be made clear to him that, though Larry presented problems, he was, after all, a man you couldn't hate? He had great gifts, great qualities; he was indeed unique, important in his own peculiar way. Could she ever get this through the Captain's head? And oh, my goodness, how she. wished she had not sent that telegram! Would it induce Larry to come on for Christmas? Sometime they'd have to meet.

The tears again welled up in her eyes. They rolled down her cheeks. And now he was doing exactly what she'd been afraid he would do. He was taking her in his arms; he was embracing her. It was most embarrassing.

"Darling," he whispered. "Darling, we'll get there in time. I'll guarantee it."

She looked at him through her tears. Then, suddenly, they were laughing into each other's eyes like a pair of lovers. How strange life was, how intricate, how unbelievable! Here, in this train, kissing George, with all these people watching them and that Indian sitting there at the end of the car, with his rugs and his turquoise bracelets, staring at them too; and these mountains, these mesas and lomas looming up out of the desert so spectral, so beautiful.

N I N E

LARRY DUMPED THE CONTENTS of a large pigskin bag he'd been attempting to fill onto the floor. He'd about made up his mind to go, but packing was the devil. Why should he have to take more than a suitcase? Would it be advisable to pack this old blue coat? He lifted it from the floor, regarded it, slung it over his arm; and what, good Lord, with all these shoes, trousers, ties, collars, books, soiled linen, goddamned laundry bags (he kicked the latter into the middle of the room), did he actually intend to do? A hell of a mess of things to dispose of. It was appalling, in the face of confusion like this, how helpless he was — helpless as a baby — always expecting someone to stand between him and the little difficulties. He'd managed all his life to get himself a nurse or a guardian (his mother, his Great-aunt Adelaide, Anne, Jerry), waiting on him hand and foot, liberating his soul for the higher flights, all of them convinced that he was an unusual fellow — spilling round their inappropriate words: "poet," "artist," "genius." Behold him now, out of his uniform, out of his nice little, tight little rut at the ordnance department — the world before him, where to choose.

He'd take what was needed for a week. But what to hell? Still in his slippers. He searched for some shoes — ah, here they were, a good strong pair of army boots. Good thing he could still wear these. He got into them. It was a raw and ugly business, leaving Jerry so abruptly. There had been, however, plenty of incidents to prepare him for it. He appeared to be leaving all the detail and disorder for the poor boy to cope with — didn't expect he'd have to send for much more than he was taking along. Jerry could pack what was necessary when he'd come to some conclusion about his plans — some books, a few clothes,

perhaps. As for the furnishings, the little gadgets and stinkets and din-
kets so dear to Gerald's heart, he could have the lot. Without a doubt
he could find somebody to share the apartment with him. There were
plenty of young men in Washington looking for a place to live. It was
going to be a bad business, getting through with it. He'd pay his share
of the rent for several months in advance and add plenty to cover in-
cidental expenses. Three hundred dollars would more than do it. It
would be horribly embarrassing. It wasn't as though these financial
matters were those of most importance. What he was about to do, he
realized, was to break the poor boy's heart. But, on the other hand, he
couldn't go on stepping on him, trampling all over his sensibilities.

Now what was he barging in here for? What in the devil did he want
of him? "Come in," he called crossly, regarding Gerald in the doorway,
arrayed in his Chinese dressing gown, his feet plunged into his
huaraches, his head thrown back, looking flushed, apologetic.

How extraordinarily handsome he was, not only the beauty of his
face, the regular, almost perfect features; but his strong and slender
body gave you the impression it had been designed for the express purpose of holding up and thrusting back from the neck and shoulders that
perfectly splendid head. The comparison to the Greek models was obvious enough. But no, he wasn't thinking of the young Antinous. He
was thinking of Pierre — seemed to see him vividly, dressed in those
oddly youthful, oddly adult clothes (short trousers, bare knees, a little
beret on his head, the natty, the carefully tailored coat), his expressive
Latin countenance, the swarthy complexion, the dark eyes, the down
on the upper lip, his gestures, the movements of his nervous undersized
body communicating instantly the fever and disturbance at work
within him. How frankly adolescence declared itself in these European
youths — their faces, their voices, their compact nervous make-up, yes,
even those queer intermediate clothes told you all about it, a process of
growth, a spiritual and physical adventure consciously entered upon.
To compare Gerald to them seemed ridiculous. Poor Jerry, always dealing with the transient, the momentary — spilling his emotions all over
the place, reducing all his loves and hates to those little "oh's" and
"ah's," busy with his small devotions to the beautiful, younger at
twenty-six than Pierre had been at sixteen. God, when Pierre had
taken him in hand what a variety of things he'd learned from that

prodigious boy — the erotic initiations had been a small part of it all; there'd been a seeking and searching for values, excursions into the mind and soul. Had he ever been naive enough to believe that he could remake this boy, model his spirit according to the pattern of those European youths?

There he stood holding out a telegram — his eyes busily engaged in roaming round the room, taking in the bags, the clothes, the disorder. "Larry," he said, "I've brought you this."

Larry took the telegram.

Very likely another missive from Anne (what did she think she was up to now?). He opened it, read it. He read it a second time, a third. It made him exceedingly angry. He wished that Gerald would get the hell out of here; but it was plain that he had something he intended to say.

"Are you coming in to breakfast?" he asked.

"God, no — not just now. Can't you see I'm busy packing? Go ahead and have your breakfast alone. I'll come when I'm good and ready." (What was this — what was this Jerry was asking now?)

"Are you walking out on me, Larry?"

The phrase irritated him. He didn't know just why. He couldn't have found more concise words for stating exactly what he was intending to do. The question was honest and direct and it had been wrung with anguish from the poor boy's heart. It certainly spared him a lot of rigmarole in the explanation of his plans. "I'm going to New York," he said, "if that's what you mean." And then suddenly, and before he could check his impulse, he'd shut the door in poor old Jerry's face.

Lord! Hilly's telegram had frightfully unnerved him — "Better not come just now," signed "Mother." His abruptness to Gerald was distressing beyond words. He'd planned to get through with this whole painful severance in as gentle a manner as possible. Everything seemed to be conspiring to reveal his own character in the most glaring possible light — this telegram and that telegram, all these decisions to make and the oddest sense upon him that situations were always repeating themselves, his behavior always the same — being cruel to those who loved him, making these scenes, precipitating these crises.

"Better not come just now," signed "Mother." What in God's name had made her send him this? She should have known it would merely confirm him in his determination to come. Her inability not to interfere, constantly wanting to arrange and manage everything, exasperated him to the breaking point. She probably thought that Anne would be disturbed. Well, that was Anne's business. Even with her uncanny ability to guess correctly, he felt sure she didn't know that Anne had sent that telegram from Reno. Hilly should stop meddling. Though she was devilish skillful in working behind the scenes, here she'd made a big mistake. He would *not* be bossed or hinted to. Seeing she'd worked so hard to get him married, it was difficult to take — the way she'd sided with Anne on the question of divorce; and, as for her having signed those depositions, there was a wound that never closed. Whenever he thought of it, his sense of injury increased.

Christ! If he allowed his anger against his mother to rage within him, it destroyed him. He was finished by it. And now, today, the brightness of the snow, the beauty of the morning, this sense of the Christmas season heightened his realization that there really was no refuge left for him — abandoned by his wife, forgotten by his son, warned away by his mother, walking out on Gerald. He was without purpose or direction, simply pushed around by a welter of conflicts.

But he must get on with his packing — all these socks, shirts, scarves, collars, winter underwear, neckties, handkerchiefs, gloves — Jerry's job, he supposed. Jerry'd see to it he got just what he needed when he sent for it. The devoted Jerry.

It was the poor boy's dear, excruciating pathos that got him down — worked on his nerves, induced the most inexcusable behavior. His gentle, slavish devotion — this habitual masochism (if you had to use the detestable word). He was filled with consternation every time he thought of the way he treated the poor fellow — couldn't go on like this, stepping all over his feelings, trampling on his sensibilities. It was those big, vague hungers in his heart — looking up to him as the only person on this earth who could fill the void. He couldn't cope with it, his need for art, for culture, Beauty with a great big B, when he didn't actually understand the meaning of these words. Hadn't it in him to understand, lacked the tragic, the religious sense of life, extracted beauty from the quaintest little oddments of experience — the hanging of a picture on the wall, the draping of a curtain, contrasting this color with that, all these pretty interior effects and decorations. He'd have to admit it, when they'd first set up this little establishment, he'd enjoyed Jerry's enthusiasm, his diligent determination to arrange everything with ab-solute perfection — charming, charming — watching his delight, shar-ing in his joy, responding to the boy's extraordinary beauty, that vibrant need he seemed to have to share vividly and at once in all these ex-quisite, small and transitory pleasures — those little cries of praise and joy, the way he tossed back his splendid head — lyric like the delight of a child; but boring, eventually boring. There was something utterly naive in his belief that they could share everything in common. The infatuation had worn off; he'd ceased to be in love with him. But the queer thing was he loved Jerry. He hated the cruelty he was constantly displaying toward him, and the boy's unvarying decency of behavior was a perpetual reproach. He was such a decent fellow, no meanness in him — admirable. The boy really was admirable. And when he thought about the story of his life, he never failed to be moved, impressed by it. The character, the perseverance he'd displayed. A touching little suc-cess story if there ever was one.

Brought up, as he had been, in that stinking little Kansas town, no parents to guess at the needs behind the big void and hunger, only his miserly old uncle to kick him out at fifteen, getting himself to Chicago, and there by hook and crook and character making good all on his own, not a damned thing to help him out but this excruciating need he had for — call it what you wanted to — beauty, art, his window-dressing talents; working in drugstores, delivering groceries, getting some free instruction in illustrating, designing, haunting the art museums; and lo and behold, finally discovering he'd become (he never could clearly ex-plain it to himself) a very successful young man, employed by a big de-partment store, decorating, buying, making plenty of money, finding his way around, beginning to associate with people who'd had advantages, education; having, to be sure, to watch every precarious step, but gen-erally guided by something (call it his feeling for beauty, his window-dressing talents), accepted for what he definitely was not, an informed young man of desirable background and education.

God, what a hasty, hungry, pretentious business it had been, nibbling at everything, grasping, looking, listening, with the museums and the radio and the records to assist him — the sensibilities always vibrating — pitching his heart to such a heaven of aspiration; for he'd snatched at everything, he'd followed every tip, he'd taken on the prevailing fads and predilections, got the names on the end of his tongue; oh, the names, the names of books, pictures, painters, composers, how one jug-gled with the names; he'd loved, he'd hated, and, as for the books, the authors, and what the critics said about them, he had it all down pat. The centuries pushed him round in the dark; he groped blindly to find his way; there were the anthologies and the open forums on the radio, and universal culture seemed forever beckoning him, nudging him in this direction and that, leering at him, smiling at him, playing such tricks and pranks upon him as would make you blush remembering all the gaffs the poor dear boy had made — such a jumble and confusion as could hardly be imagined, attempting to rearrange, to fit this rag of information onto that rag of carefully acquired taste, and to piece the whole together as best he might, getting round as he was among the so-phisticates and having to contend with the cliques and the conversa-tionalists; for there were, definitely, things he shouldn't like and preferences he should declare and having, as he knew so well, no solid structure of experience, learning, or literature on which to rely. Watching his step, keeping his nerve, steeling his character, he'd made the grade, he'd pulled off the bluff and, what with his good looks, the way he had of attracting the aesthetes, he'd got around, he'd become a great success. But always, deep down in his heart, fresh and active and incorruptible, had been the hunger, still virginal, still expectant; and then, with the readjustment and reshuffle of the war, finding himself here in Washington doing jungle camouflage, they had met and it had seemed to the poor boy that all he had yearned for had been given him, that his heart was finally fed.

Who could blame him for wanting to cling to his illusion, even though it had begun to cause him so much grief, bewilderment, disil-lusion? Why, Jerry would stay on groveling, begging to be allowed to grovel. "Larry, just wipe your feet on me as long as you want to; here I am, only allow me to remain with you," that was about the long and short of it.

But it couldn't go on; it damned well couldn't go on. It was necessary to break it up. Larry went to the desk, meditated a few moments, sat down, wrote out his check; put it in his pocket.

T E N

———

HOW IT SPEAKS TO YOU, a place where you've been absolutely happy, thought Gerald, and the sorrow in his heart was so mingled with the intense love he felt for every object, every carefully worked out detail in the charming room he was surveying that, if he'd given in to his feelings, he would have cried out passionately that he couldn't stand it, that he was going to break down and tell Larry he couldn't stand it. But he was not, he admonished himself severely, going to break down. He would make no scenes; he'd wait and see what Larry was intending to do. He'd abide by Larry's decisions.

Breakfast was ready, the coffee boiled in the percolator; the best china, with the pink and blue hydrangeas, the bright-green leaves, the curious little bridges and pagodas, the coffeepot, the creamer, the sugar bowl awaiting the empty cups looked as gay and cheerful as a garden. A fire burned on the hearth. The sunlight streamed in and played all manner of delightful pranks; it trembled in a goblet of water, dropped down on the white cloth blue shadows of the bright refractions in the glass, danced on the opposite wall, and the entire room was invaded by a wintry snow light lovely to behold.

Gerald hovered over his pretty arrangements; he moved a goblet a trifle to the right and a plate a little to the left, then he cautiously lifted a bowl of fruit and placed it in the exact center of the table and stood back to view his minor masterpiece — five fire-bright nectarines, one frosted-silver plum, three flawless peaches, three equally flawless pears, erected in a careful pyramid, over which, so disposed as to accentuate the lovely contours of the larger fruits, he had arranged a beautiful cluster of dark transparent grapes. He sighed heavily, for the love expended on these small offices and devotions seemed somehow coming back to rend his heart, since obviously they had become so meaningless to Larry.

He'd been waiting for him for over an hour. He'd fussed over this fruit and all these table appointments. Why had he stayed here, going through with the worn-out gestures? Something fastened him here — his misery very likely. It would, he knew, have been very much wiser if he'd dressed himself and gone out for the entire day, allowed Larry to make his own breakfast and depart, if that was his intention, with no further words or discussion. But then he'd got into these habits. He seemed always to be saying to Larry, "Go on, hurt me; hurt me some more. Be as ruthless to me as you want. I can stand it. If I could be your slave, if I could perform the little menial services that you require, I'd be willing to take any cruelty you might inflict on me."

But the point was this: It all got so horribly on Larry's nerves. It wasn't fair to Larry. Something had happened in their relationship; he wasn't subtle enough to know exactly what, but his affection for Larry, his respect and love for him told him clearly that the time had certainly arrived for them to separate. Larry might think that he was stupid, damnably stupid — expecting everything to go on just as it had in those first blissful months of their relationship. But he wasn't as stupid as all that. He'd never expected it to last. He'd always recognized it couldn't possibly last. However, there had been a time when Larry had shown the most tender curiosity and solicitude. He'd wanted to learn all about his life. He'd seemed so eager to instruct him — why, there had been something positively paternal about the way he'd listened and advised. He'd even shown great pleasure, actual enthusiasm, over his "little arts and arrangements" as they were now so frequently referred to. Yes, indeed, he'd taken them very seriously for exactly what they were — his way of expressing himself, his trivial little way of creating something beautiful.

He'd probably demanded too much of Larry, taken his love too much for granted, but he'd always known that his mind was inaccessible and intricate. Oh, he had none of Larry's depth. His emotions were all tied up in the personal, the immediate. He just plain wanted to cling to his happiness while it lasted and forget about everything else. And as for the war and the world in which we lived today, of course it was terrible, and, when you stopped to think about it, it brought you up short with an awful scare and horror but you couldn't think about it too much — not, at any rate, if you had beside you the one person you cared for most on earth. If you could feel that you were necessary to him, you were just not unhappy about anything. If all this had become a bore to Larry, he could understand it perfectly. The question that concerned him most was the effect he'd begun to have on Larry's disposition. This was a bad business — getting on Larry's nerves the way he did — a very serious business. He could stand it all right — the daily outbursts and sarcasms, the wounds that Larry inflicted on him. But watching Larry suffer from the spectacle of his own bad behavior, it was this that gave him pause. He shouldn't put him in a position to hate himself; he didn't like to use the word in regard to Larry, but to downright demean himself so frequently.

It was pretty heartbreaking to think that out of a happiness as complete as he had known only this misery was going to remain, this bereavement. He didn't even want to imagine how barren his life would be with Larry gone — how his heart was going to ache. Couldn't face it.

He disconnected the percolator. The coffee must be as strong as lye by now. Should he make another brew, he wondered. He reached out his hand to take the coffeepot, he looked up. Larry was coming in; he'd closed the door; he was crossing the room.

The two young men regarded each other.

Dressed in traveling clothes, thought Gerald. Must have made up his mind to light right out. Well, whatever might occur, there'd be no scene; he was set on it — not breaking down. He watched Larry go to the table and stand there inspecting the elaborate appointments. When he saw the bowl of fruit he made a familiar ejaculation, repeated it several times — "Phew," he said, "phewry-cats." He poured himself a cup of coffee and then carelessly extended a hand, lifted the grapes from their carefully balanced perch, tore the bunch apart, put a liberal allowance on his plate and threw the mutilated cluster back into the bowl.

The pyramid collapsed; several nectarines rolled onto the table, a peach fell to the floor. Gerald stooped, picked up the peach and then he took up the nectarines, one by one, and tried to reconstruct the pyramid — couldn't help it, his hands were trembling and he knew he'd flushed to the roots of his hair. Terrible to see Larry behave like this, particularly when he knew how bitterly he was regretting his own behavior — sitting there in silence drinking his coffee, helping himself to marmalade.

"Strong enough to curl the hair of a North American Indian," he said.

Gerald bit his lip. Why couldn't he let this fruit alone? He knew it irritated Larry to see him fiddling with it. Some crazy impulse to restore the beauty, the balance, was upon him. The weirdest thing about Larry was that the more he was exposed to other people's suffering the worse he frequently behaved. Oh, yes, he knew perfectly well how disgusted Larry was with himself and how sorry he felt that he had hurt him. He appeared to be devouring his grapes.

"How perfectly delicious these are," he said, "particularly so when a large portion of the human race is hungry for a crust of bread."

To Gerald's great relief, a log burned through and fell on the hearth with a thud and a little explosion of sparks. He went directly to the fireplace and remained there for some time building up the fire, trying to get himself together and decide what he was going to say. When he returned to the table he had himself in hand and looked resolute enough.

"I see you're dressed and ready for the train," he said. "Have you done all your packing — is there anything I can do?"

Yes, Larry admitted, he was ready for the trip. "But I've left a hell of a mess behind me. A hell of a mess."

The words didn't justify, Gerald realized it, the sense of relief that came flooding over him, and he couldn't disguise the note of cheerfulness, of expectation, in his voice. "Oh, don't bother about it," he said. "I'll set everything straight. When do you think you'll be coming back?"

"I'm not coming back."

"Then you're walking out on me for good?"

"Yes."

Larry continued to eat his breakfast. Silence spread between them like a gulf, and when he finally began to tackle the practical and financial aspects of his departure Gerald realized that every word he said was fraught for him with full awareness of the insensitive role he was adopting and the pain that he inflicted as he spoke. He was leaving, he explained, in a regrettable manner. It was abrupt and downright obnoxious, the way he was getting out, and to mention the financial aspects of such a break up, he knew, as far as Jerry was concerned, was like adding insult to injury; but, after all, he couldn't leave him in the lurch; they had both assumed certain financial obligations and Jerry must realize that here he did want to stick to his agreement. He put his hand in his pocket and fished out a check and handed it to him; then he said to regard it as his share of the rent and expenses until he could get himself fixed up with someone else who might want to come in with him. The deeper he got into it the harder it was for him to continue; he wouldn't, he said, want much sent after him; he'd let Jerry know as soon as he'd made his plans what he needed — some books and papers, probably a few clothes; "as for all this," and he made an inclusive, a somewhat desperate gesture with his hands, Jerry could have it all. He seemed to care less and less for things. Jerry must regard everything they'd assembled together as belonging to him.

Really, what was there he could say? Gerald got up and went again to the fireplace, tore up the check and threw the bits of paper into the flames; then he turned and stood leaning against the mantel, looking round the room, wondering about Larry. Where was he going? Did he have any plan in mind? What was his relationship to his mother? Where did he stand with Anne? He began to feel an uneasiness, a great anxiety.

"Have you any plans, Larry?" he asked at last. "Where do you intend to go?"

"I'm going to New York."

"Do you know where you'll stay?"

"At a hotel, I expect."

"You're crazy," he burst out impetuously. "The war's just over —it's Christmas time. Every hotel will be packed to the gunwale."

"Oh, there are plenty of places I can stay. Very likely I'll go to my mother's. I could stay with Peter Witt."

He knew it was audacious of him. But the words slipped out before he could restrain himself. "Don't you think, Larry," he asked, "that you're jumping from the frying pan into the fire?"

"That's my own business." Larry rose abruptly and went toward his room.

Then Gerald rushed to him. He began to plead with him. He couldn't bear it that they should part like this, everything unfinished, held back — all this reserve, this great distance between them — and he perceived at once that Larry's distress almost equaled his own. Larry could not bear it either — their separating in this unnatural manner; he was intensely glad to have him come along.

"Why not?" he said. "Go change your rig. I'll get my bag and meet you in the street.

In his own room, Jerry dressed with feverish haste. As painful as it all was, doing something about it was a relief, getting out of the apartment and starting off with a destination, a plan, in view. To get Larry safely to the train — this was the step now to take. He didn't stop to brush his hair or to look for a hat, didn't even think to take his overcoat. He snatched a pair of gloves, dashed into the foyer, out into the hall. Larry was just ahead of him, carrying his suitcase down the single flight of stairs. He followed, three steps at a time, and they reached the sidewalk together. This was not, he assured himself, Larry's walking out on him for good; it was a trip to the station. He was seeing Larry off. And there (what a break for them!) was a taxi, lunging into the street and depositing several people at a neighboring house. He made a dash for it and promptly returned on the running board. He jumped to the sidewalk, snatched the suitcase from Larry's hand, pushed him into the cab, ducked in after him. They were off.

The air was exhilarating, a holiday spirit abroad, Alexandria, Washington deep in snow, and the Christmas wreaths and decorations at all the windows. They lurched along at a good clip, passed the cemetery at Arlington, crossed the Potomac. This was the last time he'd drive with Larry over these familiar thoroughfares.

"It's a fine day," he said and he opened the window and thrust out his head. With the beautiful snow light investing every monument and building in celestial dyes, and the boughs and tree trunks casting on the white lawns and parkways a perfect maze of amethyst and indigo shadows, Washington looked wholly insubstantial, like a city in a dream. He longed to exclaim, to say how beautiful it was — "look, there's the Lincoln monument, there's the Washington memorial," and then to sit back close to Larry, to take hold of his hand and to feel once again that exquisite intimacy that used to flow between them when their hands were clasped, when they looked into each other's eyes.

But he did nothing of the sort. He talked very practically about trains and crowds and the chances of getting a seat. He advised Larry not to wait for an express — they'd all be crowded. Best take the first train he could get. Had he remembered his wallet? Did he have money enough to carry him through the holidays? The banks would all be closed. A fierce business, keeping conversation going, with the intolerable parting drawing nearer every moment. Yes, Larry said, he had his wallet, and Gerald suspected that he was longing to break down in a passion of self-accusation and ask to be forgiven. He knew, oh, he knew well enough, that Jerry didn't harbor a drop of rancor in his heart. That he cared for him deeply — would care for him always, and was grateful for all he'd given him.

"New York will be crowded to the gunwale," he insisted again. "Will you go directly to your mother's?"

"Might be," said Larry. "But, for God's sake, Gerald, stop fussing. You're not my aged aunt."

Arrived at the station, there was little time for sentiment. A train on the Baltimore and Ohio was leaving. Gerald said Larry had better take it. If they dashed, they could catch it. He snatched Larry's wallet, wedged himself into the front of a long ticket line, bought a ticket, joined him on the run, and they both got through the gates in plenty of time to board the train.

Here was a seat. Good luck. They both agreed to that. Larry was in luck finding a seat, with all the soldiers and sailors on the move. Gerald hoisted his suitcase onto the rack, gave him back his wallet.

"All aboard," called the conductor. "All aboard."

And then suddenly they were weeping. They embraced. Neither of them seemed to give a damn who was looking at them.

"Train for Baltimore, Wilmington, Philadelphia and way stations. All aboard," shouted the conductor.

Gerald wrenched himself from Larry's embrace. "Goodbye, Larry," he sobbed. The tears streamed down his face. He got himself, somehow or other, through the aisle, out of the train, onto the platform.

As he went toward the station, he had the sense of walking backward, moving with the train. Larry's car passed him and the next and the next. The train gathered speed. The last car approached. Before he knew quite what he was up to he was swinging himself aboard. Good God, he'd missed it — no, he hadn't. He had one foot on the lower step. He had the other foot on the lower step. He was clinging to the iron rail. What a fool thing he'd done! He pulled himself up.

The cessation of pain in his heart, the relief he felt, was enormous, blissful. He was on the same train with Larry. He was going to New York. "Thank God," he kept repeating idiotically, "thank God."

E L E V E N

GLAD TO BE HERE, thought Larry — liked to travel — it eased the body and liberated the mind just to sit and look out of the window, to feel at one with earth, with sky, part of the physical world, part of the mystery; the train established rhythms; your thoughts moved freely; you wished to go on and on, to have no responsibilities save to this flow, this mysterious sense of time, of space, of memory.

What town was this, he wondered — Wilmington already? Traveling in America was the damnedest — all the towns and cities so similar somehow, so ugly and exposed; this place or that place, it never seemed to matter much. A church sporting a Christmas tree all decked out with little gadgets, a house with wreaths on the door; here they made the armaments, home of the Du Ponts. And, what the devil — this sense of sudden delight, of being elsewhere, pulling up a window in a European railway carriage, a feeling resembling ecstasy creeping round his heart? Was he in Spain, in Germany, in Italy, in France — craning out his neck, repeating the place names, this nostalgia on him like a sickness, sharing Europe with Hilly, while she stood beside him at the window?

God! Would he never be able to sever these bonds — this need he had to return to his mother on terms of the old intimacy? Must he be always going back? Was every opportunity to share the present in her company, to anticipate the future with her, completely lost? These suppressions and injuries and little hoarded wounds — Lord, what they did to you! She would, he presumed, be giving a Christmas tree for Henry. There'd be a family celebration. She'd advised him not to come. If he was outside the picture, if his family life had broken on the rocks of his

220 NEW YORK MOSAIC

eccentric character, she and Anne could pick up the broken pieces; and apparently there'd be Captain Fletcher to assist.

Would this knot and tangle of his injured feelings keep on destroying his soul? Would he never forgive Hilly for standing with Anne, and in particular for that matter of the depositions? Was this journey to New York prompted entirely by a desire to be mischievous, destructive — to make Anne suffer, to pay her back in kind for that message she'd sent about her marriage to the Captain? Did he intend to play subtly and cruelly on his mother's regrets and general anguish over the situation?

No, by God, no! There were other needs within him — thank the Lord for that; needs far more profound and necessary to his peace of mind impelled him. He must, he would, go to Hilly and have everything out with her. The moment had come when this was absolutely necessary — general confession and catharsis. That's what they needed, both of them. He knew how Hilly yearned for it. And when he reached New York, he wouldn't wait. He'd take a taxi at Liberty Street. He wouldn't even telephone.

Snow, fields, trees, fences, farms, fringes of woodland dark against the smoldering sky, a flock of crows rising on heavy wings, sparrows bright on the bright still air, a man in a barnyard, a dog, some children skating on a pond — this sense of time, of space, of memory, with the train pounding out those words of Eliot's poem which, God knows why, had been haunting his mind for days on end; the revolutions of the wheels, the rhythms of his blood beating them out — repeating them again, again —

"Da
Datta: *what have we given?* . . . ."

a question that certainly wanted answer — but he must get the beat and pounding of the words, the excitement they induced, out of his system; what he needed to do was to plumb his own remorse, to look with as much integrity as possible at his own dilemma. The decency of Gerald's character, the fineness of his behavior this morning made it almost unendurable for him to remember how he'd treated the poor boy. His sarcasm and unkindness, his out-and-out sadism in pulling that bunch of grapes apart —intolerable, not to be excused. Why couldn't he free himself of the demons that possessed him? He seemed to be waging perpetual war between his pity, on the one hand, and his tortuous behavior on the other — the demon waiting to rout the angel-creature; and then, presto! after all the damage had been accomplished, behold the angel throned again within his heart, filled with sorrow and contrition; same old histories, same old battles — always putting those he loved to the torture. If it wasn't one, it was another of his victims — Hilly, Anne, poor selfless Gerald.

Demon and angel creatures. Wasn't this the central conflict of our day and age — this incessant self-examination, routing the devil, the attempt to draw up the line of battle, to discover where the angels stood and where the devils formed their terrible battalions?

> "Da
> Datta: *what have we given?*
> *My friend, blood shaking my heart*
> *The awful daring of a moment's surrender*
> *Which an age of prudence can never retract.*"

Still repeating the extraordinary lines — couldn't quite say yes to them, terribly as they always moved him. There was one word he always wanted to challenge — "surrender." Never felt that word was right. Had Eliot surrendered? We hadn't any of us surrendered to a goddamned thing — forever watching, listening, pondering the moral issues.

We'd unmasked the old Victorian moralities. We'd kicked them over, with a vengeance. We'd abandoned that Victorian God who had set a seal upon the lips, a watch upon the mind. The seal had been removed, the watch dismissed, the comfortable silences broken. We had been given liberty to walk abroad in our own souls. We'd investigated every inch and acre of that appalling journey and, although the finger had been lifted from the lips, it had never been lifted from the emotional pulse; the mind had registered every moral and spiritual vibration.

And behold us now, alone, in one enormous wide-open world. We'd lost our mothers and our fathers; we were without a home, without a country, without the usual God. We had no worldly identity whatever;

we were without sex, androgynous, anonymous, anybody, everybody, nobody.

At times life seemed to him exactly like that great Picasso show the Museum of Modern Art had staged soon after he arrived in America (God, what a wallop that had packed him!): the swift sequence and progression of the pictures, like a moving screen that passed before the eyes; the periods, the decades, one style discarded for another, such a casting off, such a reassembling, recomposing, reasserting, such an infinite, inexhaustible recombining; and all somehow precisely resembling what was taking place within your own precious psyche, disarrayed and disarranged, broken into a thousand fragments, and then again so reassembled, rearranged, that you had the sense that perhaps, indeed certainly, you had been carried past all familiar boundaries and frontiers, offered new climates, landscapes, latitudes and longitudes, placed in a new relationship to God, the world, the universe — a pretty awe-inspiring vision, abstract in a way utterly nonhuman — terrifying; but none the less exhilarating, exhilarating.

Or maybe you got shown round by Kafka, claimed by the fellow's tortured face, those haunting eyes that held reflected in their depths the loneliness and fear, the anguish and neurosis of our guilt-plagued era (a face so deeply, tragically human, so burdened with all the intricate post-Freudian problems besetting him, that you turned instinctively away from it as from too painful an exhibition of your own predicament), the poor man retreating in a kind of funk, asking for the old protections — father, mother, country, the usual God — attempting to make, in his search for these lost properties, a world as closed and ordered as Picasso's world was free and abstract and without impediments.

Through the man's uncanny allegories how you experienced not only the heartbreaking, the incredible world we'd made ourselves, but that inward world of guilt and misery we carried in the depth of us today. On what ghastly journeys, through what terrible and tortuous passages and corridors, into what walled-up enclosures and into what further prison houses he conducted you, the endless corridors extending endlessly before your eyes, while you endlessly attempted to find your way out, intercepted by what messengers, informed upon by what sergeants and officers and policemen, by what angels and archangels and ministers of God; how he marched you off for trial in a succession of night-mare courtrooms, sentenced you for sins which, though not your own, weighed on your heart with a heaviness as great as though you'd com-mitted all the hideous and accumulated crime of the human race since man was born upon this earth!

He was ready (here Larry closed his mouth upon it) to recognize the extent of his implication in the world we'd made for ourselves; he'd bear the sorrow and assume his portion of the guilt, but as for that weird laughter at our pitiable plight, the positively satanic delight in exhibiting our fruitless attempts to communicate with the inaccessible castle on the hill, where the great Judge and all His messengers and an-gels and policemen seemed to take an equal delight in frustrating every frantic effort made to get in touch with Him, he'd be damned if he'd take it. And he didn't feel inclined to have one neurotic little man, who he somehow felt was walking backward with his ball and chain attached, set up again the same old bourgeois traps that had already occasioned so much misery — less fear was needed, a bit more air to breathe.

But here, for Heaven's sake, we'd got to Philadelphia — the train stopping and a great change of passengers in progress: sailors and sol-diers, families with children, people with Christmas packages surging through the aisle, elbowing and pushing and searching for seats. It was going to be necessary to get up and allow this young sergeant, all dec-orated with service stripes and citations for valor, to take off his coat and dispose of his things.

The young man begged his pardon and not only hoisted his military and civilian properties onto the rack, but assisted an old lady in stowing away her effects and, though making no attempt to help either one or the other of them (the stir and commotion going on over his shoulder and above his head), Larry was able to scrutinize the fellow carefully. Had a good Irish face, but in spite of his genial smiles and pleasant manners he looked gray and fatigued. Had a saber cut clear across one of his cheeks —the wound must very nearly have cost the poor lad his life. Must have seen it tough. Wore on his arm the in-signia of the tanks.

No words exchanged between them, the sergeant seated and settled for the trip, the train rushing and thundering through Philadelphia.

Roofs covered with snow, chimney pots, houses flashing by, a boulevard, rows of houses, sidewalks shoveled, cars deep in snow, stores, factories, icicles, train sheds, freight cars, sidings; and now again the roadbeds clear, the glare and glitter of the open fields. And suddenly this tenderness flowing from him — great waves of tenderness and sympathy for the young man at his side, for the thousands, the millions of other young men, heroes and martyrs who'd sustained dangers and agonies which turned him sick every time he attempted to put himself in their place. How pretty he had sat, had gone to the movies, seen the shadow pictures fight the incredible battles. But, in his own peculiar way, he'd got about with the armed forces. He'd fought this war in every element and area —in the air, underseas, trapped in the flaming tanks.

A powerful desire to put out his hand and lay it on the sergeant's arm in token of his feeling for him and for all the other heroes, brave and dumb and capable of getting through with the outrageous business, was overtaking him. But what to hell, the sergeant apparently wanted to speak to him, tapping him on his arm.

"Excuse me, mister."

The young man was blushing furiously, an expression of extreme self-consciousness spreading across the good Irish face, asking again to be excused and inquiring if he was by any chance acquainted with New York.

Yes, he said, he was; he lived there, or rather he used to live there.

The sergeant's voice was lowered; he whispered; he revealed the cause of his embarrassment; he made no bones about it; came out with it bravely, brazenly. Could the gentleman, maybe, oblige him with an address — some place where he could get himself a proper woman. He had, he said, to have a woman — repeated it several times, "I gotter have a woman." And now, to cover his embarrassment, he was going into further explanations. It seemed he came from Boston. His poor mother had died while he was in the Pacific; the only person he'd find when he reached home was an aunt — a bitch of an old girl. He didn't relish getting to see her. He'd stopped in Philadelphia for a few days to visit a married sister; no pleasure there. It just seemed he owed himself a night of fun before going on to Boston.

Now to what in thunder was he committing himself — unsupplied with the required information and terribly eager to help the poor boy out — suggesting, and before he'd had any time to think the invitation out, that they dine together? After dinner they'd go to a show, then they'd go to a nightclub — and going, by God, so far as to promise him that before the night was over he'd procure that girl the sergeant had to have. Was this relief that he experienced (extending and enlarging his invitation, letting himself off his resolve to go at once to Hilly, giving the night away so recklessly), or was it a feeling of the most sorrowful regret? At any rate, the die was cast — impossible to get out of it now. He'd throw himself into plans for the young man's pleasure with all the warmth and generosity at his command —could hardly do less for the poor fellow.

The boy appeared to be immeasurably delighted. Seemed he'd never spent a night in New York. The prospect of a nightclub took on enormous luster. He hoped they'd sing some songs he knew, but there was one, by God, he wanted especially to hear — was the gentleman familiar with it? He sang the first lines in a low reminiscent voice — his friend Bill McGuire had taught it to him. He loved it dearly: "Who slapped Annie on the fannie with a flounder?"

He was a simple garrulous fellow — needed to talk. And who could do less than listen to him with attention and respect? Had seen plenty of hot spots — plenty. Fighting those island battles with the tanks was something. And the fight on Okinawa was something else — like walking straight into the red-hot jaws of hell. He and his friend Bill had had their little joke about this. They'd come to the conclusion that they'd served their term in purgatory and that Saint Peter had a right to release them from further obligation. As soon as either one or the other of the two got bumped off, Saint Peter had pledged himself to roll aside the Pearly Gates and let him directly into Heaven. And, by Jesus, he'd seen Bill burn up before his very eyes trying to get out of a bloody tank while a son-of-a-bitch of a fighter plane gave him the works and finally crashed beside the blazing tank. It was the hottest hell of a fight he'd ever seen, everything blowing up and everyone bursting into flame. He'd somehow managed to get out of his own little oven and a foot in the fray, when a son-of-a-bitch of a half-naked Jap sprang up out of nowhere. See the gash across his face? It was only one of the wounds he'd received that day. The Jap had taken him for dead and run away; and what had happened after that he wouldn't know. Couldn't remember a goddamned thing about it. They'd got him to a hospital in

Manila, where the doctors had done a dandy job on him — made him a silver rib and half a jaw built from a bone of his own hind leg. Hadn't had to fight again; but none the less, Saint Peter was going to keep that promise about the Pearly Gates. Here he winked, as though to suggest that whatever indulgences he intended to allow himself tonight wouldn't mean a thing to Saint Peter.

The train was running into Newark. Dark now, except for the remnants of the sunset scattered above the marshes. The lad had talked himself out and was looking through the window, singing his song about Annie and her fannie and the flounder in anticipation of his night of fun. The vast spread and layout of the tracks, the endless and intricate movement of the trains over the rails, the long line and assemblage of the freight cars, converging, backing, filling, shunting onto sidings, the pall and spread of steam from the engines, the fitful flame and belch of the blast furnaces, gleams of fire on the marshes, with Newark and Jersey City, their sprawling industrial areas, bridges, trellises, gas tanks, power stations, garbage-disposing plants, their abrupt irrelevant towers standing round in the infernal flats — terrifying, ominous, like Dante's approach to the City of Dis. The sergeant's phrase applied — "like looking into the red-hot jaws of hell." What had become, one wondered, of the great caravans of war matériel that had passed over these tracks only a few months since? Where distributed, how disposed? What satanic cargoes would be traveling over these same rails again? With the war over and America likely to be mistress of the situation, on what events did we wait? Was some monstrous, Spenglerian melodrama about to overtake us all? Red lights alternately flooding, dimming this large red church, the cross above it — and there, hung up against the sky, picked out in glittering letters, the electric invitation: "Come to Jesus."

Oh, God! How they tried to silence Jesus — mouthed about and mass-produced, shouted over the air, blacked-out in a blaze of electric lights — had He ceased forever to move men's hearts?

> "And in cries of birth and the groans of death his voice
> Is heard throughout the universe; wherever a grass grows
> Or a leaf buds, the eternal man is seen, is heard, is felt,
> And all his sorrows till he assume his ancient bliss."

He repeated the lines, he got to his feet, for the train had stopped and the sergeant, still singing his little song, "Who slapped Annie on the fannie with a flounder?" was taking down the luggage from the rack. He did his best to assist him but, with one thing and another, assembling and counting the young man's accoutrements, hunting for the old lady's pocketbook, presenting her with her packages, they were the last to leave the car.

Stepping onto the platform, still repeating the miraculous words of Blake, it seemed to him that he caught sight of a young man (could it have been Gerald?), hatless, appearing, disappearing in the crowd. But no, it couldn't possibly have been the case — the mind had a way of playing these illusionary tricks — couldn't possibly have been Jerry.

And Gerald, who had definitely caught sight of Larry conversing with the sergeant, ducked away from the encounter, walked to the end of the line of passengers — was lost to sight.

"No, no," he said to himself in misery, "Larry couldn't do this to me; he wouldn't have pulled it off as quick as this — after all we've just passed through together, after all we've suffered and felt." For Larry was so sensitive, so profound. He had real capacity for grief. When all was said and done, there was something about him — he'd never know his like again.

His heart was torn with pain and jealousy. He loitered; he watched them board the ferry. He'd wait for the next boat.

Or should he return to Washington? Why had he come?

T W E L V E

THERE WAS NOTHING TO DO ABOUT IT but wait for the midnight train which, if on schedule, would get them to New York, George kept assuring Anne, in plenty of time to celebrate Christmas Eve with Henry.

Yes, but would it? she questioned. Here in Chicago It was snowing. They'd already missed several trains; with the Christmas rush and everything, all the trains were late all along the line and it was unfortunate, their not getting any sleeping accommodations — sitting up all night, they were in a mess, weren't they?

"Well, yes," George admitted, they were. But he'd seen worse messes than this.

Which indeed was true and made her ashamed of herself. For there was no denying the fact that George had been through the most ghastly messes. She must not forget what the poor boy had endured. It was her business to keep this always in mind. "Of course you have, dear," she said. "I'm ashamed of myself for making all this fuss about nothing at all."

He took her hand and they both looked up at the clock in the big station waiting room. It would be a full hour before they could board the train. "Would you like another drink, dear?" he asked. "There's plenty of time."

"No," she said irritably, "I don't want another drink." She deplored her shortness of temper. Her nerves were on edge, and George himself looked nervous and tired. She must, in lots of ways, have disappointed him, doting on her as he did. He'd get plenty of shocks and jars sooner or later, which was a pity, as life owed him so much. Poor boy — it owed him everything. She ought, she supposed, to tell him about the telegram she'd sent to Larry, for if Larry should arrive in New York for Christmas (she had a hunch he'd do just this), she felt quite sure that, in one way or another, he'd let George know all about it. Well, then, why not tell him now amid this holiday crowd with all this noise, the sailors and soldiers singing and every moment or so a train being announced? In the midst of so many distractions she could tell him casually, as though it were merely something to be expected, "Larry's coming to New York at Christmastime to see Henry." He was, after all, his father.

"As soon as we arrive in New York," said George, "we'll go to Mrs. Danforth's and bring Henry directly home with us. Or wouldn't it be better for me to telegraph her to have Henry waiting for us in your apartment, dear? Delia Stone can bring him over and wait there till we come."

"Goodness no, George! I wouldn't think of such a thing — snatching him away from Hilly like that. We'll go to her apartment first. It's more than likely she's planned a little party or something. She'll expect us to stay for the celebration. We'll stay with them there a while, and then go home. I intend to let Henry remain a few nights with Hilly. We can drop in on them frequently, and when everything's in order we'll bring him back with us."

"Why in the world do you always have to call that woman 'Hilly'?"

The abruptness of the question, and something in his expression, astonished her. She had always realized that George was ill at ease with Mrs. Danforth, but why this display of animosity?

"Why shouldn't I call her 'Hilly'?"

"Why should you be so thick with her? If I were in your place, I'd leave them alone — the lot of them."

"Why, George!" she said.

He looked at her with an expression that wavered between apology and defiance.

Lord! Did his sense of proprietorship, this determination to protect them, go as far as this, excluding Hilly from their lives? She explained (and she did her very best to be quite cool about it) that Hilly was Henry's grandmother, that he loved her very dearly, and that she wouldn't think of depriving him of an influence in his life as important and valuable as hers would always be for him. "She's a remarkable — a very unusual woman, George."

"I don't like her," he said stubbornly. "Might as well tell you now, dear. I plain don't like her."

"But, George, my dear."

"Anne, darling."

A frightful moment. It was a little, thought poor Anne, like watching a forest fire and each one thinking maybe it was I who started it, and neither one of them able to put it out. A train for Cincinnati was being announced. "Train leaving on track sixteen," the loudspeaker kept repeating. There was a big exodus — people leaving for the train. Suddenly it struck her as strange beyond conception that she should be sitting here beside George, surrounded by all these service men returning home after the greatest war in all history — going home for Christmas.

"What a lot of soldiers and sailors," she said, "so many men in uniform. Look, George — there's another flyer, a captain too."

They inspected his uniform, his service stripes and decorations. George told her just where he'd probably served, the area over which he'd flown. He was in the bomber command — had probably bombed Tokyo, flown many missions.

She watched a little marine struggling with a huge duffle bag, she watched a pale young corporal with only one leg stumping off on his crutches for his train. Where had they all been? Where were they going? What had they all experienced? Christmas, 1945, she thought.

"Think of our being here tonight, and the war's being over. Think of its being Christmas and of all these veterans going home," she said.

"Where did she ever get that foolish name? What a senseless name — Hilly!" He repeated it several times.

My goodness gracious, how stubborn he was! Holding onto his grudge all this time, like a dog gnawing a bone. You'd have thought he could have forgotten it by now. She must try to remember that he was strained and nervous; but then, so was she. And she couldn't understand why he had to take it all out on Hilly.

"Her name is Hildegarde. She's had that nickname since she was a little girl. If Henry chooses to call her 'Hilly,' you'll just have to put up with it."

"But I don't want to put up with it. I don't want to put up with her. I don't see why any of us should have to put up with her."

"Of course you'll put up with her," she retorted hotly. "You'll put up with her as long as you're married to me."

"Not if I have anything to say about it."

"Well, you're not going to have anything to say about it."

They looked at each other aghast.

"You act," she said, "as though you thought that you were Henry's father. It's that that angers me."

"Haven't you given me every reason to believe that, to all intents and purposes, I am?"

"No."

"What do you call it, then? Gaining sole custody of your child, marrying a man who loves the boy?"

"It doesn't make you Henry's father, not by a long shot."

"What does it make me, Anne?"

"My husband, certainly, but not the father of my child."

He did not retort.

"Do you think" (Anne could feel the anger flame and flicker, flame and flicker, in her heart) "that you can go on living with me and escape hearing Larry referred to as the father of my child?"

"I had thought so, Anne," he said.

"Which only goes to show how naive you are."

"O.K., then — I'm naïve, let's leave it at that." She felt weak and beaten. It would be quite impossible to go further with it now, to tell George what she felt she ought to, that she'd telegraphed Larry, that he might even expect to see him, and that he'd have to accustom himself to the fact that Larry would upon occasions enter their lives, to persuade him (if such a thing were possible) that she didn't regard him, as he seemed to think she did, as an intolerable, a perfectly dreadful person. Undoing people's fixed ideas was very difficult indeed and this business of his taking it all out on poor Hilly had somehow revealed to her the extent of his prejudice against Larry — his out-and-out revulsion against him. Later (possibly), when they were on the train, she could approach the subject. She could see, at any rate, by the expression of his face, and by the dejected way he sat there looking at his timetable, that he was completely mollified.

"George," she said, "I think I'll change my mind. Let's go and have another drink."

He turned to her. "Oh, Anne, forgive me," he begged. "I didn't mean to lose my temper. I can't believe we've quarreled so." He looked positively stricken with remorse, his voice trembling and the timetable shaking in his hand.

"Forgive me, George," she said and began waving frantically — for they'd have to get somebody, she said, to keep an eye on their luggage while they left to have their drink.

He got up and went in search of a redcap.

She watched him arguing with a reluctant porter. What a business! Where would it end? she wondered.

THIRTEEN

LARRY WASN'T DRUNK. No, he said to himself, he wasn't tight. The sergeant, however, was drunk as a lord, and the problem he presented, though a minor one among the heavier problems occupying him, was nonetheless tough. What the devil could be done with the poor boy? He'd dragged him around all night, cheated him of every promise. They hadn't been able to get seats at a show, much less a table at a nightclub and, without sufficient money to finance such entertainments, even if they could have been procured, he'd merely got about with him to all these Village restaurants and bars. Hadn't so much as tried to get him the woman he'd demanded — just turned on the jukeboxes, stood him the drinks and let the hogwash pour over him. The simple fellow had taken it gratefully enough (look at his face now, all loose and open and exposed); he'd wept, he'd laughed, he'd confided in his friends; the girls had embraced him; they'd listened to his talk; his companions in arms had taken him to their hearts; he'd talked about his poor mother and about his friend McGuire. What with the maudlin confidences, the jukebox music, the Christmas carols, the drunken boys and girls, everybody standing him the drinks, and this sense he seemed to have that he'd been shown the big town in a great big way, the poor, bereaved and weary fellow was appeased. It was necessary, though, to keep an eye on him, staggering up so often to vomit in the toilet, coming back again with his face the color of a Gorgonzola cheese. And what the devil could be done with him now? Too late to take him to Peter Witt's; couldn't possibly take him to his mother's apartment; couldn't get a room in a hotel. There was, of course, the Grand Central — could sit out the night there, if they could make it.

There was the subway — riding back and forth over the rails on the subway. There might be money enough to cruise round till morning in a taxi.

"Joy to the world! the Lord is come."

A girl, with her arms around a drunken sailor, was singing the beautiful old hymn, getting through the stanzas pretty well, waving her empty glass in the air, nodding her head to the melody, and four soldiers at the end of the bar were trying to harmonize the first lines — "'Joy to the world! the Lord is come" — tum tum, tum tum, tum tum. A solitary individual pounded out the chords with his fists. Someone put a nickel in the big illuminated jukebox. The clock struck two.

He was not, he once more assured himself, tight — not at all tight. One advantage, at least, there had been for him in his European education. He could manage his liquor; he knew how to sip and space his drinks. It was certainly the goddamnedest thing the way people here in America took their liquor — simply knocked themselves out before they'd given themselves an opportunity to linger among the bright ideas, the luminous initiations.

Joy to the world! the atom bomb — tum tum, tum tum, tum tum.

The drunken voices circulated round. No, he wasn't tight — he'd defy anybody to say that he was tight. But something singular, something most extraordinary was happening to him — the anger that consumed him, his indignation and protest at this lunatic world in which we lived, was giving way to something else, to a passionate need for reverence, a desire to worship, to hear proclaimed some great triumphant declaration of faith, and the first chords of that old hymn by Sunderland had joined with other chords, they were branching out from them, blossoming forth from further chords and correlated passages; he was, he'd swear it, listening to the great contrapuntal choirs and fugal harmonies of Johann Sebastian Bach, all chorusing together, building up their mighty dynasties of praise, the notes falling upon his ear in their perfect astronomical order and succession, actually building up in his own heart the whole created universe, worlds behind worlds, constellation behind constellation, planetary systems and starry universes leading from and displaying further constellations, planetary systems, starry universes — numberless, illimitable, serenely ordered, majestically arrayed, and all subject to law, to order, to the love of God, not a star, or leaf, or bird, or flower, oh, not a little sparrow fallen to the ground but that the great Astronomer had counted it and knew its place in the miraculous design and its relationship to all the other forms and substances.

Oh, God, to possess, as men had once possessed, such unalterable, such serene, implicit faith in God, in love, in God's mysterious plan.

Joy to the world! the atom bomb. Tum tum, tum tum, tum tum.

The anguish flowed back into his heart. What he wanted most to do was to lay his head on the bar, to blubber like a baby. But all these drunken boys and girls would think he was tight. No, he wasn't tight (he was very far from being tight). However, he didn't like the looks of that little lieutenant with the dark and liquid eyes. He'd been trying for some time to make advances to him and was surly that he'd been repulsed. Looked as though he wanted to pick a fight. Well, he didn't want to fight with anyone. What he did have an overwhelming desire to do was to smash that goddamned jukebox. He loathed the awful object —all those lighted, brilliantly painted coils and tubes. Jesus, there was something infernal about it — a hellish little robot with electric intestines, going through its nasty little tricks, spilling its tunes all over you. And, for Christ's sake, if it wasn't playing that tune about Annie and her fannie and the flounder; and here was the poor sergeant returning from the toilet, rounding the corner of the bar like a seasick sailor hanging onto the rail in a high sea, green around the gills, his face all fallen to pieces, loose and disordered; but appeased, childishly appeased. He'd recognized the tune; it was swimming out to envelop him in its bliss-making airs, its gratifying intimations.

Now what were those lines of Blake he'd remembered on the train? *There* was a poet you could cling to today, a man who knew about the divisions in the human heart — the devil and the angel countries in the heart. Not like Bach — unorthodox. He'd broken with the churches and the theologians — made systems of his own. He'd walked, like Dostoevsky, through the depth of hell ("even from the deepest pits of hell his voice I hear in the unfathomed caverns of mine ear"). He'd kept, however, his unalterable faith — belief in love, in law, in Jesus Christ. You might say he'd resurrected Jesus, rescued him from the hands of the Philistines and Pharisees — the mouthers of phrases, the killers of the Word. You had to rescue Jesus from the hands of those who did the genuflecting and the mumbling, the morons and the war makers, those who neither saw nor felt nor heard — just went on mumbling the words as though there'd never been a Jesus. Blake knew the meaning of his words, his symbols, fetched them up new-minted from his heart — Jesus, Satan, Son of Man, Son of God — mixed them, mingled them, had belief in their marriage and reconciliation:

> "And in cries of birth and in the groans of death his voice
> Is heard throughout the universe; wherever a grass grows
> Or a leaf buds, the Eternal Man is seen, is heard, is felt
> And all his sorrows till he resumes his ancient bliss."

Joy to the world! the atom bomb — tum tum, tum tum, tum tum.

For everything was sundered, fragmentated, split into atoms — the moments as they assailed us, the impressions as they came. We watched, we listened, we anatomized. And now (if he could only keep his mind sufficiently clear, for he was still on the initiate's side of his liquor) he wanted to recover that remarkable experience he'd had at the Picasso exhibition. For what he'd seen was this — a moving picture of the modern soul; sounded phony enough, but that was what he'd seen — all the impressions of the world, of life, exhibited — quickly — just as they came at you, the film reeling off its millimeters, carrying your soul along with it, offering you unfamiliar landscapes, hastening you toward strange frontiers, bidding you rearrange, correlate, integrate.

But then, who ever said that there was time for integration, synthesis?

The world was shaking, toppling, tottering, and all the documents, the records, precious testimonials, memorabilia of man's experience in centuries past (passing through the decades, passing through the centuries), was presently to be reduced to ash and rubble, all the records leveled with the dust.

He ordered another drink, though he knew damned well he wasn't making himself popular, drinking alone. The little lieutenant had edged up closer and showed every sign of wanting to pick a fight. The poor fellow didn't like him; he didn't like his clothes, or his voice, or his manners — didn't like a thing about him. God, if he could only make him understand how much he loved him, how much he loved them all — all the drunken boys and girls in all the pubs and bars and dives and bistros all over the world. He cared for them so much that his heart was in danger of breaking with the love he felt for them. He wanted to get up and tell them how much he loved them — just to take them into his confidence, to unburden himself for once.

But we none of us unburdened ourselves — couldn't attempt it, too plain difficult. We carried a boulder on the heart, just like that stone on the sepulcher of Jesus — couldn't roll it away, couldn't make the effort, it was compounded of too many imponderable elements, too many people had been involved in rolling it onto the grave. We simply allowed it to remain where it was, crushing us, killing our souls, carrying us toward destruction, toward the very verge of universal death.

And here we are in our lunatic world. Easier to go ahead, speeding up the maniacal machineries we've set in motion, than to put our minds and hearts and energies into the job of rolling back the stone — a damned sight easier. The military and naval, the aerial experts, the strategists, the brass hats, the generals and the admirals and the politicians and the statesmen go right ahead speeding up the inventions, the bigger and better improvements on the big inventions, and we go right ahead listening to the maniacal, the out-and-out satanic discussions and decisions. The new words, the new names they've coined for the new inventions, the great big beautiful words for the bigger and better wonders and inventions sound in our ears, they circulate in our subconscious minds — atom bombs and the great big beautiful bombers that are going to carry the atom bombs, vastly bigger and better than those big B-29's that carried the big explosion to Hiroshima and Nagasaki, bigger bombs, bigger bombers, bigger explosions. New techniques have to be worked out, new methods of carrying hell from place to place, of course; but today's distances, the "reach" the "range," sure to be vastly increased — likely soon to be "tanker planes," rendezvous in midair (wonderful, isn't it; only think what the brain of man can achieve — rendezvous in midair), and presently there'll be fleets of supersonic bombers which can take off with their satanic freight and drop their precious missiles on any designated spot in this little world of ours. These details have to be worked out, naturally, but they're working on them — we're told they're working on them. And (we're good at that sort of thing here in America, seem to have the "know how") it's more than probable that within the coming decade there'll be "beam-riding" (that's the word they've got for it, "beam-riding"), the anti-aircraft guided missiles, traveling in stratospheric altitudes at supersonic speeds. They've got a splendid program for the development of new missiles, sure to accomplish wonders in this direction. Look into the future a bit, think of the transoceanic, trans-stratospheric missiles. No end to the possibilities, no end to the program; something devilishly fascinating in working it all out — the big problems — the big brains working it all out, this problem and that and all the obstacles that have to be overcome in planning for the bigger and better wars of the future, bigger and better than anything you could even imagine — better than the wars of the Apocalypse, better than the wars of Spengler, better than you care to believe.

For the thing that got you down, the thing that drove you to drink, was that nobody dared to believe it, nobody dared to stop and look at it, not with the eyes of the heart, the eyes of God, the eyes of the imagination — they just plain went on planning to make it bigger and better, bigger and better.

Everything in the room began to have a circular movement, his own body, the bodies of the drunken boys and girls and the bottles behind the bar and the big lighted jukebox and all the faces (double faces, disarranged faces, faces out of focus, Picasso faces, Picasso bottles, Picasso bodies, Picasso souls), and he seemed to be looking at the bottles, looking into the faces, watching them disintegrate and recompose, and to be anatomizing, analyzing, understanding the souls, with the most singular belief that they were all a part of his soul, while his own body and his own soul were jerked off and taken round with the other faces, bottles, bodies, souls — carried off and away, with limitless time, limitless space, over, under and encompassing them.

And whether his head was erect, or whether he'd dropped it on the bar he wasn't certain, though he was not, he still insisted on it, drunk — he was on the initiate's side of his liquor. To this conviction he must cling. Yes, indeed, he was on the angels' side of all the trouble and discord in his heart. He'd reached the end of his journey. It had been a long journey, he'd been hampered by a thousand obstacles, he'd met up with the sergeant, he'd been set back at every turn, but here he was at the end of the weary pilgrimage.

"Maman, Maman," he whimpered. He could feel the anger, the deliberate resentment he'd harbored so many years, dissolve within him. Tears gushed from his eyes — he was blubbering like a baby. He didn't care, the boys and girls could see him if they wanted to; they could watch him weep and the little lieutenant could stand there and stare at him with his big dark eyes if he cared to do so. He needed to weep. He and Hilly needed to talk, to speak freely and frankly to each other. He must ask her forgiveness and she, poor darling, wanted to ask him to forgive her, on, oh, so many, many scores! For she had been too young, and too beautiful; there had been too much love dammed up in her heart, too many towns and villages, vineyards, orchards, rivers, and mountains of Europe had been reflected in her eyes. Her gifts had been too exquisite for one poor little American boy to stand up against. Oh, she'd made her mistakes, her big mistakes, plenty of big mistakes. They'd spelled catastrophe. But what did it matter, so long as they could speak together with full understanding and ask for mutual forgiveness?

Blubbering again, whimpering again to beat the band — faces going round, Picasso faces, Picasso bottles, Picasso people going round and round and round; and there, by God, was the sergeant coming back once more from the toilet. And what was the jukebox playing — was it Annie and her fannie and the flounder, Annie and her fannie and the flounder?

God have mercy upon us; Christ have mercy upon us.

And had they put out the lights? Sure, they'd put out the lights; they were turning out the drunken boys, the drunken girls. And here he was; sure, here he was, assisted by the little lieutenant and doing his best to support the sergeant; here the three of them were; sure, here they were, out on the sidewalks of Greenwich Village and the air fresh and clear as cool spring water on the face, and the stars very bright in the sky ("star of the East the horizon adorning," etc., etc., etc.); sure, here, by God, they were, the clock striking four, assisting each other to the subway. Had he money for a taxi? No, he hadn't a red cent; and if he had the money, where in the devil would he find a taxi? Easy does it, easy does it, the little lieutenant with the dark eyes assisting him and he assisting the sergeant, getting to the subway, staggering down the subway stairs; easy does it, easy does it — allowing the sergeant (the poor, bereaved, motherless boy) to vomit again — standing at the booth, changing the bills. Was the lieutenant (good for the little lieutenant!) paying for them all, getting them through the gate? Easy does it, easy does it; and here was the big, thundering, lighted train roaring up on them, stopping for them, welcoming the three of them in with so much light and hospitality; and the three of them seated, collapsing one upon the other, riding the rails, riding the subway rails, up to the Bronx, over to Brooklyn — over the rails to Brooklyn or the Bronx — going to see Hilly, going to ask forgiveness, going to be forgiven.

F O U R T E E N

"No, dear, you may not," said Hilly.

"Please, Grandma."

"I don't want to hear any more about it; not another word."

"But why?"

She did her best not to drop the small hand that clung to hers as they crossed Fiftieth Street and bring Henry to terms with a smart box on his ear, but naturally she restrained herself. She'd never, she was happy to say, lost her temper with him. She'd been cross with him, yes. But she'd never lost her self-control. He was at times a very irritating child.

"But why, Grandma?"

"Now, Henry" — she stopped with him on the northeast corner of Fifth Avenue and looked him squarely in the eye — "I want no more of these 'but whyings.' You've long since outgrown that business and you're only going on with it now to anger me."

"But why, Grandma?"

She did not answer.

"But why?" he persisted.

She'd not give him the satisfaction of another rebuke.

"But *why*, Grandma?"

He trudged along sullenly beside her. Thank goodness, he'd shut up.

Why she had brought him she didn't know, and why she was persisting in her plans for the Christmas tree she didn't know either. They'd at last found the candles she'd wanted, but he'd shown no interest in them whatever; they'd braved the crowds at Kresge's in search of these blue and silver balls. But what he was still determined to do was to go to La Guardia Field. As though she hadn't told him a hundred times that his mother and the Captain were coming by train and that their train was late and that she didn't *know* what time they'd arrive.

If she was irritable, she couldn't help herself. The strain of the last two days had been too much for her. She was as taut as an elastic stretched to the snapping point. Not a word from Larry, and possessed all the time of this queer conviction that, with the usual perversity of events he set in motion, he'd turn up at exactly the wrong moment — apprehension riding her roughshod. Just what she expected was going to happen she couldn't say — something painful and disrupting. And with Anne's marriage an accomplished fact, it should be given every chance to get off to a good start. But it was this desire to see Larry, together with the certainty that he was in town, that was destroying her, and his not having answered her telegram. (Why had she sent that telegram? It had been unwise — most unwise.) If she could only subdue this excitement. For, after all, she hadn't seen Larry, or heard from him, for so long. And he couldn't go on excluding her like this forever. Better to have him come, even at the most awkward moment, than not to see him at all, to be ravaged with expectation and excitement.

At the corner of Lexington Avenue, Henry stopped her short. He was going, she feared, to make a scene. The poor child also was nervous, disappointed, irritable; nothing seemed to have turned out the way he'd expected it to, and if she'd been fond and foolish enough to think that in trimming up a Christmas tree, at such a cost of energy and fatigue to both of them, she was doing it all to propitiate him, she'd have to expect to pay for her folly.

"Daisy Mae," he said, "I think you're mean."

"Why am I mean?"

"Because you're mean."

"But why, Henry?"

"You don't let me do a thing I want to."

"You can *not* go to La Guardia Field; there isn't time for us to go."

"Why isn't there time?"

"Because your mother and the Captain might be here before we could get back. They are coming *by train*. You know this as well as I do. I've told it all to you before."

"When *will* the train be in?"

"I don't know; it's late. We'll telephone the station when we get home."

"Do we have to go home?" He pulled at her hand. "Can't we go to a movie or anything?"

"No."

"But why?"

"We have to have our Christmas tree."

"Oh, *that Christmas tree.*" Again he tugged fiercely at her hand. "Please, Daisy Mae; please; you know, it's Christmas — you ought to let me do exactly what I want to do."

They'd now reached Third Avenue. Standing there, she could see two movie houses. The one on the west side of Fiftieth Street advertised a special showing of *Snow White and the Seven Dwarfs* (an appropriate, a quite lovely spectacle for little children), and the theater across the street exhibited the well-known spiderweb, the long and bloody hand designed to grab and snatch in small fanatics of Henry's particular tastes and predilections.

"*Dracula*, Daisy Mae," he pleaded; "please, Grandma, please." (He was pulling at her arm.)

"No, dear, but if you care to go, I'll take you to see *Snow White and the Seven Dwarfs*. It's a lovely thing, and we'll just have time for it."

"No!" (He seemed to be pulling her along.) "I've seen it. It's a sissy. Come, Grandma — *please.*"

"Either you come with me to see *Snow White*, or I take you home immediately," she said with great authority.

He stopped abruptly, like a little donkey, and began to cry (poor child; he was as nervous as she was herself — pent up with waiting for his mother and the Captain). "I don't care, Grandma. I think you're mean. Mother lets me see the *Draculas.*"

"Oh, no, she doesn't, Henry."

"Yes, she does." He stamped his foot; he bawled — "Oh, ye-ss sh-ee do-es."

Was she actually allowing this headstrong little boy to drag her across the street? (There were the red lights and the traffic stopping.) Had she capitulated, or hadn't she? Dear me, she was the weakest of women; she had no discipline at all. Anne had said, however, that as far as the movies were concerned there was nothing for it but to let Henry have his own way; they didn't harm him and, moreover, they always kept him quiet as a mouse. And think what a comfort it would be to have him quiet for an hour or more. She needed an opportunity to plan things out (she was standing at the ticket booth; she'd opened her purse; she had bought the tickets).

"There," she said, "I've given in." She handed the tickets to Henry.

Into the theater they marched. Phew, how it smelled! The air was thick enough to knock you over.

Henry let go her hand. "Look, Daisy Mae, there are two seats." He dashed down the aisle, squirmed past a row of people, procured the seats, beckoned her on. Stumbling along behind him, she groped her way to his side.

Gracious, he'd already taken off his overcoat, folded it, seated himself upon it. Well, there was nothing for it but to take off her own hat and coat and settle down. What queer places these movie houses were — an extraordinary sense you had of closeness, a hugger-mugger feeling, shut up in this semidarkness with all these people, dragged along with them through so much human drama, in and out of all these beds, and rooms, and taxicabs and railway stations.

She averted her face; she didn't even intend to look at this particular picture. She'd come here to think things out. And, in the event of Larry's meeting Anne and the Captain in her apartment, she must act with great circumspection. The Captain was a well-mannered, disciplined young man, though there was something about him that had always struck her as a bit fanatical. He had never liked her, and he was certain to be prejudiced against Larry; and if Larry should happen to be in one of his insufferable moods, the situation might be most uncomfortable. The thing to do was to take it all as a matter of course, to be casual and affectionate with everybody, to maintain a gay, holiday spirit.

Impossible to continue thinking about it. Her memories claimed her. She'd been living in them for several days. A kind of compulsion was laid upon her to go into her past. Oh, it was very well for Anne to explain everything in these explicit Freudian terms, to tell her all about it. But hadn't she had the opportunity to watch this particular "case" develop, for over half a century? There were events — most important events — that had occurred before Anne or her precious Doctor

Brimmer had ever been born. And if much of this present anguish stemmed from the decision she had made in William's garden, hadn't that sudden unfortunate determination to rush off to Europe and join the relatives rested squarely on emotions undergone that other afternoon when she'd lain in the long grass and listened to her mother and Mrs. Constable whispering those dreadful mysterious secrets about Aunt Adelaide and Philip Davenport?

She placed her hands before her face and closed her eyes (Henry's whispers seemed to be fanning round her — "Daisy Mae, don't stop your ears like that! Don't be afraid. That man with a gun isn't going to shoot; and when he does, it won't make any noise; it's a quiet gun.").

She wouldn't notice him. The light that was dawning upon her was so intense, she must keep it unimpaired as long as possible. Her life on earth had been astonishing — no less; astonishing! Everything seemed to have come full circle. The wind had been sown, the whirlwind was to be reaped. Oh, there was a kind of inexorable logic about it — that she, who had been literally starved for love and beauty, for sexual and emotional expression, should have wreaked upon the one being in this world for whom she truly cared all this disaster; for that was exactly what she had done. Let her ask herself now. Had she ever been intent on giving Larry what was best for him? Had she made her plans in relation to his fullest growth and development? No, she had not — a thousand times, no! What she'd been bent on doing had been simply this: to give back to *herself*, to fill her own starved and hungry heart with the gifts that life had failed to offer her — to extract, to wrench them from this defenseless little creature. Why, she'd fed herself on his love, on his caresses, on his precocious response to her "gifts." She'd exploited every inclination, sensibility — his need for love, for joy, for beauty — oh, yes, if she must use the painful word, his sexual emotions, sensibilities. She'd played upon his emotions, drawn them out of him as you might draw music from an instrument. And then what had she done with them? She'd channeled them all one way — toward her, toward his perpetual need of her.

Oh, God forgive the mothers for the sins created in the name of love, she thought; and then, perversely, her heart cried out against Nature — against what appeared to be God's own provision, endowing the women, the mothers, with all these graces, dispensations, gifts. Where to dispense — where to withhold? Who could instruct them here? Only life to teach them, only the bitterness of their mistakes.

Ah, yes, she'd read about it in the books — this was an age of learning everything from books — think of the novels she had read. Think of Larry, the subtlety of his intelligence, the extraordinary manner in which he pried with his uncanny modern nerves into all the secrets. Think of the silences they'd kept.

She had a sudden impulse to go in search of him; what they needed now was speech, forgiveness, friendship. It was not too late for this. Good Heavens, he might have come while she was in this wretched theater! Why had she ever given in to Henry? It was more than likely that Larry was waiting for her at home. If she could only pry the little spellbound addict out of his chair!

She turned and saw, to her enormous astonishment, that Henry was on his feet. He was shaking out his overcoat — attempting to get into it. "Come, Daisy Mae," he whispered, "let's get out of here."

"What is it, Henry?" she inquired.

"Mum and the Captain," he said — "they might be coming; we don't want to miss them." He was wriggling into his overcoat.

She put on her hat; she plunged an arm into the sleeve of her fur coat as quickly as possible.

Presently they were out on the sunny slushy sidewalks, hurrying along together, with the trucks and taxis spattering them with mud. Henry's impatience was quite as urgent as her own. "Come on, Daisy Mae," he kept commanding, "hurry up."

When they arrived at the apartment, Delia Stone was at the door. "Did Mr. Larry come?" she asked, her heart thumping against her side.

"Are Mum and the Captain here?" asked Henry.

"No, nobody came," said Delia; "but a gentleman telephoned."

"A gentleman?" she questioned — "a gentleman, Delia?"

"Yes; his name was Styles — something like that. He wanted to know if Mr. Larry was here — just wanted to know. He said Mr. Larry was in New York."

F I F T E E N

THE TRAIN, THOUGHT HILLY, should now be in, according to the last word received from the station. But then, it might be even later than reported and she'd not delay lighting the Christmas tree. Delia Stone had, according to instructions, turned off all the lights in the apartment. It wasn't, as she had planned to have it, in the center of the floor, and it was not large, or decorated in the old-fashioned style, but where she'd placed it, on a table, at the extreme end of the big room, and with the long French windows just behind, it seemed, with the slender candles, the blue and silver balls so exquisitely disposed, and the silver angel shimmering at the top, to hold its own among her glittering skyscrapers and palaces of light.

"There, Henry, you can light it up," she said. She placed a chair and helped him onto it. "Look, I'll light the taper and if you'll be very careful you may light the candles."

She lit and handed him the long white tallow wand.

For some moments they were both of them absorbed. It was such a precise and pious little ritual, lighting, as she directed, first one candle and then another, watching their little tree take on a flame and flicker of its own. Suddenly, looking out at the night, the sky, the bright incredible edifices standing round, a great wave of strong emotion came surging up into her heart, for it seemed to her that these lights which they were kindling had become the central point of brightness in the splendid spectacle and that all the diamond windows, all the towers and terraces and tenements, were merely temporary civic splendors and adornments set up and brilliantly illuminated in honor of this august and tender ceremony.

"There, dear, I think that's all." She took the taper and blew it out.

"Oh, boy — some tree." Henry jumped down, grasped her hand and stood back to survey his accomplishment.

The child seemed actually awed. She'd let him take his fill of it.

"Daisy Mae," he finally said, "it's swell — with all the skyscrapers and everything; I think it's swell."

Then he jumped, and a current like an electric shock traversed her heart. The bell was ringing.

"Oh, boy! Mother and the Captain; here they are." Henry ran as fast as possible in the direction of the door.

She must make an effort to control her agitation. It hardly seemed likely that this was Larry. She hoped now that it was not (let him come later — let him come later). Delia had outflanked Henry. She'd got to the door first. She was opening it, letting in — who in the world *was* she letting in?

"It's Mr. Styles," said Delia.

Dear me, it *couldn't* be that young man — she'd never laid eyes on him. What was his name — Sykes or something of the sort? How could he have arrived at just this particular juncture? How could anything so awkward have possibly occurred?

She threw an arm round Henry. "No, dear, it's not your mother. They'll be arriving in a minute. Yes, Mr. Sykes?" She made a question of her greeting and held out her hand, a little stiffly, perhaps, but she never could be too cold to Larry's young men — she felt somehow so sorry for them. And what an extraordinarily beautiful creature, looking so agitated, so distressed, unable to say a word, just standing there and gaping at her, at Henry, at her charming room, her Christmas tree, as though there were something here — some vision glimpsed, a goal achieved, a moment arrived at, to ease, assuage the heart. He was quite unable to get on with the painful business of explaining his presence.

"What did you want of me?" she asked.

He begged to be excused for coming. He felt a little anxious, he said — he merely wanted to know if Larry had come home.

Really, the poor fellow was overwhelmed. There was something very poignant about it, feeling she had such accurate knowledge of the sorrow that was in the poor boy's heart. They loved him so, these friends of Larry's, and always on first sight; it seemed that they transferred something of this love they had for him to her — as though some power reposed in her to comfort and assist.

"He's not been yet," she said, attempting to be casual, unconcerned. "Did you come with him? I thought your home was Washington."

"Well, yes. No," he hesitated, stammered. "Well, yes. I followed him, you see; I followed him from Washington."

"Followed him? Followed him, Mr. Sykes?" Impossible to keep from displaying anxiety, agitation.

He assured her there was nothing wrong — nothing wrong at all with Larry.

This did, in a measure, relieve her mind but indicated, as she made it out, that as far as the poor fellow was concerned just everything was wrong; and she should at this point have said, with Henry pulling at her skirts, looking dark and sullen, practically commanding her to rid them both of this intrusion, that she was afraid she could do nothing to help him, that she was busy and expecting visitors. But instead she said (it was this fatal sympathy, this capacity she seemed to have to understand all that was moving in the young man's heart), "Won't you come in a moment arid see our Christmas tree? Henry and I have just been lighting the candles."

He followed her into the living room. Standing there beside him, seeing him bowled over by the beauty, the sheer astonishing drama of her exhibition, she realized the extent of her folly in having asked him in. Here he was, and how would she manage to get rid of him, with Anne and the Captain expected at any moment now? Of all the people in the world the one she *didn't* want on hand when they arrived! But the poor young man was so affected by the spectacle — these gestures (raising the hand to the back of the head, lifting the shoulders, this sudden letting forth of gasps and long-drawn sighs, this attempt to express the inexpressible), she was familiar with them; but here there was a difference, the presence of some never quiet, some prodigious need. Heavens, he didn't have to tell her anything. She knew about it all — the meagerness of his life, the hungers in his heart, the unsatiated, naive craving for beauty, culture, art. She knew his fathomless desire, the extent of his devotion to Larry: and, moreover, she knew perfectly well that what he longed at this moment to do was simply to fall down and worship. What was it he wanted to worship, with that queer look of rapture on his face? He'd seen his vision, certainly.

"Enchanting, isn't it, Mr. Sykes — my little Christmas tree, with the skyscrapers walking in through all these doors and windows?" Her voice was as silly and frivolous as Aunt Adelaide's, she thought; but then she must not, on any account, let him see how much she felt for him.

The "oh's" and the "ah's" fairly gushed from him; he wanted apparently to let her know that he was taking in each detail. He'd seen the angel, he was gushing over that, the look of trance still fixed upon his face. "The angel!" he exclaimed. "A little silver angel!"

And then, all of a sudden, she left him there, clasping his hands, expatiating, for Henry had begun to shout; he was bellowing, stampeding off. "Oh, boy! Oh, joy! They've come —they're really here!" Henry rushed, she was rushing herself, and what was happening to the poor young man, she really wouldn't know, for here they were at last, the door had opened to let them in, Anne first and Henry flying at her — "Mother, Mum" — the Captain in the rear, Henry jumping on the Captain, clamping his knees right round him, clinging like a little monkey; all three talking at once — Henry's joyous acclamation, "You're married, you really got married?" the Captain's rejoinder, "Yes, kid, we're married" — Henry unclamping himself, rushing off to Anne, the two of them embracing and Anne's voice so full of feeling, "My darling, my darling." And now Delia was standing aside to let her pass. She was taking her part in the greetings and encounters (doing it all, she hoped, with some dignity and grace).

"Anne, dear," she said, "my dear Anne. Welcome home!"

"Darling Hilly!" Anne kissed her with more than usual fervor. "Darling Hilly," she repeated, and though she didn't actually come out with it, what her face demanded of her was: "Where is Larry? Have you heard from him? Do you expect him? Is he here?"

She held Anne off at arm's length. "How well you look, my dear" (which was far from being the case — she looked thin and strained and exceedingly nervous). "And the Captain?" She turned. "I must congratulate Captain Fletcher."

She shook hands with George (oh, no, the Captain didn't like her — there was every evidence of hostility).

"How do you do, Mrs. Danforth," he said with great formality and bowing very stiffly.

"You are to be congratulated: you have won a prize," she said.

He bowed again.

She became at once practical, hospitable. She helped them off with their coats; she told Delia to hang up their things; she inquired about their luggage: Had they left it with the doorman in the lobby? Wouldn't they like to tidy up a bit?

"No, Hilly," Anne explained. "We stopped first at my apartment — that's why we came so late. We left everything there."

She was convinced that they'd been quarreling. They'd brought the remnants of their quarrel in with them; the air was thick with it. The Captain clearly had been holding out against too much association with Larry's mother.

"Come," shouted Henry. "Come. We've got a tree. Daisy Mae and I have just been lighting it. It has real candies; it's the real McCoy." Prancing ahead, he led them in to look at it.

"Oh, ah, how beautiful!" she heard Anne and the Captain cry out almost in a single breath.

And who could help exclaiming, with the room still darkened and the candles flickering and all that diamond architecture in the sky? It did take one's breath away — from this height and on this particular Christmas Eve — how could anyone help being moved?

"You're wonderful!" Anne exclaimed. "You're perfectly wonderful, Hilly. You always do everything with so much style, imagination."

"I did it too," Henry insisted. "I did it too, Mum."

"Of course you did, my darling." Anne enveloped him again in her embrace.

And then, when she'd released him, there they all stood confronted with poor deserted Mr. Sykes, very ill at ease indeed, and with his hand still raised and held against the back of his head. A difficult situation, which it was up to her to meet. The Captain had obviously taken him for Larry and was bristling with hostility, looking daggers at the poor young man, and Anne, who'd identified him at once, throwing her a glance which seemed to say, "How could you have done this to me, Hilly?"

"Let me present Mr. Sykes," she said. "Mr. Sykes, this is my daughter-in-law; and this is" (how *could* she ever have put it like that?) "my son-in-law, Captain Fletcher, Captain George Fletcher, AAF."

"Styles," corrected the young man — "Gerald Styles."

"Styles," she said — "oh, yes, of course. I'm *so* sorry. Mr. Gerald Styles."

What the Captain longed to do (she could see it perfectly well — it was written all over his face) was to take Gerald by the scruff of his neck and kick him out of the room. He didn't like his type and from now on he was going to see to it that Anne should be free of the kind of young men who apparently frequented this apartment. However, the Captain was very well disciplined. He controlled himself; he was a man of character (character was written all over the Captain's face). He had deliberately turned his back on — what was the young man's name? Styles — yes, that was it — Gerald Styles — deliberately turned his back on him; and now he had his arm round Henry (the way he appropriated that child was a bit thick — she wondered how Anne was going to put up with this). "I have something to show you, kid," he said. He was taking him back to the hall, where he'd left his overcoat.

"He's brought him some presents," Anne explained; "he wants to show them to him," and again her eyes seemed to be begging for news of Larry. If only there were time to tell her what she knew concerning him, but the first thing she ought to do was to get rid of Gerald Sykes. It would be awkard, very embarrassing (she wondered why the poor fellow hadn't gotten himself out long since) — and now, with Henry and the Captain out there in the hall, it would be doubly difficult.

And Heavens! What *was* Henry making such a noise about, rushing in with the Captain at his heels? "Greatest show on earth; exhibition tonight, La Guardia Field; newest model fighter; stunt flying, Captain George Fletcher, AAF. Exhibition tonight." The child was overstimulated; he was beside himself with excitement, and the Captain, somewhat handicapped by all those little boxes he had under his arm, trying to catch him. "Give me back that fighter, Henry — I want to show you something," dodging each other, dashing this way and that all round the table, regardless of the tree and all the lighted candles.

"Henry!" shouted Anne. "Henry!"

And now she was shouting herself — mercy, how loud her voice was; she had not intended to interfere. But the child was making for the long French window just behind the Christmas tree —"Don't go out there; Henry, don't go onto the terrace."

He made a dash for it; he opened the door. Out he ran and in came a great draft of wintry air, extinguishing more than half the candles on the tree. Heavens, what a dangerous thing!

They all shouted; everybody was shouting.

But only the Captain prevailed. He was most severe. You could see that this young man was accustomed to obedience. "Come back," he ordered. "Come back this minute. Don't you hear your mother telling you to come?"

Henry returned, meek as a lamb, cowed and sheepish.

"Shut the door," the Captain commanded. "Give me back the plane. Apologize to your mother."

He obeyed. "I'm sorry, Mum." He gave back the plane. He cast upon the Captain a look of abject devotion. "I'm very sorry, Captain Fletcher."

George put out his hand. "Okay, kid," he said, "don't let it happen again."

She could see what Anne had meant about his being good for Henry. But it was a mistake, Anne's marrying him. She would not be happy with him. They were now engaged in carrying on the discussion which had undoubtedly begun before they arrived. He'd taken her aside; she could hear him say in a none too subtle whisper, "Let's get out of here; let's get out of here at once," and, though she couldn't hear what Anne replied, it was obvious that she was trying to explain to him how impossible it was to do so, pointing to the room, the tree. She'd not do this for anything.

And all at once she grasped at an idea — it leaped into her mind as the only clear solution. Why shouldn't they go — just as quickly as she could get them out? She would approach them now, in the midst of their discussion, and very tactfully, very affectionately, and as though she hadn't heard a word they'd said, suggest it to them. She'd say that they must be very tired, that she knew they wanted to get home and take off the clothes they'd traveled in. If they wanted to take Henry, Delia Stone could pack his things and bring them later in the evening.

But they'd settled their dispute and it looked to her as though Anne had been victorious — the Captain, with all his little boxes, settling down with Henry at the big desk in the corner. Why couldn't she have acted quicker? There was, however, nothing to prevent her from tackling Anne.

"Anne," she said, "Anne, look here a moment."

But Anne was looking elsewhere.

"Larry," Anne cried; "look — here's Larry coming in."

How idiotic not to have remembered he had his latchkey — keeping her ears alerted for the doorbell. Here he was, striding up to them, and never had she been so glad to see anyone in all her life; but it was all pretty shattering, coming unannounced and at this most inauspicious moment.

"Larry — my darling."

"Mother."

"Dearest."

A loving, spontaneous reunion. His kiss, his embrace, this swift, sweet sense of tenderness that flooded her. Oh, she was forgiven — something had broken in Larry's heart. No anger toward her, no hostility. He had come for reconciliation — this she knew. What peace, what reassurance in the thought. She could get through with all this now — the awkward moments, the queer contingencies. She would simply rest in the thought that she was forgiven. Let the situation develop as it might; she would not interfere.

She released him.

Goodness, how fatigued he looked — how terribly disheveled and unshaven — his clothes as mussed as though he'd slept in them a week. And his face so ashen, standing there and taking stock of everything, exposing his sensitiveness, his awareness of them all. He knew, never doubt it, every shade of Anne's emotions and was likely to take advantage of his intimations. Now he'd caught sight of Gerald Styles. "What the devil, what to hell" — that's what his face had registered, but whether he was angry at seeing him there, she wouldn't know; he was undoubtedly surprised. His eyes went roaming round in search of Henry. There'd been no cry of welcome from the child; he'd simply disregarded his father's arrival — he and the Captain occupied with opening packages, playing with those little airplanes. Larry's eyes were resting on them. Oh, God, how strange it was that, as well as she knew her son, she could never at any given moment be certain just how he was going to act! "Larry dear" (she'd begun to pray — absurdly, idiotically), "behave yourself. It is not necessary for you to be cruel; be kind to Anne, my darling. You must not insult the Captain. You must not be insulting to anybody. Remember, dear, it will soon be over — you have come here with one purpose only, our reconciliation."

Anne was speaking to him, telling him how awful he looked, simply terrible. "Wherever have you been?" she asked — "Larry, where *have* you been?" And Gerald too had begun to question him, "You're all right, Larry — nothing's happened to you?"

He answered neither one nor the other. Went right up to Anne and kissed her, held her at arm's length, subjected her to a long and careful scrutiny. (Was he going to say to her that she looked awful too? And did he, or didn't he, know that she was married to the Captain?) Henry and the Captain were glowering darkly at them from the corner ("'please, my darling — please, restrain yourself").

"Congratulations, Anne," he said; "congratulations — thanks for telling me about it." And what was he doing now, taking a telegram from his pocket, reading it aloud? "Married this morning Captain George Fletcher AAF. Very happy. Love." He repeated the name — "'Captain George Fletcher, AAF." And then he said, "It seems you picked a hero this time, Anne. I'm here to shake his hand, to tell him what a prize he's won."

"George," Anne called, "Henry."

There was no response.

"Henry, your father's here. I want you to come and speak to him."

(Heavens — it wasn't decent of the Captain simply sitting there, with Henry waiting on him for instructions; you might think he owned the child.)

"Henry!"

No. This was Anne's business. She'd leave it all to Anne. She closed her mouth; she put her hand up to cover it — she would not say another word. But the Captain should *insist* on Henry's obedience. He'd been severe enough before, in all conscience. The two of them seemed to enjoy their defiance. Just sitting there and virtually declaring that Larry had no authority. (The way George had bound that child to him was most astonishing, incredible!)

"George, please; I beg you to ask Henry to obey me." Anne's voice had become hysterical.

And now she was adding her own voice to the protests (exactly what she'd vowed she wouldn't do) — "Henry, don't you hear your mother? Come at once; your father's waiting."

No reply from Henry. (How obdurate that child could be!)

It seemed that, as he wouldn't come to them, Anne and Larry were walking in his direction. How determined Anne looked. She must keep out of it. This was her chance to speak to Mr. Sykes. Just the moment to ask him to withdraw. She put out her hand; she laid it on the young man's arm — "Mr. Styles" (yes, that was his name, Styles, not Sykes), "Mr. Styles, don't you think — this seems to be a family situation." Goodness, there was something quite startling in the way he stared at Larry — he seemed fixed to the spot, as though you could under no circumstances persuade him to leave. How we all longed to protect Larry; and, God knew it, only Larry could protect himself. (Larry, my dear, compose yourself; do, my dear, compose yourself.)

She saw, they all saw, that Larry was attempting to embrace his child and that Henry appeared to be resisting him, glancing up at the Captain for instructions. How implacable the Captain looked. Anne had gone dead-white.

"Henry," Anne said, her voice shaking noticeably, "here is your father — speak to him."

Henry put his hands behind his back.

Larry shrugged.

Really, she couldn't endure another moment of it. She closed her eyes ("Larry, my dear son, you're acting very well. Control yourself a little longer; this will soon be over.") The silence was terribly ominous. If she opened her eyes and said something, maybe she could relieve the tension, and the obvious thing to do was to ask Anne and Henry and the Captain to go home at once. But Larry had broken the silence.

"I'm proud to meet a man with all those decorations on his chest," he said. His voice was cool, without a tremor. He extended his hand.

Really, the Captain could not go so far — refusing to shake hands with Larry! "Captain Fletcher" (she couldn't help it, the words leapt out of her mouth), "Captain Fletcher!"

Larry shrugged a second time. He was taking up one of the little air-planes, examining it, and Henry was again glancing at the Captain for instructions. You could see he felt that Larry's appropriating one of the precious toys ought to be reprimanded and that, with any encourage-ment from George, he would have snatched it right out of his father's hands. Thank Heavens, the Captain did not encourage him to do this — it would have been too raw and insolent for words. Anne's self-control was surprising — what she plainly longed to do was to rush to Larry's defense, to declare how much she loved him, and to turn vehe-mently on the Captain. Thank goodness, she refrained from doing so. She seemed, like Gerald Styles, to hang fascinated on Larry's every move. The Captain, and Henry too, were in a queer way spelled and bound by him. There he stood, seemingly disregardful of the Captain's insults and Henry's snubs, carefully examining the little plane.

"What a beautiful toy," he said — "a perfect model, a B-29." He lifted it in his hand and began to put it through some swift movements in the air — soarings and descents, very graceful and pretty, this way and that, improvising as he did so a sort of chant, words that had a beauty and rhythm of their own and which, she suddenly realized, were a para-phrase of Blake's "Early Morning Song of the Birds"; why, she'd taught him that poem years ago in their old garden at Antibes. How many times they'd repeated it together; how skillfully he was improvising on it now.

> "The child filled with divine afflatus just as the morn
> Appears, exultant waits, then springing from the
>   beauteous planet,
> Loud he leads the choirs of joy — bang bang bang,
> Mounting upon the wings of light into the great expanse,
> Reaching against the lovely blue and shining heavenly skies.
> His little heart labors with exultation — bang bang bang;
> He cries, stretching his little arm outside the fuselage,
>   every creature
> On the earth beneath him — the thrush, the linnet,
>   the goldfinch,
> The wren and robin, the young men and the maidens,
>   the mothers

And the infants in their wombs, the glaciers, and
   the tundras — trembles,
All nature listens silent to him, and the awful sun
Stands still upon the mountain, looking at the little boy."

It was extraordinary how little he'd changed the text, substituting a word here, adding a word there, making it an instrument for the expression of his grief and indignation. Every word was loaded. Why, he seemed to have taken hold of everybody's feelings and stretched them to the breaking point.

It wasn't as though any of them knew the poem, or had the ghost of an idea that it was through Blake's freshness and spontaneity, his divine wonder and joy in God's created world, that Larry had somehow been able to release his indignation. She was certain Anne and Gerald thought he'd made the whole thing up —improvised it suddenly — and yet she knew they understood it was more than just a personal thrust at the Captain, a petty show of animosity. Each of them knew how deeply Larry suffered from the world that we were living in today.

Not so the Captain, not so the Captain. There he sat, with all his little toys spread out around him on the desk, trying his best to control himself. You could see he was determined, if possible, not to give in to his anger. Every word of Larry's recitation had seemed to him an insult — an affront leveled against him and all the other heroes of the air. You could see how he hated, loathed, Larry and all this meaningless jargon he'd put together for the sole purpose of insulting, antagonizing him — a man without courage, an amoral cad, a kind of would-be-something-or-other, no good to the world, no good to anybody in it. It was all written on the Captain's face as clearly as though he were shouting his thoughts for everyone to hear. And there beside him stood Henry, responding to everything he felt, waiting for a sign.

Suddenly he got up and, without a word, strode off and out of the door behind the tree, Henry running after him.

A big draught blew through the room. Anne got up and called to Henry.

Heavens, how the candles and the branches of the tree were blown about. She called for help (thank goodness, she'd decided against all that tinsel and the paper trimmings); Gerald Styles had come to help her; there, they'd got the candles out.

"Don't let Henry stay on the terrace," Anne was calling frantically. "George, do you hear me — I want Henry to come back."

She'd begun to call, herself (it was abominable of the Captain to override Anne's discipline): "Henry! Don't you hear Daisy Mae telling you to come?"

"Larry, please," urged Anne, "use your authority" — her voice was desperate.

But here was Henry, like a small cowed puppy (thank goodness, the Captain had come to his senses). He stepped in. Gerald closed the door. She hoped Anne would not punish the child, for, after all, the Captain was the culprit. Henry should never have been allowed to follow him.

Anne grabbed hold of him. "Henry," she admonished severely, "you know you're forbidden to go onto the terrace." Larry was standing beside them. How strange he looked — Blake apparently still echoing in his mind. "Darling," said Anne, and her voice was far from gentle. "I want you to welcome your father. Kiss him and wish him a Merry Christmas."

The child regarded his father with an expression of defiance; there was something both proud and hostile in his attitude. "I hate you," he said very slowly and distinctly, "I hate you." He put his hands behind his back.

Oh, God, this was too much to bear. The situation should never have come to this pass. It was worse than she had ever imagined it could be. Why hadn't she asked them all to leave — simply ordered them out? What would Larry do now? What impulse was upon him? Clearly, he didn't intend to reprimand Henry. Anne was doing the reprimanding, sharply, and Henry (poor child, he was terribly wrought up) was bursting into a violent storm of tears.

Larry turned — there was something in his face that terrified her. He stepped behind the table, opened the door and went onto the terrace. Gerald followed him (she was glad, somehow, that the young man was with him). She wanted to follow, herself — to cry out to him. But, after all, they were grown men. This was their affair and they must have it out together.

The door was open. Henry continued to cry. Poor child, he wept as though his heart would break. There were voices from the terrace, raised but controlled. Larry so seldom indulged in violence, he hated violence — his tongue was his weapon. He would use his tongue. And the Captain was a man of the utmost self-control. It would not, it must not, come to blows.

"Larry," Anne called. "George, please."

The voices were louder. The Captain was using most unpleasant words. She was unfamiliar with them, but she understood their meaning very well — Larry didn't like such epithets.

Now it was Larry, drowning out the Captain, telling him to get to hell out of here. This was his affair, his business. He'd thank him to lay his hands off his child — and then again the string of awful epithets, words she'd certainly never heard, but from the expression of Anne's face and from the knowledge in her heart she had the key to them. How perfectly frightful was the wrath of these strong heroic men who'd fought the bloody battles of the war — one looked into the awful caverns of the soul. If only she did not have to listen. She raised her hands and stopped her ears. But still she could hear them. Now Larry's voice was ordering Gerald to get to hell out of here.

Gerald was returning, pale and trembling. She went to him and laid her hands on his arm. "Is there nothing we can do, Mr. Styles — nothing we can do to stop them?"

They'd stopped shouting at each other. The silence seemed ominous. Then the shouting began again. Anne went to the door and called, "Larry, George, for Henry's sake, for my sake, please, please!"

Suddenly she stopped calling — she stood as though she'd been turned to stone. And then she stepped back into the room and fell into a chair. She covered her face with her hands.

She and Jerry were unable to move, unable to speak to her; the same conjecture paralyzed them both. They simply stood and stared at Anne, how long she didn't know, and when suddenly Larry appeared in the doorway it seemed to them that they beheld a ghost.

He came in, closed the door, stood against it.

Gerald made a motion with his hands. Anne attempted to shake off her paralysis.

"It can not be; it is not so," she cried. (Oh, Larry, my beloved son!)

Staring at him as he stood confronting them she ranged herself with Anne and Gerald in a frantic effort to evade the awful evidence. They formed a solid front against it. Words were not necessary. They had become conspirators in thought. To save Larry. That was their purpose. Were there not three of them to prove him guiltless? They must stand united in their declaration of his innocence. He had not killed the Captain. It had been an accident — a misstep; the terrace was slippery; or it might have been the suicide of a young airman shattered by the war. With the interchange of plots and thoughts, with this perfidious will to believe their self-deception they seemed actually to have thrust the fearful truth aside, to have prevailed upon each other to believe their own denials. Larry was not a murderer.

He stepped free of the door. His eyes were fixed on hers. He was talking to the three of them, but he kept his eyes on her. "Yes," he said, and his voice was perfectly controlled, "oh, yes; I know. I have three witnesses. And all of you are honorable people — very much to be relied upon. There are various things that you could say — it might easily have been an accident; you could invent a suicide, anything you'd fix your mind upon. I know you love me. You would perjure your souls to save me. But I have killed the Captain. I pushed him over the railing. Don't ask me if it was premeditated, if I pushed him in cold blood. I pushed him and he's fallen sixteen flights. Down in the area he lies."

"Oh, but you can't!" cried Anne: "You couldn't say it, Larry. It was an accident; it must have been an accident."

"It was an accident," Gerald implored him. "I know it was an accident."

He did not look at either of them. He held her with his level gaze. "Will you betray me, Hilly?" his eyes inquired sternly. "Are you willing to perjure your soul?" Suddenly he dropped his eyes and walked very resolutely toward the telephone. (Gerald and Anne rushed at him; they both tried frantically to stop him.) "You can't, Larry — you can't,"they cried. He pushed them roughly aside.

She remained silent; she acquiesced.

He took the receiver; his voice was extraordinarily calm and firm. "I want the police," he said (those were the directions, she recollected, on the back of the telephone book; when one wanted to report a fire, when one wanted to call the police, just dial the central office). "Yes," she heard him say, "I want to report a murder." Then there was a pause

— they must have asked for the address. He gave it to them. "A witness?" (He was asking back the inquiry.) "No, not a witness — the killer," she heard him say. "Yes, I've killed a man. I've pushed him over the terrace."

She sat down. She thought she'd fainted; but no — she had not. There was Anne, leading Henry out of the room, and she heard Larry's voice, still firm, going on with further details — "You will find the body in the area. This is the sixteenth floor. Yes, my name is Danforth"; and, finally (a trifle irritated), "yes, I'm the man you want. I told you that before. I give myself up." He put the receiver back on the hook.

And now at last he'd come to her. They were united — he was beside her, kneeling on the floor; his face was buried in her lap.

"Maman, Maman," he said, "je t'aime, Maman, je t'aime."

S I X T E E N

———————

THE LIGHT CAME LATE. Hilly glanced at her watch — a quarter to eight. Over there, beyond Welfare Island, above the streets of Brooklyn and the Flushing marshes, the sun was already visible. Cold and still — hardly a ripple of breeze, the tide high, flowing strong, a boat passing with all sails stripped, lights still shining in the rigging; and now the gulls rising, descending, riding the tide, the church bells ringing and this big cloud of morning, netted with mist and frost and darkness, with snow light and river light and a million invisible beams from the rising sun, dissolving, spreading slowly over Queens, over Manhattan.

The first line of the fine old hymn (she had sung it with Larry in the little church at Antibes, and she remembered how it used to swell through the big vaulted aisles at St. George's) came into her mind — "Joy to the world! The Lord is come." It was *the* Christmas-morning hymn; one felt that it dispensed a kind of universal joy.

Emotion so powerful and overwhelming rose in her breast that it checked her breath and caused her to press both hands against her throat. Was it, she wondered, because her pain was so great, or because a mood of such extraordinary solemnity was upon her that she wished to hold it in her heart a little longer? She'd not be able to say. She was not without a curious sense of exultation. Here she'd sat for hours looking at the city and the river and the sky. She'd expiated her mistakes. The cup she'd drained was all she would possess of wisdom. Of this she was convinced. Might it be possible she could at this eleventh hour command some sapience and strength to offer Anne and little Henry? Strange she should feel this singular sense of courage. She expected that there was a core of sternness in her. The mood would pass of course — give way a thousand times to moments of anguish and de-spair. But let her hold it while it lasted. There was strength she realized in the integrity of grief.

Had she, she wondered, grasped the unadorned, unalterable facts? They had taken Larry off to the Tombs; that was, if she recollected correctly, the name of the city prison where they sent criminals await-ing bail or trial for their crimes. To even think of the ordeals ahead of her — impossible, impossible. A kind of stony courage would be given her; she'd meet them somehow. Best not to think about them. They had telegraphed George's parents — no details, just the stark fact that he was dead. They were already on their way to New York, and whether she would have to meet them and talk with them and, if so, what she would find to say to them in their bereavement were ques-tions she would have to wait on time to solve for her. There would be the hideous publicity. The papers were filled every day with these bloodcurdling histories — crime, murder, violence. This was the fare on which the public feasted. These were violent times. The appetite for crime appeared to be insatiable. But who could understand more fully, oh, who could realize more completely than she could realize now, that the facts, the headlines, the shocking public story were not what signified? It was elsewhere one searched for meaning and message — for reality.

And, in the closing moments of their fateful tragedy, she and Larry had stood together with complete fidelity. It was in the inward drama that she could rest and draw from it a kind of awesome consolation. She had realized the instant he had come in from the terrace that he didn't care a rap, not so much as the snap of his fingers, for his life. To give it up was a necessity he wasn't even questioning, and when he'd turned on them with so much disdain, realizing, as he had, that the three of them would have been willing to perjure their souls if they could, by so doing, have saved him, her shame had been excoriating. Instantly she had resolved to stand by him, no matter what he might impose upon her in his acknowledgment of guilt. She'd restrained her-self; she'd uttered not a word of protest while he'd stood there tele-phoning, giving out that fearful information. How clear his voice had been — without a tremor. Then, when he'd come and knelt beside her, waiting there together, their reconciliation had been absolute — a few

brief moments in which they had been unconscious of any need outside the necessity for physical nearness, dearness, a sense of safety in
each other's love. How long that silence, that pause in the dread inexorable events, prevailed she wasn't sure. Very likely it had been only a
few minutes before the wail and shriek of the sirens in the street below
announced the rising of the curtain on the final act of the melodrama.
Throughout it all she had had the strangest imaginable feeling that the
surface events and settings — the presence of all those policemen and
inspectors, the flashlights, the uniforms, the badges, her own familiar
interior with the skyscrapers outside, the disordered Christmas tree, the
various actors going through their roles (and even taking part herself
in the tragic drama, implicated in its grief and terror) — had been only
a series of dissolving pictures on a flickering screen, vaguely remembered, and which she was now rehearsing in a kind of troubled retrospect, for in this atmosphere of cinema, of utter unreality, they passed
from minute to minute, from scene to scene. She'd got through with it;
she'd acted her role; when it had been necessary, she'd stepped before
the cameras. Larry had been determined, from the instant the police
arrived, to prove that there was no escape for him. It had been necessary to reenact the crime, there on the terrace, with the policemen and
the plainclothesmen and the witnesses, the flashlights searching the
terrain. He had conducted them to the exact spot where he said he'd
pushed the Captain over the wall, and when Anne and Gerald had
cried, "No, no; it was an accident, he hadn't meant to do it," when he'd
said to the inspectors, fixing her with his eyes, "Yes, I meant to do it;
ask my mother," when she'd replied, "You must abide by what my son
has told you," when she had added that she'd been in the apartment
and had not witnessed the crime, but had seen, as Larry followed the
Captain onto the terrace, an expression on his face that had terrified
her (Anne and Gerald looking at her in consternation; they'd been
dumbfounded; they'd expected her support), when she'd gone on to
describe her fear, it had not been with what she'd said or done that
she'd actually been concerned. What was active in her heart, what had
filled her consciousness and would remain with her forever was this
sense she had of unity with Larry, acting in accord with him — the
constant passing between them of message and reassurance, message
and reassurance; for this matter of their private and particular tragedy,

he kept assuring her, all this present melodrama, and his getting off to Sing Sing to pay the final penalty, would be merely a part, an infinitesimal part of the monstrous, wholesale and unspeakable melodrama that was afflicting the world today, and if he had committed the awful crime of killing the Captain, he would expiate it, he would expiate it gladly, gladly. The Captain was a hero, a young man who had taken a more than honorable part in winning the war. There were many heroes in the world — millions of heroes in the world today. But who, he'd seemed to ask her again and again, could expiate the unutterable crime of putting into their innocent, their young and heroic hands, these satanic weapons, these infernal mechanisms they controlled? Somehow she had managed to convey her acquiescence; they'd been one in comprehension of the values here involved.

And when, at the last moment, handcuffed and already in the custody of the law, he'd stood beside her and she had said in a voice drained of all emotion, not daring even to kiss him, "Goodbye, Larry, my beloved son," when he'd stooped and kissed her and whispered, "Au revoir, Maman," when they had led him from the room, she had not faltered. She had kept her troth. How terrible he'd looked — unshaven, disheveled, his clothes so shamefully disordered, the outer man in a condition of complete dilapidation; but with what pride, with what great pride she had watched him go!

There was a flickering, a brightness, somewhere in the room. She turned; she lifted her eyes. The light was smiting the silver angel on the top of Henry's Christmas tree; poised and trembling, with its wings and herald trumpet shining brightly, there it hung above the guttered candles and the general disarray.

"Pardon us our iniquities, forgive us our transgressions — have mercy on the world," she prayed.

MANY MANSIONS

BOOK I

O N E

IT HAD SNOWED IN THE NIGHT, but the snow had been removed from the streets. It rained. The asphalt shone black and glistened in the rain, the tops of the taxis glistened, the umbrellas of the pedestrians and the rubber coat of the policeman at the corner of Twenty-eight Street gave off a bright metallic sheen. The air heavy with clouds and smoke and rain hung like a shroud over the city. In the tall office buildings clustered at the foot of Madison Avenue the lights shining in the assembled windows gave the effect of countless diminished suns and moons peering dead and rayless into the gloom and diffused an ominous light like the amber glow that fills the atmosphere before a summer storm.

A radio in the next room blared out the news, from the clouds above came the purr and drone of an airplane and from below the noises of the streets; motor cars grinding their brakes, tooting their horns; sirens, an ambulance, in the distance the louder siren screech of fire engines. In another room a telephone rang insistently. Wires under the pavements, cables under the seas, voices upon the air weaving the plots, weaving the calamities, thought Miss Sylvester, beating her breast in that dramatic way she had.

She was a small creature with delicate bones and transparent parchmentlike skin and her fragility lent her the appearance both of youthfulness and extreme old age. Her face under its crown of perfectly white hair was illumined and animated by cavernous dark eyes that seemed in the most striking manner to isolate her spirit from the visible decay of her body and in the play of her expression there was that immediacy of the countenance to respond to the movements of the heart which is always so noticeable in the faces of children.

Living so much alone she was in the habit of talking aloud — interrupting her thoughts — "My God, it cannot be! Preposterous. Impossible." Old age was very obstreperous indeed and life perched up here in her sky parlor amid these congregations of lighted windows, looking into all these offices, watching people sitting at desks, at telephones, dictating letters, plowing through the most monotonous tasks, was bleak enough in all conscience and with this welter of imponderable event flowing through her mind, "Good God," she frequently asked herself, "Who am I? What am I? And what's the meaning of it all, these people — all this business conducted high in air — listening to these hotel radios, these telephones and this roar coming up from the streets as though escaped from the infernal circles?" After all, she was human; she had her human needs. Caged up like this!

But now the protest and revolt that had lighted her face went suddenly blank and was replaced by gentle, reminiscent expressions, for she had had an extraordinarily beautiful experience in the night — the nights of the old were stranger than strange. She had waked from a dreadful dream, sobbing, still, it seemed to her, violently shaking her grandmother and when she had subdued the sobs there she'd lain trying to orient herself. She had touched, or imagined that she had done so, the edge of the bureau, her hand had knocked, or she'd thought she'd knocked it against the wall; the wall retreated while the doors and the single window of her room were replaced by other windows, other walls and doors, and she had had the most bewildering sense of knowing and at the same time not having the slightest idea where she was, listening to many voices while large vistas — lawns and trees and meadows and blue skies and oceans — opened up to her and people appeared and disappeared in all the various rooms through which she searched. Gradually she made out that she was in her own small bed which she had been sure was on the left of the window now restored to its proper position. Left was left and right was right. And there she was correctly located in space while a clock struck twelve. She'd counted the strokes and crossed a threshold. For it was, she'd remembered, her birthday, the first of February, 1950, and if she could believe such a thing she was now eighty-four years old. Highly awake to the inordinate strangeness of it all she'd crossed her hands upon her breast aware that gratitude was streaming from her heart. Gratitude, she might very well demand, for what? Just for this — being alive, feeling the breath plunging up and down beneath her hands — her life, this river on which she had been launched, still warm, still continuing to flow. She knew quite well that her hold on it was most precarious — she frequently prayed to be severed from it altogether, and moreover, she realized that life was not likely to offer her change or variety, here she was cooped up in her small room in this treeless iron city. Nonetheless she had her memories. The Kingdom of Heaven was within her. For after all what kind of a heaven could anyone conceive without these images of earth — these days and winds and weathers? Estimated by human events she would not have said that her life had been particularly fortunate. There had been plenty of catastrophe. She had had to bear for many years an intolerable secret which she would carry with her to the grave. However, what did these personal tragedies matter when measured up against a moment like this — fully conscious of carrying in her heart the burden and the mystery, filled with awe and wonder and rejoicing in that warm shaft of living breath plunging up and down beneath her hands?

Her condition had been a free gift. She had done nothing to induce it. There she had lain consumed with wonder, awe and reverence. What a comfort it had been to feel warm and without pain. The room must have been at just the proper temperature. The blankets felt so soft, the mattress so extremely comfortable. It had been a pleasure to luxuriate in flesh and bones that were not for the moment racked with pain.

The life of the aged was a constant maneuvering to appease and assuage the poor decrepit body. Why, most of the time she was nothing more than a nurse attending to its every need. As for the greater part of the nights one's position was positively disreputable — all alone and clothed in ugly withering flesh — fully conscious of the ugliness, the ignominy — having to wait upon oneself with such menial devotion — Here now, if you think you've got to get up mind you don't fall, put on the slippers, don't trip on the rug. There now, apply the lotions carefully, they'll ease the pain; that's it, rub them in thoroughly. Now get back to bed before you're chilled. Here, take the shawl, wrap it round your shoulders. Turn on the electric heater. It won't be long before you're off to sleep. Try not to fret and for heaven's sake don't indulge in self-pity. This is the portion of the old — having to lie here filled with cramps and rheums and agues — so aged and ugly with your teeth in water in the tumbler by your bed and your white hair streaming on the pillow and the old mind filled with scattered thoughts and memories, flying here, flying there, like bats in a cracked old belfry — haunted by fears, visited by macabre dreams.

Dear me, dear me, she thought, looking through the gloom into the lighted offices, if she could meet death upon her own terms how often she would choose to die. How beautiful to have floated away upon that tide of reverence. It was one's ignorance of just how and where death might come to take one off that made it hard to contemplate. There were all the grisly speculations.

Would she have a stroke followed by a helpless dotage? Would she die of some grave heart condition long drawn out? She might be run over any day by a taxi or a truck. She might slip on the sidewalk and break a leg or a femur. She could hear the clanging bells, the siren of the ambulance that gave her right of way, bearing her off amid the city traffic to the nearest hospital. She could see the doctors and the nurses going through their paces — everything efficient, ordered, utterly inhuman — all the nightmare apparatus attendant on keeping the breath of life in her another day — who knew? Maybe another week; maybe a month or two longer — the oxygen ranks and the transfusions, the injections — penicillin and the sulfa drugs — Heaven knew what! And would there be sufficient funds she wondered to pay for all this nonsense — keeping the breath of life in one old woman more than prepared to give up the fight? Expenses mounted to the skies. Nurses were worth their weight in gold. And as for private rooms in hospitals! All these extravagances. Dear me, dear me. Could she imagine herself in an Old Ladies Home — in a hospital ward?

She worried woefully about her finances. Eating into her principal like a rat eating into the cheese, the only capital that remained to her those few government bonds. However, she'd figured it all out very carefully. She could live to be ninety — selling out a bond when necessary and keeping something for emergencies. Was it possible that she'd live to be ninety?

Not likely at all; most improbable!

And if she did, she'd have to take the consequences. She had always been a fool with money. She knew nothing about the care of it. When she thought about the foolish things she'd done — the naive way she'd listened to all those charming philanthropic young men who knew so well how to advise the single and unguided! It made her sick at heart. But the one decision she had made — capricious, unadvised — to settle on that unborn child a gift of $70,000 she wasted not a moment's time regretting. After the completion of those arrangements if she'd had any sense she should have put her money into an annuity. They were, she supposed, fool proof. She was glad, however, she hadn't done so (she did some swift and inaccurate sums in arithmetic). She wouldn't be very much better off than she was now, and not a cent to leave to anyone. Those bonds, that balance at the bank could be bequeathed.

What a great lift, for instance, it would give to Adam Stone — how surprised he'd be, how grateful if she were to die tomorrow, to find himself heir to all she had! Poor Adam, she thought, poor Adam! And why not? Wasn't he after all the only person in her life today for whom she felt genuine concern? What if she had picked him up in a restaurant? What if she had known him only a few years? Why not?

He was in his peculiar way as much of a solitary as she was herself — an odd, unhappy, interesting young man. He seemed to stand for her as a kind of terrifying symbol, seeing behind him many similar youths who had played their part in the great war and had returned without zest or hope or faith in life. And why would it not be so — marked and marred as they had been with the impact of the dreadful years? When she talked with Adam she seemed to feel the presence of a crowd of witnesses, all the young in every corner of the world. Against his bitterness, his utter disrespect for life, what was there she could say? She imagined that in his queer way he rather liked to feed upon his bitterness. You could not disagree with him; he resented argument. He would not brook contradiction. There was something rather superb about his anger — working it all out as far as she could see in a kind of sullen passion for art, music, literature. Books he devoured ravenously. He was, she gathered from his conversation, at work upon a novel. He had cast off his family. He had cast off one girl after another, or very likely one girl after another had cast him off. There was something hard, passionate and scrupulously scientific about the way he went in for these brief affairs of love — a short interval of violent passion followed by a tremendous battle of the egos — bitter, sensual, with neither romance nor beauty, but nonetheless rewarding because of some necessity he seemed to feel to further document his vast accumulating dossier on sex, all without doubt to go into the novel he was, if not at present, some day bound to write. He seemed to be driven from one sterile episode into another.

Poor boy, she thought, poor Adam. Was she justified she wondered — "A young man you met in an Armenian restaurant," she said leaving the window and going to her desk where examining her check book and still continuing to talk aloud she muttered, "yes yes, taking that $25,000 that still remains to me in government bonds and adding my deposit, let me see, let me see, $3,497 and some odd cents, there would be in all (she added up the two figures) exactly $28,497.26."

A tidy little sum. She supposed the proper people to think about were the poor old women of her acquaintance scratching along on almost nothing. She knew a number of them — there were several right here in this hotel, unutterably dreary, desolate and brave. How wonderful for one of them to wake up some fine morning and find herself heir to twenty-eight thousand four hundred and ninety-seven dollars and twenty-six cents.

But the rub was of course how much of this would still remain when she was dead. The uncertain residue — she had practically made up her mind to it in the early hours of the morning — should go to Adam Stone. The weather prevented her from going, as she had resolved to go this very day, to Maiden Lane to see old Breckenridge.

But then there were other things that she could do and as she was thinking so seriously of also bequeathing him her precious manuscript, she really should before she determined to do so sit down quietly and read it from beginning to end. What a strange thing it was she thought as she went into the bathroom to attend to the preparation of breakfast, finishing it, laying it away, never able to reread it. And why did she feel so urged to leave it in the hands of this peculiar difficult young man? What was it that consumed her — this hunger in her heart? And was not the most astonishing experience just this — old age? When all was weariness and pain and effort, when the chief business of every day was waiting on her body like a patient old nurse waiting on an unwilling absentminded child, to feel this fierce preoccupation! Was it because she had wanted to call in her conscience — her soul, her

memory, as you might call in a priest at the last moment to offer abso-
lution, that she had undertaken the writing of this book?

Well, well now at any rate she must put her mind on breakfast — this
smuggling in, hiding away, pretending you didn't make a kitchen out of
your bathroom and a refrigerator out of your window ledge was a technique she'd mastered to perfection, she thought, stooping to fish a
saucepan and an electric plate from under the bathtub, filling the former with water and attaching the cord of the latter — putting the
water on to boil, opening the window to bring in butter, cream, fruit.
She flattered herself she pulled it all off pretty well. It wasn't that she
didn't grasp as eagerly as a child whatever pleasures life still offered her,
there was something even a little sly about her manner of enjoying her
small gratuitous blessings, as though she'd stolen a toy from the attentive nurse who kept watch over her or cake and candy from the august
angel into whose hands old Nanny might at any moment deliver her.
She made it her business to make as much out of her days as her frail
margin of health allowed, lunching or dining at a restaurant and, what
with the sandwiches, the yogurt, all the queer food that you could find
in little tins, managing somehow to sustain herself. There was something a bit miraculous about her little feats and arrangements.

It took fortitude she admitted. The old deserved to be commended
for their gallantry. Goodness, when she thought of the necessary chores
— putting clothes upon their backs, food into their mouths, getting
on and off the busses and across the roaring streets. Courage, self-
assertion, vanity were all required. As for herself how ridiculously vain
she was — always shaking off the kind and attentive people ready to
assist her, as though to say, "Thank you very much indeed, I'm quite capable of looking after myself," still trying to look as though her appearance suggested youth and vitality, never able to forget that she'd
been, and not so very long ago, an agreeable and attractive woman.
She was capable, she acknowledged it, of the most absurd behavior —
little coquetries, high and mighty airs.

But maybe she could be forgiven for believing that she had in her
eighty-odd years of life accumulated a little sagacity. She had her insights and divinations. Did she not carry all the seasons in her breast?
All the ages of man were hers; and if she liked to watch the great human
comedy with an impersonal yet highly sensitive and inquisitive eye, that

was certainly her prerogative. If she was always skipping out of her own skin into the skin of somebody else was it not her way of editing her own experience to which she'd gained at her age a perfect right? Innocent and innocuous she might appear as she sat eating her lunch or her dinner and generally engaged in saying to herself — "Oh, yes, my dear lady, my dear gentleman, you may not be aware of it, but I know practically everything there is to know about you." It wasn't that she gave herself up entirely to staring. She enjoyed her food enormously. Her luncheon or her dinner out was the great event around which she planned her entire day. But she hoped and prayed she would never resemble the positively ghoulish old ladies she often observed addressing their plates as though the only passion that still remained to them was the appeasing of their hunger. How their table manners, their bright and greedy eyes betrayed them! She ate, she hoped, with restraint and circumspection. If she sometimes allowed herself a cocktail or a small bottle of wine it was with the belief that it sharpened her perceptions. She liked to lay herself open to every breeze of insight and divination.

The old were in it as well as the young! Plenty of old ladies. They got about in the most gallant fashion — joined up in the macabre procession; birds of a peculiar feather. One saw them everywhere with their permanent waves, their little hats set on their heads at such rakish and ridiculous angles, their coats and shoes and handbags following the prevailing fashion, tottering in and out of shops and restaurants. How avid and excited they appeared as though they wished to let you know they had their own important engagements to meet like anybody else. Life seemed to jostle and push the poor old things around; pretty exposed they somehow were. The family offered them no shelter or asylum. if they had sons or daughters or great-nephews or grandchildren they did not share their homes and even if they had been invited to do so would the independent old things have accepted such an invitation? Where were they housed? How did they manage it all? The restaurants were full of them. What with the vitamins and the excitement, the movies, and the radio, the prevailing atmosphere of carnival and cocktail bar, the buffeting and the exposure didn't seem to kill them off.

It was, she remembered, under the influence of a dry martini — sipping it alone in the Armenian place on Fourth Avenue that she had picked tip poor Adam Stone. There he'd sat buried in his book, his sullen, rather beautiful face looking extremely self-conscious. And why not? For he was, she had discovered, perusing Dante's Inferno. What a pity, she had thought, that she was not young and charming, for she could read Italian too and this might have been one of those daydreams in which she guessed the young man beguiled his lonely condition come delightfully to life. "I see you're reading Dante," she had said; and when he'd taken in the situation — her ancient face together with the dry martini — he'd been quite naturally as rude as possible. However, she'd persisted. She had her ways with young men; she was not without intelligence. They had entered into conversation. Every time they had met they had continued to converse. And now, although he would not for the world admit this was the case, she helped very substantially in mitigating the solitude that overtook him in his all too frequent girl-less intervals.

Poor Adam, she reflected, examining her tray to make sure the breakfast she had now prepared was properly assembled; she'd not seen him for several months — he'd as likely as not found himself another girl and more than probably moved to a new address.

It occurred to her as she carried the tray into the bedroom, seating herself at the desk, that she would not be able to tell Mr. Breckenridge where to get in touch with him in the event of her demise. To think of making a young man her heir whose address she did not even know. Dear me, dear me, the anonymity of people's lives.

Anonymous was the word for everyone — anonymous. Why, the precious self was shattered, blown to bits a thousand times a day and it was actually the case that there was something of insolence, a kind of effrontery about it if anyone presumed to have an assured assertive self — opinions, a personality of one's own. It was incumbent on us all to do so many turns and tricks in adapting to thoughts, ideas, events, that if one showed oneself incapable of this agility of heart and mind there was a very real danger of lapsing into indifference, lack of sympathy, imagination, as though the poor battered soul were ready to lie down and say I'm beaten, numbed, dead, finished. Listening to all the assorted information, the nerves supplied with the new, the necessary antennae, the soul destroyed by the vibrations; why, the wholesale, the unprecedented calamities of the world cried out to us, shouted aloud every minute of the day. Yet who among us could endure to listen?

It was too much, too much for anyone she said, thinking as she spoke of her poor Adam. Poor boy, he held out against it all so stubbornly. He was without any knowledge of love; he did not, it seemed to her, understand the meaning of pity. He simply held out against letting it get him down. Such wholesale calamity diminished, dwarfed his little private griefs — the personal grievances and tragedies to which she guessed he clung tenaciously. It was for this reason she imagined he was so obsessed with sex. Out of his curious affairs he got but little joy, unless you could account the strife, the bitter conflict of two egos in their uneasy and anonymous roles attempting to assert there own authority, a kind of cruel self-inflicted pleasure.

Yes, Adam clung to his dwarfed uneasy self. You might say it had burrowed down in him, gone underground and as a witness of this there was that novel she was so sure that he was writing — a queer backhanded method of reasserting, reestablishing his dignity, authority. Goodness, think of all the lonely anonymous men and women there were today attempting to do the same thing; why, the novels came off the presses as fast as leaves in autumn falling from the trees and a novel was no matter what its subject matter as authentic a way of telling the tale of self as any that could be thought out.

Hadn't she, an old old woman sat down and tried for seven whole years to thrust into novelistic form the story of her life? And why, she'd like to ask herself had she when it was finished locked it up in that desk drawer and never had the nerve to look at it again? And why now did she have this strong desire to place it in the hands of Adam Stone? Vanity was certainly involved. Adam would have to revise many of his notions about her. She'd have to admit that the idea amused her. Moreover he would, she imagined, discover that it had literary merit. She somehow felt it had. He'd take it in all probability to a publisher and after she was gone it would doubtless see the light of day.

But beyond all this there was a deeper reason. Didn't she long to convey to him more intimately than she'd been able to in conversation something that she had realized in their talks together he'd not only held out against but found completely phony — her capacity for reverence, wonder, of which there was in his own constitution not a trace.

Not a trace, she said, rising with some difficulty to her feet. And was It not about to be extinguished in the human heart? Consternation, though few people would be able to recognize that this was so, standing out as we all somehow did against it, had usurped its place.

We simply stood aghast, she thought, crossing the room to get the morning paper which she must read before settling down with her manuscript (yes she was now firmly resolved to read it from beginning to end). "An excellent day for such a resolution," she said, opening the door, taking in the *Times* and returning with it to her desk.

Pouring herself a second cup of coffee she sat down and spread the paper on her lap. The headlines sprang at her — the nightmare world in which we lived — all these chimerical events through which we passed. "Impossible, impossible," she cried — "it staggers the imagination." But here in large black letters was the announcement — Truman Orders Hydrogen Bomb Built — a fact at the disposal of everyone capable of reading. Within a few hours it would be lodged in the hearts and minds of most of the inhabitants of earth — hundreds of millions of people would quail before it as she was quailing now.

But who could really comprehend the cryptic data at the core of it? The words were Greek to her as they would be to all but a meager handful of her fellow mortals — concepts of the mind, mathematical measurements, calculations of inconceivable complexity. They affected her in some odd way as though she were reading poetry; the syllables fell so sonorously upon the ear.

> "Molecules composed of two deuterons and a proton.
> Two tritons, a deuteron and a proton,
> A triton and a proton and a proton and a deuteron.
> In one of these six possible combinations —
> Triton — triton, triton — deuteron, triton — proton,
> Or a possible combination of these three
> Lies the secret of the triton bomb."

You'd have to possess the brain of Einstein to understand it.

But here it was — the perfidious, the majestic secret explained if you could get it, and the words dancing with such terrible agility in her mind and heart.

> "The triton bomb
>   is the last step
> In a six-step process
> One taking more
> Than six million years."

Could it be possible? Could it be humanly possible that the diligent, the honorable search for truth, the inquiry into the secrets of nature and the structure of the Universe would be closed and consummated with this annihilating explanation?

> "The protons are hooked on,
>   one by one,
>   To an atom of carbon
> Two of the protons
> Losing the positive electron
>   And are thus transmuted
>   Into an electron —
> As has been seen
>   A nucleus of one proton
>   And two deuterons
>   Is a proton nucleus
> This is by far
>   The most powerful reaction
>   In nature
>   And takes place
>   In the sun
>   At the rate
>   Of four pounds an hour
>   A reaction time
>   That brings it within
>   The range of possibility."

The paper dropped from her hands. She threw back her head and closed her eyes. "What is man that Thou art mindful of him or the son of man that Thou visitest him," she cried aloud.

T W O

PATSY HAD COME DOWN TO THE SIDEWALK WITH HIM. She shivered for she was clothed only in her slacks, a light sweater, and a pair of hua-raches. "There's the precious manuscript," she said, placing a well-stuffed folder in the laden pushcart that stood against the curb. Adam took it angrily from where it lay exposed to wind and rain, and repacking it with great solicitude in a nest of similar folders, turned to speak to her. But she'd gone without so much as saying goodbye. He could see her through the open door of the tenement house fleeing up the stairs to her own little flat on the third floor. To be sure, she'd of-fered to go along with him, and help him unpack his things. But he'd turned her down flat. "No, you don't, my little bitch," he'd said — the word had escaped him. There had been something in the way he'd said it that had, he expected, as good as terminated the whole affair.

He resented the note of sarcasm with which she referred to his manu-script. He was done with Patsy. He surveyed the cart on which his goods and chattels were now untidily stowed away. The sight of the fa-miliar objects was discouraging enough. How many times they'd gone with him from one place to another. A reproduction of van Gogh's *Old Shoes* peeped at him from behind an alarm clock, and a portion of Picasso's *Clowns* emerged from his old trench coat. God, how many books. There was his old victrola with a crank to wind up the turntable and a few albums of fine records. His radio was wrapped in a blanket. How had he ever managed to acquire these possessions, to move them from one place to another?

The desolation that invaded him for the moment swallowed up his wrath. The sheer discomfort of digging into new quarters, unpacking

and placing his books, setting up a table for his typewriter, rigging up
some kind of contraption where he could cook, accustoming himself to
the unfamiliar chairs, the unfamiliar bed, the general disorder and despair. A rut he could endure, but to meet with new contingencies —
that's what got him down. It was Patsy who had found the room; she
had even offered to go along with him and help him settle in. "But no
you don't," he said grimly, starting to push his cart through Jones Street
into Bleecker, "no, you don't, my little bitch," and at this moment,
turning east on Bleecker, a flight of pigeons wheeling all together and
catching on their tilted wings some diffusion of brightness from the
breaking clouds seemed to illuminate not only the dark skies but the
murk and drabness of the February day. They gleamed and disappeared
behind the belfry of Our Lady of Pompeii, just as Adam, all but
knocked down by a heavy truck, and answering with peculiar vehe-
mence the curses of the driver who had forced him and his pushcart
against the curb, experienced an extraordinary instant. Half a dozen or
more doors opening in his heart while he passed through as many moments in memory, and an accumulation of loneliness, a quite unutterable sense of his uniqueness flooding the present instant, brought him
so intense a consciousness of all he'd learned of misery, despair and solitude that he seemed to have acquired nothing short of spiritual treasure. Hounded by misfortune, accustomed by some ill star that pursued
him to the kicks and bludgeonings of fate, he would grind out of the
misery and torture a work of art; he'd wrench a masterpiece from all
that life had meted out to him. So, turned back upon himself — for he
was a young man, he felt, quite sure of genius — ravenously devouring
his experience and his bitterness, brushing the mud from several books
that had been jostled from the cart, continuing his virulent exchange
of curses and obscenities with the driver of the truck, he received so
vivid and immediate a sense of his own predicament, all the vicissi-
tudes of his late affair with Patsy, that, scrapping half the material of
his novel now in progress, he determined that he would place the first
big chapter of his book right here, in this very moment — Bleecker
Street, with the low ramshackle houses, the dormer windows, the tenements, the pushcarts, the fruit and vegetable stands, the Italian vendors, women marketing, children and baby carriages, the street cries,
the mud and drizzle. He'd make you smell and see and hear and live

with it. And in the midst of the animated scene, he'd place himself, a young man with his goods and chattels in a pushcart, shoved up against the curbing while these profanities came pouring fresh from the wells of his misery and anger — getting square with Patsy, getting square with life.

The traffic jam broke up, the trucks rolled on. Seeing an opportunity to cross the street, Adam maneuvered his cart to the opposite curbing and looking up saw the pigeons flying in close formation emerge from the clouds a second time and wheel behind the belfry and the golden cross. God, he'd snare those pigeons too, shedding their light from the cloud just like the Holy Ghost descending on the Village, and he'd introduce that newsstand there between the pushcarts with the morning papers and the headlines in English and Italian, shouting out their joyous message — the great big beautiful news about the great big beautiful bomb, the absolute weapon to blow the human race to Kingdom Come.

As he nipped into Morton Street, pushing his cart in the direction of Seventh Avenue, the truck driver's abuse and his own foul-mouthed rejoinders mingling with the rhythms of the headlines, "Truman Orders Hydrogen Bomb Built," still visualizing pigeons and pushcarts, fruits and vegetables, the belfry and the golden cross, and seeing as though he stood before him in the flesh Philip Ropes, with his chestnut-colored curls, that Byronic throat, the collar open at the neck, and remembering Patsy naked on her bed, her delicate fragile body white as a camellia, the soft red pubic hair, the red curls exquisite beneath her arms, he seized upon the plight of the planet with a kind of ungodly glee — (just another item to throw into that magnificent chapter). He'd feed that chapter all he had — this first day of February 1950 — H Day, Hell Day, Hydrogen Bomb Day, call it what you like; but it was this sweet, the acute, bitter business of the individual life that mattered. Making scenes, drawing pictures, holding imaginary conversations, he saw a series of astounding chapters, his entire novel unfolding as he marched along.

It would not be a shallow, just a surface novel. He'd throw one value up against another. He'd experienced plenty — plenty. And here for some reason or another, Mol got trammeled up in the big rush of his memories and reflections — My Old Lady — Mol — poor intense emotional Miss Sylvester. He could see her now with her big eyes and her highfalutin talk. He knew just how she'd agonize about it. It couldn't be — it simply couldn't be. The great mistake, the greatest mistake in history, Mol opined, the using of the bomb at Hiroshima. How she'd gone on about it — protesting so violently, unable to see how anyone could disagree with her. Well, if she'd marched through France or Flanders and seen those hundreds of bombers in their ordered flight moving morning after morning with spectacular promptitude into the sky — roaring like a thousand trains of cars into her field of vision and out again, on their way to Berlin, to Dresden, to Nuremberg, to murder the mothers and the babies and the children and the old people — to destroy the factories and the railroads, to soften up the job for the artillery — if she'd thrown her hat in air and cheered them day after day till the breath was drawn clean from her lungs, she might be ready to shrug her shoulders now, and say, what's the difference — a thousand bombers, or one bomber with the one big beautiful bomb — what did it matter?

Here he was, at any rate, on this first of February, in his lone and penniless condition, with the check on Philip Ropes the third, which he had intended to tear up but which as a matter of fact reposed in his pocket at the present moment fairly burning a hole in his pants.

Philip Ropes the third, for Christ's sake — he hauled up at Seventh Avenue and waited for the lights to change — there was actually no reason why he shouldn't cash that check. Patsy owed him the money. And if she'd paid him with a check on Philip Ropes, why be so stiff about it? The whole blamed business was over between them. Let Patsy go and do Ropes's typing. Miss Patricia Smith — Typing and Steno-graphy — Manuscripts — Public Accounting — that was how she advertised herself in the paper (a writer who couldn't type his own manuscripts was in any case a pain in the neck) and here Adam suddenly closed his eyes a moment trying to black out the pictures that flashed into his mind, for he did not see Patsy stiff and attentive, with her pencil poised for dictation, nor did he see her at a typewriter with her nimble fingers playing swiftly over the keys — no indeed — God no, he saw her lying on Philip Ropes's couch, beautiful and naked, and Philip Ropes beside her, beautiful and naked too — that camellia-white body, those delicately-molded thighs, that soft red pubic hair, and her mouth (the taste of Patsy's lips), the flowerlike opening mouth. God, that was what he'd paid her for. He was dead certain of it, though she'd sworn it was not the case. And how the devil could she expect him to play pimp to Philip Ropes? Lord, he'd starve before he'd cash that check. He could beat his way until he got the money from the government — only another week until the GI check came in. A man could beg. The successful beggars were always the young men who looked as though they'd had an education, whose clothes and shoes and general appearance suggested a decent background. The poor fellows, reduced to this. All they had to do was to hold out the hand an hour or more. He could work a district where nobody had ever seen his face — upper Broadway around the Seventies. That's what he would do. Everything would be scheduled, everything sacrificed for work.

Damned dangerous intersection. Were the red lights holding him up or telling him to go? Getting a cartload full of books across Seventh Avenue right here with the trucks and taxis bearing down on him was something of a feat. He might as well be the old junk man. It somehow got him down. Well, here he was. Where did he go from here? Down Morton to Hudson, or through Bedford into Cherry Lane? Again he hauled the pushcart up.

No more dalliance. He was resolved to show some guts. He'd work on schedule. The first few days would be damned hard. But just as soon as he had dumped this stuff in his new room he'd get right out and do his little stint — extend the hand. It wouldn't be difficult to pick up a few dollars every day. Think of the material he'd be getting for his new novel, the real raw down-and-out stuff.

Compare his experience with the knowledge Philip Ropes had got of life — here Adam spat. There was this urgency, this sense of being driven. All the novels, the other young men. All the photographs on the backs of the dust jackets. There were hundreds of first novels — all the handsome young men with the blurbs that blew them up as large as Tolstoy, as large as Dostoevsky. It was like a contagion, some sickness of strife and competition, this chucking about of names and reputations. Why, you could put your finger on the very pulse-beats of other people's triumphs, everything so public and conspicuous. Life came at you in every direction. It was the hungers, the hungers in the heart were suspect.

Here now was his chance to slip through Bedford with free access to
Cherry Lane. There was something ganging up on him, weighing down
his spirits — the anguish of the days ahead, getting into the rut. The
whole terrific business of mastering his craft, breaking the backs of sentences, assailed him — just plain learning how to write. What relentless memories, sitting at his typewriter for hours sweating blood, his
eyes gone bleary, tired in every bone and sinew, his nerves frazzled like
so many snapping fiddle strings, not able to write a decent paragraph,
running to the nearest bar to fortify himself with as much liquor as he
could pay for, coming back and trying to wrench his style from other
novelists. Why, he had at one time mastered all O'Hara's tricks and
mannerisms; he'd copied Hemingway, he'd tried his hand at Sartre, but
Joyce was and always would be the master who would drive him to despair. He knew what he was after, he had everything to say; he'd experienced plenty.

Philip Ropes, what did he know about anything, the little dilettante
who couldn't even type his manuscript, getting Patsy in to dictate,
walking up and down and dropping the immortal sentences? Such a
handsome fellow with his chestnut curls and his collar open at the
neck, a swell face for the dust jackets. Couldn't you just see that face
embellishing the blurbs? Hallo, the Cherry Lane theater — presenting
a play by Sartre. He drew up a moment to inspect the bill. Now there
was a writer who knew just what he was about, went directly to the
heart of the matter. He'd never have begun a novel with reveries and
reminiscences, giving you back your streets and moods and memories
— far too explicit for that. He would have started off with Patsy in that
bed in Jones Street. He'd have described the bed, warm and consoling,
and Patsy, beautiful and naked in the bed beside him on that memorable night when all their troubles had begun. He'd have guessed
exactly how she felt about Philip Ropes, conjuring up that peerless
young man, while she lay there letting him make love to her —
vicarious pleasure, that's what he'd accused her of experiencing. Patsy
had denied it. She'd said that she was sick and tired of him and his
everlasting analysis, trying to fix up situations out of every moment,
complicating everything; there was no freedom, no frankness left, no
simplicity. Well, she was right, there hadn't been. Her every tremor
now involved with Philip Ropes; you couldn't fool him about women.

Trundling through Cherry Lane into Barrow, down Barrow, crossing Hudson with the lights now in his favor his bitterness accumulated. That tone of voice in which she'd said "there's your precious manuscript," the amount of sarcasm which she'd managed to put into those few words persisted. It hadn't been too long ago that Patsy had believed he was her little genius. What a fuss she'd made about him, persuading him to give up his perfectly good job and stick exclusively to writing. She'd forced him into it. It was a crime for anyone with such creative gifts to use up all his energies on work that he despised. Where was he now? Back with his GI checks and his little course in English. She loved her little geniuses. Well, he had done with women. They didn't jibe with work. The sooner he was down to good hardpan, the better — loneliness, misery, solitude. That was his receipt. He would with the greatest willingness make Patsy over to Philip Ropes. He could have her.

Down Barrow to Greenwich Street. He looked tip at the houses. Patsy had told him they were so cute. Little red houses, dormer windows. Cute enough. Why shouldn't he cash that check? After all, whose fault was it that he was down and out? He'd paid the bills when first he'd gone to live with Patsy. He stopped and took the check out of his pocket. Made out to Patricia Smith, signed by Philip Ropes the third and countersigned by Patsy. Quite a story in it, a little story à la Chekhov called "The Check." Should he cash it, should he tear it into ten thousand bits? He returned it to his pocket. He turned the corner into Greenwich Street. The cute little houses continued; but what a difference! What a dismal street — all these trucks that rumbled past the windows and that big ugly building opposite, United States Post Office, mail trucks coming, mail trucks pulling out. Here he was, one of the little red houses all right but what a dingy look to it. Gardens behind, she'd said, and little dormer windows; cute as all get-out. But what good would they do him — living in the basement? Leaving the pushcart on the curb he climbed the stoop and let himself in with a key Patsy had procured from the janitor (he was presumably Patsy's brother) — good thing the rent was paid a week in advance.

God, what a stinking hole. He descended the basement stairs, opened and stumbled through a narrow hall to the front, opened and unlocked a sagging door, and found himself in a dark square room below the level of the street, with a very musty odor. It appeared to be furnished. There were two small windows with an outer iron grille giving on a hatchway. He threw them open. Jesus, what a hole. A closed-up fireplace with a black marble mantelpiece adorned one side of the room, and opposite a cot with a green plush spread and two green plush cushions propped against the wall. The floor was covered with a worn linoleum rug, there was a Morris chair by the window upholstered in plum-colored corduroy, very worn indeed, a wooden rocking-chair, and in the center of the room under a cluster of electric lights a rickety table with a marble top. He went to the bed, felt the mattress, sat down on it, smelled the sofa cushions. Jesus Christ.

His eyes roamed around; took in a passage between his room and one at the back which presumably opened into that garden that Patsy had boasted of, "all those dear little red brick houses opening on their gardens." He got up, went through the passage, tried the door which was locked and bolted. There were cupboards and running water — everything necessary as Patsy had said. He turned on the taps; the water ran. Well, he'd be damned. Now, what he'd have to do was pull himself together and get his junk in out of the rain.

It seemed like an interminable business, dumping first one load and then another, no order about it, helter-skelter, pell-mell, angrily making the trip to the sidewalk and back to his room Lord knows how many times. It was somnambulistic, like a dream he'd had before and expected to have innumerable times again, realizing too that he was just one in a regiment of GI brothers having their little love affair with art and the humanities. Here were these folders (the precious manuscript Patsy had been so sarcastic about). Under the bed with it, safe from the rest of the litter. Well, to what else could you turn your allegiance, if you didn't turn to art? Perambulating the room, taking up this book and that and his eyes roaming round, it seemed to him he was surrounded by masterpieces, cheap editions, the big Giants, and the smaller volumes. God, the room was filled with masterpieces — translations, anthologies — that banged-up box was stuffed with masterpieces, if you turned the right knob at the right moment, they flew into it from the very air you breathed. The records, the victrola, Picasso's *Clowns*. Did the fellows making up statistics in the government bureaus get wind of all this, so many GIs at this university, so many at that, all his brother veterans attempting to drink from every spring at once? For here was art, the aristocratic, the inaccessible commodity, suddenly made cheap, mass-produced like everything else. You had to hasten, there was a fearful and immoderate haste about it. With the whole of society geared up to the organized production of murder, wholesale slaughter, you had to choose your horse and mount in haste, art and death running it neck and crop.

Suddenly he seemed to hear again that incredible accumulating volume of sound, and to see the heavens literally sundered to let pass above his head the majestic procession, thousands of planes roaring like express trains through the sky. God, the perfect synchronization, the order and the majesty, morning after morning at the punctual hour, all those bombers on their way to murder old men, children, babies, women, to blow up munition factories. It wouldn't be so majestic the next great show they staged. Likely to be silent, out of sight, out of sound. Some solitary bomber silent in the stratosphere on its way, God knows where, carrying God knows what infernal freight. Well, stick to the horse you've chosen, hurry, hurry like the devil. The race was not entirely reputable either, there were the rivalries, the jealousies, the triumph so public and conspicuous and he saw, though it was the very last thing he wished to see, the picture of Philip Ropes decorating the dust covers, all the blurbs, all the handsome young men who had snatched right out of the jaws of death you might say their little moment of success, flying into the magic beam, gyrating crazily in the public neon.

God, life came at you from every direction — all the thirsts and hungers that beset you. There was this Babel of voices — literatures, philosophies, distractions — there was the music, wanting to hear it all. It was free now — loose on the air, incised on the rubber discs, canned for your convenience if you had the price for it. Hurry, hurry. And there were the pictures, the exhibitions, the museums, the art shops. No, it was not just the drive to create something on your own; it was these little empires of beauty you needed to build up in your solitary soul, call it culture if you wish to, universal culture, poets, scholars, anthropologists, historians, theologians, philosophers contradicting, asserting, and the musicologists, the art critics, the reviewers — such a babel of tongues, such exquisite distractions, clutching at them all. Good God, thinking you could read, hear, see, *get* everything all at once, these thirsts and hungers to be assuaged, wanting to drink from all the springs at once, snatching at universal culture, being, as you damned well knew you were, the most solitary, the most lonely individual that ever at any moment in the march of mad events had trod upon the earth.

It was multitude from which we suffered, all that everybody had to tell us, buzzed around and blown upon by all the conversations and the arguments. Our traffic with each other, what a queer attempt to protect our aloneness. Christ, how we loved our own aloneness. We did plenty of howling about it, it was a central theme of all our art expressions. None the less we hugged it jealously. We were incapable of giving because there was so much within our reach to grab and snatch and gather for our own, our solitary souls.

Take his relationship to women. Always the same old story. There was Patsy now — her fresh, her lovely body; yet the more he ravished it, the closer he drew to it, the farther she retreated with her loneliness, the more she cherished her little empire of selfhood, extending it, hoarding it up, subjecting each experience to analysis, to some damned way or another of getting wise about herself. It was just this of which she had complained to him about his own behavior. What was it she had said had made her sick of him, sick and tired of this way he had — taking the pulse of each vibration?

He flung himself down on the bed. He was mortal fagged. This putting the energies and muscles to work on tasks so uncongenial drained the life blood out of him. He'd never set this place to rights. God! — what a hole in the wall — the worst he'd ever had. He buried his face in the green plush cushions. Phooey, how they stank! Imagine sleeping on a bed like this. He groaned.

My Old Lady — Mol! Why not call her up and ask her to cash this check? Simple enough. Hadn't he been suppressing his resolve to do so right along? Sure he had. The money was his. It wasn't as though it came to him from Ropes. It was the payment of a debt. Patsy owed it to him. Why be so stiff-necked about it? Ridiculous to think he could beat it, beg his way until he got the GI check.

Mol — what a queer, eccentric bird she was. He had a real affection for her. When he came right down to it, he'd have to admit she was the only human being in this benighted city who really cared for him. Absurd she was, caring so much about the bloody world, so dramatic about everything, beating her chest and flashing those astonishing eyes. "If you'd lived as long as I have, my dear boy," always getting back at him with her age and her experience. She seemed to him, in spite of all the books she'd read and her fine assumption of knowing all there was to know, innocent as a May morning; virginal he'd swear.

The longer he lay here and tried to make up his mind to telephone, the less likely he'd be to find her in. It must have stopped raining by now. Very likely she'd be out. He got up, and going to the window, craned his neck to see just what the day was like.

Jesus, you couldn't see the sky. There above the area railing was the sidewalk and the pushcart, and both quite dry. He supposed he'd have to trundle the old cart back to the ice and wood man from whom he'd rented it.

Okay, the sooner he was out of this black hole, the better. He searched his pants to find the check, looked at it, put it in his waistcoat pocket, buttoned up his coat. Now to discover if he had some change. Why, he'd be damned. The Lord was on his side. Here was fifty cents, here was a nickel. He'd go out now and find the nearest drug store.

Mol — My Old Lady — he said, as he groped his way through the dark hall to find the outer door. She'd let him have the cash.

T H R E E

THERE HAD BEEN OF COURSE, thought the old woman as she reflected on her childhood and the manuscript she was about to read, the two large inhospitable houses where she had been so lost and so unhappy, the Fosters and the Chamberlains and all the rest of them walking about among their splendid properties. But there had also been the outdoor, the open world — certain experiences looked forward to each year, annually repeated and becoming, as the seasons circled round her completing the cycle of the years and memories, the very essence of life and anticipation. Winter and spring, summer and the autumn: yes, that was their sequence in her memory.

Winter! — it was the cold smell, the no-smell, snow smell, the first flakes falling on the mittens, on the coat sleeves, and never one exactly like another, it was those storms that changed the rhythms of the blood and the behavior of the nerves, the wind blowing the white dust off the drifts, swathing the lawns, whirling the snow up in a great darkness, sucking it like a typhoon into the cloud, sweeping it from the roofs of houses, from the boughs of trees, creating such a dark the flying flakes were lost to sight. The lull, and snowfall seen again, that soft accumulation of the flakes. It was the clear cold days that followed, the glitter of the sun upon the snow, the lambent shadows on the lawn, the fiery incandescent atoms dancing, gyrating by their billions and quadrillions in the air. It was the breath that streamed before her as she walked, the snow creaking beneath her shoes, the numbed face and feet and not a thing to smell but the sharp keen no-smell of the cold. The sudden thaws, the drip, drip, dripping from the eaves, the sound of icicles shattering as they fell, snowballs easy to manufacture, the mittens soaked, the coat hem drenched. It was scent returning to the breath, memory stirring, rain and again the cold and all those crystal exhibitions, groves and gardens, fountains, pavilions, palaces of ice — sights glittering and splendid but unrelated, severed from the flow. And finally, finally, communications, whispers, that little mesh and maze of sparrow voices and the whir of sparrows wings, the gutters running rivers and the grass exposed, feet sinking in the mud, rubbers sucked clean off the shoes, roots stirring — intimations, memories, buds swelling on the boughs of trees.

Spring was that swamp where all the violets grew in such abundance, variously tinted, poised and spurred, the large deep blues, those with large white faces delicately penciled, the short-stemmed red variety, and always when she saw them that sense of having been divinely conducted to some secret ground.

It was that search for flowers in the woods, the spell cast over her, the light dim, the stillness of a place enclosed. Above, the brown buds sheathed in their brown casings casting gloom upon the light that filtered through the boughs, and on the ground to the right and to the left all the adorable green shoots and tendrils, the little antic flowers of the woods springing to life and vigor among the skeletal leaves, the dry dead needles of the pine, ferns pushing their unfurled fronds above the earth, standing about like little wool-clad gnomes in the grotesquest attitudes, stems of the moss tipped with the minutest blossoms. And there on that bed of rusty, far from springlike leaves, arbutus, perfect and precise as stars, pink as though they had been washed in the pure waters of the dawn, peering up at her — kneeling to pick them, burying her face in the evanescent, the ineffable fragrance, that sense she'd had of waiting on some memory, some intimation, of having been — but when but where she could not tell.

Summer was that field on the high shelf above the ocean, the meadowlarks rising, the bobolinks swinging on the timothy. It was that dance of joy, that dance of life, that perfect union with the summer day, exact accord with all the little flying creatures and the business they accomplished, something physical about it, visceral, planted very deep in memory, singing with the larks, skimming with the swallows, everything barging up, blowing up, buzzing, humming, floating — all the white, the innocent daisies, the oxeyed daisies, the buttercups, and the grasshoppers transparent as the grass, hopping, springing, squatting, working their horses' jaws, making spittle on the grass blades, and some of them with wings shaped like little fans, opening and shutting them with such a clack and clatter, flying in every direction, the butterflies descending noiseless on this flower and on that, spreading the velvet and the satin, here the yellow, there the purple, the cat's eyes, the tiger's stripes. Running here, running there, and something in her crying out to that blue, mysterious element beyond the dunes to wait, to keep its distance, to allow her still a little longer to belong completely to the earth.

It was that swift descent upon the beach, the surf strong, the waves breaking. Something pretty terrible about it — getting it in one fell swoop, the fury of the breakers carried back to crash and echo in the dunes, waves running up the shore in all their sound and smother, the wild cold smell of the salt spray inducing maniac excitement. Up the path of the waves shrieking, down the hard wet slope again, the waves springing, leaping forward, and one more terrible than all the others standing up in its intolerable beauty, seeing the jellyfish and seaweed and the flung sand churned within its glassy caverns, hearing amid the roar and thunder that little dreadful music of the bubbles breaking, opening their lips on air, on sand, on stone.

Autumn was the orchard where she used to come to bury katydids and spiders, and a state of the clammiest contentment — the air webbed with all manner of tiny tunes and gossamer occurrences, gnats humming, flies and bees and hornets droning, shining threads attached to no visible bough or leaf or spider slack in the bright air, wings flash-ing, vanishing, bits of down and fluff and feather disappearing in the blue, appearing in the sunlight, those fat worms squirming loose from the grave she opened, and the sepulchral smell of the autumnal earth.

But not a word of all this recorded in that manuscript, she thought as she rose to take her novel from the desk where it had lain so long unread.

F O U R

MISS SYLVESTER TURNED THE PAGES of the manuscript, and moved at once into that dim abyss of time where recollections dawned, where rooms gave off their smells, their voices and associations. That sense she'd had of coming from nowhere into somewhere very large and most important back upon her in all its original assertiveness, she seemed to be groping rather blindly through her grandmother's home in Brookline.

How large the rooms had seemed — immense, falling away into echoing vistas, overfurnished, over-subdued by the weight of all those Victorian possessions. There was the wide hall, with doors opening on the double parlors, the library, the dining room, and at the end of the hall, and directly opposite the front door, that staircase, of splendid proportions, branching off with carpeted stairs and a balustrade on ei-ther side to meet a balcony halfway up and ascend again in all the majesty of its double flights to the floors above. Here more than else-where the large and lavish manner of the household had seemed to her exhibited. People ascended and descended. Some took the flight to the left, some the flight to the right. Maids in black dresses tricked out in clean white caps and aprons answered bells; they ran up and down in a flutter of apron strings and messages to be delivered; they came bearing boxes of flowers, candy boxes, boxes from the milliner's and huge im-portant-looking boxes from the dressmaker's. Something about that stairway — the echoing rooms above and the echoing halls below that intimated the cramped, the meager, the not to say demeaning nowhere from which she had emerged into all this hustle and bustle, and how frequently she must have wondered, peering through the banisters, traveling up and down, what in the world she was doing amid all this important traffic.

Downstairs the large rooms, their lofty doors and ceilings, the high windows draped in heavy lambrequins and curtains, seemed to diminish her height and give her a curious sense of walking very lightly on her feet. All was reflection, scintillation — mirrors, chandeliers with pendant lusters, lamps, statuary, porcelain vases, marble busts, marble mantelpieces reduplicated down a vast extension of the scene.

There had been — most awe-inspiring of all the apparitions — old George the butler, carrying trays, announcing visitors. There were uncles, cousins, acquaintances engaged in animated conversation. Some sat down, some stood up, and anyone was likely at any moment to make a grab for her, to hold her at arm's length and exclaim, "Oh, *this* is the Sylvester child." The difference in the behavior of the sexes was very noticeable indeed. The ladies' laughter was light and musical, they affected the most decorative attitudes, their dresses fitted them closely, their waists were incredibly small, they wore the loveliest of hats. The gentlemen guffawed and gesticulated. They were extremely elegant. Some had beards carefully trimmed, some had mustaches meticulously combed, some wore clothes that gave them a curious robinlike appearance, some were dressed in coats which lent them a grave, ministerial look. The young men, with the notable exception of Lucien Grey, had clean faces and were more graceful and appealing than their elders. Young or old, male or female, they all had the unmistakable look of being very fashionable indeed.

Arriving with a heart from which all references had been erased, and bringing with her not a sight or sound or smell that might illuminate the past and thus explain the present, she'd had perforce to reconstruct it all as best she could. Vaguely realizing there was mystery behind her and a conspiracy of silence imposed upon a time when with a legitimate equipment of parents she must presumably have lived elsewhere, she had been accompanied by a curious sense, not only of trying to rediscover them, but in a measure of attempting, you might say, to find herself.

All was at first confusion, people holding her attention, flitting off again, an inflection of speech, an exaggeration of dress or gesture, the bird on Cousin Cecilia's hat, the way Great-Uncle William shrugged his shoulders, the scent that issued from a gown or handkerchief, a reprimand, some emphatic expression of opinion — figures, personalities, characters coming at her, retreating, coming at her again with an accentuation of their tricks of speech or gesture, their private queernesses and mannerisms, until, lo, behold, what with piecing all the impressions together, responding to them with the uncanny sharpness that her position of insecurity somehow or other induced, she became acquainted with her grandmother and grandfather, the formidable great-aunts and -uncles, her beautiful Aunt Eleanor, and Lucien Grey, with Cousin Cecilia Ware, and her pretty, frivolous Aunt Georgie. She observed them with a kind of spellbound attention and was never without a feeling that they were actors taking part in a series of improvised scenes and exhibitions, fascinating but not altogether enjoyable. Something seemed to be lacking, some warmth, some sense of being attached to people and things, and not just suffered to walk around among them.

Difficult to tell what exactly happened when in that crowded world to which she had become attached, rooms, conversations, people and the manners they carried about with them, shifting and changing as they did in memory, but there was a certain emotional climate which persisted throughout those first winters in Brookline, induced by plans, postponements, preparations — bringing Aunt Georgie out into society, getting her successfully married. The entire house vibrated to these events, and as it comes back to her, all this stir of talk and preparation seemed to have sharpened and increased a feeling she carried uneasily about of being somehow or other responsible for holding up the schedule of events, arriving as she had in a shroud of mourning that suspended all festivities and left all projects hanging in the air. It must have been the "coming out" which her arrival had actually delayed. But nonetheless, the great occasions became inextricably combined in mood and in memory, and as far as her responses to them went, they seem now to have taken place but once, and to have brewed in her heart exactly similar impressions. And how she had been able, amid those glittering displays of family pride and power, to make out that she in her small person represented something that had run amok in worldly calculations it is impossible to explain. Wandering about amid those tides of merriment, congratulations, laughter, and with the strains of flute and fiddle, the fragrance of innumerable hothouse flowers, the subtlest perfumes wafted to her from the circulating ladies, heightening her emotions and inscribing on her sensibilities God knows what of melancholy pleasure, she had been most certainly aware that she stood somehow for misfortune, not to say disgrace.

That daughters must marry into their own class and maintain their position in society was an essential doctrine held by both her grandparents. For what earthly reason had they elected to marry and bring them into the world if not for such alliances? The roots and reasons for these assumptions she was, naturally enough, unable to plumb, but somehow or other she had been able to pluck from the very air around her, through hints and inflections, through words and phrases far from clearly understood, the realization that her mother had brought disgrace upon the Fosters and the Chamberlains, and though she was completely ignorant of the story attaching to her parents, she seemed to have suspected very early in the game that her mother had never been properly "brought out" nor decently married.

Some talk overheard among the servants about a runaway match should have set her right on the details, but knowing nothing about matches except that she was forbidden to strike them because of fire, and runaways in this connection suggesting fire engines — horses running to a fire, the phrase served only to confuse. All this was presently cleared up, but for a while she knew only that her mother had died and "gone to heaven," as good old Irish Annie frequently assured her, "to live with God," and as she heard nothing at all about the other parent she simply had taken it for granted that he was also dead and residing happily in heaven.

An inclination on everybody's part to act as though she had come parentless into the world could not, very naturally, persuade her that this was the case and there was that house that had for some time had the power, whenever she so much as thought about it, to scare her out of her wits, a symbol of her dreadful, her demeaning past. This nightmare sense of it came to her full-fledged out of that incident that had occurred on a spring morning in the nursery when certain shabby trunks and boxes from "the house in Pinckney Street" were brought down from the attic to be unpacked. Grandmother Foster supervised the whole performance and there had been something about her expression, the way she handled, smelled and sorted out the various articles — blankets, sheets and little undergarments, dresses, coats and jackets, undoubtedly her own — that had suggested as she watched her from the floor where she remembers she was seated the very direst kind of poverty; and when she heard her add, "These will be quite suitable for Joe, I understand his daughter has a brood of little girls," the final touch of the macabre and dreadful was put upon her speculations. For was not Joe, the old man who came out from Boston to assist the gardener (Dago Joe as Annie called him), an Italian as well as a Dago and had she not somewhere ascertained the fact that her own father was an Italian and learned moreover that he was a musician, and was it not most logical to jump to the conclusion, having in this musical connection only a hand organ to rely upon, that he was a Dago organ-grinder? Anyway it was thus she'd made it out, leaping wildly from one association to the next, as she sat there on the floor and watched her grandmother handling, sorting, *smelling* those little garments, and heard her in that high and lofty way she had bestowing them upon that scary old man, and from that day on and for some time afterwards poverty, parents, Pinckney Street were trammeled up together, to breed in her imagination a series of the most sordid and frightening pictures — men and women with tattered sleeves and toes protruding from their shoes and wearing the most disreputable of hats, lurking in area-ways, poking in the ashcans, children with uncombed hair and uncouth manners playing in the gutters and in the vicinity of garbage cans, and naturally enough, the Dago organ-grinder with his organ and his monkey and his cup extended grinding out his scary tunes.

Just how long this ghoulish sense of her forgotten past prevailed she cannot be quite sure, but she remembers perfectly the day that it was dissipated and the delight and surprise that she experienced and how then and there her mind escaping the dark and horrid speculations seemed to run at once toward new and happier conclusions and how she was immediately furnished with a succession of the most romantic, comforting, and comfortable beliefs.

Oh, the vividest memory of that experience comes back — the cold crisp weather, the sharp astonishment, the unutterable relief, driving on one of those rare occasions when she went to town with her grandmother in an open sleigh, that delicious sense she had of almost sliding along on air, all so smooth and swift and sunny. Her grandmother beside her silent in her sealskin coat, then suddenly leaning forward and saying to the coachman in her peremptory way — "Turn here into Pinckney Street — stop at twenty-eight."

Pinckney Street! To say that she was filled with horror, with a kind of dreadful expectation is to put it mildly. The sleigh turned. My goodness gracious! How astounding — bewildering indeed! It was a very pleasant kind of street, not perhaps as elegant as other streets she'd seen, but none the less tidy, clean. They stopped at twenty-eight. Could this be perhaps the house, the awful house of her imaginings? There were curtains in the windows, the stoop was well swept. The footman jumped down, climbed the steps, rang the bell. What a pleasant house! What a pleasant street, clean, tidy — people on the sidewalks were dressed in the most respectable clothes, no uncouth children played in the gutters, there were no terrifying women in tattered clothes with unkempt hair picking over garbage cans; not a drunken man in sight.

The door was opened, a maid appeared and took the letter. The footman descended the steps, clambered to the box. The horses neighed and shook their bells and pranced away.

What relief, what joy! Her parents had not lived in a place of horror, in a dreadful slum. Her father was not, he had never been a Dago — no Dago could have lived in such a street! And then and there her mind went skipping in and out of words, incidents, references she didn't even realize she'd remembered; and with a speed, a brilliance that was nothing short of unbelievable, piecing this and that and utterly discarding all that had been distressing and confusing, the runaway horses and the fire engine as well as the monkey and the organ-grinder retreating forever into limbo, her parents' gallant little love affair came to her as clear as day and infinitely brave and true. Of course that runaway match meant simply this, that her mother had run away with the Italian musician, who had married her and brought her to Pinckney Street to live. Just to think of her having had the courage to do such a thing — defying and standing out against Grandmother Foster, who, as far as she'd been able to discover, nobody dared so much as contradict. Gracious, how she must have loved him! Why, he had not been an organ-grinder at all. Far from that! Suddenly, in a flash of what must have been sheer clairvoyance, she'd got it all exactly right, brushed as she had been in that miraculous instant by the memory of what Grandfather Foster had said when he'd come upon her in the parlor at The Towers sitting on the musical chair, "The Overture to *William Tell*, your father's favorite tune," receiving instantly (the silvery tune the chair gave off perhaps assisting in this feat of memory and intuition) the picture of a dark Italian elegantly attired standing up before her straight and slender, playing on a flute.

Doubtless the fact that he had played in the Symphony Orchestra got hitched to all these intuitions at a later time, so curiously do recollections lapse and come together in the mind, but in retrospect it seems to her she'd got the whole thing in that bright moment straight. The sleigh continued to slip merrily along, and oh how proudly she surveyed Pinckney Street, how she regretted that she was not living there as she must have done before she remembered anything about it. However, she could bear to be without her parents if she could cherish in the thought of them such a romantic story — keep them forever beautiful and brave — mysteriously touched by death.

F I V E

———————

THE YEARS DID NOT DIMINISH HER TREASURE, which due to the consolations of good Irish Annie added the joy of anticipation to the satisfaction she somehow felt in the possession of parents who had, according to Annie, so beautifully "gone before." The idea of joining them in heaven began to dawn, and presently took on all that could be imagined of the gala and familiar as well as the supernatural and divine. Heaven became for her a very actual place, and she found no difficulty at all in combining the joys of earthly greetings on the part of those long separated and bereaved with states of more seraphic and transcendent bliss. It seemed simple enough to imagine an ambient where they were invested with the human as well as the angelic condition. Since it existed both in her mind and heart and memory, she required for its architecture no more than what her eyes had looked upon with wonder and delight — the morning and the evening clouds together with all the bright stars strewn upon the sky and all the lovely flowers growing in the grass. It was a place immense and capable of infinite extension, with clouds perpetually opening to reveal unending corridors — vistas of mountains, valleys, rivers, seas. So vast indeed as to allow all the dead and all the living, those who had died before and those who at some time in the future would be dead, to meet and recognize each other and to renew their earthly ties at just that instant when clothed in their flesh and bones they had been so rudely torn apart and where among all these human and bodily reunions divine and incorporeal changes were perpetually taking place — children turning into angels, parents flying about on angelic wings and God Himself at the center of all the light and splendor forever welcoming the newcomers — bidding them draw a little nearer to His throne.

Yes, that was about as she had pictured it — dying and going to heaven — and though she was by no means frequently visited by these divine anticipations nonetheless they vaguely fringed her reveries whenever she dwelt at any length on the thought of her parents, both of whom, for she had heard nothing to the contrary, had died and gone, as Annie used to tell her, to heaven to live with God.

And it was certainly because of these bright mansions of her imagination that Easter became the day of all days in the year to be anticipated. How vividly she gets those Easters back, the beauty of the season and her delight in being dressed as gaily as the spring. That drive to Boston accompanied by her grandparents, and oh, so happily aware of the new shoes and coat, the straw hat trimmed with its bright wreath of Easter flowers, the special sense she'd had of it, spring and joy and resurrection, gaining momentum as they drove along, the church bells on the air, the children on the sidewalks carrying pots of flowers contributing enormously to her peculiar joy. Why, by the time she arrived at church and alighted from the carriage, it had reached a peak of the highest solemnity. Walking down the aisle behind the grandparents, she was, you might say, drenched, baptized in Easter sentiment. What with the profusion of spring flowers massed beneath the windows and banked upon the altar, and that cool sweet smell of Faster lilies flowing through the other perfumes like the very breath and fragrance of the day, the glory spread, became a great effulgence streaming from her heart. The organ voluntary rolling through the aisles and arches seemed to be rolling back the clouds of heaven. They bloomed, they burst asunder. Aware that her acquaintance with loss had left her open to receive the glory and the splendor, she was translated, lifted in her new spring coat and hat right into heaven.

On this memorable Sunday Easter was as she recounts it unusually late, and the drive home after church delightful with the trees in leaf and the birds caroling away. But what stood out so clearly in her mind was her grandfather's high spirits and that after-church solemnity that enveloped her grandmother, and how suddenly out of a portentous silence she remarked, "Let the dead past bury its dead. Do not speak of it again. Treat the event as though it had not occurred." To all of which her grandfather, continuing his whistling, folded his arms without rejoinder.

This had left within her heart an area of apprehension, some sense that it could not go without a sequel, an expectation carried with her to the dinner table, and she cannot now go over the dramatic disclosures that finally ensued without feeling she is there in that familiar room, seeing the picture, vivid, animated, before her eyes — the table drawn out with all the extra leaves set in to its extremest length, the damask cloth of incredible dimensions, the napkins folded to look like Easter lilies, displaying their embroidered monograms, and all the plates, the knives and forks and spoons, the goblets and wineglasses set to such absolute perfection, the flowers in the center of the table so fresh, with the ferns, the daffodils and freesia and narcissus doing their best to conceal the painted eggs so discreetly hidden in their midst, all the festival decorations, the gold-and-lace-fringed snappers, the place cards, the bonbon containers adding a touch of the naive and childish to this positively regal laying out of the best family glass and napery and china.

There they all were, the various members of her extraordinary family, Aunt Georgie, Charlie Lamb, Aunt Eleanor and Lucien Grey, Cousin Cecilia Ware, the great-uncles and their wives, Uncle William and Aunt Mary, Uncle Richard, Aunt Amelia, Uncle James, Aunt Harriette, and she in their midst, with Lucien on one side of her and Great-Uncle William on the other, perfectly certain that something was about to occur.

Dinner went on as usual. The familiar jokes and platitudes from everybody, the change of plates, and finally the arrival of the champagne, Grandfather accomplishing his part of all this business with his usual grace, extracting the first cork and then out of the smoking bottle, without so much as spilling a single drop, pouring a little of the sparkling wine into his glass. With equal grace he opened a second bottle and a third.

The wine went round the table. Everyone's glass was filled. The Easter toast, "To the family, the living, and the dead," was downed. Then Grandfather got up. "Let us drink," he said, "to the burial of the feud."

And then all the voices, all the questions, everything so quick, so surprising — getting the startling news trying to adjust to it, sitting there stunned, bewildered. "Horace!" her grandmother's voice so sharp and so peremptory, and Aunt Eleanor, "What feud, Papa?" and all together taking up her grandfather's announcement.

"Silvestro's dead. He's had the grace to take himself off."

"You mean to say," Uncle William sputtered it out, "Silvestro's dead?" And Uncle Richard, "I was under the impression that he was long since dead — or as good as dead." And Uncle James, "Suicide, eh? the poor fellow did away with himself?" — "James!" Aunt Harriette, she remembers, casting an eye in her direction.

"He couldn't have done *that*, Papa," from Aunt Eleanor.

And here it was that Lucien Grey had laid his hand on hers, the two of them caught up together, listening.

"Oh," Grandfather said, "we needn't call it that. The poor fellow fell off a cliff. You know they have 'em in the south of Italy — lots of cliffs and vineyards on the top of 'em."

"Horace," from her grandmother, reprimanding him down the length of that long table.

"Lucky thing!" muttered Uncle William, still gobbling his lamb. "No more trouble from that direction."

"Well, I can't say," her grandfather corrected, "that we did have any trouble from him, since he took himself away to Italy — signed the papers and all."

"Horace!" Grandmother's voice had risen to a shriek.

"But you never can tell," he said, "it's a good thing for everyone concerned the poor fellow's out of it."

How could she possibly have digested it? The ice cream, she remembers, was presently brought on, a great pink and white and chocolate colored lamb, with flowers for ears and spun sugar all around the platter, and everybody, happy enough to change the subject, exclaiming how beautiful it was, and Grandfather giving her one of his famous winks, remarking that they'd slain the paschal lamb especially for her. Sitting there stunned and wondering who she was, Sylvester or Silvestro, and what she could make of a father who had not all these years been waiting in a condition of angelic expectation for her in heaven. He had been right here on earth, and made no attempt to get in touch with her — just taken himself off to Italy.

Now he was dead. There was something unforgettable about it all, trying to accommodate herself to the information, and with Lucien caught up in it, knowing the way she felt — sitting there and watching the ice cream go round the table, his hand on hers.

S I X

———

SHE CLOSED HER EYES and gave herself up to meditation. It was a curious thing, she thought, but she could not for the life of her remember — really remember Lucien. There were of course the amber eyes, the dark mustache, the mobile, enigmatic countenance, but when she tried to reconstruct his features, the expressions of his face, she could not make an image clear enough to bring him back as she had known him then.

For her now he represented all that overwhelming passion, that ecstasy and anguish, the sorrow and the severance which was to say the lamentable story of her love for him, and there were in this connection so many things still left to be conjectured, the fact that he belonged to that closed world, the world of Chamberlains and Fosters, of people walking about among their splendid properties, was naturally to be taken into account.

"Ah well." She looked out at the familiar buildings. The lights were extinguished except for a few scattered windows still bright in the Metropolitan Tower. "Ah well," she said, and there appeared upon her face an expression of profound gravity. Life was tragic enough in all conscience, but it had its exquisite comedy, and it was on this threshold, delicately poised between a comic and a tragic sense of it, she had first become aware of her friendship for Lucien Grey.

The chance and change of circumstance! Would her own personal tragedy have gathered to such a climax if she had not been seated next to Lucien on that particular Easter Sunday? Well, she concluded, very likely yes, what with those long summers he always spent at The Towers, each of them addicted as they were to scrutiny and observation, and their being thrown together among that gallery of characters.

It was not only his sympathy but his sensing what a show it was, that exhibition of family obtuseness, that had made her feel for him such an ecstasy of gratitude — appreciation.

This exalted young man whom even Grandmother Foster held in such high esteem that she found it necessary whenever she spoke of him to say his name twice over, had all at once become a close companion, the two of them by some magic distillation of their qualities capable of passing signals, exchanging messages. How he had assisted her in her enjoyment of the human comedy, confirming her in a knowledge of something she had somehow from the very start seemed so intuitively to know — that there were no frontiers at all between the realm of laughter and the realm of tears. It was only necessary to meet his gaze, set up an interchange, a conversation which the very lack of speech converted into code, tossing the amusement back and forth between them, lifting the shoulders, and sometimes during those interminable midday dinners flicking little crumbs of bread across the table, and wanting desperately as she had on many an occasion to overturn the tumblers, to smash the china, to upset the general pomp and ceremony with a series of loud guffaws, saying as they often did between them, "Oh, really now, you do not mean to say so. We've heard all this a hundred times before." And watching Grandfather Foster as they might have watched a little monkey on a string, wishing that he would go to any length in his absurdities so they could appreciate the show the more, and always conscious of her grandmother, not unaware that there was something here more than a little frightening, as though she might at any instant come down upon their irreverence with some appalling reprimand, for she always seemed, with all her money and set round with these fine exhibits and displays, to have God upon her side; a presence to be feared, never letting anything escape her, and mistrusting the new relationship — her entering into cahoots with Lucien Grey.

To think of Lucien was always to think of those summers at The Towers. How clearly that incredible house of her grandfather's comes back to her. Shingled and clapboarded, perched up behind the hills and hollows of the dunes, with lawns in front of it and the blue ocean stretching off to meet the paler blue of the horizon, it stood, an architectural cross between the Kremlin and a cuckoo clock, adorned with towers and turrets, verandas, balconies, pavilions, the whole monstrous and elaborate structure painted various shades of green and yellow.

The rooms so full of voices, people long since dead, crossing the thresholds, leaving upon her as they passed the impact of their characters and eccentricities. Pretty rooms they were, frivolous and elegant, and filled with a prevailing pinkness, blueness, as of roses, hydrangeas, cupids generously distributed — flowery chintzes, Dresden ornaments, fresh-cut flowers, baskets upheld by cupids, little love seats, whatnots, shepherds, shepherdesses so gaily juxtaposed, and always the pleasant smell of sea and sand and honeysuckle freshly blown about.

The days were filled with people, arriving, departing. Festivities repeated themselves year after year to form one pattern in the memory; what with the garden parties, the tennis parties, her grandmother's afternoons at home, they seemed to merge into a single shifting panorama, the color and the movement all creating in her the same interior vibration and response. How vividly she visualized, how sharply she responded to it all again, those incredible green lawns, the flower beds, planted with ageratum, geranium and portulaca in the shape of anchors, hearts and half moons, set neatly in the grass, cannas waving from the borders and pink petunias fluttering above veranda rails, ladies carrying colored parasols, dressed in flowered hats and ruffled dresses, strolling about engaged in conversation, dappled with sun and shade, and gentlemen whose white ducks and flannels shone as bright as bright, passing refreshments, assisting in the general elegance. The movement, the voices, the cries and laughter, the ships and clouds and whitecaps, and the ocean breezes intermingling, wandering about in the deep recesses of her heart, accentuating that sense she carried with her of summer and the sea and heightening her excitement at the knowledge that among these alien people there was one voice, one face, one presence.

The only variation in the inward drama as the years progressed had been that increasing certainty she had that Lucien had made himself the guardian of her sensibilities. Being one of them himself, belonging to their world, how curious it was that he had been able to share her appreciation of those personalities, to watch them with her as though the two of them were nefarious spectators at a fascinating and continuous drama, the grandparents sharing the honors of the principals in the incredible performance.

What an astonishing pair they were! To think of them was to see them large as life and perfectly satisfied with themselves. How their presences assailed her even now. Her grandfather's elegance was simply beyond description. Even his mourning could not diminish it. When she encountered him first he affected, she remembered, broad black cravats adorned to strike the official note of grief with a large black pearl. He was small and dapper, and all this smartness and perfection assisted by the fragrance of eau de cologne and expensive soaps and pomades gave him a little breeze of his own which he wafted before him as he hurried here and there. His white hair sprang back from his head, framing to their very best advantage those fine features, that perfectly exquisite white mustache and the large dark eyes, the eyebrows impressively black were startling indeed — theatrical. Despite his mourning he was tuned to the enjoyment of life. What a lot of antic tricks and jokes he had, sticking his fingers in his ears and wagging them in a most alarming manner, and how he used to boo at her from behind closed doors and portieres. She had never been able to tell whether his exuberance or her grandmother's severity had been the more difficult to endure. The ordeal of sitting beside her grandmother in church was something to remember. Those Sunday clothes, that clean starched smell she had, the immaculate summer dresses without a spot or crease or stain, her little hats trimmed with such restraint and yet looking as though they'd cost a great deal of money, and the white gloves, so tight on the stout hands. There she'd sit, her hands folded in her lap, communing with God, never moving until some change in the service necessitated her standing up or falling upon her knees. Very pious she was, believing so implicitly that God was with her in all she did and said, and that towards the rich and the wellborn He extended His particular benevolence. How long she remained upon her knees, and when she'd got to her feet again, there was that look upon her marble countenance as though she were now doubly fortified in her belief in God and her own opinions.

Then there was Cousin Cecilia Ware, the ubiquitous poor relative, always managing to say the right thing at just the proper moment, "Yes, Cousin Amelia; yes, Cousin Horace" — making herself useful and somehow or other managing to keep herself so young and fresh and fashionable. Her outings with Grandfather Foster were, the weather allowing, a regular feature of those summer afternoons. She could see them starting off together as clearly as though the lively tableau were going on before her eyes.

Under the brightly painted porte cochere, the high, the brightly painted phaeton, the impatient horses, the small footman holding them in check. Then suddenly her grandfather making his appearance in spotless white, a flower in his buttonhole, his hat cocked a bit to one side, mounting to the driver's seat, putting on his gloves, taking up the reins, while Cecilia Ware clambered up to sit beside him, seated herself, opened her parasol, and the little footman, with the agility of an acrobat, jumped into the rumble as the horses reared and bolted off, adjusted himself to his precarious perch, crossed his arms upon his breast.

There on the sunny veranda stood her grandmother, her hand raised against the light, watching the animated spectacle. Laced and hooked and buttoned into her well-fitting costume as tightly as her emotions were packed into her breast, her face in some queer way resembled her figure. No betraying emotions save that look she had of paying strict attention to every detail. She noted with satisfaction that the footman's breeches were well chalked, his boots well shined, that the horses were in prime condition. She approved the cut of Grandfather's coat, his way of handling the reins, she approved even of Cecilia, who bore herself in a manner that befitted her position.

She was well aware of the sentiments they entertained for each other, but she did not allow this to disturb her. Cecilia assisted her with her lists and made herself useful in many necessary ways; besides, she knew on which side of the loaf her bread was buttered. As for her little husband, if he wished to have an affair of the heart, much better to have it carried on right here beneath her eyes than in regions farther afield. She knew him to a T. He would never cross a single line she chalked for him. Moreover, he was always a perfect gentleman, an ornament to society. She regarded him, by and large, as the most elegant of all her appointments and accessories.

How Cecilia loved those drives, sitting there beside her dashing relative, fully conscious of the splendid appearance they presented to the world. It was not only the public show. She enjoyed his confidences, saying "Poor dear Cousin Horace," and making all those pretty sounds of condolence and acquiescence. The thought he was a creature of the deepest feeling, and as he had just such a notion of himself, his sensibility, his great capacity for suffering, no wonder they were never at a loss for sentimental conversation.

For years they had carried on a little affair of the heart. Fanned by all the breezes of mutual attraction, never allowed to go too far, each preserved unimpaired a sense of the other's charms. The glances they exchanged, the delicate breezes of sensuality they set afloat, did not, as she reflects upon it, escape her, and the fact that Grandfather Foster was as they used to put it "sweet upon Cecilia" created just another of those situations that she and Lucien shared together, and constituted some portion of that curious sense she had that matters of a nature somewhat secret and suppressed were under observation. Sex, if indeed she could speak of it as belonging to an age entirely unacquainted with the word, was for her a matter of the licensed exhibition, the small scenes and tableaux enjoyed with Lucien, all of which — the ladies in their low-necked dresses at the dinner table, their behavior at the garden parties, Charlie Lamb's lady-killing manners, Aunt Georgie's undisguised jealousy — savored more of the absurd and the ridiculous than of the passionate and profound.

Very dark and secret they had kept it. She had been led to understand that there were certain subjects under no circumstances to be mentioned. "When the proper time arrived," all would doubtless be revealed. She had been singularly lacking in curiosity. Her mind had been bereft of concrete facts, concrete sexual images. Perhaps it was the gallant little story of Silvestro and her mother where romantic love had captured her imagination as something belonging to the higher reaches of the soul, connecting it somehow with sorrow and her orphaned state, with evening and the falling of the dew, the scent of flowers in the garden. How oddly in her adolescence she had been assailed by longing, rushing off at twilight into the garden, or more often to the solitary beach, where she would throw her arms out wildly, invoking winds and waves: "Swiftly walk over the western wave, Spirit of Night" — what extraordinary power that particular poem had had, to fill her full of yearning, immense, unutterable, vague — "Out of the misty eastern cave / Where all the long and lone daylight / Thou wovest dreams of joy and fear / Which make thee terrible arid dear / Swift be thy flight!" And those ardent invocations at the end of every stanza, "Come soon, soon." For what was it she had waited? For love, for the arrival of a lover to whom she would yield up all the rich, the undiscovered treasures of her soul? Love had seemed to her as riotously, romantically incorporeal as those kisses of Shelley that mixed and merged with winds and waves and sunsets, leaving the soul quite free for unimpeded flights of poetry.

It had seemed to her quite possible that if two people actually in love with each other should, by some rare circumstance, be left long enough unchaperoned, their love might reach a climax of such soulful unity that the exchanging of a kiss, the extending of this rapture beyond the limits of propriety, might very possibly result in the shameful, the unlawful bearing of a child. It was thus she remembers she had interpreted that child, that scarlet letter pinned to the breast of Hester Prynne. And it was probably, she had made it out, to save her from just such ignominy that she was always so rigorously chaperoned, never allowed to be in the presence of a young man without Cecilia or Aunt Eleanor or someone of a proper age to see that the proprieties were kept.

How could she have been prepared for it, loving Lucien with her innocent, exclusive heart — that August afternoon when they had lain beside each other on the sand, the joining of their hands, their lips — the sudden tracks of fire traced along the secret pathways of her nerves, the secret channels of her blood?

How could she possibly have stood out against it, that sudden passionate love that consumed and overwhelmed her — those stealthy meetings under the lee of the dunes where very occasionally they used to lie together in the hot dry sand?

There were those words he used to whisper to her, "You are part of all things great and quiet, my beloved." She had thought them very beautiful. They were, he told her, taken from a Rumanian folk song. She had, to be sure, been very far from quiet. Her heart had beaten wildly when he took her in his arms. But after their love had been consummated, when all that passion was spent, there she'd lie, very quiet and meditative, listening while the waves approached and, breaking, drew back the pebbles with that mesmeric music that carried her away, floated her off across the waters, across the limitless horizons. Then it had seemed to her indeed she had become a part of that open world of childhood — those moments that were timeless and imperishable.

S E V E N

VERY MUCH ABSORBED she read on. Good gracious, she thought, her predicament had been incredible. Who would be able to believe in it? She found it difficult to believe in it herself and her mind running back to dwell on certain incidents that had preceded that memorable trip from Rome to Florence and which had so absorbed her thoughts upon that April day, she went over them again with all the old astonishment.

That morning at The Towers when Lucien and Eleanor had appeared so late for breakfast and something it had seemed to her between them — Eleanor with that look, hard to define it, in complete possession of her face and looking, if such a thing were possible, more beautiful than ever. Lucien pale, determined; he'd not looked up — he'd not looked at anyone and no sooner had he spread his napkin over his knees than he announced casually that he and Eleanor were leaving for the mountains — Eleanor he said had been suffering from lassitude. She needed a change of air. Eleanor kept her silence, that look of which she'd been aware spreading on her face and she remembers how she'd searched the other faces — Grandfather's evident surprise, blustering out his protest, "What, leaving for the mountains, wasn't the air here good enough for anyone?" and her grandmother sitting behind the coffee urn without a quiver of expression on her face — Lucien had done most of the explaining — a little as though he'd been talking to himself — for he'd looked at no one and it was sea level they'd seemed to be discussing — Eleanor had had too much of that — she needed higher altitudes and as the protests and expostulations had come entirely from her grandfather it was to be assumed that Grandmother Foster was in agreement — Eleanor must have a change.

At any rate, they had departed for the White Mountains that very afternoon. She'd had no word from Lucien. She had not laid eyes on him again until Thanksgiving when, politely, decorously, they had met in the big house in Brookline. At Christmas she had seen him, and during the winter they had met occasionally in the same casual family way, and he had discussed with her and the rest of them the plans her grandmother had made for her to spend accompanied by Cecilia a year in Europe just exactly as though nothing out of the ordinary had occurred. She would love Europe. He hoped she'd go to Italy. Not a word from anyone regarding her condition, merely that relentless carrying out of plans for Europe, and then, in February, his coming with all the others to see her off.

And oh, that moment on the steamer when they had been left alone together on the deck standing beside the rail. "Child," he'd said, his voice so broken he could not go on; the beating of her heart so loud she dared not look at him; and then Aunt Eleanor's arriving in a flurry of excitement, "Lucien, who do you think is on the boat — the Milton Steeles." She'd borne him off with her and that was the last she'd seen of him save for his face upon the pier among the other faces in the crowd.

Utterly incredible — never having mentioned her plight to a soul on earth and Cecilia playing her part to such perfection. Why no sooner had she been safely planted on foreign soil than she'd taken on the status of a respectable young matron — always referred to while they stayed in France as Madame and in Italy respectfully addressed as Signora. Goodness how Cecilia had loved it all — she'd positively doted on the coy little references — going in Paris to the dressmaker's to order the new spring clothes. Did Madame hope for un fils or une fille? and making the rejoinder as it were by proxy, "Oh, un fils, of course." And then in Rome how she'd enjoyed that too, being so conspicuous in her care of her — toting her about to see the sights and making such a feature of the fact that she was, impossible to disguise it, about to have a child.

So there, thought the old woman, continuing to read and to remember she'd been on that lovely day in April traveling from Rome to Florence and Cecilia beside her very smart in her Parisian outfit, the new spring suit and the fashionable hat that set off her little head and the blonde, the pretty puffs and curls so admirably, her manner arrogant and frivolous, playing the woman of the world. She was no longer the poor relation. She was acting the great lady for all she was worth — the garrulous, the asinine conversation, "Look, darling, the Maremma oxen, the beautiful Maremma oxen. Your grandfather loved the oxen. No wonder, with his beauty-loving soul."

There, opposite, was that sprucely turned-out little gentleman, who was, and it could not have escaped Cecilia's notice, an Italian version of Grandfather Foster, every move she made and every word she spoke a patent bid for his attention. "So good of your dear grandparents to send you to Italy at just this impressionable age. I wish I were seeing Italy for the first time." The old gentleman had crossed his knees and discreetly extended his well-shod foot in the direction of her pretty ankles.

Sooner or later, she had thought, they'd pick up an acquaintance. She'd given them however but scant attention, going back and forth among her memories, asking herself the same old questions, never able to answer them. Who had known exactly what, and above all, had Lucien been informed of her condition? She would wonder, what with his cousinages and connections, knowing he shared the same collateral relatives with Grandmother Foster, and remembering how she repeated his name twice over when she introduced him, "My son-in-law, Mr. Lucien Grey; Mr. Lucien Grey" — had not her grandmother let him off the final information? Could it be possible that Lucien had not known about the child? That was the all-important question.

On and on Cecilia prattled, "Look, darling, at that old monastery; see the priest under the cypresses reading his breviary. See the splendid villa, the stone pines along the avenue. Isn't Italy adorable?" And so on, and so on, until finally she'd leaned forward and tried, with a solicitude manufactured entirely for the benefit of the gentleman opposite, to place that little traveling pillow behind her back.

Was he or was he not informed? It was a question nobody was likely to ask or answer, so decorously and discreetly was everything proceeding. Round and round in a circle went her thoughts. What was going to happen next? The only thing she knew for certain was that Florence was her destination, and that Cecilia was carrying out her orders from behind the scenes, her grandmother's skillful hand directing every move. How supine she'd been about it all, never able to trump up the courage to have a showdown with Cecilia. What scenes and conversations she'd invented as she sat there, "See here, Cousin Cecilia, it's my right to know what you're planning to do with me and with my child," or, "Let's put an end to all this secrecy and make-believe" — forcing the issue in imagination as she sat beside her listening to the silly prattle.

She'd managed, as she knew she would, to get into conversation with her fellow traveler, and was doing her level best to draw her into it. "This gentleman has been so kind. He's been telling me about the places we must see while we're in Florence," and she'd turned to ask the name of that interesting little village he had spoken of.

"Borgo alla Collina." It meant, she'd explained, little town among the hills, and wasn't that perfectly charming? A very famous man was buried there. He was mentioned in Dante. They must not fail to go.

"The Signora is," she'd explained, "very interested in poetry. She intends to study Dante when she's mastered her Italian."

"Bravo," said the old gentleman.

She'd made no rejoinder whatever. She'd simply sat there, looking through the window at the broad, the spacious plain, the mountains, those celestial clouds and snows that lay upon them, and suddenly she'd felt consoled, carried beyond, outside her grief and her bewilderment. This is Italy, she'd thought, rejoicing in her Italian parent and in the radiant beauty of the Italian spring, all those blossoming fruit boughs, peach and plum and almond, pear and apple, with the lights and shadows on them from the clouds and snows and mountains, and all those little Tuscan views and landscapes, valleys, olive groves and vineyards, hills crowned with their towns and towers and churches, lifted from the earth, transilluminated there before her eyes.

It was just before they got to Florence that she'd had her moment of rapture, ecstasy, call it what you would, remembering that small Annunciation just as plainly as though she'd stood before it in the Vatican Museum, something about the Virgin's attitude, her hands folded upon her breast and that movement she seemed to be making, a drawing back in awe and denial as though an announcement so great and so astonishing could not by any possibility be true; and the angel, the rush and spread of wings, the garments full and flowing, the hand upraised,

had all but overwhelmed her with that sense she'd had of the surpassing mystery, the miracle of birth.

It was just then the door of the compartment opened to let in that
ridiculous little courier. What was his name? Fratelli, that was it.
"Scusi, scusi," he'd exclaimed, continuing in his nervous, broken, ob-
sequious English. They were nearing Florence, would the ladies permit
him to take the luggage from the racks and place it in the corridor? He
smiled, and, addressing Cecilia, said that the carriage for Fiesole would
be waiting at the station. All the arrangements had been made, the
drive in the cool of the evening would be delightful.

"But delightful," he repeated, and, turning to her, expatiated on the
joys awaiting her. "When the Signora arrives in Fiesole," he declared,
"she will find herself in paradise," and he kissed the ends of his fingers.
"But in paradise," he said.

Again the old woman shut her eyes and closed the manuscript. Ah,
there was more to it than just the recounting of her quite incredible
little tragedy, that laying bare of the secret she had kept through all
these years, and which was so faithfully recorded in these pages. It was
on the place names now she lingered — Firenze, Fiesole, those months
she had spent with the nuns in their convent overlooking Florence.
Why, they had a heartscape, a horizon that closed her in with memories which left her vibrating now to an intensity of response entirely
unique — to Italy as she'd experienced it at that time of poignant sorrow. To be sure she'd been in Rome but that ancient city had been too
large, too crowded with history — the Forum, the Coliseum, the cata-
combs, St. Peter's and the Vatican, all the Christian churches, dragged
hither and thither by Cecilia, telling her about it in her uninformed,
irrelevant manner, and her own thoughts but seldom free from her
predicament.

But here in the fine weather with the spring rioting wildly in the
vineyards and the gardens and the nightingales singing all day long as
well as through the night! There had been those drives to Florence
down the long hill in the big landau with Fratelli on the box beside the
coachman pointing out this sight of interest or the other, and Cecilia
next her talking the usual nonsense, the Judas trees in blossom and the
wisteria dripping over every wall, passing the contadini in their rattling
wine carts, cracking their long whips, shouting their jokes and gay

obscenities; then the entrance into the old town, clattering over the cobblestones through the dark streets between the great palaces with their overhanging roofs. And all of a sudden coming out on the Piazza del Duomo, that astonishing display of architecture, the great cathedral with its enormous dome, the baptistry and Giotto's lovely tower intricately overlaid with flowery patterns of mosaic, as though with that happy exuberance of the Renaissance it had been necessary to proclaim in these wondrous structures that this was the city of flowers, the city of youth and renascent spring.

Oh, she couldn't get away from it in Florence, that sense she'd had that one participated in the celebration of life itself, its perpetual renewal. As she scanned the faces of the young women who passed her in the streets and saw their features and expressions again and again repeated in the faces of the Virgins and Madonnas in the churches and museums she became increasingly aware that the masters of the Renaissance had expressed, in their beautiful Annunciations, Nativities, and Assumptions, as much their pagan adoration for life, fertility, as their ecstasy in the presence of the great Christian myths and mysteries. It was here on every side, you couldn't escape it, the declaration of joy in the beauty and mystery of life. She was young and uninstructed historically, and she hadn't so much got it through her intellect as through her senses, through every fiber of her being, so that now she had only to think about that extraordinary time to feel it flowing back to her through all the tides of memory — the language, the voices, the smells, vistas down the long dark streets, sunlight on the palaces, in the piazzas, clattering over the pavements, walking past the monuments. crossing the bridges, going into museums, entering churches.

She had not, of course, been able to have it out with Cecilia. Day after day had passed, keeping up the same old farce, going in and out of Florence like any other pair of avid sightseers; and then, when it grew very warm and she had found it difficult to be so much upon her feet, the sisters had urged her to remain in the convent garden, and Cecilia had sustained them in this advice. Oh yes, she'd said, she must make herself comfortable in the lovely garden and let her do the honors of the town.

E I G H T

CERTAIN MEMORIES ARE NEVER STILL, thought the old woman. They are like clouds, they move and shift about, they emit their lights and shadows. You suffer them; they come and go and after a while establish a climate, an ambient all their own.

And there had been a trancelike spell about that convent garden which, even as she thought about the anguish she'd suffered there, began to work upon her — sitting day after day in that long chair, the heat intense, the roses blooming, fading away in such profusion that she'd heard the little sound of petals falling through the hedge. The soft petals accumulating under the hedge, that mass of purple iris, the tall buds, and the blossoms standing up like moths above the broken chrysalises, the pigeons walking up and down beneath the cypress trees engaged in ceaseless conversations, the sisters coming on little errands, bringing her this and that — speaking to them, dismissing them, never allowing her reveries to be disturbed, and seeing, while they retreated down the path between the cypress trees, over the edge of the garden wall, floating off and away into the distance of the skyscape and the mountain ranges, the immense, the lovely panorama, with Florence lying below her in the valley of the Arno; asking herself the same insistent questions. Was Lucien informed or was he not? Did he know that she was about to bear his child? Had he allowed himself to be maneuvered by the same powerful hand that moved her puppets with such skill and deliberation? What would happen to her child? And why, why, why had she not been able to have it out with Cecilia?

So the days passed. And then that day, that moment — impelled by the almost suicidal impulse to get up and go to the parapet. Standing there looking down on Florence — the churches, the bridges, the river flowing golden through the plain; and suddenly with no warning, no preparation for it, those sharp pains ripping through her abdomen. It has begun, it has begun, she'd thought, and clutching her side, holding her breath, she'd managed somehow to get back to her seat in the shade, seeing Cecilia, scaring up the pigeons in front of her while behind her they descended in an arch upon the shadows, coming towards her along the path between the cypress trees. How determined she had been not to let her know her labor had begun. She'd braced herself, she'd taken those long deep breaths, and she had vowed that she would play this game of silence to the bitter end. She'd counted one, two, three, four, five, six; and suddenly it was over and there was Cecilia closing her parasol, kissing her lightly on the forehead. "Oh, darling, here you are," she'd said, "how *comfortable* you look." She was on her way to Florence. She wouldn't be long. There was a call that she must make, a *most important* errand. She'd turned and, waving gaily, traveled down the path that led her to the gate in the garden wall as though bent upon angelic business.

How long before the nuns discovered her condition she has not the ghost of an idea. And as for that tragic childbirth, in the big bare room above the valley of the Arno, her labor had been so long and unremitting, the Angelus ringing, and later the same bells ringing for the matin services, that she had never been certain whether it was the call to morning or to evening prayers to which she listened.

Would her anguish never cease? Could it be possible that it was evening — that it was dawn? Was it a feast day? Was it Sunday? In Italy they rang the bells for all the great occasions, for birth and death and burial, and it comforted her to think that they were answering each other across the hills and valleys while she labored with this painful birth, tugging with all the strength remaining to her at the sheer tied to the bedpost, hearing the doctor say "*Coraggio,*" sinking back among the pillows, and in the intervals between the spasms experiencing that extraordinary exaltation. The intervals grew shorter and the pains intolerable. If she listened she could locate the various chimes. A little way down the slope the bells of Settignano. Those nearer, louder, rang in Fiesole, farther down the hill the bells of San Gervaso. Ah, the tolling of the great cathedral bell in Florence and such a curious sense of being lifted up in the moments of exaltation between the brutal spasms, of floating out, drifting away with the church bells, distributing herself among the olive groves and vineyards, of being one with earth, with the processes of life, renascence. If she held to the thought that she was assisting at the greatest of all life's miracles it would help her to be brave, for the pains returned with redoubled violence.

She'd sat up, the sweat beading her forehead, streaming down her face.

She heard the doctor, "Pull, Signora, pull with all your strength."

The sister came with a wet cloth and wiped her face, her hands. "Oi, oi, oi," she'd screamed.

And still the doctor's voice, "*Coraggio.*"

"*Oi, oi, oi,*" and the voice of her anguish mingling with the voices of the church bells answering one another with their ancient earthy tongues, and then that sudden stream of sickly sweetish air, breathing it thirstily. Taking another and another breath, the gradual annulment of the torture. And had she or had she not above her exaltation and her anguish heard the doctor saying in Italian, "*Un bel maschio, Signora,*" falling into deep abysses of fatigue and sleep?

And then that rude awakening, thought the old woman, and she moved in her chair and stretched out her arms as though she still implored Cecilia to let her have her child, being to all intents and purposes back again in that cool dim room, the shutters closed against the midday glare — hearing voices drifting through the windows, seeing the sunlight dropped in rungs like a bright ladder tremble on the floor and on the wall against her bed and aware that her cousin looking very fresh and energetic sat beside her — that she was telling her — what was Cecilia telling her? that she looked *so* rested after her refreshing sleep.

She was unable to speak the words — "Where is my baby? I must see my child." They were on her tongue, her heart was bursting with them, but she was listening to Cecilia. What was it Cecilia was saying, prattling on so brightly, stressing certain words and going on with such enthusiasm? "Darling — it's *all* right; it is your grandmother's doing. You must give your grandmother credit for it — that *lovely* couple being here in Florence and at just this moment. Think of it, coming *all* the way from America, the *loveliest* people. I met them by your grandmother's appointment; but the *loveliest* couple, people of excellent family. I am *not* going to tell their name. They want to adopt your little boy, to give him their name and bring him up *exactly* as though he were their own. They have *plenty* of money and they will give him the happiest of lives."

That was word for word exactly what her cousin said. And there she'd lain, paralyzed, unable to speak or move, looking blankly at Cecilia while she went on with further explanations. She had brought the couple up from Florence. There was nothing to do but sign some papers, make some promises, it had all been made *so* simple for her. It was her grandmother that she must thank; all too good to be quite true. Grandmother had managed it with such perfection. She wanted her to stay in Europe for another year. When she returned it would be *exactly* as though nothing had occurred. "Tabula rasa," she had said, repeating the phrase as though she'd coined it.

"Tabula rasa."

Miss Sylvester closed her eyes, and there before her was the angel in the Annunciation she had seen that day upon the train — the rush and spread of wings, the garments full and flowing, the hand upraised.

And then suddenly the poor woman jumped as though she'd been struck a violent and unexpected blow, for the telephone was ringing, stridently demanding her attention. "Dear me," she said, "dear me," and with the greatest difficulty she got up, went to the desk and lifted the receiver from the hook.

N I N E

SHE ROSE FROM THE TELEPHONE and began to pace the room. Dear me, she was highly irritated. Adam was a most exasperating young man, and there was little consistency about her own annoyance since she had been eager to get in touch with him. Now they'd dine tonight together and she could at once discover his address. Capricious enough of him not to have let her have it on the telephone. Where was he living? Oh, he'd said, in a new dump, a hole in the ground below the sidewalk in a street she wouldn't know.

He'd moved, he said, and her supposition about that love affair was, presumably, correct. He was in the bitterest of moods and very exigent about that check he wished to have her cash. She looked at the clock upon her desk. There had been plenty of time for her to have cashed it, if she had wished to do so. Her bank was most accessible, and why she'd been so contrary she didn't know. Surely he could wait until tonight. Down to his last red cent, he'd said. It was his mood had set her off, to say nothing of his having broken into her flow of thought and memory. Well, well, she musn't let her irritation work upon her thus.

It was the way he had responded to her when she spoke to him about the morning's news. It was quite all right by him, the sooner we got blown to Kingdom Come, the better it would be for all concerned.

My God, she said, my God. This world in which we lived, these past decades, unprecedented, unparalleled in history. She had no patience with those who retorted that other ages had been comparable, nothing new or different in this. What utter nonsense! The nightmare of our lives today had no parallel in history. Those monstrous images of terror and the dark, Geryon, Belial, Beelzebub (what were the other names?), prophetic images of evil riding the whirlwind in the Apocrypha, were not to be compared with the shapes that stalked the world today. The skies above our heads were crowded with them, the seas beneath the earth, and in the satanic mills, Los Alamos, Oak Ridge (heavens, there were so many others located who knows where), what shapes, what forms were now materializing. Voices, voices over the air, announcements, appropriations, threats, phantasmagoric images of wars to come. Everyone listening, waiting, and this simultaneity, hearing it together all around the world, shuddering, turning in our sleep, walking through the dream, pure nightmare in which the whole world walked together, pushing the horror down, letting the usual events, the joys and sorrows, the expectations, the personal desires, the vanities and the ambitions, submerge it, hide it deep, deep down, away from our investigation. All in the dream together, every man Jack of us, big fry and little fry alike: and now, for one reason or another, she saw the face of Einstein, its uncanny beauty, the white hair like a halo circling the countenance of a charming, an innocent child. On which of the terrible horses would he be mounted? she wondered, for certainly he rode in the forefront of the procession, along with the politicians, statesmen, the brass hats, the military strategists, and in the rear she saw the rest of the inhabitants of earth, unnumbered, unidentified, running full tilt like so many Gaderine swine, head on for destruction. Mad it was, an insanity unprecedented. Was there in it a self-determined will, a drive towards general, wholesale suicide? No, no, she cried aloud, and again she struck her breast. It was not so, nobody wanted it.

What if, she thought, there could come a moment's pause, everybody ordered to halt, big fry and little fry alike? What if some voice of supreme authority, a voice that could be heard in every corner of the earth, ordained a general pause, a moment's halt in the inexorable procession? What if, in that silence, the wheels of these satanic mills should cease, the voices in the air, the threats and proclamations? If in the silence all could drop upon their knees and pray, pray together for five minutes, give due thought and due consideration to the general madness, might we not somehow or other find that we were saved? But no, we didn't dare, we hadn't the nerve to look it in the face; the only thing was to prepare for it, to accelerate the procession. That seemed to be the great idea. This

side and that side of the curtain that divided the world into two op-
posing camps, the monstrous, the subhuman mechanizations, material-
izations continued, the whole world geared to the wholesale production
of death. Once more the old woman put her hands before her face. Was
she trying to drive away the pictures that came into her mind, or was she
attempting to visualize them? They staggered the imagination.

No wonder that Adam shrugged his shoulders and asked her why she
got so worked up about it all, intimating by his voice and his expression that since she was so soon to exit from the scene forever, there was
no need for such agitation. "Well, it matters to me," she said aloud, "it
matters more than anything " and again she seemed to be engaged in
one of those endless arguments that she carried on with the young
man. He belonged, in his surly, stubborn manner, to the wars-have-
always-been-and-always-will-be school of thinking. He liked to quote
history and trot out his greater knowledge to confound her. Nothing
different in the human situation, only on a larger scale — that he
would concede, the scale of it. He was a Spenglerian and used to quote
those passages about tile great Khans and the epochs soon to dawn
upon us, the bigger and the better wars about to come. It was apparent
enough to her that he was sick to death of the whole dreadful subject.
Had he not, poor boy, seen enough of it already, waiting there in
France for them to soften tip the enemy's resistance, and later marching into Germany over the Remagen bridge, and seeing the wreck and
ruin of all those bombed-out cities?

What the eyes of the young men had seen, the abhorrent scenes, the
pictures pushed down into the deepest wells of memory; and hereupon
she began enumerating the great terrains of battle, islands in the
Pacific, the beachheads, the battles in the desert. She too had seen
them, comfortably seated in her armchair, at the movie theaters; but to
imagine it, the nerves, the senses — eyes, ears, the shuddering flesh exposed. It was a marvel to her that so many of them still preserved their
sanity. No wonder they challenged the years to come with the supreme
insolence of disregard.

No wonder that Adam was disconcerted and irritated when she
dwelt upon it with such persistency. He was determined to snatch eagerly, hungrily at all that he could get, living on so little, attempting to
complete his education, and writing of course that novel which de-

voured him. The moment was pregnant with possibilities. Was her interest in Adam, she asked herself, a kind of substitution? He was the same age as that young man she would never lay her eyes on, stamped with the imprint of the same horrendous years. More than likely he too had been flung out into one or another of the outrageous areas. Perhaps his bones were bleaching on the Libyan desert. Maybe he was lying under a nameless cross on some island in the Pacific. It might be — and this seemed to her more right — that his dust was scattered among the vineyards and the hills of Italy.

Well, the less she thought of him, that child to whom she had so rashly decided to leave the bulk of her fortune, the better for her state of mind. Anonymity was, when she reflected upon it, a condition she should now be willing to accept. Had she not kept her secrets to herself, and was there a soul alive to care whether she had a past or not? Anonymous she was, and somehow always had been.

Anonymous was the word for the lot of us, she thought, as she continued to gaze at the accustomed view, the office buildings with their bright panes reflecting the scudding clouds, and behind the windows countless men and women in their busy cells. She seemed to see the entire world, the human hive collapsing, falling in upon itself, the integuments melting, disappearing, cities, insolent skyscrapers falling, falling. The bees swarmed; the cities fell, and, attempting to blot out the dreadful pictures fringing her imagination, she remembered how she had read, she didn't know exactly where, that, measured against the aeons, the endless procession of evolving species, the birds were practically new arrivals on the stage of life, and how it had pleased her to call them little John the Baptists, singing in the wilderness, prophesying, preaching the gospel of one to come, the latchet of whose shoes they were not worthy to unloose.

Ridiculous, she thought, for Adam to assert so stubbornly that this age did not in basic experiences differ from the other ages. It was the simultaneity of our responses to the catastrophes, what with the very waves of air transporting us, riding us round the habitable globe, photographs flowing through space, and voices, voices. Try to press the pictures and the voices down, to hide them in the deepest wells of the subconscious. The world was too much with us, it had entered the secret, the most uneasy placing of being — conscience.

And here we were, hawking our souls about, writing novels, our own little autobiographies (all the novels were, in one way or another, autobiographical), young and old alike engaged in it, dissecting, anatomizing, breaking up the moments, and there was something not to be passed over lightly in the startling fact that the splitting of the atom and the splitting of the soul, the long, long range of human memory, had been contemporaneous, all in the open world together, no shelter for us, no place to hide. And suddenly there was a poem upon her lips, she couldn't for the life of her remember where she'd read it, but the words seemed, as she recited them, the very voice of her apprehension.

> "Put out the stars an instant, Lord,
> Lest all these swords and scimitars
> Frighten this snail who goes abroad
> For the first time without his mail.
> Behold him laid along the slim
> Green blade of grass too frail for him.
> He has no home, no church, no dome
> To shelter him. He goes alone.
> Put out the stars an instant, Lord,
> Lest all these swords and scimitars
> Turn him to stone."

She repeated the last two lines, and found to her astonishment that she was standing in the center of the room, attempting to collect her wits.

What had she intended to do? She must get herself some lunch. Stepping rather unsteadily into the bathroom, she looked about her. Here was a can of soup, here were biscuits, there on the windowsill was fruit. When she'd had something to eat she'd get back to her chair and go on with that manuscript to the bitter end.

But where, where in the world was the can opener? She searched frantically among the queer utensils under the tub. It was these wretched little gadgets she felt unable to contend with.

BOOK 2

O N E

———

IT WAS A CLEAR EVENING. Miss Sylvester stood at the window. She had finished her manuscript and she sighed heavily. Her novel had left her with a feeling of incredulity occasioned not so much by the fact that her story savored of the unusual, if not to say the melodramatic, as by the positively imponderable strangeness of the human condition, one's existing in this world at all. There was something about this winter hour when the lights were bright in all the assembled windows which never failed to impress her as entirely unreal, especially if as was the case tonight a small slice of the wintry moon could be seen sailing round the corner of the Metropolitan Tower.

She had told the story of her life and, she must admit it, it had moved her profoundly — left her as novels frequently did with a residue of emotion that she often carried in her heart for some time after she had finished them. But oddly enough she was irritated that this was so. If her book should fall into the hands of others addicted as she was to the habitual reading of novels, what exactly would their feeling be? Doubtless they would regard her history as a very tragic one indeed. Poor girl, or more likely poor unfortunate woman, they'd think, what a sad time she'd had of it, and would they not be liable to carry away from the perusal of her book something of the same soft and not unpleasant ache of love and sympathy that she felt herself for her poor heroine?

Well, well, she reflected, peering at the young moon and the incredible citadels of light as though in the face of such a spectacle it was something of an impertinence to indulge oneself in personal tragedy at all. New York had been her home for over fifty years, nearly three-quarters of her life. Think of the changes, think of the events! Why, on her first arrival she had lived only a few blocks north on Fifth Avenue. All these neighboring streets had looked considerably like the Back Bay — low three-story houses with high stoops, maids at windows pulling down the blinds, front doors opening to let in children and nursemaids, ladies in long skirts alighting from carriages, gentlemen with canes and top hats walking down the stoops. Very decorous and stable, more or less rooted in tradition, no intimation of this neon-lighted metropolis hung crazily in air, people inhabiting a few cubic feet of sky and regarding it a valid piece of real estate.

Taking up the manuscript and holding it as though she weighed it in her hands, the old woman reseated herself. Book One, she said aloud, Book Two. Yes, that had been, she thought, an excellent device — skipping all those years, giving but short shrift to that anguish, that complete death of the heart (the year in Europe with Cecilia, her return to Brookline, her final severance from family ties), and placing her heroine, after nearly two decades of residence in New York, there on Fifth Avenue in that memorable parade. And she'd achieved it admirably, looping up into a single chapter the thoughts and resolutions with their backward and their forward glances, and setting her novel in motion again on that tide of faith in human nature and the future of the race. That had seemed to her on that May afternoon to have reached its highest flood, loosed as it had been from the hearts of all those men and women walking up the avenue. With Mary Morton at her side and that group of Italian working women she had browbeaten into taking their part in the great demonstration forming a small battalion, she had asked herself if it was possible in a world where there was so much human misery, so many wrongs to right, for one woman to cling tenaciously to her own particular griefs. Today I turn my back upon the sorrows I have known, I shall forget my past. Those were the words to which she'd set her feet to marching and, with the band only a few sections ahead of her playing almost exclusively as she recalls it "The Battle Hymn of the Republic," "Mine eyes have seen the glory of the coming of the Lord," getting the rhythms of her body somehow or other swung into the rhythms, not of the familiar words, but of her own brave resolutions, she had been borne buoyantly on and up the avenue.

Ah, thought the old woman, we are inclined to laugh whenever we see the pictures of those old processions. What funny hats we wore, those high collars, the long skirts that swept the ankles, the stance of all those standard bearers, the resolution in those faces, all that seriousness, that dedication. But if the world could recapture it again, that buoyancy and hope, all that faith and optimism, the protest against injustice, inhumanity, the comradeship, the pledging and resolving, the banding together in unity and friendliness which somehow or other on that particular afternoon had joined and gathered to a tide. It spread along the line of march, it communicated itself from heart to heart, that sense one had that the world was getting better, that new visions and concepts were abroad. She remembers what joy she had experienced thinking of the splendid women marching with her in the same procession, of the distinguished men who had laid themselves open to the jeers and insults of the crowd to march along with them in this demonstration of their strength. Everyone, she'd thought, with vision and with courage is out today rejoicing in a common faith — a belief in the future of the world. There was a spirit in the air she could not well define, participation, comradeship — joy at being alive and able to consider oneself a useful member of society. So on and up the avenue behind the bands and banners she had marched, making her own brave resolutions, embarking as it seemed to her upon a new life, a good life.

In the beauty of the lilies Christ was born across the sea. Today I turn my back upon the sorrows I have known, I shall forget my past. As though one could forget one's past, exclaimed the old woman, looking up to see that there rested on the Metropolitan Tower and on those citadels of life insurance at the foot of the avenue the cool bright glow of winter twilight. You might as well tell a river to stop flowing as to say to anybody, now forget your past. Your past was contained within you, a part of this moment or the next; the scent of a flower, the song of a bird, music as you entered a room, some sight on which your eyes were resting, and back it rushed into the mind again — as though she had not been all the way up Fifth Avenue, even while she was saying those brave words, swinging her body into the rhythms of that glorious hymn, remembering her past, passing this landmark or that, and finally halting with her little band of working girls directly in front of the house that had actually been her first home in New York. Somewhat washed up it had looked to her, with the shops to the right and left of it, and offering quite a different appearance to its aspect in 1895 when, just one of many similar mansions presenting their high stoops and brownstone fronts to the avenue, it had offered her shelter and refuge from her misery. There she'd waited, standing first on one foot and then on the other, telling herself so gallantly that she was on this day to turn a leaf in her book of life, and the associations rushing over her, mixing and mingling with the memories of those early days in New York, the distressful remembrance of the two years that had followed her return from Europe.

Awful had been that return to Brookline, not indeed as she had imagined it with Lucien in the picture and having to pretend that nothing had happened between them, none of that anticipated agony which she had told herself a hundred times a day she could not face, never a sight of Lucien. She had passed him on the ocean. He and Eleanor were off on an extended trip. And all this dropped casually into the conversation a few hours after her arrival and just as though it held but little interest for her. They would not return for several years. "Your uncle has developed an extraordinary interest in Chinese pottery (or is it temples, Horace?)" her grandmother had elucidated. "Your Uncle Lucien is," she'd continued, "a very cultivated man." And with this to make him as inaccessible as possible she changed the subject quite abruptly. Life went on. Lucien never again made an appearance, driving out from Boston as in the old days to make those sudden calls that had always furnished her with so much joy. He never appeared on Sundays for the usual midday dinners. No sight or sound of him. And when the time came finally to go to The Towers that was what she had not been able to endure. Why, she'd almost died of it. The less she thought about it now the better, being there where every scent and sound and sight had brought the memories back so swiftly, lying awake at night and listening to the waves and always trying to stop the words from coming (they were a portion of the very breath she drew), "You are part of all things great and quiet, my beloved." She hadn't cared what happened to her, and returning for her second Brookline winter she'd simply allowed life to be taken out of her own hands altogether. She'd become the victim not only of nervous prostration but of a romantic and disastrous love affair which it was presumed she had sustained while traveling in Europe. Toted about from doctor to doctor, listening with complete apathy to that astonishing array of lies and allusions, and finding her life embellished by a romance quite different from the sorrow which consumed her, she had paid no attention to the advice of the doctors or the stern admonitions of her grandmother. She must take an interest in life, she must go out into society, she must find some kind of a hobby, she must stop reading so much. She had made it her deliberate business to pine away, cherishing a vague hope that, like the heroine of the romance trumped up around her, she might presently die of a broken heart.

And then suddenly when life was at its very lowest ebb her grandmother had in her desperation brought out of the unknown and the unsuspected into the very forefront of those plans and decisions as to what in the world to do with her next that neglected and forgotten, that impoverished relative, Miss Leonie Lejohn, who had turned her pleasant home on Fifth Avenue into a very select and suitable boardinghouse. Leonie should chaperon her. There could be no better place to send her than to New York. It developed too that she was to take up singing. She had had a father who had played the flute, her voice was very pleasing, she had an excellent ear, it was not unlikely that she could develop a genuine talent for music. And so, subscribing as apathetically to the scheme as to any of the other prescriptions for the condition of her soul, almost before she knew what it was all about she had found herself at Cousin Leonie's.

For once, she'd said to herself, getting into line and step and casting a backward glance at the high stoop, the brownstone façade still standing there amid the shops and restaurants, her grandmother had struck it right, she'd made the perfect choice. There'd been something about it, something, and breathing again the smell of asphalt, that smell of the Avenue in the 'nineties, hearing again the vast rumble of vehicles, carriage wheels, cart wheels, and the descent of horses' hooves, plunk, plunk in the asphalt, she'd lived through it all again, stepping out of a morning with the large impersonal roar of the great city in her ears and that sense within her, though she wouldn't for the world allow herself to acknowledge that she felt it, that she was still young, that life had an interest, a positive fascination for her. And how extraordinary it is, she thought, keeping step, keeping step, He is trampling out the

vineyards where the grapes of wrath are stored, the vitality, the recu-
perative power of youth, just being there in New York with her talent
flowering and blossoming, how exciting it had seemed, with Eva
Winters (yes, there had been poor Eva, what a part she'd played in all
of it), Eva, whose passion for music equaled her own and whose voice
had been not much better or maybe not much worse than hers, and
who, if she cared to take a backward glance, had probably put into the
head of Cousin Leonie in her correspondence with her grandmother
the idea that singing lessons might be the best anodyne to apply to a
heart that was almost at the point of breaking. She and Eva had had at
any rate the same singing master, Signor Vittorio Locatelli, who raved
with almost equal fervor about the voices of both talentless pupils.
Under the inspiration of the fiery-eyed little maestro what a passionate
enthusiasm for music they'd each of them worked up. Music-crazed
they'd been, starting off together in the earliest hours of daylight to
procure for themselves if possible seats in the very front row of that
topmost, neck-breaking, back-breaking gallery of the Metropolitan.
What Wagnerians they became. To hear "The Ring" again and still
again as many times as it was given, that had been their idea of bliss,
sitting there imagining themselves impersonating those famous heroines, Isolde, Brünnehilde. Strange, exotic had been those agonies, in-
tensities, resting her chin upon the rail of that uncomfortable "nigger
heaven," while the music pouring from the lighted pit and the stage so
far below became not so much the score of Wagner as the inexhaustible
stream of emotion welling from her agitated heart. She'd swooned,
she'd swayed, she'd practically melted away in an ecstasy of remembrance and delectable indulgence in her grief, and, let her admit it
now, even while she'd thrown herself with complete abandon into the
splendid agonies of those majestic heroines, she'd been quite well
aware that Eva, who she knew to have heard the legend of that fictitious heart-breaking European love affair, was watching with the keen-
est awe and interest the spectacle of her abandonment to grief. For
there had been, she must confess it, much sweetness in holding in her
gift and even while she kept her secret locked within her breast the
sympathy which at that period everyone was so ready to bestow upon
her, and although she knew, with that habit of silence long built up in
her, that her story would not be whispered to a soul on earth, she had

felt enormous satisfaction in being pointed out and noticed as a creature so young and so afflicted.

Fantasy, catharsis, call it what you would, a necessary phase perhaps,
a way in which she'd learned to find her grief endurable. Glamorous,
exciting it had been walking among the crowds on those enchanted
New York pavements, living in her cloud of dreams. And so, swinging
along in time with the brave resolutions (today I turn my back upon
the sorrows I have known), continuing in step with her beloved Mary,
she'd rehearsed it marching up the avenue.

T W O

———

WELL, IF SHE HAD TO SAY IT, thought the old woman, that had been quite a tour de force. She'd done it very well indeed getting her heroine all the way to the Plaza and trailing the memories along with her, the story so clearly told and the scenes so vividly rendered. None the less there had been something omitted. Suddenly she began to beat her breast with the familiar emphasis. Something felt, here in the heart and along the channels of the blood, a sweetness, a quickness, some suppressed excitement, why those early years in New York had had a pulse-beat entirely their own and, she'd have to acknowledge some surprise in the realization of this, they had been thoroughly pleasurable, delightful. The flow and rhythm of one's life could not be communicated. It was carried here. Again she pounded her breast, here in the heart.

How could she possibly describe that house of Leonie's — it was all in entering the front door, walking up the long flight of stairs to her room, passing that bronze statue of the Venus de Milo in the niche at the curve of the stairs, getting that sniff of escaping gas, old carpets and ancient plumbing in the hall, stopping as she entered her big sepulchral room and before turning on the gas to listen to the roar and rumble outside. Nothing so exciting as that had ever met her ears, the loud, the assertive voice of New York, whispering to herself that she was here on her own, leading her own life. Something about it, that extraordinary domicile, that had from the beginning spelled adventure, the front rooms looking out upon the avenue and that endless procession of vehicles, the horses' feet descending, prancing up and down the pavement plunk, plunk, plunk.

There was the faded shabby elegance of the long drawing room and, at the back, the other side of the folding doors, the long dark dining room which constituted the stage and center of that fascinating drama — life as it was led at Cousin Leonie's. The long table always covered with a white cloth, changed each Sunday and stained with many grease spots towards the end of every week. Cousin Leonie dispensing coffee from a large old-fashioned urn at breakfast and soup from a large china tureen at dinner, toying delicately with the teacups at the luncheon hour ("One lump, Mr. Langley?" "A dash of cream, Miss Playfair?"), doing her level best to keep up the tone of her establishment and Mr. Langley on her right doing more than his best to support her endeavor — a funny eccentric little man with a waxed mustache and very shiny trousers. Interested in genealogy, he spent most of his time at the public libraries investigating family trees. Cousin Leonie had a perfect genius for knowing without having to study it up exactly who of any importance was connected with whom, so that conversation, if the two of them had their way, consisted entirely in enumerating and recapitulating names. Then there was Miss Playfair who, they used to intimate, was a mere parvenue. She kept her own little brougham and inhabited the largest room in the house. She tried to make it out that Miss Leonie's was her own residence, and was driven to the oddest expedients in explaining to her visitors the intrusion upon her private scene of such a queer assortment of characters. Last and least of all was Mrs. Canfield. Supported by a small group of friends and relatives whose monthly subscriptions made it possible for her to inhabit a tiny hall bedroom on the top floor and to enjoy three meals a day, she regarded it a privilege to breathe the air surrounding her, and was always saying "Dear me," or "Yes," or "No" at what seemed to her the appropriate moment. Offsetting, spellbinding, disconcerting and generally discombobulating all these odd had-beens and would-be's were Mary Morrison and her queer friend Morty (Mr. Martin Morton, as Miss Leonie never failed to call him).

Ah how vividly she could see dear Mary now, that face, the cloud of dark hair around it, and the black eyes that seemed to give off a kind of sulphurous smoke, the nose broken at the bridge, and that glow of health and vitality, as though somehow or other her love of life and her interest in it had been gathered right up into her countenance, where it gave off its warmth and glow like a hearth at which the sick and the self-centered could come to warm themselves. How passionately Mary loved the fullness and variety of life, how passionately she loved the world, and with what eagerness she dedicated herself to reforming it, for making it better, as she used to say, for the next generation to live in. She could not sit down at that table without knocking the proprieties and absurdities and conventions into a cocked hat. She discarded conventions, she discarded all the rules and orders of her day. She'd been, she had to acknowledge it, pretty appalled by Mary at first, and though fascinated, fascinated, had tried to stand out against her. All her recklessness and daring, all her scholarship and seriousness, with none of her warmth and humor and humanity impaired. And what a mind she had. A woman with a mind like that! — taking all those courses, reading all those books, a freak, a wonder, a phenomenon. And with the eager, the factual, the estimable Morty so head over heels in love with her that the rooms the two of them inhabited together positively rocked and shook with what, they made no bones about it, appeared to be going on between them. What commotion her very presence in their midst incurred.

The way Mary used to air her opinions. How she liked to shock, astonish, always bringing the underprivileged into the discussions, and her belief in trade unions. What other weapons had the poor industrial workers but their collective strength? she'd ask. And she'd usually turn to Miss Playfair. Did she have any idea of the conditions under which the clothes she had on her back were manufactured? No, she'd bet she didn't. And Miss Playfair turning a very cold shoulder would try to incite Mrs. Canfield's indignation, the poor bewildered little lady nodding her head or shaking it as she thought most expedient, muttering "Dear me," "Yes," "No," "I never did," and Mr. Langley who knew every root and branch of Mary's family tree (was she not a Morrison, one of *the* Morrisons?) expressing unutterable consternation, looking at Miss Leonie as though to implore her to show Mary the front door at once.

With Eva there was something else — jealousy. Eva had somehow sensed from the first that there was a kind of kinship between herself and Mary. "I don't like her," she'd say, "she frightens me. I don't see how you can be so fascinated by her. I think she's dreadful." She'd denied it. No, she'd said, she wasn't fascinated. But Eva had guessed it right. She'd loved her from the first. However, it had taken that friendship a long time to declare itself; and it caused her the profoundest remorse to remember how when Mary used to say to her, "Come along with Morty and me to one of our meetings," she'd sneak out after dinner hoping nobody had seen her go with them. The meetings were dreary enough in all conscience, held in smoky rooms and among what had seemed to her the most unrefined and unattractive people. There they'd sit, smoking, discussing, organizing, and Mary and Morty so familiar with them. Pretty lacking in glamor it had been when she compared it to the hours spent in Eva's company at the Metropolitan.

Poor Miss Leonie was rather at her wits' end, for Mary's mother was an old friend and she'd promised to keep an eye on the wayward girl. She kept the place in perpetual ferment. Miss Playfair was always declaring ultimatums, "Either I go or they depart." Such a pair endangered the repute of the house. Why, Mr. Morton visited Mary in her room. They smoked cigarettes together! It was an outrage. As for her effect on the other young women in her charge, well, that was Miss Leonie's lookout. If she didn't write to Miss Sylvester's grandparents she would undertake to do so herself.

Finally Mary and Morton solved all the problems by simply lighting out together one fine day in the second winter after her arrival. Heavens, what a to-do. Miss Playfair made a big scandal out of it even though the first thing they'd done on leaving was to go directly to a justice of the peace — imagine it. She wouldn't give a snap of her finger for such a marriage. They were living in open sin, and a good thing it was for Miss Leonie, bringing down the repute of her house and everybody in it by keeping such a pair beneath her roof. But gracious, how sadly she and all the rest of them had missed dear Mary. Nobody to shock and scandalize, to make the very breath of life begin to circulate around that stuffy dinner table. Even Eva felt at a loss, having to listen every night to Miss Leonie and Mr. Langley exchange genealogical data, putting up with Miss Playfair's pretensions and Mrs. Canfield's subservience.

And as for herself there had been a hollow in her heart — that suppressed anticipation at the thought of seeing Mary every night at dinner now extinguished. There had been the queerest void. Even her music began to wear a trifle thin. An intimation that there was in

Mary's gift something that might stand her in better stead than that very reedlike voice about which Signor Locatelli raved so extravagantly began to announce itself as actual fact. How she had missed her! And when she turned up one evening with Morty and invited her to go out with them, "Come along with us on a spree," what joy she'd felt! How exhilarating she had found it to brave everybody's disapproval and start boldly off with them. That was the night that dated for her the actual beginning of their long and steadfast friendship, that sense that Mary'd had of her as of a poor benighted creature in need of just exactly what she had to offer somehow declared itself that winter night — it became a warmth within her, sweetness, joy.

For who can say, thought the old woman. The love that fills our hearts has its tides and overflows mysteriously, disperses itself in so many and such varying channels. One's passion for art, for nature, beauty; and always, always that feeling one has for life itself with its insatiable hungers, its overwhelming sympathies. And if she must confess it at this late hour of her life, with all the central founts of love — sexual passion and maternity — so disastrously cut off, had not this deep, this steadfast friendship for Mary been the one human relationship where love had never failed to nourish and replenish her?

The spree on which they went consisted in going to the slums. "We're taking you into the ghetto," Mary explained. Ah, that was a night she had not so much as mentioned in her novel. How could she have done so? Too swift, too fluid in the memory the scenes and the emotions — that sense she'd had walking between her friends, arm linked in arm, that there were being opened up for exploration large and hitherto unimagined areas of life. Grand Street, Division Street, Delancey. A cold night with occasional flurries of snow and the blue flames from the small acetylene lamps that dimly and intermittently lighted the pushcarts and the faces of the crowds blown off into the wind like birds, like flowers. Such crowds, such an assemblage of strange peoples teeming, pullulating, boiling over, the pushcarts drawn up in a double line on either side of the curb, the dark mass of the tenements looming up to right and left — that feeling she had had of being closed in by tenements stretching off in solid blocks to north and south and east and west — multitudes out that winter night haggling, bargaining, pushing — the laden carts displaying every variety of merchandise — hairpins, shoestrings, pickles, aprons, dresses, bars of nougat, kitchen utensils, mounds of nuts, rugs, linoleum, fruits; Mary explaining, "It's the bazaar, the ghetto." The bazaar it was, the ghetto, but something else that teased the mind, ancient, Biblical — those faces, the pushcart vendors with their eyes rapt back on some fixed point of meditation and their beards blown in the wind — Isaiah, Jeremiah, Abraham; fish for sale, ribbons, vegetables, children's apparel — the vigor of those women, their grasp and strife and surge, the large deep-breasted mothers of the race sorting, bargaining, picking over the merchandise, jostling you off the sidewalks, milling round with their indomitable vigor; Mary beside her, "No room for all these people, look at the tenements, see the homes we give our immigrants — in they come, thousands by the month"; Morty waving a vague hand in the direction of the harbor, "That's our industrial civilization for you." Mary, who had told her in a whispered conversation on the streetcar that she and Morty were going to have a child, warm, well clad against her arm, "You should see these streets in daylight. You should go inside some of these tenements. You wait, I'll take you with me, I'll show you children. What our industrial civilization does to children. I'll show you mothers. You wait, I'll take you with me," showing life to her, trying to sell sympathy to her, to sell love to her, to give her you might say the whole wide world to take into her arms, the wind blowing and the snow increasing and the blue flames caught in the wind like birds, like flowers, and memory bringing to her mind remembrance of that early dawn in the big room overlooking Florence, that sense she'd had of distributing herself among the vineyards and the orchards. Had Mary maybe got some inkling of the nature of her grief? Between them there had been something, a sympathy as though with her quick intuitions she had guessed or very nearly guessed her secret.

   That then had been the real beginning of her long and remarkable friendship, her association with Mary in her work and interests. The shifting of allegiances, abandoning Eva and Locatelli for the great business of trying to reform the world, had of course been gradual, but Mary and Morton had seemed bent on introducing her to the sufferings of the poor. They wished to have her see it at firsthand, to actually get it as they used to say "circulating in the mind, in the imagination, a part of the heart's blood," and it was in connection with that branch of her own work dearest to her heart, the attempt then being made to do away with industrial processes carried on in the tenements, that Mary got her first to visiting the homes where children, little boys and girls scarcely more than babies, were kept all day long at unimaginable tasks.

Loading dice, finishing coats and pants, making willow plumes, artificial flowers. Ah, she could see those children now, clad in scanty clothing, eyes dulled with mortal weariness, little hands and minds conditioned to the various coordinations. There in those bare kitchens she used to find them, their eyes mirroring only what they saw reflected in the eyes of the driven, the exploiting parent — fear, urgency, hunger, terrified by the intrusion, looking up like frightened beasts. Afraid of what — of penalization, punishment? In all those eyes, the mother eyes, the dull eyes of the children, the same expression, as of souls already killed, creatures already thrown upon the waste heap, finished, exploited to the very last shred of human endurance.

And so, one thing leading to another, she had finally become a part of that great movement, the stirring in the hearts of men and women, at the turn of the century, of indignation at the evils of society, that hope in human nature, the belief that it was capable of improvement, the desire to right the wrongs, to make the world as Mary used to say with head thrown back and sudden fire in her eyes a better place in which to live. She had found the right, the perfect occupation, and presently she'd had a stroke of luck, she'd become the beneficiary of a will. Let no one ever tell her that money contributed but little to the enjoyment of life. Why, when she'd found herself with money of her own, dependent on nobody, capable of making her own choices, doing what she wished with what she had, it had made all the difference in the world. All so unexpected too, her grandfather dying suddenly and his fortune entailed to be divided, left in equal parts to his children and their issue, and as both aunts were childless there she was at twenty-eight with a decent little fortune of her own, the income to be hers till she was thirty and after that the entire principal hers to squander as she pleased. Good luck it was indeed, let no one say it wasn't. No time at all before she'd bade goodbye to Cousin Leonie's — egged on by Mary ("What, wait and let your grandmother dictate to you what your life is going to be — with all that money yours. I never heard of such a thing"), she'd made her declaration of independence; she'd taken an apartment not far from Mary and Morton. She'd walked breast to breast with them in all their plans and leagues and projects.

And so on that fine afternoon in May 1915 life had seemed to her a pretty glorious affair. It had been good to her, it had given her Mary and all these Italian working girls marching along with her, keeping step, keeping step. Today I turn my back upon the sorrows I have known. I shall forget my past.

THREE

WELL, IT HAD BEEN ONLY A FEW DAYS after that parade that the past had
come barging up at her in the most extraordinary manner. The curious
thing about it had been that she'd recognized the fact the moment
she'd held that blue heavily-scented envelope in her hand. Eleanor,
she'd thought, looking at the Boston postmark, recognizing the handwriting. Opening it, seeing the gold monogram with the crest above it,
enveloped by the still familiar scent — heavens, her aunt might have
been in the room with her — she'd read the little missive, large letters
scrawled across the page with a great many words heavily underlined.
"My *darling* little niece, it's so many years since you and Lucien and I
have seen each other. We shall be in New York Saturday next staying
at the Plaza — and *will* you come at four-thirty to have a cup of tea
with us? We *must* hear all about you. We *suppose* that you are quite a
songstress now."

How upset she'd been, put out of her stride all day. Why revive those
memories, she'd asked herself, and during that interminable committee
meeting and amid the endless discussion she'd resolved many times
that she would not go; she'd changed her mind as frequently — since
the request had come from Eleanor why and for what reason could she
possibly say no? Tortured by indecision she had not answered till the
following day when she'd written the briefest possible reply — yes,
she'd be there. It would be nice to see them again. In the interval she'd
wondered why in heaven's name she had not turned her back on the
proposal (the old unanswered questions had pursued her. How much
had Eleanor known? How much had been kept from her? Did Lucien
know about the child?), and when she'd come to dress for the appoint-

ment how undecided she had been about her costume. Should she look
her dowdiest and simply rub it in that she had turned her back upon
the world of foolishness and fashion or would she wear her new spring
clothes? She was forty-nine. That was, if anyone asked her opinion, the
moment when a woman was at her very prime. She'd scrutinized her
face with care. She was not by any means a beauty like Aunt Eleanor
but still she had her points. She'd made up her mind that she would
look her best.

She'd been early for the appointment and had gone into the park and
sat down on one of the green benches close to the entrance, pretty appalled at being there at all and rather inclined to get up and go directly
home. The day was perfectly lovely and she remembers how she had
looked with the tenderest affection at the flowers of the maple trees,
yellow and red, crushed on the pavement by the feet of the passersby,
and then up through the boughs above her head, deep, deep into the
blue sky between the leaves thinking how perfectly exquisite they were
— the leaves and buds and blossoms spread out like flowers in water on
the air.

She was pervaded by the spring, that sense of being still endowed
with youth — the same old heart in ferment. And suddenly dropping
her eyes she'd seen emerging from the mists and all the lacy greenery
and in the procession of the other vehicles about to leave the park (it
could not be, she thought, yes, it certainly was) Aunt Eleanor and
Lucien Grey. There they sat behind the chauffeur in that high landau
with the top thrown back, Eleanor grown a great deal stouter, dressed
with extreme elegance, and Lucien still slender, wearing a Homburg
hat in the jauntiest possible manner, about them both something unmistakably European as though an afternoon drive and in exactly those
lazy, lolling attitudes had become the habitual order of their days.

No, she thought, I can't go on with it; why should I? But even while
she said it getting up. How weak she'd felt, her knees shaking under
her. Trying to keep her eyes on them, she crossed the street, saw the car
swing round the Plaza and stop in front of the hotel. There seemed to
be some delay about their getting out and she'd had ample time to
watch Eleanor while Lucien assisted her to get out of the car. How
stout she'd grown, florid, and her hair, no question about it, dyed that
startling copper-gold. And Lucien, dear me, dear me, it was all in the

way he moved, the way he helped, handled her, you might say, as though assisting her in and out of cars and carriages, trailing behind her into dining rooms, picking up her handkerchiefs had become (where had they been? What had they done with themselves all these years?) the chief business of his life. They gave their orders to the chauffeur, dismissed him, and stood an instant on the sidewalk looking vaguely out across the Plaza. Then just as they were about to turn and go into the hotel Eleanor caught sight of her and coming forward with her arms outstretched, "My darling little niece," she drew it out affection-ately. Pressed against that ample bosom, positively drenched in the somehow familiar odor of her perfumes, she felt herself kissed first on one cheek and then on the other, conscious all the time that Lucien was standing there beside her. Eleanor let her go and turned to him. "Why, Lucien," she drawled, "she hasn't changed a bit."

Lucien came forward. Would he kiss her or would he not? Good God, he extended his hand, he took one of her hands, lifted it to his mouth, kissed the back of her white glove. "Margaret," he said, and she might have been wrong but it seemed to her his voice was shaking, "Margaret, let me look at you."

All three started up the steps, went on into the hotel, Lucien re-gaining his savoir faire (if indeed he'd lost it), tripping round her with considerable agility in his endeavor to assist Eleanor who was a bit un-steady on her feet. Thus the three of them walked through the spacious airy hall (she could never go into the Plaza through that particular door without reenacting the entire scene), she and Lucien in the wake of the large, beautiful, perfectly possessed woman drawling out her little questions and comments as though they'd been the only people in the place. Would they like to have tea in the little or the big dining room? What an extraordinary hotel, so large and *American*. "Look, Lucien, at those absurd jardinieres."

Miraculous at moments are the powers of insight, the ability to put this suddenly with that. Certain it is that in those four or five minutes, trailing along behind Eleanor and with the oddest feeling that the spring, the green trees outside, all that movement of boughs and the passing of vehicles was somehow still a part of the poignant experience, seating herself (they finally decided to have tea in the little dining room) at a small, prettily-appointed table and a great to-do about who should order tea and who should take chocolate in process, she appeared to have found an answer to many of the questions that had so tortured and bewildered her throughout the years.

Lucien had, there was no doubt of it in her mind, even while enjoying with her their delightful secret interchange, even while bored to death by all the banality and repetition of the family scenes, belonged to that world of Chamberlains and Fosters — he had been tied and bound to it hand and foot. She had watched him push back Eleanor's chair, rearrange her scarf, had noticed she remembers that he carried in his pocket a small French novel and even while she was attempting to make out the title on the cover she'd got it all in an astounding flash, her mind traveling back with the most extraordinary conviction to the moment that held for her the clue to her bewilderment — that morning at the breakfast table when Lucien had announced so suddenly that he and Eleanor were leaving for the mountains. For what she'd seen again was Eleanor, that look she'd worn upon her face — sensual, possessive, triumphant. It was Eleanor who'd forced the issue. Ah, she had known, this dull, this repetitive woman, what was hers to give and to retract. She had taken her shrewd and well-calculated risk there as they'd lain beside each other in the summer night, for about that seldom if ever mentioned word, which more than likely had at that time never so much as passed her lips, Eleanor had known all there was to know. He should choose between the two of them. That's exactly what she'd told him, not with anger but with all the persuasiveness of her beauty, her passion, and her desire; he could go on with it if he wished to, but he must face the music out alone.

"Darling, would you like tea or chocolate? The chocolate here is perfectly delicious. Let me recommend it," she'd prattled on, treating her exactly as though she were taking a child off on a spree.

However, her attention was immediately distracted. The Plaza did not provide the kind of tea that Lucien preferred. There was conversation among the waiters, the headwaiter ran up. "Your Uncle Lucien," she explained, "since his visit to China, has become a connoisseur of teas." "Let it go, let it go," Lucien said, noticeably put out. And as she watched them she had seen a series of small tableaus taking place in hotels and restaurants all over the continent of Europe, waiters rushing up with wine lists, waiters hovering over menus, for what they ate and what they drank had become a matter of the greatest moment to this childless pair. "We should have gone as you suggested to the St. Regis," said Eleanor. Stealing a glance at Lucien, Margaret had done her best to make what she could out of it all. No, he had not changed too much, grown older of course, and he was rather stooped, but there was still a look of distinction about him, the same fine features and that plasticity about the molding of the face under the cheekbones and around the mouth that showed the signs of suffering. Or had it, she'd wondered, become boredom? The same amber eyes, the same dark mustache. And suddenly there she was saying to herself, while Lucien put his finger on an item in the menu — this was the tea that he would take, "You are part of all things great and quiet, my beloved," hearing the waves drawing up, retreating from the shore. Did this man know, she wondered, he was the father of her child? No, she came suddenly to her conclusion, he did not. He had no inkling of such a thing. Eleanor was talking to her now of China. "Your uncle knows *all* there is to know about China. You must see his collection of Chinese pottery. We have it in our villa at Mentone." He was, she confided, writing or was about to write a book on Chinese art. "Darling," she turned to Lucien, can't you tell Margaret something about Chinese art?" But the tea, the chocolate, little cakes and sandwiches arriving all together, she plunged rather greedily at the plate of cakes. "Do try some of these," she exclaimed, helping herself before anyone else to a large cream puff, "they are perfectly delicious. Nothing I enjoy so much as a good cream puff." Lucien meanwhile looked critically at the tea. "Little bags," he said in a voice of great disgust; nothing he deplored so much as tea in little bags. And drinking the good tea (for in spite of all the fuss he had made about it the tea smelled fragrant and delicious and she kept on wishing she had not allowed herself to be bamboozled into ordering that rich, too-heavy chocolate) he began to change his mood. Suddenly and with a jaunty self-conscious gesture he put his hand into his coat pocket and drew out the paper-covered novel she had noticed that he carried. And she might have been wrong but she imagined he was attempting to describe a little circle round the two of them as he handed her the book. "Have you read this, Margaret?" he said. No, she had not; was it good, she asked. He closed his eyes an instant as though attempting to gather up and then express if possible something of the exquisite pleasure he was still capable of snatching for himself and even in the midst of an existence spent mostly in the company of this foolish, garrulous woman. It was remarkable, in his opinion the greatest novel ever written. "But the greatest?" she'd expressed astonishment to think she'd never even heard of it. "Your Uncle Lucien is," said Eleanor, bridling a little, "a connoisseur. He knows *all* there is to know about books." "You must read it," said Lucien. "You will like it, Margaret," and he looked straight into her eyes.

She leafed through the little volume. *Du Côté de Chez Swann,* she read, making a note of it for future reference, by Marcel Proust, and the situation in which she found herself presenting her with such a staggering list of questions, it seemed to her impossible to cope with them. Had Lucien prepared this little incident in advance, placed the book in his pocket with the intention of drawing it out at exactly the right moment? Had he thought thus to tell her that after all he had a life of his own, and that this imbecile chatter was not the whole of it? Was he not somehow or other trying to tell her that he had not actually changed, that this was the same Lucien who had at one period in her life been her mentor, taught her the love of good books, developed in her that passion for poetry that had stood her all her life in such good stead? Was he not attempting to say to her in those few brief words, "You will like it, Margaret," that he and she, not he and Eleanor, were the pair who really should have spent their lives together? And was he not at the moment experiencing the most excruciating chagrin at having her see him in his role of slave to Eleanor? "'You'd *love* our house in Mentone, you simply must come some day for a visit. It's crammed with books. Lucien has a splendid library. Haven't you, darling?" Eleanor laid her hand on his arm. The twists and turns of life, the irony of the moment could hardly be rivaled. Sitting here with Lucien, with whom she had once shared the high comedy of the family scenes, their humorous observations, glancing off from Grandfather Foster to Cecilia and then back again as always to her grandmother, seeing now as she could not but see in Eleanor a creature who somehow combined the salient points of all three characters, her grandfather's extravagant good looks, his self-indulgent and naive pleasure in the good things of life, Cecilia's idiotic chatter, and what was really most appalling, knowing her grandmother loomed so large in this sensuous, powerful woman — her indomitable will to command, her eagle eye on every situation. Why, why, it was Eleanor who had known all there was to know, who had herself assisted her mother to keep Lucien in the dark about the child.

But why, she wondered, why on earth this particular meeting? At whose suggestion had that letter on the bright blue paper been sent off? How the questions came at her. She couldn't beat them off. What vistas seemed to open in her speculations. Had Lucien expressed a desire to see her before they returned to Europe, or might it not have been some extremity of boredom, a sagacious, well-calculated attempt on Eleanor's part to vary the monotony of their days — those drives and taking tea together every afternoon? After the meeting was over there'd be plenty to talk about. They could discuss it for weeks on end, and since she now felt certain Lucien had not known he was the father of her child it might well be that Eleanor, with the ability of complacent, comfortable people to forget the tragic and the painful, regarded the whole sad story as a kind of midsummer madness, and might even enjoy her chance to show them both, herself and Lucien, that she had you might say won the day.

She gave Lucien back the book and watched him put it in his pocket, almost it seemed to her with resignation, as though to shrug his shoulders — books, his library, this precious little volume, the exquisite pleasure he was still capable of extracting from literature, were his at any rate, even if he was unable to share them with anyone on earth. "But wouldn't Margaret," Eleanor insisted, "*love* our villa at Mentone." Lucien to her surprise practically took the words out of her mouth, launching out upon a lyric account of the beauties of the villa. It looked right out on the Mediterranean. "The sea comes blue and full," he said, "over the terrace wall; it floods the rooms. The Mediterranean is the sea," and he looked vaguely into the distance, "that always seems to be brimming over, full, full," he said, "full to the very brim." He half closed his eyes while Eleanor, you could see at a glance that the foolish, worldly, powerful woman was still head over heels in love with him, looked up into his face much as a mother might gaze on an odd, precocious, gifted child. She patted his arm as though to say, "Really, Margaret, isn't Lucien wonderful?"

But he relapsed presently into silence and conversation had for an instant flagged. Eleanor however, allowing only the briefest silence, transferred her touch on Lucien's arm to her own. "*Tell* us," she exclaimed, trumping up a gush of enthusiasm, something about *yourself*, Margaret. You must be an accomplished singer by now," and she looked around the room as though expecting a grand piano and an accompanist to appear at once. "I *wish* we could hear you sing."

It had been too much for her, the questions and intimations, and such a flood of memories accompanying them, and now remembering how she used to feel in Lucien's presence, longing to do something, to smash the plates and tumblers, to throw some kind of bombshell into the midst of all that talk at the dinner table, she did literally throw her bombshell, and with a kind of fiendish, hysterical delight in watching its effect upon the two of them. No, she wasn't singing any more, she said. She thought surely they had heard she'd given up trying to be a singer. Eleanor was nonplussed. "Not singing? What *are* you doing?" And it was then she'd shot her bolt. "Why," she said, "at present I'm swamped — immersed in labor unions." Lucien put down his cup of tea. "In what?" said Eleanor. "Labor unions," she repeated. What devilish delight it gave her to pronounce the words. "I don't understand." Eleanor was obviously bewildered. There was a big strike on, she explained to them, a laundry strike. She had as a matter of fact taken the afternoon off. She should at the moment be assisting the girls on the picket line. "The what?" asked Eleanor. She reiterated the explanation, "the picket line," pronouncing the words precisely. Eleanor and Lucien exchanged an outraged glance, and she perceived at once that he had, and with appalling suddenness, as though taking cudgels up against a common peril, joined his indignation up with Eleanor's. Something indeed was going on between herself and Lucien, a kind of flashing of swords, a crossing of lances, just as though he said to her, "What, you, Margaret? Betraying your own class?" forgetting as he apparently had what in the past had been apparent to them both, that she was not, when all was said and done, and never had been exactly what you might call one of them.

The rest of that poignant little tea party had been all but intolerable. She had shocked, she had wounded, betrayed them. That was the substance of their exchange with her, and though they made an effort to recover a semblance of geniality it was difficult to get on with conversation. Life was, she kept telling herself, a business. She must not allow these little ironies to get her. They were inherent in the social comedy. Life was full of just such little incidents. A remarkable scene, she remembered thinking to herself, for a novelist. What a good novelist could make of such a situation. Why not? What was to prevent her from putting it some day into a novel? She finished her chocolate, Eleanor gobbled up the remainder of the cakes, Lucien allowed his tea to grow cold, and they did their best to turn the dreadful information off with a kind of affectionate banter, an assumption that it wasn't true, that, being as they still conceived her to be no more than a foolish misguided girl, she would presently become a more disciplined member of society and regain her sanity. And when at last they all got up to go, they accompanied her out of the dining room and through the wide hall to the door at which they'd entered. There had been the liveliest exchange of little jokes and pleasantries, and when it came to bidding them goodbye she was again enfolded in that ample bosom. The invitation was renewed, she must, the next time she came to Europe, come and make a long, long visit to them at Mentone.

And then again, the whole experience was something she had read of in a novel; not her own, oh not her own. Lucien took her hand and kissed it in his gallant European manner, and there was, believe it, she had said to herself, or not, a note of reproach in his voice, as though she had been the one to deal the mortal injury.

F O U R

PHEW, MISS SYLVESTER EJACULATED, making, she was aware, exactly the same sounds that she had made that spring evening as, turning her back on the Plaza and the park, she'd walked at a very brisk pace down Fifth Avenue, taking long deep breaths, and presently muttering to herself, "Thank God for Mary and Morton. Thank God for Felix Isaacs. Thank God for my work"; thanking God in fact for everyone and everything able to assist her in the forgetting of her past. And if, thought the old woman, on that particular night Felix Isaacs had asked her to marry him as he had on so many previous and later occasions, she thinks it. very likely she would have answered, "Yes, indeed I will."

But an end to all these ifs and might-have-beens. Let it be, let it be, she said aloud. At any rate she'd walked all the way down to Ninth Street and then east to Second Avenue, and at St. Mark's Place, in front of the high iron fence that enclosed the tombstones and the old brown church she'd stopped and looked up at Mary's lighted windows, allowing herself to rest in the comfort they brought her, for Mary's apartment across the way on Tenth Street, with its spacious, high-ceilinged rooms, its charm and warmth and welcome, had been the place in New York she'd loved the most, and there had been something about it, lingering there looking into the churchyard, the chestnut trees in leaf, the shadows of the leaves and branches thrown upon the gravestones and the church, with Mary's windows glowing warm behind the boughs. It gives her back in all its fullness, thinking of it now, that brief period before the First World War when in association with a few friends and a great many people of various religions, nationalities and classes she had shared the same expectancy, as though under the ministering direction of all that hope and work and effort one might actually expect to see a better, braver world emerge. A small holding in time, she thought, for was one not at liberty to speak about an era as a home, a bit of spiritual property now demolished and which one had once regarded as one's own?

She was late, and much to her surprise and pleasure had found Felix there when she arrived. They'd sat down without her and were excitedly discussing the strike. Several young women had been arrested and, according to Mary, cruelly beaten up. One of them was she firmly believed in a critical condition. She had herself laid hold of a policeman and called him a brute and a bully, and he had struck her across the face. Why she had not been taken off in a Black Maria she wasn't able to tell. She was standing bail for all the young women, and Felix, whose knowledge had brought him in to be of help in the problems arising from the strike and the arrests, had forgotten the legal technicalities and all that difficult jargon and was together with Mary and Martin letting himself go. He was angry and excited. He wanted to get the facts before the public. He was determined to write an article and was questioning Mary, who had, the fine, intrepid creature that she was, worked all the previous summer in a big steam laundry just to see what the conditions were and was telling him about the heat, the long hours, the meager pay.

The windows were open. The smell of the chestnut trees in the churchyard together with the smell of heat-drenched pavements came drifting in. How delicious it was, this first hot summer night, sitting here in Mary's pleasant dining room with the roar and cry and rumble of the city rushing at her, experiencing this perfectly delightful sense, glancing out now and then at Second Avenue, the bright lights, the restaurants, the theaters, the bakery shops, all those Bohemians, Austrians, Hungarians crowding the pavements, that the whole of Central Europe was impinging upon her. Listening to the conversation, to the outdoor laughter, the voices, she kept saying to herself, this is real, this is my life, these are my friends.

She did not take a large part in the discussion. Every now and then she'd say "How terrible," "It's an outrage," or something of the sort. She was intent on watching Felix. He paced up and down the room, lighted one cigarette after another, questioned Mary, stopping occasionally to make a note of what she said. He was she'd thought a very extraordinary looking man. There was something about him different from most of the intellectual Jews of her acquaintance. He did not have that familiar gesture, the lifting and arresting of the arms and shoulders, assertive and at the same time repressed, as though the impulse towards emotionalism in conflict with habitual repression induced an awkwardness, a kind of bodily malaise. He had a peculiar bodily grace. Tall, blond, with that curious stiffness of the arm, throwing it out abruptly, the fingers held together, the thumb at right angles to the hand. He made her think of those figures in ancient Assyrian bas-reliefs, asymmetric, stealthy, the body under strict control. She had seen the type in the ghetto. It differed from most of her Jewish friends whose Semitism seemed to lie upon them in a more self-conscious, brooding manner, something younger about him as though he'd skipped the experience of the ghettos and the persecutions and had gone back to the youth of the race. His face was long and pale and he had a blond pointed beard and full red lips. Really what an exceptionally interesting creature he was. To marry him would be an excellent way to begin life anew, to turn her back completely on her past. She'd kept saying to herself, "Mrs. Felix Isaacs, Margaret Sylvester Isaacs." What a nice, what an extremely interesting name that would be. Or she might perhaps take up Silvestro and assert her Italian origins. Mary was always saying to her, "You're a perfect fool. What's the matter with you that you refuse to marry Felix? He's one in a million. What? You think you're too old for him? He's nearly ten years younger than you? Stuff and nonsense. You say you're not in love with him? What does that matter at your age? Think of growing old and solitary! What devotion, what friendship you will find with Felix." Watching him intently she'd thought it was perhaps those full red lips above the pointed beard, so sensuous in the ascetic face, that troubled her. Once he had lost control of himself altogether and kissed her passionately on the lips and she had recoiled at the thought of his passion. Passion had been burned right out of her, that was what stood in the way of her saying yes to Felix. But none the less, none the less, after her experience of the afternoon she must forget all that, she must lay herself open to love, to passion. Felix was, there was no doubt about it, a most attractive man.

When he'd walked home with her that night she'd hoped, contrary to her accustomed desires, that he would stop in the midst of their conversation and say as he had done so many times before, his arm thrown out stiffly, the fingers held together, the thumb at right angles with his hand, "Margaret, will you marry me? I love you deeply. I feel quite sure I can make you happy." But he had done nothing of the sort, walking west to Fifth Avenue through the soft summer night and up the avenue to Twelfth Street with that wash of cool moonlight engulfing them, he'd gone on about the laundry workers and Mary. What a remarkable woman she was. Why, when she'd worked in those laundries, he'd had it from a reliable source, not a one of those women with whom she'd been associated had so much as suspected that her background differed from their own.

"More than you ever could have done," he'd said, and at her door he'd left her quite abruptly.

She'd let herself in and walked up the two flights to her apartment, and when at last she'd got undressed and into bed there she'd lain, feeling as though she'd walked all day through a long, incredible dream. Today, she'd said, and yesterday; tomorrow. The strangeness of life had overwhelmed her, and there had been that pear tree in full bloom drenched in moonlight standing up between the clotheslines in a yard on Eleventh Street. It had seemed to her she had never seen a sight so naked, forlorn and lovely. Suddenly and to her surprise she'd found the tears were streaming down her cheeks, She'd stretched out her arms in the direction of the pear tree. "Give me back my child," she'd sobbed.

FIVE

———

IF FELIX HAD ASKED HER TO MARRY HIM on that night in May she would most assuredly have said yes and on the impulse of the decision and with that need upon her to shed her past she would doubtless have started off in his company the very next morning to procure the marriage license and gone with him as soon as possible to find a justice of the peace to pronounce them man and wife.

Strange are the vagaries of chance. He renewed his invitation on many other occasions, "Margaret, I love you profoundly." She could hear his voice now and see the look that used to suffuse his face, the pupils of the eyes dilated, the forehead and the cheeks noticeably flushed; his hands trembled and his voice shook. Whenever she saw him so overcome by emotion and sensed the depth of the passion she aroused in him she would invariably say to herself, no, no, I can't go through with it, and she would say — (it had become almost a formula) that she was too old for him; he should find a younger woman; and moreover, she tried to state it as gently as possible, she was not in love with him, nor did she feel inclined to fall in love with anybody. Sometimes he would cry out with undisguised bitterness that she was a cold and passionless woman.

She'd treated him abominably, taken all he had to give and given nothing in return. She must have made him suffer cruelly. It was better he used to tell her to have her on the terms she imposed than not to have her at all. And so it was that their companionship continued. It is only in looking back upon it now that she begins to realize his persistence was founded on the hope that his devotion might become so necessary to her that she would eventually change her mind. He pur-

sued her thus for nearly twenty years and in his company she enjoyed
New York in the most free, familiar and delightful fashion.

He was, like many Jews whose sense that they belong nowhere in particular makes them as much at home in one place as in another, a thor-
oughgoing cosmopolitan. He was determined to extract from the city in
which he lived the very best it had to offer. There was a kind of arrogance in his demand for excellence. He seemed to be perfectly at home
with all the arts and his response to them was sensitive and fastidious.
A man untiring in civic duties, a busy lawyer, where did he come by so
much knowledge of music, art and literature? Did he pluck it from the
air — was it bestowed upon him at birth? she would ask him. His answer was interesting and profound. "We are born old, my dear."

Yes, that was the key to the riddle, she thought, and seemed to see
her old friend again, the slender, asymmetric silhouette, the abrupt gestures, the arm thrown out stiffly, the long fingers, the long face, the
pointed beard, his resemblance to some youthful figure in the old
Assyrian bas-reliefs. Well, his looks belied him; he had escaped no iota
of his heritage. He was born very old indeed. There were realms of his
spirit which she was inclined to think she could not even imagine. He
had given her a liberal education, free instruction in the arts and humanities. When they went to concerts or exhibitions together she had
the curious impression that he had heard the music — seen the pictures many times before, that nothing was new to him and that he was
incapable of a purely fresh response; whereas with her, dear me, exactly
the opposite was the case. She had had, with him for her interpreter, a
sense of seeing and hearing everything for the first time.

She and Felix enjoyed New York tremendously. To remember certain places is always to be accompanied by him — the Metropolitan
Museum, Carnegie Hall, Central Park on Sunday afternoon. To think
of one of those high, uncovered Fifth Avenue busses is actually to be
sitting on the front seat beside him engaged in animated discussion,
clinging on to her hat, the breeze in her face, the bus plunging and
lurching like a spirited horse beneath them. From that vantage point
on how many hot summer evenings or afternoons in spring they had
viewed the city together. The sky was then uncrowded with the great
midtown skyscrapers. There were no towers in air, no tiers of windows
in the clouds. There was the recessional architecture and they caught

glimpses of it down the side streets and the prow of the Flatiron Building pushed aside the traffic at Twenty-third Street and appeared to be sailing straight up the Avenue as they descended upon it. You had a sense that the city was growing like a giant. You had belief in it — confidence. The terror and awe that inspired you today was absent. Instead there was an excitement — expectation, a feeling which she knew she shared with Felix, almost of owning it — certainly of feeling for it some responsibility. Their firsthand knowledge of its slums lent strangely enough a special edge and sharpness to their enjoyment of its areas of pleasure and delight. To be as much at home in Hester and Elizabeth Streets as at the Metropolitan Opera House or on Fifth Avenue was somehow to feel for it a very special kind of love and devotion.

Something was in the air, some connivance with the future, a naive feeling that they were assisting personally to improve the world. God knows just what it was. She believed in what she was doing. It seemed to her that every time an Italian working girl joined a trade union there was a feather stuck in the cap of progress and reform, and when any of her Italians were out on strike there she was at strike headquarters making speeches, urging them under no consideration to turn traitor and become scabs. "Donne Italiane," she'd begin, invoking them to march breast to breast with their Italian sisters, for only in numbers was there any hope of bettering their conditions and their lives — all for one and one for all. Felix came to listen to her. He admired those speeches extravagantly. He used also to go with her into the worst of the tenements she visited — a kind of self-appointed truant officer. He assisted her in getting those miserable little slaves of industry back to their schools again. Heartbreaking were the scenes they witnessed. They wrote reports and articles. Wherever they could wax indignant, wherever they could try to "do something about it," there it seemed to them they were helping to build their city on the hill.

Take it by and large, Felix was the most interesting man she had ever known. There were many layers in him of sensibility, intellect, and emotion. She could meet him on so many different levels of experience. What they enjoyed most was dining together in a leisurely Bohemian manner. They did not then drink any of the present alcoholic favorites — generally beer or a bottle of wine. They smoked a great many cigarettes, drank a great deal of coffee and talked late into the night. They were familiar with each other's tricks of thought and conversation. That tightrope on which she'd always seemed to walk poised between humor on the one hand and tragedy on the other, treading it lightly, like a dance on air, was a line not quite discernible to him. His tragic sense of life was on a deeper level, he kept it in a compartment separate from his laughter, and what she was capable of finding extremely humorous he often relegated to the department of his grief; and this because there burned within him a deeper passion for perfection. It was humanity that troubled Felix. He could not separate his ancient tragic knowledge of the human heart from his faith in what a just society might accomplish in making men good as well as happy. His kingdom of heaven was like Christ's situated right here on earth.

There had been that night she remembers with especial poignancy when she had almost but not quite been able to break down and tell him the secret that she had kept so long. The scene comes back with all its urgency, that need to speak so strong upon her. Little Bohemia on Second Avenue, the outside door opening and shutting to let in the cold, the lights of Second Avenue bright through the windows and that little old man playing his violin standing right up in front of them; over and over the familiar waltz from Weber's "Invitation to the Dance" and that handsome boy blown in on a blast of cold air carrying a tray of violets and gardenias; Felix buying gardenias, violets, burying her face in them, "Oh, how lovely" — breathing the draft of perfume; then that conversation infused with the fragrance of the flowers. "Something about you that reminds me of a child"; the old man with the violin stepping closer, the "Invitation to the Dance" continuing; "You've never lost your sense of wonder, you respond to certain things with all the freshness of a child." And suddenly her telling him about those flowers in the woods, the fields in summer, and how she'd stood before the waves; and all the time that powerful desire to let go, to tell him everything — her love for Lucien, the birth of her child, giving him for adoption; his saying "But that is pure Wordsworth, Margaret — 'moments in the being of the eternal silence' — is this enough for you?" her answering "Yes, yes, it is enough," longing all the while to come out with it, to tell him everything, but telling him instead of that experience she'd never told a soul — how once in Italy when she was trying to recover from an intolerable sorrow she had found a volume of Wordsworth on a hotel table and how she'd opened it and for the first time read the "Ode on Intimations of Immortality" and how the effect on her had been instantaneous, how the meters and the movement of that marvelous poem, like the measures of a dance had carried her straight back to childhood and to those moments of which she'd spoken, the words had been for her the declaration of a creed, they had established in her heart a faith; and there was that little man still playing the familiar tune and the ineffable smell of the flowers hovering around them and Felix laying his hand on hers — drawing her hand away quickly, fearful lest she break down and tell him everything.

There had also been that night the following August when the words "Yes, Felix, I *will* marry you" had actually been moving through her mind while he begged her so earnestly to reconsider her decision. Luchow's the night the First World War broke out in Europe — sitting by the open window, a stifling heat upon the city, newsboys shouting "Extry! Extry!" a tension in the air like waiting for a bomb to burst, Felix white and stricken. "It will be long, we'll all be in for it. People like you and me will suffer, Margaret. There will be times we'll be unable to endure it. We shouldn't be alone. We could be a comfort to each other"; hearing the voices crying "Extry, extry," seeing his face so white and stricken and people getting up to buy the papers, coming back with them; thinking yes, he's right, we should suffer this together; but getting off (so firmly rooted in her this resistance, this feeling she could not go on with it) the same worn-out objections; she was too old; he should marry a young woman; he mustn't, he positively must not ask her again — his getting up and going out to buy a paper.

S I X

———

IT HAD ALWAYS SEEMED TO HER, looking back on her existence, that as far as personal history went, outward events and associations, she had had as many lives as the proverbial cat, one quite separate from the other, this epoch and that, and if she examined her experience it was always to inquire could it be possible to crowd into one human span such a shattering succession of eras and events. The incredibility of it, the accelerated speed with which changes and calamities marched on! Why, if she tried to bring any sequence to her personal story after August 1914 it got so whirled round with history that the only thing to which she could compare the process was a kind of crazy newsreel of the soul — pictures collapsing, colliding, careening madly off into time, into space — faces, personalities, voices — the Kaiser with his plume and helmet, Lloyd George, Clemenceau, soldiers of France, German soldiers, dugouts, trenches, American soldiers, Wilson with his top hat, his lady with her orchids.

As for the human side of her life in those years of the first great war, they were still so poignantly associated with Mary that to think of them was to live in them and through them all with her — standing on curbs and street corners with her, watching the young men pass. How those old tunes to which they'd marched, with their enormous emotional content, carried her back to the hour and the mood. That sense she'd had after the long waiting, the fear that war might after all not be declared, the strong conviction that *this* was a just war in which one should be willing to sacrifice one's son came surging back to her, for she too had had her personal stake in all of this — did she not also have a son of fighting age? "Over there, over there" — "It's a long way to Tipperary, it's a long way to go."

And even while that music and those words assailed her she heard again those bells that rang on that November day; she lived again through that fictitious peace, sitting there at lunch with Mary and her little grandson Matthew, the bells continuing to ring, and Mary laying down her napkin, their looking at each other, uttering the word together, "Peace," each rising from the table and running through the hall to the front of the apartment, opening the window, craning to look out; and Matthew there between them, the bells still ringing and men and women running through the street; Matthew sensing the excitement, asking questions. "Peace," they'd told him, "Matthew, it is peace"; the child seeing the people, hearing the bells, catching something of that high excitement and intensity, insisting "But I want to see it," while they turned from him to get their coats and hats and he behind them, questioning; "It's peace, Matthew," they'd insisted, running to the door, the child crying out "I want to see it, please let me see peace"; leaving him there and rushing into Twelfth Street: the weather cold and gray with occasional glimpses of the sun, not too many people yet assembled, but everyone communicating, passing the word along, running in this direction and in that, not exactly sure just where they wished to be, getting themselves to the subway and presently finding they were in Greeley Square, the big bell ringing out above the statue of Horace Greeley, the pigeons fluttering in confusion and that amazing sense they'd had of being like everybody else a vessel of joy, pouring it out incessantly, the squares, the streets, the whole town flooded with it like some high tide arising; and then that motley, disordered, spontaneous parade somehow or other set in motion, and all marching together in the direction of Fifth Avenue. Into the streets and through the streets, God knows from where, from the business sections, the residential districts, streaming out of the slums, trucks, taxis, wagons, private cars, public vehicles, and on the trucks and wagons all those improvised floats, the Kaiser set up in effigy and people dancing round him, the crowds in the streets gone mad, shouting, weeping, embracing one another, boys in uniform lifted aboard the trucks and taxis, onto the shoulders of the marching crowd, flags, trumpets, paper hats, confetti, all the paraphernalia of celebration instantly supplied, she and Mary borne along, caught up in the contagion.

The marching songs persisting, the war to end all wars presumably over, there again she was with Mary on Fifth Avenue to watch the troops pass by — the Seventy-seventh Division that had fought so gallantly in the Argonne and Mary's Martin among them. She saw dear Mary's face, the eyes closed, the tears streaming (dear Mary who was dead and little Matthew killed at Okinawa), she saw the boy erect in his brown helmet, shouldering his gun.

S E V E N

AND THEN THE ASTONISHING YEARS, the jazz bands, the bootleggers, the speakeasies — new morals, new behavior, new indulgences. Everyone seemed somehow to recognize that there had been betrayal. Wilson's fine phrases had turned to gall upon the lips. The world would not be made safe for democracy, but there was this knowledge hovering around the heart, that the world encroached upon it, was indeed about to enter in with its insuperable problems; a crazy spendthrift will to pleasure was abroad.

She and Felix spent a great deal of time together. They looked around them in alarm, attempting to adjust to the changes that had taken place in their own hearts as well as in the exterior scene. The restaurants on Second Avenue with their pleasant Central European charm saw them no more. They frequented the speak-easies. An inordinate need for alcohol was upon everyone.

Just to think of those speakeasies is to get back again the climate of that nervous, febrile time. There were signs and signals, a behavior to which one lent oneself without a qualm, waiting at those grilled doors (uptown the brownstone stoop, downtown the basement area) and the door opening a crack and through the crack the face, the whispers, giving the password and the door opening with the greatest caution and there you were inside the overheated and somehow oversilenced place, certain of your drink. There was all that whispering with the waiters, consulting the menu with such earnestness as though while giving the illegal orders you were making up your mind whether to have soup or antipasto, and then at last beholding with satisfaction that spread undisguised across the countenance that awful bootleg liquor as it appeared, served up in the oddest crockery, upon the table.

There was about all those dreadful cocktails, that illicit wine poured from a crockery teapot into a crockery teacup, the most peculiar effect. It gave a sharpness, an attentiveness to everything and everyone sur-rounding her. She seemed closed in with her guesses and intimations. It might be her fancy, probably was, but remembering it now she thinks it was about this moment that something extraordinary took place in her as though she had somehow been supplied with a new equipment of nervous feelers — picking up the messages, the intimations, the way one looked and stared, received the sudden answers, exposed oneself to insolence and to initiation.

They were a noticeable couple, Felix with his marked Semitic coun-tenance, his rather intense way of talking, obviously in love with her and she so much older. Even the way they talked arrested attention. They were interested; they liked discussion. The young were around in those days, very conspicuous indeed, determined to squeeze to the last drop of enjoyment their suddenly acquired reputation for belonging to a lost, a desperate generation. They were alert to everything; they had their ears back like little bird dogs, listening to scraps of conversation, making their quick appraisals, requiring but a glance or two to come to their conclusions. They regarded the two of them with their straight assessing stares. You could positively hear what they were thinking — "The man's a Jew. Talks well. Where did he get the blond beard and those arresting gestures? The woman is no slouch on looks. A good-looker. Getting on in years but she's got something."

It was a curious thing but at just that time she was aware that she did have something. There were sympathies and curiosities brewing in her which in a most subtle manner flowed out and brushed the minds, the hearts of these young people and in particular went out from her to the young men. There were many influences, strong currents of repressed emotion that set afloat upon the air an intricate network of inquiries and invitations and on these tenuous lines of communication she drew the young men's glances. Stare for stare, they set up the wordless ex-change. She seemed to hear them saying to her, "You've got something; give us what you've got," and from the hungers of her heart, out of the love that had never found a place to rest, the questions wandered from this young man to that as though she asked of all of them "Have you something to tell me of my son? Do his nerves resemble yours? Has he this same acuteness of perception, this awareness, quick and sharp and new and born apparently of your generation — does he frequent these places and drink himself night after night into the same state of drunken sensibility?" They were in the oddest way drinking from her wells of sympathy and not without a realization of the interest their lost condition inspired they played right up to her; they dramatized their plight.

Felix was definitely averse to these glances and exchanges. He seemed actually to think that she was carrying on some kind of airy intrigue with these charming, tipsy, rather disreputable young men. Considering how little she had ever permitted him to display his amorous inclinations his jealousy was, if these were his suspicions, understandable. It made for something of a strain between them.

There was a place in Morton Street they used to go to occasionally, Dante's Inferno, and most appropriately named it was. Goodness what a hole. Approached by dark area steps, dimly lighted, never aired, phooey how it smelt. The food was good, the drinks were cheap. It was very hushed and not too well policed. She had a preference for it because it was the hangout of a little group of young people in whom she had become specially interested. Felix objected to it strongly and on the night which she has never ceased regretting he had protested vigorously as they groped their way down those infernal stairs.

They were all of them there, the young man with the chestnut-colored hair, the young man with the dark countenance, tall, slender, distinguished, the nondescript boy with the freckled face and red hair; and there were the girls she'd seen before except that the young man with the chestnut mane had acquired a new partner. She was slight and exceedingly pretty — difficult to make out. Was she just another of those girls one saw so much around the Village, their youth already frayed, burning their candle as swiftly as possible at both ends? She obviously responded with joy and immediacy to the attentions of her young friend whose lovemaking appeared to be very explicit indeed. Charming he was if one ever saw a charming young man, easy, graceful, witty, with an air about him of having issued, like Venus from her shell, full-fledged from his lost, his desperate generation.

The group pricked up their ears and laid them back as soon as she and Felix got seated and began to talk. They listened attentively and seemed ready at any moment to break into the conversation with or without invitation. Felix was talking about *Ulysses*. He didn't like it — a dangerous tendency, to reduce a novel to the stream of one man's consciousness. The Russians were for him the greatest of all the novelists. They had, he believed, exhausted the novel, drained it of about all that could be said. Weren't they the first to explore the subconscious mind, the angel country and the devil territory? They'd broken down those neat integuments, they'd let in the dark, the new dimension and managed to keep it all within the framework of a novel, a novel, mind you, he said, in which men and women play their various parts, display their characters, move around, do this and that, get something going, action, situation, denouement. But this kind of thing, no good, he said, and he threw his arm out in that abrupt arresting manner. Why, it's an association test, a matching up of literary associations. To really get it, to understand it and follow it to its source you'd have to know every book that Joyce had read, to have seen and heard everything that he had seen and heard and thought about. God, you can't make a novel out of that, the flow and eddy of the individual mind. You can't get order out of that chaos.

"Hell," said the young man with the chestnut-colored hair, and he drew out the hand which under the young girl's blouse had been caressing her pretty, slender breasts. "Why can't you? He *has* reduced it all to order."

This made just the opportunity the young people were looking for. Suddenly they were all of them shouting and Felix found himself the center of their attack. It was impossible to make out what anyone was saying, no one listening to anyone — new phrases, new names, new reputations that had got suddenly circulating in this strange postwar world where everything, even the books one read and the thoughts one had, seemed to have expanded and taken on a new dimension, were thrown vigorously about. The young man with the red hair was giving a monologue on Freud. He insisted on being heard. "Hell," he said, "wasn't it Freud who'd thrown the fat into the fire?" Felix reminded him and pretty irritably that Freud had come into the picture long after the Russians. If it hadn't been for them there might never have been a

Freud. They'd started the analysis and investigation, they'd begged for this descent into Hell, or if you wished to express it according to Freud — the subconscious. Nobody appeared to listen much to him. Each of the young men seemed to be an advocate for something or for somebody. The young man with the chestnut-colored hair shouted an inquiry which brought her quickly to attention recalling that slender little volume Lucien had taken from his pocket that afternoon at the Plaza. Had his friend with the beard ever heard of Marcel Proust? *There was a novel to put an end to all novels — the greatest novel ever written, A la Recherche du Temps Perdu.* He waved a graceful hand and draped his arm around the pretty girl beside him. "Have to wait to finish it," he said, "still waiting for it to come off the presses. The stream," he glanced at Felix with his mocking eye, "of one man's consciousness. *A la Recherche du Temps Perdu.*" He kept repeating the title not without awareness of his fine French accent. The dark distinguished-looking boy shouted the loudest and apparently most effectually, for presently an actual conversation was under way.

She had not contributed a word to the general babel, but now that the shouts and monologues had more or less yielded to discussion she realized that the young people were expecting something from her and was uneasily aware that they had taken it for granted that she was somehow or other lined up with them, indeed that they expected her to understand the habits of their thoughts, the associations they shared and the predilections they espoused. How they could have believed this to be the case she couldn't imagine, but it was evident to her from their glances, from those curious tremors and vibrations that passed on their tenuous lines of communication, that they did. She hadn't at that time read a single one of the books about which they'd been shouting and wrangling, she'd been in no position to enter the fray, but now they were talking about a book which Felix had lent to her only a few days since. Now I shall be called upon to say something, she'd thought, remembering how she had agreed with Felix that the book was difficult — very nearly impossible to understand, and that she had shared to some extent his indignation.

The young men had conceded him the floor and he was expressing himself in no uncertain terms. "A pedant," he said, "his poem is another example of the association test — trotting out all those private incommunicable references. Who wants to be jerked around on the vehicle of one man's wandering reflections?" He turned to her. "Why don't you speak up, Margaret? You're familiar with this masterpiece." "Well," she replied, and she can never think of that answer without acute regret, "after all, Felix, it is their waste land. If these young men can find their way around in it, and it's clear enough they can, maybe we'd better back down. It's a landscape with which we are not as familiar as they — it's the world we made for them. We ought to have some respect for the disgust and grief they feel in having to inhabit it."

She can see now the gesture with which Felix summoned the waiter. Her answer had not only been ambiguous and trite, it had lacked a decent loyalty, for surely the future towards which he had worked and aspired was not, he was intimating as he paid the bill, counted out the change and tipped the waiter, this land of Eliot's poem, and if these young people wished to indulge themselves in their drunken and conspicuous sorrow that was no reason for her to imply that he didn't suffer too. It was not a world he had made and he didn't like it any better than they did, and as for this infernal hole, he seemed to be implying as he helped her on with her coat and bade goodbye to the young people, he hadn't wished to come and he did not intend to return.

It was over a fortnight before she saw him again. When he finally telephoned her his voice showed no sign of injured feeling. There was no reference to the night at Dante's save for the fact that he said "We won't go to any disreputable hole in the ground." Mori's on Bleecker Street was the place he chose.

It had been recently done over and there was an air of elegance about it, with the big spacious dining room and an open gallery above, the walls white and severe and all the appointments in excellent taste. The tables were against the wall and they sat next each other, which lends a peculiar poignancy to her memory of that night. They had cocktails and wine served here as elsewhere in crockery pots and teacups. Felix was gentle and quiet but she saw at once that he was agitated. She knew that some kind of an outburst was coming and was preparing herself for one of those painful proposals. Dear me, she'd thought, why must he keep this up for so long. He ought to know by now it's hopeless.

"Margaret," he finally began. She waited, reluctant to help him out.

"I have something to tell you," he stammered, and laying down his teacup spilled his Chianti all over the tablecloth. "I am going to be married."

It was like a blow straight between the eyes. "Oh, Felix," she exclaimed, aware that her voice expressed more consternation than delight, "I am so glad. It's what I've always wanted for you." She placed her hand on his. "Is she young?" she inquired. "Do I know her?"

"She's not so very young," he replied, attempting to disguise his agitation. "Yes, you do know her, or at least you've seen her once or twice. You've talked to her over the telephone."

"But who is she, Felix?"

He came out with it quickly, a little defiantly. "She's my secretary, Rachel Weil."

"Oh," she exclaimed again, "oh, how nice."

"Yes, Rachel Weil, my secretary," he stammered again, grabbing his napkin and mopping up the wine. "She's been," he blurted it out painfully, "my mistress for over ten years."

Again she felt as though he'd struck her between the eyes and, it was utterly lacking in decent appreciation of what he had endured at her hands, she'd felt grieved, shocked, indignant. Felix of all people! Such infidelity from him And there it all was written across her face as plain as day. "All these years?" she asked when she had gained her breath.

"Yes," he said, "all these years. She's a warm and passionate woman. I have asked her now to marry me."

She is certain she would not have experienced so accurately all he underwent had she not been seated so close to him. He was determined if it was humanly possible to control himself, but all the restraint she had so long imposed upon him broke down. His feeling surged up and mastered him. He put his hands before his face and succumbed to a succession of sharp, convulsive sobs. A more distressing moment it is impossible to imagine. He did his best to pretend that something he had eaten was choking him and seeing this she summoned a waiter and asked for a glass of water. "This gentleman has swallowed a fish bone," she said.

What with the commotion the little drama had stirred up, getting and gulping down the water, the waiter hitting him, vigorously on the back and each of them engaged in carrying off the pretense, it wasn't too long before Felix had himself well in hand, and presently they appeared to be conversing in the calmest possible manner.

Then there had been all that intimacy, that gentleness between them, which each had tried desperately to cling to and prolong. Her indignation had passed as swiftly as it had come and how humanly, how exquisitely Felix had understood her shame and chagrin for having felt it. It was upon that core of finesse, delicacy, and depth of feeling in him she'd rested gratefully. He had allowed her to feel that he rested and reposed on what he knew he had in all fullness and sincerity — her friendship and affection. She was concerned about everything he told her of his plans. He was moving to Washington to go into partnership with a friend. A good arrangement for him he believed and he had high hopes that his knowledge of labor relations might result in a government appointment. That was as she knew well what he had always wanted most. There was on the whole a better future for him in Washington than in New York. To this they both agreed. She kept assuring him that he was not old, that he would have a successful and a happy life. She hoped that he would have a family. Was Rachel she asked too old to bear him children? No, he said, and with the greatest earnestness, he hoped, he trusted not. They both of them desired children. And so they talked together there at Mori's until the waiters began to whisk the tablecloths off the empty tables, positively inviting them to leave.

He took her home as he had so many, many times before. They walked up Sullivan Street and crossed Washington Square. It was a pleasant April night and the spring mist hung about in the trees and shrubbery. The pavements were wet and gave off a smell of spring. There was a special smell they both agreed that hung about the Square. It was a bit too damp to sit down. They were very loath to leave a place so crowded with memories, with nostalgia for an epoch — beliefs and hopes they knew had gone past all recall.

Outside her stoop on Twelfth Street he took her hand and held it for some time. "Good night, Margaret," he said, "goodbye."

"Good night," she said, "goodbye, my dear, dear friend." And that was the last time she ever laid her eyes on Felix.

E I G H T

THAT FEELING SHE HAD had of being somehow protected from anonymity and rootlessness suddenly gone from her heart. The long accustomed habits, calling Felix up, knowing that Mary was always at hand with her wisdom and her companionable wit, the basic reliable love still regulating the behavior of her thoughts (I must tell this to Mary — Mary would adore that, I'll call up Felix) and on the brink of all these feelings, thoughts and impulses the knowledge that she would not see her friends again and the great need to see, to hear, to have the usual talk, the old exchange.

Gone they were, vanished before she was prepared for losing them, and the shock of Mary's death the more unbearable because it might so easily have been avoided. If she had taken the trai' as everyone advised instead of going over those bad roads in that rattling old Ford, the day so wild and rainy; or better, if she hadn't gone at all. It had been unnecessary to attend that hearing, everyone had told her so, but determined she had been to go and in that car she so adored. Why, the moment the boy had brought the telegram and before she'd even opened it (what an uncanny thing) she'd known exactly what had happened — all day long that heaviness of heart upon her, that foreboding.

She'd been the first to get to Beacon and only just in time. Clear enough from the look on the doctor's face and the looks on the faces of the nurses that there wasn't a chance, and Mary waiting for her in that immaculate bed, whiter than the sheets that covered her, had conveyed the same intolerable message. She was conscious still and fully aware that she was dying. "Are you scared, Margaret? Well, don't be, darling. I am not," she'd whispered as though she were husbanding her strength for further conversation. She had taken her hand, but she'd been unable to utter another word. She'd closed her eyes. What could she possibly have said to Mary? Just being there with her, holding her hand while she lay dying seemed enough for both of them. The great experience had been rounded off by Mary's words. Gallant she was in her life and in her death. Beloved Mary Morton. Miss Sylvester drew a long breath as though she wished for a moment to hold her love and close it in her heart.

Life had struck at her again; but that was its behavior. It struck one blows and as far as outward events and circumstances went she seemed to have had, as she so frequently remarked, as many lives as a cat. The world which had confronted her was very feverish indeed. It invited to change and experiment — everybody running frantically about in search of distraction, and after a nearly unendurable year of trying to master her loneliness and adjust to life and its new conditions she too was caught up in the contagion. There had been that something brewing in her, God knows just what it was, she was over fifty and she discovered what honestly had come to her as a great surprise, that there was as you grew older no letting down emotionally. The hungers and thirsts increased, they struck at one with sharper thrusts. At any rate she used to regard herself in the mirror and see reflected there a not uncharming woman. Yes, she had some power to charm and to arrest attention; a gift with people. If she made an effort she could collect new friends, she could make the acquaintance of people who would interest and amuse her. New York was crammed with men and women one wanted to know and perhaps could. She might, and the idea struck her, she remembers so well one evening when she was feeling particularly bereaved, buy herself a house (real estate was a good investment). She could do it over, live in half of it and rent the other half. She might give little parties. She might make it a center for finding interesting companions — people with gifts and creative talents.

And so, and so. The heart has a way of renewing itself; life had at all times its gifts and invitations and New York at that quite dreadful moment dangled them conspicuously before the eyes — everyone spending so much money and extra dividends appearing so unexpectedly as one ruminated over one's breakfast. Why yes of course, that was exactly the thing to do — to buy a house. It would give her something to think about. A home that actually belonged to you — what could make you feel more secure and permanent? It should be west of Sixth Avenue, it must be in the Village proper. And following this decision she got to work at once to search for the new home. Accompanied by that voluble young woman from the real estate office who, armed with keys and authority to let them into houses, to knock at the doors of private apartments and as soon as they entered to begin to act as though the house, the premises and everything but the chairs and tables of the lessor were already in the hands of her client ("you can knock down a partition here, you can throw out an extension there, you can add a bathroom, excuse me, you don't mind if I open this door?"), she found herself beguilingly employed. It was exciting enough imagining herself leading so many gracious and decorative existences in so many different houses, rooms, gardens.

Finally she found on Grove Street precisely what she was after — a Victorian house, nothing especial to look at from the outside, brick with a high stoop and ornate ironwork, built probably in the 'eighties. It had been unnecessary for the real estate lady to tell her a word about its possibilities — she saw them at a glance. The house was constructed according to a familiar pattern and she knew its layout so exactly that directly on looking around she was able to choose her own quarters and dispose of her tenants in the most satisfactory manner. Ah, this was to be hers, she'd thought, as she entered the ground floor apartment. She'd always liked space — here she had it. The two long rooms and an extension; and ah — a garden, a pear tree. She'd knock down the partition between the two big rooms and she'd keep both fireplaces exactly as they were, marble roses and lilies and acanthus leaves intact, and between them she would run up her bookshelves (books she thought and winter — open fireplaces, flowers). Ah yes, and the extension; she'd draw all this space out towards the windows and the garden. You couldn't knock down the partitions, but you could perhaps widen the doors. Anyway she'd leave them open. There she'd sleep; there need be no visible trace of her dressing or sleeping arrangements, for on the right was a small room she could use for dressing and a bathroom leading from it; and as for the bed, well that should be magnificently disguised. There and then she saw her lovely gracious suite decorated in relation to her fine old piece of needlepoint which she would throw over the low, the comfortable divan, the walls were painted, the curtains hung, books, rugs, lampshades taking up its subtle shades and colors; furthermore, furthermore, the ugly doors would be replaced by long French windows and beyond and through them the pear tree, that spot of beauty and delight, would guide the eye of the entering visitor down the vista of the room to rest upon its shining beauty. My home! she thought, and her heart warming to it and her imagination continuing to embellish it she constructed between the extension and the second fireplace a graceful little stairway and below, white and severe and quite Italian, her dining room with open archways leading to the large, bright, pleasant kitchen — all somehow arched and aired and sunny and filled with the joy of that perennially blooming pear tree. And yes of course, oh yes of course, there were the tenants to consider. Behind the kitchen there'd be ample space (she'd put in a bathroom and kitchenette) for a small apartment at the front which she could rent to a nice neat quiet bachelor or perhaps some unobtrusive woman and upstairs the two floors which she could admirably adapt for renting. She figured out, the real estate lady assisting her, the total yearly rentals and, naturally, much exaggerating the price she'd ask the tenants and underestimating the upkeep and repairs, they added to a total sum of such splendid proportions it appeared the whole exciting venture was not only a satisfactory solution to her problems but an exceedingly sagacious investment of her money.

What a business the enterprise had been, selling securities, taking out a mortgage, searching the title and, after that, remodeling and discovering that the estimates made out with her contractor proved quite different from those she'd sketched in her imagination. She'd chosen, take it by and large, a man she liked, Mr. Kopf, a fat, genial, moon-faced creature, honest on the whole, inclined to be generous and say he'd throw in this little bit of painting or that little job of carpentry that wasn't in the contract. But slow, mortal slow. It had all taken longer than she'd figured out. She'd been kept in town through the entire summer.

She'd enjoyed it, the walk from Twelfth Street over those sizzling sidewalks, lingering in the Square, improvising schemes about the house and meeting Mr. Kopf in Grove Street every morning, scolding him or buttering him up as the case might have been. Pleasant it was walking through the rooms she'd presently call hers, looking out the windows on that tiny plot of city property — her garden, and the summer heat casting over her tree, her garden and on the backs of all those houses, all the little gardens, its peculiar spell — some intensity about it hearing saws and hammers and the voices of the carpenters and plumbers busy in the house behind her and thinking how she'd feel at home in Grove Street.

It was autumn however before she was able to move in after plenty of brushes with Mr. Kopf, hurry and strain and nervousness. But finally in the late September days there she was inhabiting her house. To say she'd loved it was to state it mildly. What a delight to wake up on those autumn mornings with the windows open listening to those sounds, believe it or not, thought the old woman — hens, a rooster crowing, for what with all the Italians in the vicinity, Antonio's lot behind that boarding at the junction of Bleecker and Grove Street, where he kept his hens, a donkey and a horse, there'd been something almost bucolic about life in Grove Street. How she had enjoyed getting to know her neighborhood, starting out to market, the smells on Bleecker Street — cheese, oil, garlic — carrying her off and away to streets in Rome or Florence and that bright display of fruits and vegetables on the pushcarts and the stalls outside the vegetable vendors' — a veritable market garden, the lettuces and fruits so freshly watered, sidewalks wet, Italians in the crowds haggling and jabbering away in their various dialects and returning home with her market bag spilling over like an autumnal cornucopia.

She'd been loath to start the search for tenants. To complicate the pleasures of her new life with business seemed a shame, and so she put it off. Over her furnishings and final decorative touches she'd lingered as long as possible. Why she'd never been so extravagant in all her life, though to be sure she'd tried to justify every purchase with one rational explanation or another — this was the place she'd live in for the remainder of her days, and after all she was planning to entertain, to give other people a chance to enjoy her home. And so, sitting first in one chair and then in another, viewing the big room from every possible angle, she'd attempted to think out her decorator's problems. There was one thing she felt was missing. She'd known it from the moment she moved in — a grand piano. She must have a grand piano; the room cried aloud for it. Moreover it fitted in so well with her schemes for peopling her life with new acquaintances. No difficulty at all in imagining the winter nights with both the fires lighted and some young pianist playing as though he'd been inspired. Ah, she knew exactly where she'd place her instrument — there, backing on the stair rail and behind her softly lighted bedroom, the garden dark beyond.

And so, and so (it took a month before she bought it) she got her new piano. It looked as well, and even better than she'd imagined. Ah how she used to love to sit and strum upon it. She was nothing of a pianist, but what delight it gave her, lightly touching the keys and how the little tunes she played enticed the dreams. A bit melancholy they were, for there is always a touch of melancholy in the daydreams — lovely, soft and satisfying to the soul; there'd been in them fulfillment of one kind or another. And what, she would wonder as she played, was it exactly that she wanted? Perhaps to be — well, not exactly that, but something similar, a kind of patron of the arts — to have, ah well, you couldn't use that word, it sounded too pretentious, a kind of salon? No, certainly not that, but to cultivate charming creative people. She had a gift of making others easy with themselves, a gift for entertaining, getting the right kind of friends together. Felix had always told her there was the making of an artist in her. Yes, yes, she had always known it, she had an artistic temperament. Too old to be creative, but — but, there was this way she had with the young — with young men in particular; and if her life had had its bitter sorrow might it not be possible that she could draw on this bereavement? Was there not a depth, a rich fund of understanding — sympathy? Her heart was full, it was flowing over she assured herself, touching the keys, trying to remember a Chopin Prelude, a bit from one of the Beethoven sonatas; and seeing as she played, the curtains by the long French windows (they were just as she had planned them and the pear tree leafless there beyond) move lightly in the breeze that stirred them.

N I N E

FLOTSAM AND JETSAM, thought the old woman, and she beat her breast, flotsam and jetsam. Those were the words, try to drive them away as she invariably did, that came to her mind whenever she thought about her basement apartment. And why should she have gone out of her way to furnish it, taking so much pains to make it resemble the boudoir of an interior decorator? If she'd left it unfurnished there would have been more permanency, the tenant would have had to bring in his bed, his desk and books and chairs and tables and after he'd hired a van and got his things transported, there would have been some obligation to pay his rent and stay. But to go out of her way to furnish a basement and in the Village in those days; why, it had been an invitation to trouble. She began to conjure with the ifs and it-might-have-beens, and again she beat her breast. If she hadn't rented the basement at all, just kept that front room for herself as she had seriously considered — a little guest suite. It was putting those friends of hers into the two floors above, giving them the duplex instead of keeping each floor a separate unit and just because they'd overpersuaded her, and asking them less than she'd planned to, and then thinking she could make up the deficit by furnishing the basement and demanding a good round sum for it.

To call it naive was mild indeed. Those discreet and careful furnishings, the pretty Chippendale desk, the expensive rug and hangings, those good prints she'd found and framed with such particular care. Ah, ah, she put her hand to her heart as though her thoughts were becoming too painful to endure. The only things that were apparently necessary in the basement apartments were the beds. Yes they needed beds. They were all that was necessary; and for her to think now of that narrow mahogany four-poster with the box mattress and the handsome spread she'd finally settled on was, she said and caught her breath, too ironic for words.

Suddenly she began to mutter to herself swift incoherent words, "My dear, my dear one," as it came back again, the excruciating story, just as she'd narrated it in her novel and feeling it here, here in her heart — memory flashing back those scenes and situations — and seeing that charming boy ("Yes, yes indeed you were, you were charming, beautiful"), letting him in herself that winter evening — the young man with the chestnut-colored hair. There he had stood, hatless and without an overcoat, throwing back his head, trying to brush the snowflakes from his shoulders, smiling, showing his fine teeth, his face responding with pleasure to the warmth and firelight as he came into the room.

It *had* been a surprise! He was a most beguiling young man, but she'd been determined under no considerations to have him dwelling in her basement floor. "Yes?" she'd inquired as coldly as possible and implying she hadn't the ghost of an idea what he was there for, just exactly as though there'd been no sign "Apartment to Rent" tied to the area rail.

"We meet again," he'd said and with that touch of impertinence that somehow or other enhanced his charm he'd taken his cigarette case from his pocket and looked around.

"Yes?" she'd repeated, not so much as offering him a chair, allowing him to stand hatless, covered with snow.

"Where's your friend?" he'd asked and he'd outlined with his thumb and forefinger the shape of Felix's beard, then he'd dropped his hand offering himself, as she had failed to do so a comfortable chair, and with the same incomparable gesture suggesting that she too might like to sit down he'd seated himself and lighted a cigarette. "Sorry your friend isn't here. He was a good talker. Something to his remarks about Joyce," he'd said, observing everything around him — the books, the bowl of roses on the desk. "A nice place," he'd vouchsafed and he might just as well have added as he took her in from head to foot "and you are, my dear lady, an extremely attractive woman. I like your gown and the sleeves showing your pretty arms. I like your dress. Gray becomes you."

Ah well, ah well. The old woman sighed and a look of infinite tenderness flitted across her face. She mustn't linger too long over that conversation. She'd recorded it, she felt sure, word for word in the manuscript. Ah, but the intimacy, the warmth of it — the two of them there in that beautiful glowing room and the snow falling so fast outside, the firelight casting shadows on the walls and ceiling and playing over his perfectly delightful countenance. "Young man," she'd kept saying to herself, "I am simply *not* going to allow you to inveigle me into giving you my basement apartment," knowing perfectly well that he knew, though they'd not so much as said a word about it, she knew what he was there for and had firmly made up her mind not to let him have the room he wanted. Plain enough to see that he was playing for time. "Give me long enough" he seemed to be saying with every word and gesture "to melt away, well, if not all your objections, at least every vestige of your resistance to my charms." There'd been a playfulness and humor about the situation which curiously enough they'd both of them enjoyed.

Finally he'd come right out with it. "Now," he'd said, "tell me, why is it you're so determined not to let me have a look at that room in the basement?"

"Oh," she'd parried, "oh, my basement?"

"Am I so objectionable?" he'd asked.

"No, no, not at all," she'd assured him. "Quite indeed the contrary." But she had already made up her mind not to rent the apartment to a young man — not to *any* young man.

And suddenly he had laughed and she had laughed. Wasn't it foolish of her then, he'd inquired, to rig up that sign and hang it on the area rail? There were plenty of young men in Greenwich Village searching for rooms — best place in the world to put them, they could come, they could go, keep whatever hours they pleased. "Why," he'd said, "you'll never be the wiser, never lose a wink of sleep."

And thereupon she'd laughed outright. "But I want a lady," she'd explained. "You wait till you see the little place. It isn't for a bachelor at all, it's for a single lady."

Well, if she was looking for Bernard Shaw's Prossie he'd said and they'd continued to laugh, why hadn't she advertised in *The Churchman* or gone to the YWCA to put in an application. "Your procedure is, my dear lady, if you'll allow me to say so, extremely naive." And so there they were laughing together. Was it at his wit or at her folly in putting up that ridiculous sign or simply the fact that he knew perfectly well that she knew she was caught. "Oh come," he'd begged her, and he'd risen, "let me take a look at the place. What possible objection can you have to a young man at work on his first novel? Is that such a disreputable occupation?"

"That depends," she'd said, bursting again into a laugh (he had a faculty of making her say the silliest things) and all at once and to her astonishment she'd seen that he was moving toward the little staircase.

"Come, let me see the flat," he'd urged.

"But that isn't the tenant's entrance," she'd reprimanded, "— the tenant can't go through my apartment, my dear young man."

"Oh, just this once," he'd begged, "I'll never do it again." Why, you might have thought she'd already rented him the place. And down they'd gone together through the dining room and into the little flat.

"Nice place you've got," he'd said, and he'd looked around, examined one of her dining-room chairs, taken a glance into the kitchen. "Pleasantest place in the Village," he'd said, following her through the door and into that neatly decorated front room.

"Quite a place," he'd looked about, and then he'd gone directly to that small four-poster, felt the mattress carefully. "Good springs," he'd said. "Comfortable bed. Expressly made for Prossie." And once more they were laughing both together (playing into her hands like that). "Well," she'd asked, "isn't that just what I've been telling you? the room, you can see it at a glance, is not for a young man."

"No, no it isn't," he'd acknowledged, "but all the same I want it. What's your top price?" He'd made it plain enough he knew she was about to soak him.

"Fifty dollars," she'd said, adding ten to the rent she'd figured on asking and as though to justify the sum opening the door to the bathroom to display the tiling, the porcelain tub and all the shining brass. "Look at this beautiful bathroom" she'd said as she'd opened another door — "Here's the kitchenette."

"Splendid!" he'd exclaimed, "a bathroom and a kitchenette! I'm game for it." He'd fixed her squarely with his eyes.

"But I'm not going to let you have it," she'd assumed the playful note, tried to be a bit coquettish. "No, my dear young man, you really can't persuade me."

Unabashed he'd gone to the bed and begun again to press the mattress and at that she'd turned, and left the room.

Gracious how glad she'd been to get out of there, to precede him through the dining room and up the stairs, talking all the way and with a feeling of defeat already taking possession of her. "You know, my dear young man, I don't intend to take you. Tell me now, what do I know about you? I've seen you round at restaurants, I expect you keep late hours and have expensive habits, most young people do."

And so there again they'd been, the two of them together in her pleasant room, fencing, bantering, somehow taking pleasure in it, the attraction they'd felt each for the other; and she remembers how she'd fancied that he somewhat resembled Byron. Well, under no consideration would she have him in her basement.

Yes, he'd said, he wrote. He was at work upon a novel. Oh he was a hard worker. He worked terrifically. It seemed his book had been begun in Paris. He hoped to finish it here in New York and afterwards return to France. Examining his mobile, interesting face she'd wondered if the lines of fatigue under the eyes, dragging the flesh down below the cheekbones, could perhaps have been occasioned by hard work — writing took it out of people. Sometimes it left upon the countenance the same kind of marks as those traced by dissipation. Well, well, whatever his habits he was irresistible and she would have to play her hand with the greatest care or there'd be no extricating herself from the net he was casting round her.

Finally he'd looked at his watch and risen briskly. It was getting late. He was due at an appointment. And hadn't he by this time persuaded her that though his sex might be against him he'd be the best of tenants. To be sure he'd beat the typewriter, but he didn't believe she'd so much as hear him do it, and he'd drawn out his checkbook. Well, she'd thought, the young man's got a checking account. That's more than some of them have. "Do you mind?" he'd asked, and he'd gone to the desk and sat down, taken out his fountain pen. "My check is good," he'd said. "Here's an advance, and if I don't pay my next month's rent just kick me out." And back he'd come with that check for fifty dollars, the ink not dried upon it. "There," he'd said and she had taken it, looked vaguely at the signature. An interesting handwriting, she had thought. Signed by Philip Ropes Jr. Why, of all things in the world. She knew the Philip Ropeses, the stuffiest, positively the stuffiest, most conventional Bostonians. Delighted she'd been in a queer way — there was something so amusing about it, that the Philip Ropeses could have had a son like this. Hard to believe it but then young people these days sprang surprises on one. She'd been on the point of saying she knew his parents but then she hadn't, she'd never liked opening those old connections.

"Good for fifty dollars, my name is good for that the first of every month," and then he'd asked with the greatest politeness for the keys.

Weak she'd been, as weak as water. "But it isn't the first of the month," she'd protested and she'd got up: she'd gone to the desk, she'd searched for the keys, found them, put the two of them on a ring and conscious that he had risen and was standing beside her she'd turned, she'd given them to him.

How earnestly he'd thanked her. The only reason he'd asked for them he'd explained was so that he could slip in without disturbing her. He intended to be, he'd assured her, as quiet as a mouse. He'd put them in his pocket, he'd smiled; he'd held out his hand and she has to this day the firmest conviction that what he'd really wanted to do was to stoop and give her an impertinent but none the less grateful kiss, for there had been warmth between them — yes, yes she is sure of it — a kind of warmth, a mutual attraction.

"But when are you coming?" she'd inquired holding his hand an instant. "When do you intend to move in?"

"Oh," he'd said, he hadn't much to bring, only his typewriter and his manuscripts, some socks and shoes and pants. He'd soon pack up, he'd be along. She could expect him almost any day. "And mind you," he'd added, going to the door, "we've made a deal: the rent is paid." Then out he'd gone, hatless into the snow.

Well, thought the old woman, why go over it when she'd just finished reading all about it? Ah but wasn't there she wondered just this difference — letting the memories give it back? There in the novel had been the words carefully arranged, scenes, situations, and she expected she had done them well: but this, she placed her hand against her breast, this flow, this going on with it. Ah she remembered how she'd waited for him to put in an appearance. She'd deposited the check, she had even called up her bank to see if it was good and wondering all the time what had delayed him. It had been almost a week.

And then, gracious what a surprise, looking out the window on that February morning and seeing, why she wasn't even sure it had been altogether a surprise — seeing him there in the area accompanied by, who in the world but the same girl he'd had with him that night that she and Felix dined at Dante's Inferno. He'd let her through the gate and off the two of them had walked together in the direction of Seventh Avenue.

Had it been indignation? What was it she had felt? To be sure there'd been nothing illegal. Why she hadn't even made him sign a lease. Just that check on Philip Ropes the bank assured her had been credited to her account. It had been, as he insisted, a deal and as for leases, you rent an apartment and unless the contrary is stipulated it is yours to do with exactly as you please. You can bring in your girl, your dog, your pet monkey. It was this knowledge she'd had that he had tricked her. Never, never in the world would she have let him come if he'd told her he was planning to bring along that girl.

Little she could do about it. There apparently they were and she'd have to say they had given her but slight annoyance. Sometimes she'd heard his typewriter but not to be sure too often. It had been this uneasy sense she'd had of it, not of him in particular but of the lives of the young, having them there in her basement documenting, as she'd felt they were, the whole irregular and spendthrift era. For of what were they not, she began to wonder, spendthrift, of youth, of time, of money? And of something else she could not so easily put her finger on.

The clicking of that area gate got strangely on her nerves. They came in at all hours and slept, she gathered, the larger part of every day. She seldom heard them stirring till after noon. Well, it was none of her business she'd tell herself. When his month was up she'd have a talk with him. Maybe she'd ask him to move. She dreaded it — encountering him again. There'd been between them a mutual desire to avoid another meeting and after all you didn't often have to meet the tenants in your basement. And when one evening she had met him emerging from his room and without the girl how blithely he had hailed her. "Hullo, Miss Sylvester," he'd cried out as though delighted to see her again. Chilly was not the word for it, the way she'd nodded to him. Why she'd not so much as spoken, just that little nod. Well, she'd registered at least her feelings towards him and glad she'd had the chance to do so. Presently she'd have the courage to ask him to get out.

Then when the month was up it had gone on just as she'd expected. They had not paid their rent. Should she go down, knock on their door and ask to speak with them or would she write a note? Cowardly enough to write and besides she had some curiosity about that room, just what they'd done to it. Well well, she'd let it go a fortnight; and then one morning about twelve A.M. she'd heard them stirring, and down with sudden resolution she had gone and knocked peremptorily upon their door. "Come in," he'd called, his voice quite blithe and casual and she'd heard a protest from the girl. She'd found the door unlocked and opened it and there he was tying his necktie, apparently preparing to go out and the girl lying on the bed smoking. Casual they both of them were, the girl not so much as getting up. "Won't you have a seat?" he'd said and then seeing there wasn't a chair in the room unencumbered by some garment or other he'd swept the girl's pajamas and bed shoes and heaven knows what else from a nearby chair and invited her again to seat herself. She'd come he knew to ask him for the rent but — but, he'd said, embracing with a gesture that untidy room, the girl on the bed, and the dire situation in which she had presumably found them — the whole irregular establishment as though it had been something for which she should by every standard of human decency have felt concern and sympathy, he'd asked her to be patient. He was at the moment waiting to get a check for a story he fully expected to sell. Just give him a week or two he'd pleaded and though he did not say "You simply cannot throw us into the street," the words were implicit in the demand and the girl lying there smoking leaving it all to him. She had not so much as looked up. Pretty she was even in her dishevelled condition. She had on a bathrobe and had not made up, but her hair which was cropped was the purest gold and seemed to fit her small head like a shining cap. The features were delicate. Yes, there was no mistaking it, the face was sensitive, a little sulky, petulant perhaps at seeing the plight in which life apparently had plunged her. But it was the face, she felt, of a gently born and gently bred young creature. Somehow it had made her heart ache — the whole situation had made her heart ache heavily. She'd wished to turn her back upon it. She'd hated to haggle with them for her rent and so, and so, she'd been quite lenient. She'd said that she would wait, but she had hinted broadly that she wished they would do their very best to find another place. "I had not been prepared for two," she'd added and she'd taken a good look at that slovenly room. They should see, she'd said, what they were doing to her pretty flat. Yes, yes, he'd agreed, they were a sloppy pair, but they'd try to mend their ways and she had to admit she'd given them no warning she was coming. Not a chance to tidy up.

So she had left. There'd been little else to do, nothing very satisfactory accomplished, she'd reflected. He'd promised to pay as soon as possible and then she had said, but weakly, weakly, that if they hadn't paid by the end of the month she would be forced to take measures to evict them. She was giving a large party on the first of April and just why she had thought it necessary to tell them that she didn't know. She hoped they would be out before that date, she'd said, rather as though she'd considered them too disreputable to be in the same house with her while she was entertaining guests. The whole thing had been sickening to her. It had made her heart ache.

And her party; well, what could she say about that party but that it had been the most beautiful occasion? Something extraordinary had occurred, an event — moments passing one into the other, little tableaus of the heart, the desires, the dream images coming suddenly to life, and there in the midst of them she'd been, in them but outside of them, the genius in fact that had conjured them into being and looking around her, saying to herself "Can this actually be true? Have I pulled it off?" Why, it had been exactly what she'd wanted, the evening soft and springlike, the windows open and the fires lighted and all those flowers, yellow, white, pale ivory, and amber. She could see and smell them, daffodils, freesia, white hyacinths, narcissus, Easter lilies, all the Easter constellations clustered and assembled there in her room — her home.

Her dress too had been quite perfect, pale ivory and amber with a touch of young spring green and as she'd walked about she'd had that curious feeling of unreality — the compliments and the perfection. And she had managed to procure what had been the very core of her ambitions, a string quartet, one of the very best in town — there had been music with the fires lighted and all her guests responding to the magic just as she would have wished to have them. Ah, unforgettable, forever unforgettable the "Heiliger Dankgesang" in the Beethoven 132. That music, what was it, she had asked herself, occurring in her heart, feeling it climb, ascending to what celestial heights she did not need to ask, but let it climb, let it continue climbing, let the clouds burst and the effulgence stream behind the breaking clouds while she experienced such joy as never was or could be quite imagined, running as she seemed to be backward into childhood with that music, with those intimations and the remembrance of that day in Siena when she'd found and read the incomparable Ode, and being there again in that grove in Brookline picking those spring flowers, being in the summer fields above the ocean, a part of that great dance of life. And from whence came such music, she had asked herself, from what fount of knowledge and intuition, yielding herself up to it, letting the heart climb higher, higher, and saying to Felix yes, it is enough, it is sufficient.

After that was over, the spell had been cast, shed on all the guests, and she had walked through the rest of the party treading it had seemed to her upon celestial clouds, the pleasantest compliments in her ears and that delicious sense that everything was going as she'd planned. She'd had in a man to serve and a caterer had furnished the refreshments and with her own Daphne Jordan assisting everything went on without a hitch. Champagne, she had thought, looking at her guests, at the daffodils, the freesia, the narcissus — the perfect wine for such a night as this and she had lifted her glass to drink, as someone had suggested, to the spring and there at her side the young cellist who had played, it was the only word for it, like an angel, and she had told him that his performance was perfection and he had bowed and said "My dear lady, it was because you were there with that expression on your face that I performed so well." A lovely compliment she had thought carrying it with her through the evening while this little tableau melted into the next and the whole airy, fairy dream went floating away from her until the last guest had gone and there she'd been alone in her big room thinking of it all with such extreme delight.

And then because she must find somebody to talk to she'd gone downstairs in search of Daphne Jordan and found her stacking up the dishes on the dining table just as she had ordered, tired, considerate, and more than a trifle tipsy, what with all the glasses she'd emptied.

Her lady must sit down and have a cup of coffee for she hadn't, she'd
reminded her, had a bite to eat. "Now there," she'd said, returning with
salad, sandwiches, and coffee, "eat, my lady, eat them sandwiches," and
back she'd gone into her kitchen to finish with the dishes.

Glad enough she'd been of something to sustain her. Pitching into
the sandwiches and salad, trying to gather and assemble the various
fragments of that lovely dream her party, which for once in a way had
been so completely successful, and becoming suddenly aware that
something was going on in the front room she'd felt annoyance, irritation. Why should those two young people disturb this mood of happiness and satisfaction with their ugly quarrels? They were in the midst
of a regular fracas. She'd not wanted to listen to them, but as a matter
of fact she had done so; she'd listened attentively. She could hear them
plainly, for they'd raised their voices and oh, she wished they would
not use all those ugly words, throwing them at each other like that,
words only associated in her mind with certain passages of the Bible
and in the mouths of these young people revolting, revolting. The girl
was apparently weeping and what was she telling the young man? That
she was going to have a baby. Oh God, oh God, she couldn't bear it,
and she'd put her hands before her face. "All right," he'd said, "you're
going to have a baby. All right, that's your responsibility. No reason at
all for me to believe it's mine." At this the girl had shrieked hysterically. It seemed that she was on the bed. She could hear her moving
about and the springs creaking. "But Philip, you liar, you bastard, you
know there's nobody but you." "How do I know it?" he'd shouted back
and he had called her one of those names it had seemed to her she
could not tolerate upon his lips and all the while she'd been aware that
Daphne Jordan was just behind her listening at the kitchen door. She
wanted to command her to go away, but then how could she? The
young man was banging about, opening and shutting doors, bureau
drawers, making a big racket and the girl continuing to shriek at him.
"God knows, I'm crazy about you." "Shut up," he'd roared at her. "I'm
getting out," and then the girl must have got up from the bed, for they
were having an actual physical tussle. "Philip," she'd shrieked, "you
bastard," just pelting him with the dreadful word, and there was a great
sound of slaps and blows. Maybe she was slapping him, maybe he was
hitting her. And then suddenly it seemed that it was over and Philip

was talking in a slow thick voice while Daphne listened there behind her, mumbling this and that, and while it seemed to her her blood congealed, her heart stopped beating. "All right," he'd said, "I am a bastard, and the son of a bastard and the offspring" — he'd used the word which had turned her heart to stone, maybe sitting down on the bed or on a chair, for what she'd needed was to get a physical picture of him. What she'd needed was to have him there, folded in her arms, longing so desperately to rush through that closed door and claim his love and his foregiveness and the word piercing her heart as though he'd aimed an arrow at it, hearing him brutally, rather drunkenly, but obviously with some need upon him to redeem, to excuse himself, telling the girl the secret she had kept so long, how he'd been abandoned by his mother in Fiesole, sold as he'd put it to save her precious chastity. Then their voices growing lower, the anger diminishing, she'd been unable to hear much of what they said. But certainly the quarreling was over, mostly she heard the girl's voice declaring that she loved him. "Philip, Philip," she kept saying, and she was crying still and there had been kisses and then again the shutting and the opening of doors and bureau drawers and both of them, it dawned upon her, packing up, preparing to get out.

And there she'd sat at that table with all those stacked-up dishes round her, but frozen, paralyzed, wanting, oh desperately, to get up and rush through that door and not even knowing if Daphne was still standing there behind her. Only scraps of words and phrases and all to be put together, pieced out by her imagination, "not paying the old lady," "running out on her," "getting out of here." Had she heard something about Europe, Paris, about the story that had been accepted? Maybe, perhaps she'd made it up. There she had sat and listened and finally she had heard the door stealthily opening and then feet as cautious as a pair of thieves, the boards creaking in the basement hallway, the opening of the outer door; then faint but audible the latching of the area gate behind them.

T E N

———

MISS SYLVESTER REGARDED her little patch of view. She had never been able to accustom herself to it and tonight it was of such transcendent beauty, the air, the sky so clear and that small slice of a moon sailing past the tower, the stars quivering, this astonishing array of windows building up before her eyes their citadels of crystal light. Strange it should have been her portion to look out on such a spectacle as this. Strange to have lived on earth through these last eighty years. And an altogether extraordinary business writing her book, laying it away unopened and then rereading it today, sitting here turning the pages as one might turn the pages of anybody's novel, all the while reliving it, giving it back to memory, to that stream that still continued flowing. It was, she thought, looking out upon the moon, the stars, and all the glittering windows, as though they challenged her, something of a cheat — a cheat, the cutting her story off, rounding it to a finish with all that tragedy and melodrama in the basement.

Life carried on and that knowledge to which she'd been so brutally exposed became as time went on an item of familiar baggage in her heart. How long had she stayed on in Grove Street, three years or four? She wasn't sure, and the year she'd sold the house and moved to that comfortable place in Eighth Street would probably remain uncertain were it not for the fact that luck had been involved, getting out before the crash, selling the house at a good profit and making all those arrangements about the legacy, the settlement of seventy thousand dollars on the grandchild she'd never seen, completed in the spring of that same year, the funds invested soundly, capital and accruing interest to be paid at his majority and all achieved without so much as breaking that agreement never to reveal herself either to her son or to his issue.

And the years that followed her moving out of Grove Street, goodness gracious, more than twenty of them. What with the world events that rushed upon her out of the headlines, off the celluloid, out of the air, collapsing, colliding, careening madly off into time and space, how could she possibly keep track of them? After the crash that period of depression, queues of the unemployed and that soup kitchen right around the corner on Green Street, never emerging from her door without the sight of hungry men. Then there had been Hitler and all the terrifying rumors (just when had she first heard of Hitler?), then Roosevelt and the moratorium, the first inaugural speech, that voice in which you somehow trusted, then suddenly the rolling of the beer barrels so jolly in the midst of all that apprehension, and behold the bars, the mirrors, bottles, the ladies with their glasses, and all the time the rumors growing louder — youth movements, storm troopers, Jews in liquidation, windows broken in Berlin, shops raided in Vienna, the burning of the Reichstag.

How many years since she'd divested herself of her personal possessions and moved into this singularly impersonal room and here, confronted with her lone estate, resolved to write her little story, to sit down every single day and try to tell the secret she had kept throughout the years? Was it the anonymity of her life against which she'd rebelled? One had a right to one's personal history; if one had experienced strong emotion, endured one's special brand of agony, one was entitled to express it. At any rate with all the *Schrecklichkeit* that marched upon the world — Hitler entering Vienna, rolling across the bridge with all that show of military might, Czechoslovakia, Munich, Berchtesgaden, Chamberlain stepping from his plane carrying his scroll and his umbrella — switching on the radio, sallying forth to see the newsreels, how determined she had been to stick to her resolve. Why, it had obsessed her utterly. All the rumors from the air, that sense that everybody had of waiting on some dread, calamitous, unprecedented moment had not been able to deter her. Desperately she'd stuck right at it, working each and every day. It had, she is free to confess it, almost killed her, but when the spring arrived, exceptionally soft and lovely, she'd felt on certain days a curious joy, as though her heart had been assuaged, her spirit given wings to soar, to mount. There, spread upon the Flushing marshes was the great World's Fair — the fountains and the palaces of peace, and she had walked among them in the warm spring weather, an old, old woman in her declining years with something slowly growing, taking shape within her.

The King and Queen had visited the Fair, had eaten frankfurters with Mrs. Roosevelt and returned to England safely. Finally in August that cloud that hung above the world exploded, burst asunder — Poland invaded, England, France at war with Germany, Warsaw bombed, the whole world waiting for Paris and London to be strafed from the air. During the long winter of the phony war with what dogged perseverance she had labored at her task. She could bring no order, no organization to her work, it simply fell to pieces in her mind. Up and down the floor she'd paced telling herself she was the greatest fool alive. Then out of that dead calm, ah God, with what swiftness came those bolts of lighting, Norway invaded, the overrunning of Denmark, the occupation of Belgium, the overrunning of France, Sedan, the fall of France, and the miraculous Dunkirk; then a pause before the crisis and finally, staged forever on the screen of air and sky, the battle of Britain, all those nightly bombings, conflagrations, the show put on for everyone to see — that English bravery, with Churchill looming like Colos-sus, and all America invited to stay at home and listen to those cheerful voices of the bombed-out people in their shelters, jovial as though assembled at some pleasant nightclub, London every day in flames at all the movie theaters, and there she'd stayed to watch it, with her novel weaving through the holocaust and the horror.

After that to cap the climax Rudolf Hess flying to Scotland, and then to cap all climaxes and all surprises Hitler invading Russia, nothing to think about but Russia, those place names tolling in the mind like dirges, Kiev, Smolensk, Nizhni Novgorod. Would they hold, had they fallen? That meeting — Churchill shaking hands with Roosevelt aboard the battleship, the Atlantic Charter. And on a Sunday, the seventh of December, breaking through the music. Was it a prank by Orson Welles — a jamming of the radio? Pearl Harbor. Where exactly was it? What did it mean? Were we at war, lined up against the Axis, in it with out allies to the finish?

Disaster falling on disaster, Wake Island, Bataan, the stand at Corregidor, the sinking of the English ships, Hong Kong, Singapore, the Malay Peninsula, the Dutch East Indies; and presently the celluloid offering the eyes the visual images, the far-flung lines of battle, that wilderness of snow in Russia, the armies fighting in the snow, the cities holding — Moscow, Leningrad, and in the spring those corpses on the leafless trees in the demolished hamlets, convoys in the Atlantic, sinkings, aircraft carriers in the Pacific, dogfights in the waste of sky and ocean, landing craft, soldiers disembarking on the lonely beaches, battles in the jungles, flaming tanks, the boys arrayed in leaves and branches, with Mickey Mouse and Donald Duck and Popeye running in and out of Armageddon — sitting in that macabre twilight, wondering if she had the courage to complete her novel, Alamein, Guadalcanal, Roosevelt and Churchill at Casablanca, our landings in North Africa, and Stalingrad, the bleak, the desolated city, Eniwetok, Tarawa, Okinawa, Truk, Stalin under the palms with Roosevelt and Churchill.

And then again the voices, the announcements, sitting beside the radio — the channel safely crossed, the epic beachheads, Caen and the channel ports. And in the summer, voices that announced the Russian conquests, cities taken back, that gathering sense of safety, victory approaching, the Battle of the Bulge and hopes set back at Christmas, confidence restored, that softening up, the ceaseless strafing of the German cities, our armies on the march, the crossing of the Rhine (victory so close that you could touch it), Stalin, Churchill, Roosevelt at Yalta (the black cape, the skeletal face) — peace and the spring approaching. Suddenly that voice that struck out like a blow — Roosevelt dead at Warm Springs, the funeral train (lilacs in the dooryard blooming), the crowds at stations weeping. Then spring with all the blossoms; peace in Europe long awaited. And summer with the victories in the Pacific, the Philippines regained, the islands hopped. Truman in conference with Attlee. Truman's announcement on the sixth of August, those words reverberating round the world. Alamogordo, Hiroshima.

Nagasaki; peace.

Peace, repeated the old woman, peace, and remembering the news that she had read that morning, said aloud, or thought that she had said it, "What is man that Thou art mindful of him, and the son of man that Thou visitest him?" and she attempted to get up, for she was late and Adam waiting for her (dear me, dear me, how much money had he said he wanted? She must go to her desk and get it. Fifty dollars was the sum? No, no, she would not leave her manuscript to Adam, she would destroy it when she returned from dining. Plenty of novels in the world already. She had had the experience of writing it — that was sufficient, quite sufficient) and had she risen to her feet, had someone dealt her a stupendous blow and was it Nanny at her elbow urging her, "Yes, now, take another step, the money's in the desk, go there and get it," or was it the august angel with his hand upon her shoulder?

She fell, her head escaping by the fraction of an inch the corner of the desk and there she lay stretched out upon the carpet while the telephone upon the table by her bed began to ring, continued ringing.

And Adam who was mad and standing in the booth at the Armenian restaurant cursed roundly. "Damn the old woman, damn Mol," he said, banging the receiver onto the hook and then as he heard the coin click in the cup beneath the telephone, he pocketed his last remaining nickel and went back into the dining room to wait for his old lady, under the impression that she was on her way.